DANGEROUS
WATERS

DANGEROUS WATERS

TONI ANDERSON

Montlake
Romance

Published by Montlake Romance
P.O. Box 400818
Las Vegas, NV 89140

ISBN-13: 9781612186078
ISBN-10: 1612186076

To Gary, my wild Irish husband.
For love, support, and hero inspiration.

PROLOGUE

1982 – Bamfield, Vancouver Island, Canada

Towering pines loomed menacingly overhead but nothing stirred. The shadows unnerved her. Bears were common on the island, and she didn't fancy meeting a hungry one. A branch snapped in the woods and she whirled.

"Mama, Mama! Look at me!"

Bianca forced a tired smile as her daughter jumped off a log at the side of the gravel lane. She stopped the stroller and applauded the little girl's bravery. "Wow. Look at you. You're flying." She grinned as Leah took off, spinning in circles with her arms flung out, head thrown back in wild abandon.

Was everyone born that joyful? Did it leach out with tears and failure or simply vanish as life piled on worry and disappointment?

A strident cry came from the stroller.

"I just fed you, you glutton." They were headed for the local library, but considering the strength of six-week-old Tommy's escalating cries, he wasn't going to last that long. Every wail pierced her skull until she couldn't take it for another second. "Come and sit over here, Leah. I'll feed your brother before he drives me nuts."

She pushed the stroller to the side of the road and brushed off the loose dirt and pine needles from the base of a felled tree. She undid Tommy's straps, and his angry red face became even more frantic. "Feed me, and feed me now, huh?"

She sat heavily on the flat surface, pulled up the T-shirt she wore under her thick denim shirt, unhooked her bra, and helped the baby latch on. She should have listened to her mom and just given the little monster formula.

Guilt was a terrible thing.

Her heart clenched as two tiny hands cradled her breast and he looked up at her with big, innocent eyes. The utter silence of the forest pressed down on her as her son suckled hungrily. An itch of awareness crawled over her skin. Her head shot up and left. "Leah?"

She craned her neck as far as she could without standing. "Are you playing hide-and-seek, baby? Because Mommy can't come and find you right now. Just give me two minutes…" How often had she said those words to her patient little angel over the past few weeks? She pressed her lips into a tight line.

Worry tugged at the corners of her brain, but she was tired, and even though she'd just reached the so-called terrible twos, Leah was a great kid. She wouldn't go far. Tommy suckled some more. His warm contentment made her drowsy.

The first lick of panic hit out of nowhere and she snapped upright. There were cougars as well as bears out here. "Leah? Leah! Come back here right now." She stood, Tommy fussing as she headed into the brush where she'd last seen her little girl.

Had she fallen and hurt herself? Was she sitting behind a bush waiting to be found, a mischievous smile lighting her face?

Bianca walked deeper into the forest, protecting little Tommy's head from getting scratched by branches, spinning around, looking for a glimpse of the red jacket her daughter was wearing. Tommy started to bawl against her shoulder, and she cradled his head, trying to hold him securely as an icy wave of desperation sliced its way down her spine. "Leah." She made her voice singsongy even though she wanted to shriek. "Sweetie, come to Mommy. We have to go to the library now. You want some new books, don't you? Please don't hide."

She stopped at a clearing. It was empty and the leaves were undisturbed. No one had come this way. She swung back, and a figure stepped out of the bushes between her and the road. Fear drenched her to the bone. He wore a black mask, a tool belt riding his hip, a hammer balanced in one hand. Her mouth parched. The thump of her heart detonated mini-explosions through her body and she shook. She wanted to run. Couldn't move.

"What have you done with my little girl?" Her voice was thick and gravelly. She was pinned in place with indecision, so scared her bones rattled. She couldn't leave her little girl, couldn't escape while holding the baby. The man pulled his other hand from behind his back and dropped something to the ground. A flash of scarlet. Leah's jacket.

"Where is she?" Scared but angry, she took a half step forward. She wanted to rip into him. Where was Leah? What had he done with her? She took another step closer and recognition hit. The rush of relief made her knees melt and she stumbled. Relief, regret, rage.

Why was he wearing that stupid mask? How dare he try to scare her like this? "Where is she?"

Birds flapped out of trees. A short burst of startled feathers.

He said nothing, and she huffed out a confused breath.

Why didn't he speak? She didn't understand. She grabbed his shirt with her free hand and tried to shake him into a response. He smelled like the woods—smoky and earthy.

She looked down at her beautiful son who seemed beguiled by the stranger.

Was *this* what he wanted?

Uncertainly, she held the baby a little higher. Her son's first smile was the last thing she saw as something violent and heavy crushed her skull.

CHAPTER 1

Present Day

Finn set out the dive flags and made sure the lights were on. Anchors secure. "Ready?"

His boss nodded and did a final equipment check.

Finn handed him a dive light. "Don't turn it on yet." He glanced around the rocky cliffs that surrounded the sheltered cove. The outcrops were topped with craggy pines and Douglas fir. Crow Point—it was remote and sparsely populated, no chance of rescue should things go pear-shaped.

It was creeping toward dusk and would be full dark when they came back up. He was in charge of dive safety and dive training at the local marine lab, and it went against every principle not to have a surface crew on a dive this dangerous.

Conditions *were* perfect.

On the low edge of a neap tide cycle. Flat calm and nothing in the forecast to cause any concern. But there was a reason this part of Vancouver Island was called the Graveyard of the Pacific, and relying on forecasts was for fools and novices. Barkley Sound was notorious for violent squalls and surging swells that came out of nowhere and sucked you down into the pitiless black depths and never let go. "You sure you want to do this?" he asked.

Professor Thomas Edgefield, director of Bamfield Marine Science Center, nodded and stood awkwardly with his three air tanks secured to his back—two cylinders and a pony backup.

If ever there was a need for *margin of error* and *built-in redundancy*, this was it. He shuffled over to the dive platform at the stern of the boat. Finn checked that his buddy's hoses were secure and not liable to get caught on the wreckage as Thom pulled on his fins. Thom returned the favor, patting Finn on the shoulder when they were good to go. Thom put his regulator in his mouth, held his mask, and stepped off into the sea. Finn took a last look at the brooding cliffs and dropped in behind him.

The first thing that always hit was the flash of cold as the Pacific struck exposed flesh.

He signaled, and Thom returned the thumbs-down gesture. They began descending the gerry line to the anchor line, swimming toward the area where ten days ago they'd discovered the wreckage of an unknown, previously undocumented ship.

The second thing that always hit was the ominous quiet. The muffled, deadened version of sound that amplified awareness of body, breath, heartbeat. A deceptive quiet that lulled the mind and softened the very real danger of a nighttime wreck dive without proper surface support.

But Thom had been insistent and he was the boss. Worse, he was liable to do it alone if Finn refused to help. Classic case of damned if he did and damned if he didn't.

He flicked on his flashlight and shone it along the anchor line, checked his gauges, turned to watch his buddy do the same, and they both gave the OK signal.

They headed straight down, air bubbles streaming out of their mouths. Ten meters. Twenty. Clearing ears as depth increased. Thirty meters, and they were almost there. Pressure pinched the neoprene tight to his skin. At the bottom, he tied in the anchor, making sure it was secure. He attached flashing strobe lights and clipped off a line reel so they could more easily find their way back. He might not have told anyone what they were doing but he sure as hell wasn't playing fast and loose with their safety.

The hull was a dark, menacing shadow, riddled with cracks, but inaccessible. Potentially treacherous. Unwilling to give up its secrets. The research he'd done suggested the ship was a relic of the nineteenth century. He'd learned little else. Why had no one ever heard of it? Why hadn't some of the crew escaped?

Finn didn't like mysteries. He liked things straightforward. Direct. No bullshit. But it wasn't the first shipwreck in this part of the world to be found with no record of survivors or crew.

Most wrecks on the west of the island were pummeled by wave action and pounded into tiny pieces or flattened in the sand. But in this sheltered cove, the waves were buffered, and at this depth, in this remote, protected part of the Pacific Rim National Park Reserve, the hull had remained intact, the wreck undiscovered for all these years. Until he and Thom had checked out an unusual sea otter sighting in the bay and done some impromptu diving, just for the hell of it.

Serendipity? Thom sure as hell thought so.

Finn looked up through the water column and saw nothing but obsidian blackness at these chilling depths. He shone his beam over the metal hull, picked out starfish and anemones that shimmered in gemstone colors. But they weren't what had made Thom nearly choke on his regulator last time they were down here. Finn moved cautiously over the deck to one of the doorways and tied off his reel. Inside the wreck the line was more hazard than help. The pitch-black opening consumed him with a tight swallow. He felt Thom move close behind.

A shiver of dread picked its way over his vertebrae. He shook off the feeling and moved farther into the ship. They had to move with *extreme* caution. Otherwise, sediment would completely destroy visibility and they'd have to rely on touch to get out of the deadly maze. A good way to die on an unfamiliar wreck in the middle of the night with no surface crew to miss them.

His heart thumped impassively in his ear. Years of military training had taught him how to control his stress levels. He'd taken plenty of risks diving military targets in enemy-rich environments, but this situation didn't feel any less deadly. And Thom might be an experienced diver, but he was too old and...*frail*...to do this alone.

Thom drew level with him and stopped, shining his dive light under his chin and pulling a comic horror face. Suddenly he looked happier than Finn had seen him in years, and the worry lightened. Maybe it was worth it. This discovery would make Thom famous rather than infamous, and it was about goddamn time.

He signaled his buddy to take the lead in the hunt for the treasure. The water started to get cloudy so he slowed, gliding with precision so as not to disturb the insidious layer of silt that shrouded every surface. The flashlight beams penetrated the gloom by only a few meters, slashes of brightness in the heavy, claustrophobic darkness. Finn checked his wristwatch and air gauge, every movement controlled and cautious.

Shadows swarmed through the water, schools of fish darting in and out of the beams like flashes of sunlight off the edge of a blade.

They headed along a stairwell and into the bowels of the ship. Into the engine room, Finn scanning for sharp edges that could cut through rubber hoses or neoprene. At nighttime, the ship was a dense absence of light, and he felt like Jonah in the belly of the whale. Except he had a knife and he knew how to use it.

Thom started taking photographs, the flash startlingly bright in the void of the silent tomb. This was the most hazardous time. Thom's attention was rapt on his prize, oblivious to everything else. Finn had to think for both of them.

He let the man work, stayed perfectly still in the background as Thom wrote in his underwater notebook, took water temperature readings, more photos, before carefully collecting his treasure. Cold started to seep into his muscles and he flexed his fingers. He didn't wear gloves—didn't like how they reduced his dexterity. Five minutes later, he rechecked their gauges. Saw Thom was guzzling air in his excitement. He tapped him on the shoulder and gave him the thumbs-up, the signal that meant it was time to surface. Thom scowled and shook his head. Finn tapped him again—with his fist. Gave him the thumbs-up signal once more. It wasn't a question. Thom might be his boss, but Finn was dive master. Down here he was God.

Thom nodded with a glare and slipped his prize into a bag at his side. He started swimming for the exit. Finn caught a flash of something in a shaft of his flashlight and paused. He shone his beam over the same spot and picked out the object. Frowning, he went down for a closer inspection.

It was a weight belt, worn by divers to reduce buoyancy. He swore and swam swiftly to Thom. He didn't want his buddy popping to the surface like a cork when he got out of the wreck. He didn't want to spend the night in a decompression chamber or have to explain what they'd been doing down here. He grabbed his mentor and friend and physically turned him—but Thom's weight belt was securely in place. Thom frowned in confusion, and Finn swam back to the bottom, picked up the belt, stirring up silt and swearing silently with each noisy inhalation. He glided carefully back to where Thom floated beside the door.

Thom ran his own light over the belt and his brow wrinkled. Then he looked up, past Finn's shoulder, and his expression morphed into horror. He screamed, panicking as he lost his regulator, banging against the doorframe in a frantic effort to get out. Finn shot a quick glance over his shoulder before sediment obliterated the view like an ink cloud.

Shit.

He didn't have time to deal with it. Thom was in deep trouble. He'd banged against something sharp, and a confusing swathe of bubbles now engulfed him, stirring up grit and muck all around them. Finn's training took over and he grabbed Thom's pony tank, turned it on, and shoved that regulator into his mouth, gripping him by the chest so he didn't disappear. Something had pierced Thom's manifold and emptied both air tanks. Finn shook him hard to get his attention. Kept them orientated with the hatch so they didn't lose their way in the velvety, encompassing blackness. Panic would kill them as surely as lack of oxygen, and he wasn't dying like this. Thom sucked air like an asthmatic, eyes bulging from the awful choking experience Finn knew all too well.

In zero viz, he hauled his buddy through the hatch. The twisted wreckage pressed tight around them, making it hard to move, suffocating and sinister.

This was the danger of wreck dives. You had to expect the unexpected. They bumped up the narrow stairwell. Every frantic movement stirring up more sediment and silt that crowded them, obliterating every particle of light, every hint of shape and form.

His heart beat louder in his ears, still steady, but reinforced by the *oh fuck* factor. Flashlights were useless. Finn used touch and had to trust his innate sense of direction. With an iron grip on Thom, he made it out of the stairwell, through the wheelhouse, and free of the shipwreck. Sediment cleared as they hit open water. Darkness still surrounded them, but it was different. Less oppressive. Less claustrophobic. He pulled Thom swiftly to the strobe lights that marked the anchor line. They didn't have much time on the pony tank, but if that ran out, Finn had plenty of air in his backup. Just so long as Thom didn't freak.

He had to hold on tight when the man would have shot straight to the surface. *Dammit.* He dragged him back down. His dive computer said they needed to decompress for a few minutes or they'd face the very real possibility of getting bent. He held Thom determinedly in place, stared into his eyes, and willed the man back from the ledge of crazy.

Thom's skin was so waxy that, up close, his face shone like a full moon. Finn had never seen him so distraught—well, not in decades.

They'd known each other a long time.

They'd trusted each other a long time.

He willed Thom to trust him now. To get him safely to the surface and out of this mess alive. Slowly, Thom's juddering breath settled and his eyes calmed. Finn checked his watch, his gauges. He flashed him the OK signal, silently asking the question.

Thom nodded, gripping Finn's arms and closing his eyes, drawing in a huge lungful of air. Finally he returned the signal, thumb pressed to index finger, other fingers upright. OK.

Everything was going to be all right.

Finn gave the signal to surface, taking it slow, forcing air out in deep breaths to stop his lungs from exploding as the air expanded. He had to remind Thom to do the same, which told him the guy—an experienced diver—was in bad shape.

Breaking the skin of the inky surface, they followed the gerry line back to the boat that bobbed gently on the incoming tide. Neither said a word. They threw their fins up on deck, climbed aboard, and shucked off their heavy equipment. Sat breathing heavily, looking at one another for a long, drawn-out moment. Ghosts lingered in Thom's eyes.

"I have to report this to the police," said Finn. The image of the diver hanging lifeless in the water burned through his brain.

Thom swallowed thickly. Nodded. He pulled out a small sample jar and looked at his prize floating gently in the water. Then he rested his head in the palm of his hands and started to cry.

Holly Rudd stepped off the speedboat and looked around. Vancouver Island was the size of Scotland, but with a population of only three-quarters of a million people, most of whom where based in the provincial capital, Victoria. The rest were scattered among tiny outports and communities like this one—Bamfield, population one-hundred and fifty-five hardy, adventurous souls, according to the last census.

"You can't moor that there."

She looked the guy up and down. Surfer blond hair and bare feet. Rugged good looks and attitude to match. She dumped her bag at her feet and turned to the guy who'd ferried her over from Ucluelet. Tipped him fifty bucks. "Thanks for the ride." He waved as he sped away.

She turned back to the dude who stood with arms crossed over his broad chest, radiating impatience and hostility. Sexy as hell. She was tired from lack of sleep, exhilarated by the thought of what the day might bring, but she sure as heck wasn't blind.

"This is private property." Blue eyes glittered. Pale hair glowed like white gold in the rays of the rising sun. Hot, tanned, gorgeous. Just her luck.

She raised a brow and checked her watch. "I'm meeting someone here."

"Public dock is another minute that way." He jerked his thumb down the inlet.

She smiled coolly. Twelve long years on the job and she was still dealing with macho bullshit. "Except someone's dropping a car off for me *here*." She pointed up at the Department of Fisheries and Oceans sign on the side of a large wooden building and started toward it.

He blocked her path. "There's no one there today."

She rocked back on her heels, let her eyes range over the square jaw and heated eyes. "You're not very friendly."

He didn't crack a smile. "Not in my job description."

Not in hers either, but she found smiles worked better than growls when gathering information.

His mouth pinched, then he backed off, relenting. "Tell me who you're supposed to meet, and I'll get someone to track them down."

"Who are you?" She had a feeling she knew.

He blew out an impatient sigh. "Look, lady, I don't have time for this—"

"Sergeant."

"Excuse me?" Those pale brows formed a formidable line.

She held out a hand. "Sergeant Holly Rudd. I'm with the Vancouver Island Integrated Major Crime Unit."

"You're a Mountie?"

A proud member of the Royal Canadian Mounted Police by any other name. She nodded.

He stood stock still, nothing moving but the glitter in his eyes. Finally he sucked in a breath and shook her hand. "Nice uniform."

She glanced down at her ragged old T-shirt, cutoffs, and thongs. "I was caught a little unprepared this morning, as I was officially on vacation. Thankfully, I always pack a uniform." She tapped her bag with her foot, smiled widely, and watched his eyes grow a lot more friendly. And then they shifted straight back to suspicious as he realized she was cataloging his expressions like a facial analysis program. "And *you* are?"

"Finn Carver."

Ah. Her fingers tightened on his when he would have let go. "You called it in?"

"I did." He forcibly disconnected her fingers.

"I'm going to need all the gear you wore last night and the other diver's. Forensics will want to check it out."

He regarded her with one of those silent, steady gazes people used when they wanted to argue but couldn't. "I'll need it back ASAP. I have a busy dive schedule this week."

"You can use something else for a day or two, right? I'll make sure they do a quick turnaround." She needed this guy on her side.

The little time she'd had before the boat trip she'd used to pull up background information on the two guys who'd found the body. Finn Carver had been in the military. Right now he looked ready to go into combat. "Any chance the dive team arrived yet?" she asked.

"No. Their ETA is eleven o'clock. West Coast Marine Service had a call north of Prince Rupert last night. It's going to take them a few hours to get back here. So far you're it." His eyes scraped her form. He didn't look impressed. She should be insulted, but she worked best when people underestimated her.

"I want to check out the crime scene ASAP."

His face gave away nothing but skepticism. Those arms crossed again over that muscular chest. Mouth pressed into a firm line. She let her eyes wander over him. He really was very attractive and absolutely untouchable. Knowing that gave her a distinct advantage.

"*You* can take me down," she suggested.

He gave her one of those sideways glances. Not hostile. Not friendly. "Whoever is in charge of the investigation probably wouldn't be very happy about that."

"Me. I'm in charge. On the ground anyway." Although she was the newest member of the major crime unit here on the island, she had plenty of experience. She let her grin reach her eyes this time. This was her first case as primary investigator in a murder investigation, and she didn't usually have to work this hard to charm anyone. "I just helped solve a case down in Blaine." RCMP, municipal, and FBI collaboration. A hell of a big deal. "Guy murdered his wife, dumped her in Semiahmoo Bay. We found enough evidence to prove he was lying and he confessed." To her, at the end of a bloody knife. She rubbed the newly healed scar on her arm. "I've been working with forensic experts in Burnaby for some time, looking at decomp after seawater submergence."

His lip started to thin. He was definitely not buying it.

"If you're too scared to go back down there…"

He snorted and whirled away. "What am I, eight?"

"If you don't take me down, I'll find someone who will," she called to his retreating back.

He stopped, tension stretching the muscles tight across his shoulder blades. "I thought people who found the bodies were suspects?"

Knowledgeable about police investigations. Check. "At this stage, everyone's a suspect, but I can take care of myself."

A harsh sound was forced out of his mouth. "Just what a potential dive buddy wants to hear." He swiveled back to her and moved so close she smelled his scent and felt his body heat. She held her ground, watching his nostrils flare. He was trying to intimidate, but she'd been a cop for over a decade, had grown up with cops. There wasn't much she hadn't seen or dealt with, and brawny guys with bad attitudes did not scare her. "This isn't some macho pissing contest. Wreck diving is dangerous, especially at this sort of depth. Only experienced divers should be down there."

"I can handle it." Her voice was sharp. He wasn't a pushover for female charm or pretty smiles. Perhaps proving she was damn good at her job would work instead.

He went to walk away, but she reached out to touch his arm.

"I have dive training." She spoke softer this time. She'd learned to dive exactly so she could pursue this sort of investigation.

He paused, those eyes of his diamond hard. "Prove it."

She let go of his arm and bent to pick up her bag. Unzipping the tote, she pulled out her brand-new PADI diving certificate. "I just completed the basic dive training yesterday."

"Fortuitous." He plucked the book from her fingers and flipped through it. "You did four open-water dives and think you're ready for a thirty-meter wreck dive?" He shoved the book back in her hand and stalked away. "Not on your life, Sergeant Rudd."

"I checked you out, Mr. Carver."

"I bet you did."

She followed him into a low-slung single-story building, the room full of tanks and neoprene. The desk overflowed with papers, keys, coffee mugs. Where was everyone? The place was quiet as a graveyard. He picked up the phone.

"I heard you're the best dive instructor this side of the Pacific. If anyone can get me into that wreck, it's you."

"Getting you into the wreck wouldn't be the problem." His eyes flicked over her, unmoved by flattery. He started talking on the phone. "Johnny? Finn Carver here. I've got a woman called Holly Rudd claims she just completed a PADI course with you?"

It went silent, and Holly leaned against the doorway, straining to hear above the background sound of running water.

"What was she like under pressure? Think she could hold her own on a thirty-meter wreck dive?"

She watched his face, trying to gauge the answers, but his impassive features gave nothing away.

"Would you trust her with your life?" The reply made Finn smile. "That's what I figured. Talk to you later." He hung up.

"What did he say?" She could have kicked herself for asking.

He stared at her, then bent down and started filling an air cylinder. "You don't want to know."

Her eyes widened despite her efforts to conceal her emotions. "Well, it won't be anything I haven't heard before." She lived in a man's world and never forgot the fact, but she was done playing games. "Are you taking me down or not? So far we've only got your and Professor Edgefield's word a body even exists. And even if there's a body, it doesn't mean it's a homicide."

He snorted. "Trust me, it's a homicide."

This was her first murder as lead investigator, and she would not be thwarted. Checking out the crime scene with the body still in place was imperative, as long as she didn't contaminate the scene. The guys on the Underwater Recovery Team were no more likely to take her down than he was. She geared herself up for an argument.

"You do *exactly* as I say. No pulling rank or cop bullshit when we get down there. And you'll owe me." Carver disconnected one cylinder and began filling another. His eyes were flat and hard.

"You're going to take me down?" A rush of adrenaline shot through her. "As long as it isn't illegal, I'll owe you." She nodded.

"Down there I'm boss. You have to trust me implicitly." He took a step closer and her mouth went dry. "If I put my hands on you…" He rested both hands on her hips and she felt the imprint of each burning hot finger. She forced herself not to react. This was a test. She didn't fail tests. Ever. "If I grab you, you *don't* freak out. You help me do whatever the hell it is I want to do. You follow my lead exactly and we'll both get out of there alive."

She found herself staring up into those bright blue eyes, only inches from hers. Energy sizzled between them. A sudden wave of sexual awareness mixed with mutual mistrust, a subtle perfume of complication.

Red burned his cheekbones. He released her. He hadn't expected it either.

"I have to trust you. Think I can do that?" Blue eyes held her gaze.

She didn't make a joke about putting her hands on him because suddenly it wasn't funny. One, he was a suspect, and she refused to feel anything for him that wasn't strictly professional. Two, they were going to dive a hazardous shipwreck at thirty meters with a rotting corpse at the end. It wasn't the sort of treasure most divers dreamed of, but she wasn't most people. She kept her mouth shut. Nodded.

The shipwreck looked different by day. At this depth, in pristine water, the hull took on a romantic aspect, an adventure, a mystery. But it was also a coffin, and the thought of entering it willingly twisted Finn's guts. He looked at Holly. Indicated she stay still while he circled her, checking that the hoses were taped down tight against her body. He tested her by poking and prodding to make sure everything was secure. She held fast, tense, but doing what he'd told her to do even though she didn't like it.

She went up a notch in his estimation. Not because he liked women docile, but because he liked people smart.

The advantage of her being newly qualified meant she should treat her instructor like God because the basics had been freshly drilled into her mind. The disadvantage was he was about to put his life in the hands of a novice who'd never gone inside a wreck before and would probably screw up the dive before they even got to the engine room. Which was fine as long as neither of them ended up dead in the process.

He'd found her a dry suit and rigged them both with double tanks with separate regulators, plus an independent pony rig. They had as much safe air as a person could carry, and still it didn't guarantee they'd survive the experience.

But a Coast Guard vessel acted as the surface crew this time, and there wasn't much current. Twelve hours later and he'd hit another low tide. Lucky him.

Nothing for it, he approached the wreck the same way as before. He turned on his light and flashed her the OK signal. She mirrored her reply, gray eyes serious now.

He pointed to his flippers and shook his head. A reminder not to fin inside the vessel. She nodded, gave him the OK signal. So far, so good. He used momentum to drift into the broken ship, used his hands to pull himself slowly and steadily along. It was so tight and dark they had to go single file. He couldn't believe he'd managed to get Thom out of here alive last night. It had been a close thing, and he'd been foolish to bring him down.

Yet here he was again with a frickin' novice.

He entered the wheelhouse and waited. There was plenty of light here, but inside the stairwell there was almost complete darkness for about five meters. He'd talked Holly through it, but the reality was different. He checked both their gauges. Her eyes tracked him, looking for something he couldn't define. Weakness? Aggression? Guilt?

She didn't trust him, and he didn't blame her.

It wouldn't be hard to pin her down and pull the regulator out of her mouth and watch her suck in water. If he was a killer, taking out a fresh-faced girl who was also a cop would probably get his rocks off. Then he'd let the sea take her body and say she panicked on him and took off. No one could prove different. Or he'd disappear. It wasn't that hard. He'd rather slit his own throat than raise a hand to a woman, but she didn't know that, so being wary of him was a smart thing, just as long as it didn't fuck up their dive.

He could tell she thought she could take him on if she had to. Crazy, even for a cop. A quick background check wouldn't reveal much other than the fact he'd been in the army.

He checked their gauges, made her switch tanks because she'd guzzled more air than he was comfortable with, and if there was a problem with the second tank, he wanted to know before they went farther. Exasperated patience shone in her eyes now, and it caught him so unexpectedly he grinned. Then sobered. This was not the time for amusement on any scale.

He led the way, holding his beam of light aimed straight at the hatch they needed to go through. The unwavering light was their beacon, and he hoped Holly had the nerve to follow through with it. He waited at the opening and felt a current next to his body as someone came alongside. Holly squeezed his arm and flashed the OK sign in his beam of light.

He steeled himself to what lay inside the chamber. He carefully inched forward, using the sides of the hatch to pull himself through and into the heart of the shipwreck.

Holly followed, bumped into him, and he gripped her around the waist to stop their forward propulsion. He felt her freeze at the contact and then force herself to relax. She watched him through the bubbles, questions clear in her eyes. He maneuvered her until she faced the right direction and held tight as they both took in the corpse. The diver hung in the water with his arms and legs dangling. He wore a shabby old wetsuit and his mask was askew. His air cylinders were gone. A big-assed knife was strapped to his thigh.

An even bigger knife stuck out of his chest.

Finn let Holly go with a warning squeeze.

He'd seen plenty of death in his time, but he didn't know what sort of person would purposefully pursue it. Homicide investigator seemed like an odd choice of career for a beautiful young woman like Holly Rudd. She flinched as she got close enough to run her light over the damage the fish had wreaked on the guy, which proved she was at least human. There was frayed flesh where his lips should have been, teeth prominent in the murk. Flesh on the hands had been eaten away too. Holly took a series of photographs. Finn edged closer. The knife jutting out of the diver's chest was pretty indicative of murder. The hilt was heavy and black, the grip worn down by age.

Shit. He frowned, his heart contracting extra hard. He recognized that knife.

He checked his gauges then tapped Holly on the shoulder to do the same. She glared at him for a moment. She was caught up in cataloging the details important to her, much the same way Thom had been caught up in his treasure last night. Finn pointed to the dial. Her second tank was almost empty, and she blinked in surprise. Her body wasn't used to this depth; she should have been checking more regularly. This was why novices didn't do their first wreck dive at thirty meters or their first thirty-meter dive in a wreck. A double whammy.

He passed her the regulator to her half-full first tank and adjusted the discarded regulator until it sat under her chin. While he had her attention, he pointed to where he'd dropped the weight belt. She nodded and was about to dart off when he tightened his hold and pointed to her flippers, which had stirred up a wave of sediment. They couldn't afford to whip things up if the dive unit hoped to find the body when they arrived. He didn't appreciate how much he enjoyed touching the confident, sexy cop. Given time and the right circumstances, she was exactly the sort of woman he'd like to explore in much more detail. But he didn't have time, and these definitely weren't the right circumstances.

He checked his dive computer.

Time to go. He tapped Holly on the shoulder after she took another set of photographs of the weight belt, but she shrugged him away. He did it again and she batted his hand. Pissed now, he stuck his hand in her face, giving her the thumbs-up signal. Her body tensed and she blew out a plethora of bubbles. She flashed him back the same sign.

He waited for her at the hatch. It felt wrong to leave the dead guy dangling in the breeze, so to speak. Holly reached his side, and he indicated she should lead the way out through the stairwell. They both paused, watching a school of small fish feed on a long pink blob. It took a moment to figure out the blob was an eyeball. A reflex gag hit him, but he choked it down. Holly's face was ashen in the beam of his dive light, but at least she hadn't thrown up. He dug in his bag for a sample jar and captured the object, putting the exact nature of the thing out of his head. That was how he coped. That was how he'd learned to do the things that scared the shit out of him. He slipped the jar into a bag, then tilted his head to get her to swim out ahead of him. He followed her slender form through the dark tunnel.

When they exited the ship, four black-suited divers were waiting for them. They'd just started photographing the ship's exterior. Finn used hand signals to ask one guy to take Holly to the surface. She shook her head vigorously. Trying to defy him.

He dug for the eyeball jar, knowing there was a chain-of-evidence thing she needed to follow. She took it with a blast of air bubbles. He pointed to her air gauges, which were approaching the red zone, and repeated the thumbs-up gesture, then indicated on his computer screen how long and where she would need to decompress. Her expression was livid, but he ignored it. Keeping her alive for the duration of this dive was his responsibility, and he knew how to do his job.

With another huff of air, Holly finally followed the cop up the anchor line. Finn turned back to the vessel. He checked his air and pointed to the other men to follow him. Police divers were professional and experienced, and he didn't worry about telling them what to do. He'd show them where the body was and leave. This was the very last time he was ever going into the bowels of this cursed wreck.

CHAPTER 2

Holly broke the surface and nodded thanks to her escort, torn between gratitude to Finn Carver for taking her down and resentment he'd made her surface so quickly. The diver from the Underwater Recovery Team slid back into the water and disappeared from sight. When she looked up, she found eight pairs of eyes glued to her, a group of officers hanging over the side of the Coast Guard ship, including one pair she'd hoped never to see again—Staff Sgt. Jimmy Furlong.

Shit. Inside, her heart squeezed into a tight little ball, but outwardly she smiled and lifted her hand in greeting, mentally tallying her favorite swear words, and swam to the small boat Carver had brought them out on. She climbed on board and carefully disposed of her equipment, stacking it the way Carver had earlier.

Jimmy Furlong. Of all the twists. In this part of Canada, murders were investigated by a group of dedicated police officers led by a primary investigator—her—but overseen by a team commander. She'd transferred to the major crime unit on the island when she'd heard Furlong was moving to the integrated crime unit in Surrey, and yet here he was. When resources were stretched, they sometimes pulled personnel in from other sections. She had to be the unluckiest woman alive. The realization left a bitter taste in her mouth.

Her heartbeat slowly settled. She could get through this.

The victim was more important than her own fractured pride. She'd pushed her luck with Carver in the wreck. He'd been pissed with her at the end, but she'd got what she needed and neither of them had died, even though she'd almost swallowed her tongue when that damned eyeball had bobbed their way. Human eyeballs shrank in seawater. The prof she'd been working with at Simon Fraser University was going to be very interested in the fact that it had come loose.

She found the zip of her suit across the back of her shoulders and tugged to get it undone. Pulling her way out of the neck seal was like trying to pry a turtle out of its shell, but eventually the neoprene stretched over her head. She swore as it ripped out a handful of hair.

A small inflatable sped toward her. Staff Sergeant Furlong was driving, and it was just moments before he pulled up beside the marine lab's boat.

"So do we have a homicide or not?" he yelled over the wake and engine noise.

"Knife to the heart suggests we do, sir." She schooled her features to give nothing away. "If you give me five minutes, I'll get dressed and bring everyone up to speed."

There was a thick pause. "How are you, Holly? I heard you got injured during your last assignment."

"It was just a scratch. I'm fine, sir." She picked up a towel and scrubbed at her hair. "How's Penny and the baby?" she asked brightly.

"They're great." His teeth gleamed as his eyes ran over her in a familiar way. Nausea swirled in her belly. "You got here fast."

"I was in the right place at the right time. Dad and I decided to take our yearly vacation before I started the new job in Victoria.

We were learning to scuba dive near Tofino. We cut the trip short when I heard about the case." She locked her teeth together.

His lips compressed. "This is your first case as primary, correct?"

"Yes, sir." *No pressure.* She plucked at her sopping, bedraggled hair. "I need to get dry before I get too cold." She picked up the evidence jar and pressed it into his hand, taking care not to connect with any skin. "Meet the victim. Part of him, anyway."

"I see." A frown furrowed the skin of his tanned brow. "Is this going to be a problem—us?"

She laughed and was pleased at how it came out, all tinkling and light rather than rabid and nasty. "There is no 'us,' so there's no problem, sir."

He nodded, and a rush of water at the end of the boat made her flinch. Finn Carver hauled himself on board the dive platform and started peeling off gear. How long had he been there? What had he heard?

Staff Sergeant Furlong gave her a nod. "I'll see you on the Coast Guard vessel in thirty minutes. They've offered us space to begin our preliminary work."

She stood straight. "Yes, sir," she clipped out. And then he was gone.

Silence hung in the air. The blue sky and gentle lapping of water against the hull seemed inappropriate for her mood, but a hurricane wouldn't be good either. "Thank you for taking me down today, Mr. Carver. I can appreciate why you weren't so keen."

A sexy dimple appeared in his cheek as he casually stripped down to board shorts. "Call me Finn."

"Finn." She must have been distracted earlier because she hadn't noticed the sheer quality of muscle packed into that body. This was a man in peak physical condition, with superb observational skills. He caught her looking.

"Checking me for weapons?" He raised one Viking brow.

She was a little unsettled by the thought of frisking him in any capacity, especially so soon after talking to Jimmy *forgot-to-mention-I'm-married* Furlong. "Just keeping an eye on you, Mr. Carver." She peeled off the wet neoprene and realized she stank. She sat there bedraggled and shivering and figured there were days when the deck was heavily stacked against being a woman.

"There's a shower downstairs. Go grab one before you have to report in."

Considerate men were the most dangerous. Jimmy Furlong had been a hell of a considerate guy, all the way to the bedroom. And it must have given him a goddamn heart attack when he'd found out who her father was.

She pulled her wet hair off her forehead. "You need to come over there too. I need to take an official statement."

He grunted. "I need to get back to work, Sergeant Rudd. Come by the marine station when you're done here. You can interview me and my dive buddy from last night at the same time." He looked over toward the two boats guarding the scene. "I'll even tell the cook to put on a big pot of stew in case your guys get hungry. Students can eat it tomorrow if you don't."

Her brows hitched in surprise. People rarely defied her, but this plan made sense. She grabbed her bag and started down the steps.

"Guys like that always cheat. You know that, right?"

She froze.

"You should pity his wife." He'd spotted the ring Jimmy Furlong hadn't been wearing the week they'd met during a FBI Academy training session.

Her fingers curled tight around the banister. "I don't know what you're talking about."

"I hope you nailed his balls to the wall when you figured it out."

She stood frozen on that top step as if it were a hundred-foot drop beneath her. She looked over her shoulder, but she kept her mouth shut tight. A hint of sympathy twisted his lips, but she didn't want pity. She'd rather get a punch in the face. She nodded and headed for the shower.

She'd been played for a fool, and it had been a hell of a lesson. In truth, she was grateful to Staff Sgt. Jimmy Furlong. He'd taught her one of the most important lessons in life. Trust no one, not even her fellow cops.

Finn tied up the boat. His jaw ached because it had been clenched ever since he'd gotten a look at the knife sticking out of the dead man's chest. He needed to refill cylinders, check seals, and hose down the equipment to prevent salt damage. He needed to pack up the equipment they'd used on the dive last night so the cops could test it for god knew what. To log in, check nothing important had happened in the last few hours, and make sure everything was ready for tomorrow's rescheduled dives. As he'd told Holly, he had work to do.

A black cormorant sat in judgment on the end of the pier. Gulls were curiously absent.

The smell of brine washed through the air, a constant in this damp, temperate region. His feet pounded the wooden boards as he scanned the surroundings. It was quiet. No one was around. They were running two courses, but both had switched to lectures and labs today as opposed to scheduled fieldwork. Seeing no one, he went inside the dive shed and straight to Thom's locker. He checked rapidly through his stuff. His hand lingered on the brand-new dive knife on the top shelf of the locker. *Fuck.*

"Finn, you in here?"

He turned slowly.

Mike Toben, whose family owned the hardware store, stepped through the open doorway, eyes sharp. "Got the RCMP cruiser outside. Thought I might leave the keys with you?" The cops kept a vehicle stored in town in case the West Coast Marine Service needed to do land-based inquiries. The Tobens rented them storage space in their warehouse.

Mike reached up above the desk that held a whiteboard full of the week's dive schedules. There was a rack of keys on the wall.

"Leave 'em behind the sun visor."

Mike's eyebrows climbed halfway up his forehead as he held on to the keys. "How come? What's going on?"

"I'm going to start locking the outside door."

"Why? Something been stolen?" Unlike Finn, Mike had never left the area. They had beers occasionally, but that was as far as it went.

Finn wasn't about to confide in the guy. "We've got a lot of expensive equipment here. I don't want it walking." He herded Mike outside.

The younger man eyed him narrowly. "Something's going on. What is it?"

Finn strode down to the boat and started hauling equipment up to the shed.

"Need a hand?" Mike offered.

Finn stared unsmiling at the other guy. He didn't want to talk to anyone right now. "I can manage."

On cue, a car horn honked, and Mike turned to wave at his dad, who was waiting for him at the top of the hill.

"See you at O'Malley's later?"

"Sure." Finn turned on the hose and started washing down the dry suits. He wasn't going anywhere near O'Malley's or any other damn place where he'd be interrogated by the natives. He needed to figure out how Thom's old dive knife had ended up hilt deep in the body of that diver. And he needed to make sure no one else knew about it.

"Any clues as to the identity of our vic?"

Holly shook her head as she handed her underwater camera over to Cpl. Steffie Billings, the exhibit custodian for the command group that had been set up to investigate this murder. She'd worked with Steffie in Chilliwack years ago, and they'd been close friends ever since. She was looking forward to working with the no-nonsense blonde again. "Download these, will you? There's a timestamp on them. You got the eyeball?"

"I did." Steffie gave her an arch look over her spectacles. "Thank you for that."

Holly grinned. "Sorry. We couldn't exactly leave it floating around being nibbled on by baitfish—"

"Too much information." Steffie held up her hand. "I'll get to see all the gory details during the postmortem, so I really don't need to hear about it now." She gave a shudder. "Floaters are always the worst. Well, except for children." She stopped talking for a moment and they both paused. Certain aspects of their job made grim look like sunshine. The only thing that made it worthwhile was incarcerating bad guys so they didn't hurt anyone again.

"I passed the eyeball on to the guys from forensic identification." She pointed to one side of the room where three IFIS guys were unpacking an array of machines and tubes. One had the sample jar next to some monitor. "They drove in from Port Alberni. Said the road's a bitch."

Holly's lips tightened. Nothing she could do about the road or the location, but it made everything more complicated. Most officers had flown in from Victoria via Comox. She hadn't even made it into headquarters to start her new job. But she relished the chance to prove herself, and this was exactly the sort of case to do it.

"You gonna be OK with you-know-who?" Steffie asked.

Steffie was one of two friends Holly had confided in about her affair with the rat bastard. Right now she was wishing she'd kept her mouth shut. "Everything will be fine." She lowered her voice. "Especially when he goes home and leaves us to do our jobs."

The sheer number of personnel was making it difficult to move around the ship. Most would leave as soon as the body and evidence were recovered.

On deck they had a coroner from the BC Coroners Service, plus two of his assistants. None of them were divers, so they were in deep discussion with members of the Underwater Recovery Team, who hung over the rail, waiting for their teammates to surface. She'd spoken to the pathologist, given him details about the condition of the body, substrate, temperature, and depth. Passed on the name of the prof at the university who might be willing to consult on the case. Now they just had to raise the body. The main fear was if the abdominal gases hadn't already dissipated, they might expand and...well, it wouldn't be pretty.

There were three officers from the *Nadon*, one of the boats that acted as mobile police cruisers along this coast, operated by the West Coast Marine Service. Coast Guard people wandered about, but none in what she was thinking of as the incident room. The command group who'd be investigating the crime consisted of herself, Steffie Billings, four other investigators from the major crimes unit, plus their team commander.

She squared her shoulders. She could do this.

The job of team commander was more manager than investigator, in charge of staffing levels, overtime, special expenditures, etc. Cases like this were hardest on the budget, which put everyone under added duress. Furlong also liaised with head honchos, and with a bit of luck, he'd head back to the mainland just as soon as the body was recovered.

Her braided hair made a wet line down the center of her pale gray shirt, a damp sliver of discomfort. Furlong looked over some heads and caught her eye. She made herself join the group as he introduced her. "Sergeant Holly Rudd is the primary investigator. Do you know everyone, Holly?"

She shifted from a formal stance into casual.

"I recognize a couple of faces." She smiled at Jeff Winslow, who she'd graduated with from basic training many years before.

"Corporals Ray Malone, Freddy Chastain, and Rachel Messenger." Staff Sergeant Furlong pointed out each individual, and she nodded hello. The rank structure was left over from the police force's origins as a paramilitary group back in the late-nineteenth century. Steffie waved them over. She'd set up a large computer screen that showed a picture of the outline of the wreck.

"Cool," said Chastain.

"Know anything about the shipwreck?" asked Furlong.

"Nothing as yet. We need to talk to the Coast Guard and discuss the potential for raising the ship—"

"Hold on now." Furlong put both hands in the air. "That's a pretty serious operation. Any reason to think lifting it out of the water will aid the investigation?"

"Pretty hard to gather all the evidence when the thing is sitting at thirty meters."

"But you're going to lose most of the evidence as the water drains." He shook his head. "Talk to the Coast Guard, but don't proceed until you've talked it through with me. I'm not convinced it'll give us anything useful."

True, and she didn't want to waste time sifting through centuries of debris, but being shot down by the boss was never a thrill.

"Go on," she said to Steffie, who flipped to the next image. Finn Carver was in the shot. An enigma and someone who intrigued her on several levels. Definitely someone to avoid unless it was directly related to the investigation.

"What we know so far is two divers were inside that wreck last night and found more than they bargained for. This guy is Finn Carver. He's dive master at the Bamfield Marine Science Center. The other guy, I haven't met yet. He's the director of the marine lab. I'm going to interview them as soon as the body is recovered."

"Any clue as to the identity of the victim?" asked Furlong again.

Steffie clicked, and the gruesome image of a corpse hanging in the water greeted them. Faces were pulled. Holly was grateful she hadn't eaten. "He's not wearing a weight belt or air tanks," she said. His mask was askew, the lack of one eye obscured by shadows.

Freddy Chastain pointed to the knife protruding from his chest. "Whoever stuck him with that had to be tremendously powerful."

Holly agreed.

"We found an eyeball floating around, and IFIS people have it. Hopefully that'll get us DNA."

"Can we be sure that's his eyeball?" asked Jeff Winslow. Jeff was the detail person. The nerd with a black belt in jujitsu.

"You think someone else might have lost one?" Chastain joked. Furlong laughed along too. Jeff's cheeks grew pink.

"It's a good point, Jeff. We need to double-check and confirm DNA." Holly backed him up.

"So someone stabbed him, took his equipment, and just left him there?" Corporal Messenger asked, perplexed.

"I've seen stranger things." Furlong leaned closer to the screen.

Holly cringed at the hero worship she recognized in Messenger's gaze as she stared at their team commander. She'd probably stared at him the same way, and now the thought made her sick.

"It's possible the equipment could be used to identify the victim in some way." Holly had been mulling it over. "Maybe that's why they took it."

"Or it was borrowed? Maybe from the killer," Jeff piped up.

"That guy, Carver." Furlong frowned at the screen. "He recognize the vic?"

"Not to my knowledge." She stood straighter, almost eye level with the boss. "I intend to interview the men who discovered the body just as soon as the victim is recovered," she repeated.

Furlong pressed his lips together and stared at the face of the corpse on the screen. "It's not a lot to go on. What's your plan of action?"

"First thing we need to do is ID the victim. We're going to need dental and DNA tests expedited. Hopefully, the postmortem can give us a window for time of death." Notoriously difficult in marine submergence cases. "We'll take photographs of the dive suit and the murder weapon and float them around locally, see if anyone recognizes them. Start interviewing the locals. Find out who else knew about this supposedly undiscovered wreck. Look at missing persons."

She let out a breath and caught the watchful gazes of her colleagues. "Steffie is evidence custodian. I want Jeff as file coordinator. We'll get public relations to draw up the press release and get a hotline set up. Corporal Messenger, see what you can find out about the shipwreck. Chastain, Malone, and I will start conducting interviews."

There was a commotion outside the window.

"Looks like they're bringing him up now." Chastain peered out the window.

They all turned and headed out on deck.

Furlong touched her shoulder. "I have something for you." His smile was lopsided, probably supposed to be boyish. He reached into a bag and pulled out an object. Pressed it into her palm.

At first she flinched, then she realized it was her nine-millimeter Smith & Wesson. She focused her attention on attaching the holster to her belt and not on the fact that she wanted to smack him for touching her. "How'd you get it?"

"Your father called ahead and had Corporal Messenger pick it up from your gun safe in your apartment. She gave it to me."

Holly had spent only one night in her new place before she and her dad had taken off on their annual father-daughter vacation. Weird to think Messenger had also been there. "Thanks."

Furlong looked around before saying quietly, "I take it he doesn't know about—"

"No." Holly sucked in a sharp breath and swallowed the shame that splintered in her throat. "You didn't tell him?"

"I've got seventeen years of service. I'm not going to risk that for a—" Furlong stopped short. *A quick shag. A roll in the hay. A piece of ass.* Her stomach roiled. His expression remained impassive. "If I'd known you were the deputy commissioner's daughter I'd never have touched you."

Her dad was the commanding officer of "E" Division, the largest division within the RCMP, with about one-third of its total employees under his control.

She didn't point out to Furlong that he was married and shouldn't have gone near anyone who wasn't his heavily pregnant wife. "I don't want him to find out."

He leaned a fraction closer. "He won't hear it from me."

She'd slept with a married man. Even the idea made her seethe with self-disgust. What if his wife found out? Her father?

Finn Carver had figured it out. Would he try to use it against her?

Furlong touched her arm again, and she forced herself not to snarl. But she could *do* this. Jimmy Furlong would be gone soon and she'd be running the show. She raised her chin. They joined the rest of the team on deck as the body was hauled awkwardly from the Pacific onto the deck of the Coast Guard vessel. Another victim of this deadly stretch of coastline.

But it wasn't Mother Nature doing the destruction this time.

Mother Nature hadn't shoved six inches of honed steel between this man's ribs and into his chest cavity. It was Holly's job to figure out who had.

Finn walked into the local school and headed down the wide corridor to the central atrium. The beat of running feet reverberated around the gymnasium. Good. The kids were out of the way. Fewer people to notice him.

Thom had been on a conference call, so he had to wait to ask him about the knife. They often left the dive shed wide open and accessible because different dive teams came and went at different times. He locked it at night when everyone was done for the day, but the rest of the time anyone could get in, and everyone knew it.

Not anymore.

Was that Thom's knife? Had someone—i.e., the murderer— been inside Finn's place of work and grabbed the first blade at hand? Or had they deliberately set up the old man?

Thom had spent the last three decades digging up the town's secrets, looking for answers about his wife's and child's murders, trying to find any trace of the daughter he stubbornly believed was alive. During that time, he'd managed to implicate almost every family in town with his various theories. Then piss off the cops by bombarding them with leads and publically berating their lack of progress. He reported *every* unusual activity and, in doing so, had helped prevent organized crime from getting a foothold in the community. He hadn't exactly made friends. Two years ago someone had been pushed to the limit and had tried to silence him permanently.

Finn rounded the corner and tapped on the glass door where the librarians worked. He walked inside the office.

"Hello, gorgeous." Gina Swartz stood and came around to his side of the desk. "What can I do for you today?"

"Did you tell anyone I was in here last week?"

She crossed her hands over her chest and dipped her chin. "Now why would I?"

He put his hand to his forehead, suddenly feeling incredibly foolish. He'd figured maybe Gina had taken a look over his shoulder and seen the websites and reference books he'd been browsing while trying to identify that wreck, and blabbed to someone. It was stupid. "No reason."

She laughed. "You look awful worried for *no reason*. Is this something to do with all the police activity over at Crow Point?"

He shrugged but kept his mouth shut. No matter how deep the town buried its secrets, news always spread like wildfire. The wreck and murder wouldn't stay secret for long, but he didn't want to get into it. Let the police do their jobs for once. He rested his hand on her shoulder. "You seen Brent recently?" He tried to keep the question casual.

She rolled her shoulder and he dropped his hand. "I told you I'm not seeing your brother anymore."

"You've been saying that for years. You guys always get back together."

She tugged her blue cardigan over her neat cotton blouse. "Not this time." Her eyes looked haunted. She tried to smile. "I guess I picked the wrong brother, huh."

He pulled her into his embrace—small, fragile, too sweet for any man with Carver blood. He kissed the top of her head. "You're too good for either of us."

She gripped him tight for one long second before pulling away. "Actually I'm seeing someone else. A boy toy. More stamina. Less scruples. None of the angst."

"Better have some damn scruples. Who is it?"

She grinned at him, still pretty, though the brilliance of her eyes had dimmed over the years. "None of your business—I'm having some fun. He isn't hurt, is he?" she asked suddenly.

"Who?"

"Brent." She blew out another sigh as he shook his head.

"I need to go visit him." Not something he was looking forward to. Finn shoved his hands in his back pockets.

"He won't welcome you." She went and sat back behind her desk, the prim and proper librarian who'd waited years for his brother to get out of jail. Then, when he had, the bastard had dumped her.

"He never wants to see anyone. But he'll talk to me this time."
He didn't have a choice.

Twenty minutes later, Finn walked into Thom's office and closed
the door softly behind him. Their relationship was complicated,
and he owed Thom more than he could ever repay.

Thomas Edgefield had raised him from the time he was thirteen years old, when his brother had hit their father over the head
with a beer bottle and killed him. Thanks to a ruthless prosecutor,
a shitty defense attorney, and a harsh judge, sixteen-year-old Brent
Carver had been charged as an adult, convicted of second-degree
murder, and ended up serving twenty years. Those years in prison
had changed Brent from a loving and overprotective brother to a
hardened ex-con who'd refused every overture of friendship Finn
had made in the years since his conviction. When Brent got out
three years ago, he'd been a cold-eyed stranger with none of the
easygoing attitude of his youth. He'd gradually forced everyone
who'd ever cared about him out of his life, and even though Finn
had been back in Bamfield for nearly two years, they still hadn't
really spoken.

Finn intended to change that, but first he needed answers to
some hard questions from Thom—a man generous enough to take
pity on a smart-mouthed, snot-nosed brat when he'd still been
suffering from the loss of his own family.

Thom gave him a tired smile. "The cops been to see you yet?"

Finn stared at him closely. Thom's face was an unhealthy color
that might just be exhaustion, deep grooves lining the leathery
skin. The last twenty-four hours had been grueling.

"I took an officer down to see the body. They're all out at Crow
Point gathering evidence. I told them they could eat here if they
wanted and interview us then too."

"Good idea. I have another piece of information I wanted to
give them about the time Bianca disappeared—"

"I don't think this is the right time for that, Thom." He let his impatience show.

Thom must have traced the movements of every person in the village the day his wife had been murdered. It was either a stranger who'd attacked Bianca or someone from the village was lying. Thom had spent his life trying to prove which.

"You think I'm being insensitive?" Thom snapped. "Using this new murder to stir up interest in one they haven't been able to solve in nearly thirty years?"

Jesus. Finn's thoughts screeched to a halt. Would Thom kill to rekindle interest in his wife's death? He'd been badgering the cops to reopen the investigation for years.

He narrowed his eyes. Most people thought Thom was unhinged in his obsession. Finn had only ever seen desperation. What if he was wrong?

Finn stared out the huge picture window in Thom's office. It overlooked the Coast Guard station and the Broken Islands. There probably wasn't a more spectacular view in the world, but neither of them was admiring it right now.

"I got a closer look at the corpse when I took that cop down." He watched his boss carefully.

Thom pressed a hand to his stomach. "God. What a terrible thing." He looked up, cheeks as hollow as teacups. "I wouldn't have got out of that tomb alive if it wasn't for you. You saved my life. Thank you."

"I should never have let you talk me into a goddamn night dive."

Thom had the grace to look ashamed. "If I'd had any idea there was a dead man down there, believe me, I would never have insisted—"

"When did you get the new dive knife?"

The older man looked puzzled by the brusque interruption. "I picked it up in Tofino last weekend." He stood.

"Why?" The question was a shotgun blast and Thom flinched. Finn didn't like being lied to or manipulated. Not by the one person he trusted.

Thom leaned heavily against the windowsill. "Because I couldn't find my old one." His lips pressed together, bloodless. "What's the matter?" he asked quietly.

Finn moved closer so no flapping ears could eavesdrop. "I'm pretty sure that's your old knife sticking out of that corpse down there."

Thom turned so pale Finn worried he was about to have a heart attack, but dammit, he needed answers. "Did you kill him? Did you set this whole thing up to get the cops back out here?"

Thom shook his head. "I would never hurt anyone."

"Seriously?" Finn's lip curled. That was so not his mantra. "All those bastards who've mocked and maligned you over the years? The guy who almost beat you to death? You wouldn't want them to suffer even a little?"

"I don't believe in violence. You know that." It was a whispered, vehement hiss.

"Not even for the man who smashed in your wife's head with a hammer, murdered your infant son and daughter?"

Thom's face crumpled into a network of fine lines, and Finn wanted to stop pushing but couldn't afford to. There was too much at stake.

Thom sank his face into both hands. "I don't want him dead. I want justice. I want the truth." His jaw worked frantically, as if he was trying to persuade himself. "God, maybe I do want him dead." His breath started hitching in his chest, and Finn's anger evaporated. He shook his head and pulled the old man into an awkward embrace.

"Don't tell the cops about the knife," he whispered quietly into Thom's ear.

Thom pulled away, his mouth agape. "I can't lie to them."

"You will be top of the suspect list, and we both know how many people would be happy to throw you to the wolves."

Thom's eyes were bloodshot and wide. "I didn't kill anyone."

"Maybe this is just another way to try to get rid of you. They can't get past me, so they're trying to get you out of here any way they can." Two years ago, someone had beaten Thom nearly to death, and Finn had given up his career as a soldier to make sure it didn't happen again. It still wasn't enough.

"I'm not that important."

Finn laughed. "You've single-handedly kept organized crime out of Bamfield for years."

Thom shook his head again. "I can't lie to the police. What if the reason they can't solve Bianca's murder is because someone told a little white lie that no one thought would do any harm?"

"They can't solve Bianca's murder because it happened thirty years ago and no one saw a goddamned thing. She was caught alone in the woods by a maniac with a hammer." Why wouldn't the guy just leave it alone? It was horrific and awful, but why couldn't he just drop it and move on?

But it was all Thomas really cared about.

"Forensics weren't what they are now." Thom doggedly dug into one of his many recurring arguments.

There was only one way to do this, and Finn hated himself for it. "Listen, if you tell the cops that your dive knife is the murder weapon, you're going to end up in jail. Then who's going to carry on looking for Bianca's killer? The RCMP?"

Thom's expression hardened. "They gave up a long time ago."

"Exactly. She'll be forgotten by everyone." Finn gripped his friend's arm, doing this for his own good. "Let's keep it quiet and figure out how and why someone stole your knife before we tell the police, right?"

"You're right. We know we didn't kill him." The older man nodded vigorously. "I'll plead ignorance. People always seem convinced I haven't got a clue about what I'm talking about anyway."

His faded gray eyes held self-deprecating humor. Thom Edgefield was a good man, but there was no doubt he had moments of madness.

"Let's just keep a lid on it, huh? Try to act like neither of us is fucked up."

There was a knock, and a moment later Sgt. Holly Rudd poked her head around the door. "Can I come in?"

Thom took one look at her and fainted dead away.

CHAPTER 3

"What the hell? You have that effect on many people?"

"I've knocked a few on their ass, but...no, I don't normally make them pass out." Just what she needed.

Finn bent over the incapacitated man, checking his pulse.

"Is he all right?"

"I don't know. Pulse is strong. Breathing steady. No history of heart trouble. His color isn't great, but we were both up all night, so he might just be tired. I think he's coming round." He sat back on his heels. "Gladys!" he yelled.

"Is that the secretary? She isn't there anymore." Holly craned her head to see into the empty outer office.

He pulled out his cell. "You should probably leave. I'm getting the doc up here."

She noticed the way he hovered protectively over the guy. Oh, man, had she ever read him wrong earlier. A rush of relief swept over her. "How long have you two been together?"

"I came back to work here a couple of years ago." He paused for a moment and his pupils flared as he looked at her. Then his lips tugged into an annoyed smile. "You think me and him are..."

"Gay?" Her voice cracked.

"Really?" He let his eyes wander down her body, and she felt a sudden flush of heat as blood infused her skin. "You really think that?"

"Well, you're fussing over him like an old maid, I just figured—"

"*Ha*. An old maid?" Those bright eyes looked like blue ink. "Well, you figured wrong, Sherlock. He's a friend of mine. I take good care of my friends."

Holly felt foolish on too many levels to even think about. And slightly threatened, even though he hadn't moved an inch. There was something about his powerful frame and the controlled way he moved that suggested he could dominate any situation. A black belt in aikido and boxing champ at her weight, she wasn't scared of much. She knew he could hurt her if he wanted, but she wasn't about to wimp out just because a guy was bigger than she was. Pain was a part of life; it was how you dealt with it that mattered.

The look on his face was fierce. "Are you supposed to be a good cop?"

Her lips tightened. "I *am* a good cop."

"Well, your instincts are screwed."

"And maybe you're in the closet."

His laugh sent a shiver of heat down to her bones. She was bluffing and they both knew it. "Do me a favor and look for solid clues rather than making half-assed assumptions. Thom is like a father to me. I'm as straight as you are." Their gazes locked, and her mouth went dry as sand. She had to drag her eyes away.

She'd wanted him to be gay. Being a hot gay guy would be absolutely fantastic, but once again luck wasn't going her way. It amused him, she could tell. And he was obviously less than impressed with her deductive skills, because, despite everything, the frisson of attraction crackled between them, as obvious as forked lightning on a moonless night.

She raised her chin. "It was a possible scenario."

"Bianca?" Thom Edgefield's voice rasped in his throat. She'd almost forgotten about the poor guy. His eyes popped open, and he stared at her as if he'd seen a proverbial ghost.

Finn's gaze sharpened on her features. He looked back at the older man. "That isn't Bianca, Thom. This here is Sergeant Holly Rudd. She's a cop."

"Who's Bianca?" she asked.

Professor Edgefield tried to climb to his feet, but Finn pressed a hand on his chest. "Just rest easy. It isn't her."

"Who's he talking about? Who's Bianca?"

Neither man spoke. When the old man wouldn't calm down, Finn helped him to his feet and he lunged unsteadily toward her. She was suddenly aware that she was alone in a room with two possible suspects. Her hand rested on her stun gun.

"Don't," Finn said firmly, though he didn't move toward her. *Smart guy.* "He's not going to hurt you."

"Sir," she told the professor sharply, "you need to take a step back." Thom clasped her fingers as if he wanted to hold her hand. Disquiet crawled over her skin in size twelve boots.

Finn must have recognized her decided lack of amusement because he grabbed the man and hauled him physically into a seat. "It isn't Bianca, Thom. That isn't her. Bianca's dead, remember?"

Whoa. "Dead?"

The old man stared at her as if he'd gone deaf and dumb to reason.

"His wife. Murdered years ago, along with their infant son in the woods." Finn jerked his head in the general direction of town. "His little girl's body was never found, and although I didn't see it before, you're a dead ringer for the woman."

"My father is alive and well in Vancouver." His DNA shaped every day of her life. Every decision she'd ever made.

Thomas Edgefield's gray eyes locked on hers, and it was disconcerting to realize hers were the exact same stormy shade. "I'm sorry about your family, Professor, but I'm not your long-lost daughter. I'm the primary investigator in a homicide." She swallowed her pity for the man. She had a job to do. "I have to ask you some questions about last night. About the body you found. Are you up to it or should I wait until after you've seen a doctor?"

"*After* the doc examines him," Finn said firmly.

"I'm not sick. I just had a bit of a shock." Edgefield's eyes latched onto Finn's, and he patted the hand that held a fistful of his shirt. "You can let me go now. My marbles came back." He huffed out a soft laugh that made Finn scowl before releasing him.

Finn threw Holly a tight-lipped glare and shook his head in exasperation. "You want to talk to me or him?"

"Him first. If that's OK, Professor?"

"I'd be delighted to sit and chat with you, Officer."

She took out a digital recorder and a spiral notepad. "Mind if I record this session?"

"Not at all. Not at all." Edgefield rubbed his palms up and down his thighs.

She shivered. He repelled her on a subtle level. And that shamed her because he'd clearly suffered tremendous loss. She turned her attention to Finn. "Where will I find you when I'm done?"

His eyes glowed with controlled emotions. "I'll wait for the doc and send him in." He obviously didn't want to leave them alone, but she was the one in charge. "Cabin sixteen. They're all numbered so you won't have to use too many detective skills to hunt me down."

Funny man.

He pointed a stern finger at his boss. "The doctor will be here in five minutes. You'd be dead if it was a real emergency, but make sure you let him examine you anyway."

Thom nodded. His secretary suddenly hovered in the doorway with a shocked expression on her face.

"Holy mother of God." She crossed herself as she stared at Holly's face. "I can't believe I didn't see it before."

Well, *that* was unsettling.

"Get us some tea or coffee, would you, Gladys?" the professor asked.

Finn Carver didn't take his eyes off Holly's as he headed toward the door. He had beautiful eyes. Direct eyes that seemed to see right into her mind. Just when she thought he was going to leave quietly, he stopped beside her. Leaned close to her ear and she forced herself not to back up. "He's been through a lot over the years. Borne more than any man should have to bear. Treat him gently, or…"

"Or what?" She jerked around to face him. Blue eyes turned flat as stone. His lips were a bare inch from her own. A shiver of something primal slid over her skin.

"Or you'll have to deal with me."

"Mr. Carver, are you threatening me?"

His lip curled. "I don't threaten women. I just don't want you making a bad situation worse with your cockeyed powers of deduction."

"Don't tell me how to do my job." Her jaw locked in anger as they glared at one another.

"Then do it." His gaze drifted to her lips. Another shot of sexual excitement sent tingles spiraling through her body. Her heart pounded harder, but she straightened her spine. He was using basic animal attraction to prove how wrong she'd been earlier. But he could be faking it. Hell, guys seemed able to turn it on and off like a faucet. Either way, she was pissed.

"It would make a helluva change for the cops to actually catch a killer around here."

She matched his grim intensity with some of her own. "I'll find this killer, Mr. Carver. Whoever it might be. You can count on it."

Gina Swartz rested her head on her lover's chest and trailed her fingers over his sternum. They only had an hour. He'd started out fixing her plumbing and ended up fixing her broken heart instead. "Finn Carver came to see me today."

A grunt.

"He asked if I'd told anyone about what he was looking at in the library last week."

Muscles tensed beneath her hand. "What did you tell him?"

Her hands slid over taut, smooth flesh. "I told him I hadn't said a word to anyone. Do *you* know what's going on with all the cops?" Her hands slipped beneath the covers, and he groaned and closed his eyes.

"If you keep doing that there's only going to be one thing going on." He dragged her mouth to his for a long, hot kiss. "Don't tell that mad fuck about us, or the cops. I don't want to deal with Finn Carver or his crazy-ass brother."

"Anyone would think you're ashamed of me." She squeezed her fingers, tight and low, part punishment for mentioning Brent while naked in her bed.

Heels pressed against the mattress, thighs strong and muscular. He moaned. "I don't want people poking their noses where they don't belong." The moan turned to a growl. He was sweating and straining in lust-filled agony. "It's nobody else's business."

"I'm not going to say a word. Why would I?" This was her business. It had taken a long time, but she felt whole again. She'd finally left her past where it belonged. She traced his earlobe with her tongue. "It's so soon after last time I think you might need a little assistance here." He laughed as he twitched hot and rigid against her palm.

"Feel free to help me out." A wicked dimple appeared at the side of his gorgeous mouth. "I can't keep up with you anyway."

"Good." She slipped beneath the covers and took him in her mouth. She'd done things with this man she'd never imagined possible until a few weeks ago, and it made her feel powerful. His hands cupped her head as he urged her to take him deeper. She reveled in the power it gave her, in the knowledge that she could bring him to his knees with a few well-placed strokes. He filled the empty places inside her. Made her forget about the one man she'd loved with all her heart her entire goddamned life.

Not anymore.

Some days, her new lover brought her flowers and treated her like a lady. Other days he was rough and fucked her like a whore. They played erotic games. It was exciting, and she never knew which way his fantasies were going to veer. She'd discovered she had a few fantasies of her own that he didn't mind exploring. She craved the distraction of him like a drug. Rode the highs with wild abandon, but she wasn't addicted. She was never going to be addicted to a man ever again.

They had tea. From a pot. With china cups and saucers. It reminded her achingly of her mother, who'd died eighteen months ago from pancreatic cancer. Now there was just her and her father, their all-consuming work, and their annual father-daughter vacation.

He was all she had. She would not let him down.

Professor Edgefield's color was better, pink brightening his cheekbones. The local doc had been and gone, telling the professor he needed to come in for a full physical ASAP.

Now they sat in comfortable chairs facing one another in uncomfortable silence. Edgefield's gaze never left her face.

She sipped her tea then began. "So tell me what happened."

"The police have copies of all my files. I send them regular updates." He went to stand up and reach for something, but she stopped him.

"No, Professor." She waved him back to his seat. "About last night. Tell me what happened last night."

Understanding slid over his features. He closed his eyes as if in pain. "I'm sorry. It isn't that I don't care that poor man was murdered, I'm just so used to thinking about my own family."

"I understand."

There was another uncomfortable pause—because how could she really presume she understood what he'd gone through?

"Do you look like your parents?" he asked.

"This isn't about me, Professor."

"Of course not." His Adam's apple bobbed up and down in his gaunt throat. He had the look of a sick man—hollow, slight, insubstantial. "Well, let's see. Last night I ordered the marine station's dive master—that would be Finn—to take me out to Crow Point so we could dive a wreck we found there about ten days ago."

"You told people about this wreck?"

"We did not." His eyes were keen with intelligence now.

"Why not?"

"Because I didn't want them disturbing it."

Why not?

"Did you find treasure, Professor?"

"Call me Thom. And, yes, we did find treasure." A twinkle appeared.

She sat back in her chair. Getting information out of this guy was like playing a game of chess. He was hiding something. "There are rules for salvage. Is that why you didn't tell anyone? Did you break the law and now you're worried you'll be arrested for it, maybe lose your job? I don't care about treasure, Thom. I'm only concerned about how that man died."

His expression was almost pitying. "It's not what you think."

Holding on tight to her patience, she frowned at her notepad. "What exactly do I think?"

"That Finn and I found gold or precious gems down there. That maybe we discovered someone else down there and killed him to protect it. But I can assure you that is *not* what happened."

The dead guy hadn't been killed yesterday, so they hadn't killed him then. Coroner figured he'd been dead four or five days at least.

"The Underwater Recovery Team didn't find any treasure, Thom. So what happened to it?"

"One man's treasure is another man's..." another irritating pause, "...junk. We didn't tell anyone about it because I didn't want anyone disturbing the wreck." His expression morphed into deep concern. "The damage done already is probably irreparable."

"Especially to the dead guy," Holly said wryly.

"How old are you?"

She frowned. "I don't give out personal information."

"Thirty-two?"

She jolted. It was just a lucky guess. "You see anyone else while you were on your way to the dive site?"

Thom's eyes went up and right as if searching his memory. "We saw a few boats in the distance. No one on land or in the cove."

"And you're certain you didn't tell anyone about this wreck?"

"I am absolutely positive."

"What about Mr. Carver. Did he tell anyone?"

"Finn wouldn't want the wreck to attract inexperienced divers. The fact he took you down is quite the compliment, by the way. How long have you been diving?"

She gave up telling him her personal life wasn't any of his business. "You and Carver seem pretty tight."

"We are 'tight.'" The word sounded wrong coming from his lips. "I took him in when his father was killed."

Killed? She had so many questions but needed to stay on track and figure out what they'd found in that wreck. "Why did you take him in?"

"There was no one else. I had space." His laugh was mirthless.

She needed a lot more information than she'd been able to gather so far. About Edgefield. About Carver. The former was an eminent, if whacky, scientist; the latter had been in the military and had never been in trouble with the law. There was little else so far, but she'd requested deep background checks on both of them. "Tell me about this treasure."

"I'll do better than that." A grin lit his face as he stood and grabbed a windbreaker. "I'll show you."

Holly pulled on her dark blue patrol jacket and followed him to the door. The secretary threw Holly another of those wide-eyed looks, then told Thom she was leaving for the day. Other people wandered in and out, giving her curious stares as she followed the director down a thousand stairs then pushed open a door and was jostled by the brisk wind coming in off the sound. She looked across the inlet to the Coast Guard station. A bald eagle sat at the pinnacle of a massive pine, staring out to sea. It was still light, but the sun was starting to set across the horizon. Down more steps until they reached the water. He typed in a code and entered a square, modern building. There wasn't a soul about.

The interior was dimly lit and silent except for the background drone of appliances. He flicked on the light switches. "It's very quiet down here this time of year, which is perfect for what I need."

Suddenly the silence and isolation pressed down on her. Holly had made a tactical error. Winslow, Malone, and Chastain were conducting door-to-door interviews. Staff Sergeant Furlong and Cpl. Rachel Messenger had gone to talk with the aboriginal community just south of where the wreck was located.

The professor pressed his finger to his lips and urged her inside.

The chill in the air at her back was preferable to the unease she felt at being alone with this eccentric man. She unclipped her Taser and rested her palm on the weapon. She hadn't called in her position to fellow officers, hadn't expected to leave the main building. She eyed the back of the professor's thinning hair. She could take him.

They walked up a set of stairs. The place stank of antiseptic and brine. Warning signs were posted on every wall about chemicals and radiation.

"In here." The light in his eyes bordered on feverish. The guy was looking at her as if she were his *long-lost* daughter or, worse, a reincarnated wife straight out of the grave.

She steeled herself to blast fifty thousand volts into his body.

"Go on." She jerked her chin to indicate he move farther ahead of her. She half expected Finn Carver to leap out of the shadows and push her to the floor. Every sense was on high alert, and her heart thumped erratically. She adjusted her footing and braced herself. He could damn well try.

The professor strode to a fish tank. "You can't tell anyone about these yet," he pleaded earnestly, as if she had a clue what he was talking about.

He leaned closer to the tank and flicked on a light. Slowly the aquarium came to life, and she spotted several unusual creatures floating around in the water. They were black with yellow spots edged with purple.

"Exquisite, aren't they? We saw them the first time we dove the wreck, but I had to set up exactly the right conditions in the lab before I could risk bringing any to the surface."

"Sea slugs?" She tried to keep the doubt out of her voice.

"A previously undiscovered species of nudibranch." He beamed.

"*This* is your treasure?" Her heart thumped so loudly in her ears she felt like a damned fool.

He nodded. "So you can see there's no monetary value in the treasure for anyone. And certainly no motive for us to tell anyone about it."

Damn. It made sense. Or it was a hell of a ruse because she didn't know one sea slug from another. She'd check it out. "Thank you for your time, Professor."

"It's been a pleasure, Sergeant Rudd." And still his eyes roved her face like cockroach antennae. "Will you be reopening my wife's murder investigation?"

The guy was tenacious, she'd give him that. "I'll review the files looking for similarities when I get time, but I doubt there's going to be anything there."

He grabbed her arm, nails biting through the sleeve of her jacket. "Aren't you even remotely curious?" His eyes burned with some indefinable fervor.

She broke his grip and refrained from arresting him for assaulting a police officer.

Pity was foremost in her mind. "I'll look at the case, but after this length of time, the chance of solving your wife's murder is extremely slim."

Grief swam in his bloodshot eyes.

"I'm sorry." She turned on her heel and stalked away. She didn't like being unsettled. Didn't like being knocked off her stride. That wasn't how cops solved cases. The sound of gut-wrenching misery followed her down the stairs and out the door.

Finn sat in darkness, nursing a cold one. He concentrated on the woman creeping up his stairs. She moved quietly, maybe trying to catch him off guard. *Good luck with that.*

She rounded the corner and released her breath as she spotted him sitting in a canvas chair outside his front door.

"Wanna beer?" He reached down for an unopened one on the floor beside him.

She shook her head. "I'm on duty."

He put it back on the deck. "And what do you do when you're not on duty, Sergeant Rudd?"

She examined him as if she was trying to decide which angle to take. Hard-ass or friendly. "Last week I learned to dive."

"Why?"

She laughed and the sound brushed across his skin like electricity. He wished she'd gone for hard-ass.

"Why does anyone learn to dive?"

To covertly infiltrate enemy positions. To plant explosives and cripple ships people didn't want sailing. To insert listening devices and/or tracking devices. To take out enemy communication systems. To look at pretty creatures underwater. The list was limitless.

He leaned back in his chair, watched her as carefully as he'd watch a hammerhead. "You did a good job today"—she started to smile at his praise—"until you got stupid at the end."

Her lids dropped lower over her eyes, masking her reaction. "You're right. I was out of line. I'm sorry."

Contrition didn't sit naturally on those features and didn't last long.

Her grin was infectious. She meant it to be, and that bothered him. She used her smile to sneak beneath people's guard, and he didn't like the fact that it worked on him the same as anyone else. "You're pretty funny, Mr. Carver. I tell you I'm coming by to interview you about finding a body and you try to switch tables by critiquing my dive performance."

"Dive performances are my specialty." He held her gaze without smiling. The words were full of sexual innuendo, and he let those images settle around them. He wanted her unnerved, distracted. He was willing to use whatever it took to put her off her game. Same as she was using that smile of hers to get what she wanted.

Her grin deepened. "Did they teach you that in Special Forces?"

He finally smiled back. *Touché.* "You fishing, sweetheart?"

"Your military records say Special Forces."

He never dropped her gaze. "I'm not allowed to discuss it. It's against the rules." He took another swig of beer, which tasted dark and bitter on his tongue.

"Do you always play by the rules, Finn?"

"I do, *Holly*, always." He didn't say whose rules.

"So why didn't you report you'd found a wreck?"

His shoulders kicked up. "Thom wanted the chance to collect a few specimens before we contacted the Coast Guard. As soon as the dive world heard about a new wreck they'd swarm all over it. I assume he showed you his treasure?" She nodded. "Hardly worth killing for, is it?" He shrugged again, feeling the weight of guilt abrade his shoulders. "I didn't think it would matter if we waited a couple of weeks."

Her hair was jet black in the shadows, caught in a severe braid at her nape. No nonsense. Professional. Still, she looked hot in that uniform, with her police insignia and that gold stripe running down the side of her pants. And she looked well able to handle the weapons riding her hip. He liked people who could stand up for themselves and who stood up for others. Her features were unadorned, but a face like that didn't need makeup or glitter. He'd always preferred the natural look. Her confidence and air of authority was also a turn-on, he hated to admit. And despite what he'd said to her earlier, he'd bet she was a good cop.

None of it mattered.

The only thing that mattered was keeping her far away from the marine lab and, more importantly, far away from Thom. Her uncanny resemblance to Bianca Edgefield was a wild card the older man did not need. The rekindling of a hope that had all but burned out.

"Wreck diving gets addictive. Think you'll get addicted?" He let his gaze wander lazily around her body; long legs, trim waist, nice round butt that would fit nicely in his hands as he—*Whoa!* Not where he'd meant his mind to go.

"It was fun." She leaned against the railing, not hunching up or hiding, but not extending an invitation either. "I can see why it gives people a buzz."

He swigged back a mouthful of beer, hoping to cool off his imagination. "For what it's worth, I was impressed this morning. I'd rather dive with a novice with grit than an experienced diver with no spine."

"Are you giving me a compliment, Mr. Carver?"

"Maybe I'm just trying to get into your pants."

She laughed, but her gaze slid away. "That's not going to happen. You'll just have to fantasize. I'm a cop and you are part of this inquiry."

"Is that the only reason?" His voice came out gruff.

She didn't answer. The night air was cool around them, but he wasn't feeling the chill.

"Am I a suspect?"

"I told you earlier. Everyone's a suspect. Did you find out anything about the ship? What she was called or how long she's been down there? What she might have been carrying?"

He shook his head. "Coast Guard will probably figure it out in five minutes, but I couldn't find anything."

"So you did inquire?"

"I searched online databases and checked out a bunch of maps at the local library and some historical references. I did *not* ask around."

She pulled a face. That had been her next question.

He wasn't about to tell her that Gina might have seen what he was up to. No way would a sweet woman like Gina skewer a guy with a big-ass dive knife. And if she had been going to murder anyone it would have been his brother, years ago.

"Did you recognize anything about the equipment the dead man wore?"

Finn tipped back his beer and took another icy swallow. "No."

She was eyeing him sharply. "Could his equipment have come from the marine station?"

"Sure." Finn shrugged. "But his tanks were missing, which would be the main thing I'd recognize." He was very careful about tanks and regulators, not so particular about all the rest. "I'll do an inventory tomorrow if you want, but we have a lot of equipment and a lost-and-found people dip into. I didn't recognize the weight belt, but the suit was something I'd have used to make patches."

"What about the knife?"

"Looked like a thousand other dive knifes." He got to his feet and took a step toward her. "How was Thom when you left him?"

Her eyes tracked him carefully. "Upset."

"He ask you to reopen the investigation into his wife's murder?"

She nodded. Bit her lip.

"I figured." The silence stretched for a few moments. "He'll get over it. Believe me, he's used to disappointment."

"The professor said you went to live with him after your dad died. When was that?"

Tension crackled between them. Her lower lip looked wide and bee-stung. His gaze hooked there and he couldn't look away. "Is that part of the investigation, or personal?"

She straightened her shoulders. "There is no *personal*, Mr. Carver."

He leaned against the railing beside her, not touching, but close enough to unnerve anyone with half a brain. Holly was firing on all neurons and swung around to face him. "When did your father die?"

Old familiar anger made his chest tighten. "Nineteen eighty-nine. I was thirteen."

Busy eyes watched his face. He didn't kid himself she was besotted. "You must miss him."

"I hated the sonofabitch."

Her eyes narrowed.

"We don't all get to grow up in happy families, Holly." He clenched his fist against his side. "Count your blessings."

"I do."

"Do you have brothers and sisters?" He wanted to know more about her. Wanted to figure out what made her tick. Wanted to distract her.

She shook her head. "I'm an only child." Her mouth pulled down as she looked up into the night sky. "Spoiled rotten by loving parents. My dad's a cop too. Mom died, almost two years ago now." She looked a little lost when she mentioned her mother.

"You miss her."

She nodded. Then she looked pissed, as if she hadn't meant to tell him a damn thing. He took another swallow of beer to stop himself doing anything stupid, like trying to find out how that plump lower lip of hers tasted.

She switched the subject. "Has the professor always been so…"

"Messed up?" Finn nodded. "Ever since he found his wife and child with their heads smashed in, he's clung to the slippery edge of sanity. The only things that keep him going are his research, searching for the killer, and maybe finding out what happened to his little girl." His eyes swept her features. "You really *do* look like Bianca Edgefield, you know."

"You knew her?"

"I was six when she was murdered, but she was one of those women who always made a fuss over us kids. Bought us bags of candy and ruffled our hair."

He'd liked her. Everyone else had treated him like he was stupid. Thom had fixed that.

"What did your mother think of her?"

"My mother?" A strand of her hair had come loose in the breeze, and he tucked it carefully behind her ear. She looked like she was thinking about removing his balls with nail clippers, but she held still. "My mother wasn't around."

"Where was she?"

"I have no idea. She took off when I was little and never came back."

He watched as another note was added to her mental to-do list. Did she think his mom hadn't really run away from her dickhead alcoholic prick of a husband, leaving her kids to his nonexistent mercy? "She mailed a postcard a few weeks after she left. Postmarked Florida."

She nodded, but he could tell she was going to check it out anyway. What did he care?

"Did you see anyone on the way to the dive site last night?"

"Nope."

"Did you tell anyone where you were going?" Back to rigid cop mode.

"No." He frowned. "But I *did* write our coordinates on the dive sheets in case we didn't come back. It's SOP."

"You wrote them down that first time too?"

"Sure. There was a sea otter sighting, which was unusual in that bay. We checked it out but didn't find anything. Decided to do a quick dive while we were out there so the trip wasn't a total bust."

"No surface crew?"

"No surface crew either time. Thomas was emphatic the ship-wreck remain a secret. Nudibranchs are more active at night—hence the night dive." He wished she was watching him so closely because she wanted him, not because she wanted to catch him lying. Heat spread through his body. Muscles tensing with unwanted attraction. Plenty of good-looking women came through the marine lab, but he didn't believe in abusing his authority. He'd be quite happy for Holly to abuse hers, though. He wanted her. But he had to make sure she stayed far, far away from them all.

"Do you have any theories about who the victim might be?"

He crossed his arms over his chest and shook his head.

"Right. Thanks for the information." She stepped away from him as if he'd given her some big clue in this investigation.

"Holly?"

She paused on the top step.

"Are you involved with anyone now?"

"No." Her eyes glinted suspiciously at the reminder he'd over-heard her earlier conversation with her boss. Too bad.

He raised his bottle. "Well, if you ever want to go diving when you're off duty, let me know."

"I'm not looking for a relationship, Mr. Carver. I'm here to solve a murder."

He opened his front door to go inside. "Who said anything about a relationship? I'm just offering a no-strings recreational dive."

A light came on from the next cabin and an icy glow washed over her features. "Good night, Mr. Carver," she said with remarkable composure for a woman who was angry enough to spit nails.

He grinned. "'Night, Sergeant."

Bianca Edgefield's body was rotting beneath rich prairie grass, but the woman who strode to the police 4x4 parked on the side of the road was her doppelganger. The gossips had been right, and a shot of unholy fear stabbed through muscle to bone.

How many times did the bitch have to die?

Hatred stirred for that pretty face, those long, graceful limbs that liked to open wide and tempt the weak. Edging closer, silently weighing the possibility of killing her now, again. It was quiet. There were few people around. This might be the only chance. Another inch closer as the woman spoke into her police radio. Eyes shot to the cabin where Finn Carver lived and found the man watching from the window. Too close. That big bastard was sneaky and dangerous and couldn't be trusted.

Easing back into the shadows, one with the night. Patience was a virtue. Good things came to those who wait. The cop drove away, and a branch cracked in the deep, dark wood.

Maybe the cop would be gone by tomorrow. Maybe she wouldn't dig. But *if* she stayed, *if* she started to dig, she was dead.

CHAPTER 4

Lights from the houses across the inlet glistened in the water. It was full dark now, twenty-four hours since they'd found that body. Exhaustion grated along Finn's nerves, but he couldn't put this off any longer. He headed down to the dock and climbed into the rowboat. He wanted to figure out who the victim was before the cops did—only one person to ask. Trouble was that person hadn't spoken to him in years.

The dip of oars in the water was the only sound even though it wasn't late. Bamfield-west was quiet, and unless there was a poker game tonight, most people would be tucked up in front of their satellite TVs, nursing a cold one.

The sea was calm, saving her energy for her next blast of destruction. A whale surfaced only a few feet away, releasing a blast of spray that showered Finn with fine droplets of water.

"Son of a—" He held his breath until it dove beneath him and the boat again. Wasn't much that could creep up on him, and it was ironic that something so large did it effortlessly. He carried on rowing, glad for the adrenaline rush that fired up his nerves.

He tied up to the public dock but kept his face in the shadows as he moved swiftly along the village boardwalk. Up the road, past the Coast Guard station. The ship wasn't back yet. He figured they'd be out at Crow Point for another day or so, protecting the wreck, making sure they got all their evidence—evidence and information he didn't have access to.

He started jogging along the gravel road, not needing lights or signposts to guide his way. He knew it, the way a salmon recognized home.

There was nothing but forest around him, with the occasional house buried deep in the woods. There were hidden trails, but tonight it felt necessary to use the road. Five minutes later he came to a massive two-story log cabin topped with cedar shingles.

It was a house no ex-con should be able to afford.

No law-abiding ex-con.

A shiver of unease stroked his spine.

The driveway was level and graveled, not pitted and overgrown the way it had been when they were boys. The shack had burned down years ago—a pyre of childhood memories. He ignored the ripple of antipathy that rose up inside him and the bombardment of images that flashed through his mind as he walked down that driveway. It was all ancient history now.

There were no lights shining on the property; Brent might not even be here.

He circled to the back of the house through the woods, watching for signs of movement. A flicker of red glowed on the porch that faced the Pacific in a head-on dare.

That was how his brother faced every challenge in his troubled, rage-filled life.

Finn stepped out of the woods and approached the bottom of the steps. The red glow burned brighter for a second. A cigarette.

"Figured you'd turn up sooner or later."

Two years later to be exact. They hadn't spoken since he quit the military. The day Brent had been released from prison, Finn and Thom had turned up to bring him home. Brent had wanted nothing to do with them. Finn had tried to talk to him a few times since but had been constantly rebuffed. It had gotten to the stage where it simply hurt too much to try to repair their tattered relationship, even if he'd known how.

"How've you been, Brent?"

A harsh laugh cracked the shadows. "I've been great, Finn. Fucking great. How was the army? Kill anyone?"

Anger simmered too close to the surface. "I did what I had to do."

"What you were ordered to do." Bitterness laced his brother's tone.

"We *both* did what we had to do."

The scrape of a chair grated across the deck as his brother climbed to his feet. "Is that your version of forgiveness? I don't need your fucking forgiveness."

"My *forgiveness*? You *saved* me." Their father had beaten Finn unconscious with an iron bar. If it hadn't been for Brent, he'd be dead. Worse, because Finn had been unconscious for much of the attack, the prosecuting attorney at Brent's trial had created enough doubt in the jurors' minds to suggest Brent might have been responsible for Finn's injuries too. But Finn knew exactly who'd hurt him, and guilt expanded in his chest every time he saw his brother. Most days it almost suffocated him.

Waves washed against the nearby beach—the sound so reminiscent of childhood, he choked. "You're the one who wouldn't let me visit you in prison. You're the one who shut me out." Finn stood, breathing hard. Thirty seconds of togetherness and they'd said everything that needed to be said.

"I should've just let him hammer away at you, you runty little bastard." The red glow settled malevolently back into the shadows.

"Maybe you should have." He wasn't a runty little bastard anymore.

"Get lost. I don't want you here. I haven't seen you for half a goddamned lifetime and you turn up like the prodigal son? Get off my fucking land."

Brent had made it more than clear over the years he wanted nothing to do with him, but he wasn't running away this time. "Our land," Finn reminded him grimly. Not that he wanted it. Brent had earned that and more over the years. "I didn't come here to fight. I am sorry for screwing up your life."

There was a long, taut silence as shared memories connected them. They didn't need to say the words; they'd lived through good and bad times by relying on each other. Then Finn had let them both down.

"You had that asshole professor looking out for you. It worked out all right for you in the end." Brent sounded snide and bitter, just like their old man. His resentment toward Thom had been palpable from the start, and Finn didn't know if it was because Thom had given him the life they'd both craved or if Brent just didn't like the man.

"He taught me how to read." Dyslexia had made him an easy target for bullies at school. Brent had tried to help but hadn't been much better at reading himself. Finn doubted that had improved in prison.

"And I killed for you. You're a hell of a lucky guy."

"Lucky?" His voice cracked and an old embarrassment welled up inside him.

Emotion finally penetrated his brother's ex-con hide, and Brent let out a deep breath. "You were just a kid. I didn't want you coming to the prison and seeing that…filth, that ugliness. And by the time I got out, you'd joined the army. And after you came home…" His brother swallowed audibly. "I'm not good to be around, Finn."

Finn took a step forward.

"Come any closer and I'll blow your head off."

Finn's night vision had kicked in, and the moon had risen over the water. His brother's face was lined with age and experience. Lean and mean. Beloved and familiar.

"You wouldn't shoot me."

A bullet scored the earth to his right.

"I'm not the same stupid asshole who protected you from that fucker. I don't want you here." It was the desperation rather than the anger that had Finn backing down.

Finn swallowed the razor blades that lodged in his throat. "I don't need protecting. Not anymore."

The harsh breathing eased. "Good." The cigarette bobbed as he nodded and exhaled. "Good."

"I found a dead guy in a wreck at Crow Point last night."

Brent sneered out a laugh. "Should've known."

"Known what?"

"That you'd only come here because you wanted something."

"You just shot at me, which was exactly the welcome I was expecting. You know anything about that dead body or not?" Brent had connections in low places and, according to Gina, had received enough death threats over the years to pay attention to everything that went down on this part of the island, criminal or legit.

"I haven't killed anyone recently, if that's what you're asking." There was a feral flash of teeth. "I did get a phone call a couple of days ago asking if a guy called Len Milbank had been over to see me."

Shit. Finn didn't like the direction this was going. "And?"

His brother's eyes were hooded. "You know who he works for?"

Finn nodded. Len Milbank was an enforcer for Remy Dryzek, a scumbag who ran drugs and drink and anything else that paid, out of Port Alberni. Milbank was also Finn's best candidate for the person who'd beaten Thom to a pulp two years ago.

"I haven't seen the bastard in months. Last time Len visited, I broke his arm."

"Social call?"

Brent's lips curled up in a half smile. "Well, it wasn't tea and biscuits." His expression turned flat.

"You hear anything about a shipwreck out on Crow Point?"

"I haven't heard anything about nothing."

And wouldn't say if he had. Finn looked at the moon and remembered staring at it as a child. That huge silver orb that hung over the midnight sea. He'd often thought about walking into that ocean when he'd been a scared little boy. Brent had saved him. No one had saved Brent.

"The cops are in town asking questions."

Brent grunted.

"I gotta go." He turned away.

"Finn."

He hesitated and looked over his shoulder.

"It was good to see you." His brother's face softened for a moment. "Don't come back."

"What've we got so far?" asked Staff Sgt. Jimmy Furlong.

Full of nervous energy, Holly paced the floor. They'd set up shop in the local hotel on the west side of the inlet. It wasn't open for the season, but somehow Furlong had persuaded the proprietor to put them up. Easy money because they'd barely see their beds.

"The body has been transported back to Vancouver for autopsy. Coroner figures the TOD is at least four or five days, but he hasn't given us anything conclusive yet, except that the victim was a mature male Caucasian," she told the officers clustered around the makeshift conference table.

"All those years of medical school weren't wasted, then?" Freddy Chastain quipped.

Furlong laughed.

"Corporal Billings accompanied the body to Vancouver and should be back by lunchtime tomorrow," said Holly. "A professor I know from SFU is going to observe the autopsy in the hopes she can help him identify marks caused by invertebrate predation." Various faces were pulled.

"Evidence?"

"A weight belt was recovered from the floor of the shipwreck. Murder weapon we assume is the knife still protruding from his chest. Wet suit, knife, and vic's body are the only evidence we have so far."

"Witness statements?" Furlong pressed.

"I've interviewed the two divers who found the body. Shipped their equipment for a once-over by IFIS in Port Alberni. Professor Thom Edgefield is the director of the Bamfield Marine Science Center; he's a leading figure in his field. The other guy, Finn Carver, is an ex-Special Forces soldier who is now the dive master for the marine lab. They say they came across the wreck ten days ago when they were looking into an otter sighting. Edgefield claims to have discovered a new species of sea slug while they were down there and that's why they wanted to keep the site quiet."

"You're kidding me." Furlong shook his head. "I thought I'd heard it all."

"You believe them?" Jeff Winslow asked.

"It's a pretty convoluted lie to construct—he even showed me the aquarium he's set up for the creatures." She shrugged. "But, like all witnesses, I don't think they're telling me everything. The professor is an odd character." She didn't want to analyze Finn Carver too much. She didn't like being attracted to someone involved in an investigation.

"Professor Edgefield is the guy whose wife was murdered?" This from Corporal Messenger, who kept flashing Furlong idolized glances from beneath her lashes. Holly gritted her teeth.

"Yeah." She forced a smile. "He freaked me out because he thinks I look just like her."

"Really?" Furlong's eyes gleamed with interest.

"You do look like her—more than a little." Corporal Messenger was turning out to be an encyclopedia of knowledge on that particular case. She pulled up an old photo online and Holly blinked. It was like staring in a mirror, except Bianca Edgefield had brown eyes. They even wore their hair the same way.

"Wow." Jeff Winslow shot glances back and forth.

"He must have had heart failure," Chastain said seriously. "You're like her twin."

Holly felt a little embarrassed at being the center of attention. She knew who her family was and where she came from, but she tried not to remind everyone of it in case they thought she was getting special treatment. "Well, he did faint," she admitted.

"Dammit," Furlong swore and rose to his feet. "Did a doctor check him out before you interviewed him?" He was thinking about the big picture of an investigation—which made him a good administrator. But she didn't like being treated like a rookie.

"He did, and Edgefield was quite happy to talk on tape and show me his prized sea slug collection too."

Furlong grunted. "I want thorough background checks on both of them. Any other interviews turn up anything? Any missing person reports that might fit?"

"Nothing. But I started compiling a list of people who currently reside in the town," Jeff offered. There were a lot of holiday homes in the area. A lot of empty properties. Fewer suspects, assuming it was a local who'd killed the guy.

Holly pulled up a map of the area. "The land around the cove is heavily wooded. There's no road. This guy had to have traveled there by boat. What are the odds he just stumbled upon that shipwreck only days after Edgefield and Carver? He had to have heard about it from someone."

"Maybe there was treasure down there...real treasure, gold and silver," Chastain suggested. "And someone decided they didn't want to share."

Holly glanced at her watch. The first twenty-four hours of a murder investigation were crucial, and they were already well behind the curve ball. A headache ground at her temples. "Chastain, talk to the Coast Guard and see if you can figure out what that wreck is and what she might have been carrying. There're more doors to knock on in the morning—that's going to be Malone and Messenger's job."

Malone nodded. He was closemouthed and intense, but she'd heard good things about him.

"Jeff can keep the data compiled and talk to the local cops about any known criminal activity in the area."

"What are we going to do, Sergeant Rudd?" Furlong asked.

She hoped to hell *he* was leaving. "Until we get a hit on the vic's ID, I'm going to keep interviewing the locals. See what I can shake out of the tree."

"I'm heading back to base in the morning," Furlong said. *Yippee.* She kept her face straight. "I want progress reports every couple of hours. And immediate updates on any serious breaks in the case." He had to report to senior management, including her father. The thought made the headache pound harder. "I want this case solved and off the books ASAP. Understood?" He was staring at her, and she stood to attention.

"Yes, sir," she clipped out, feeling shame wedge under her skin. She'd slept with this guy, and while they hadn't been working together then, they were working together now. She hated making mistakes and detested errors in judgment.

"Good." He checked his Rolex. "Might be an idea to get a couple of hours' rest—see if the pathologist can come up with an ID to help us in the meantime."

Holly nodded and watched her team murmur and gather their stuff and head up the broad staircase. She was intensely aware of Jimmy Furlong watching her from the corner of his eye. The thought of him making a pass at her made her stomach twist. She hurried to her sparsely furnished room and quickly got changed. No way in hell was she going to rest. She slipped out the front door and headed down to the dock.

Ten minutes later, Holly walked into the local bar and snagged an empty stool. The place was rough as shark skin. Dark, dingy, the faint whiff of weed hanging in the air. Enough faded denim and scuffed leather to start a Hells Angels clubhouse.

"What'll you have?" the barkeep asked.

"Bud Light."

He passed her the open bottle, and she paid him, told him to keep the change. She kept trying to catch his eye, but he seemed determined not to chat. She sipped her beer, trying to blend in and absorb the conversation.

"You new around here?" A dark-eyed, dark-haired guy in his late twenties, worn jeans, red plaid shirt, squeezed between her and the next stool and ordered two beers. He smelled of expensive aftershave even though there was a shadow of a beard on his jaw.

A ladies' man.

"It's my first time in O'Malley's." Holly gave him her friendliest smile. She didn't know how old she'd been when she'd figured out her smile was her greatest asset, but it had been before kindergarten.

His eyes lit up. "Studying at the marine lab?"

"I'm learning to dive." That wasn't a lie, and officially she was still on vacation. "Are you from around here?" she asked.

A dimple appeared in that shadowed jaw. "Born and bred in this little town." His mouth tightened slightly. "Although to be honest, I can't wait to get out of here." He paid the barkeep and lifted two bottles off the bar.

"What's stopping you?"

"Too many responsibilities." He took a long swallow of beer, stuffed the other bottle under his arm, and reached out a hand to introduce himself. "Mike."

"Holly." She slipped her fingers into his grip, cold and damp from the beer bottle. "So do you dive?"

"Sometimes." Mike shrugged and grinned, knowing exactly how handsome he was. "But I usually wait for the water to warm up."

"Know any good wrecks in the area?"

Despite her smile, his eyes changed and he looked at her differently. Backed away almost imperceptibly. "That's not really my thing."

She felt a presence beside her and recognized a familiar deep voice. "I see you've met Sergeant Rudd. I've been driving myself crazy wondering what she looks like in her red dress uniform."

Her new friend reared back as if she was a rattlesnake. "Seriously? You're a cop?"

"You wanna shout that louder, because I don't think they heard you over by the jukebox." Pissed, she swung around on the stool, bumped her knees into the very solid thighs of Finn Carver. She didn't know how long he'd been there or how he'd snuck up on her so easily. She'd hoped she'd seen the last of him for the evening. He unsettled her in ways that had nothing to do with the investigation.

"Catch you later." The guy escaped back to his table.

Why had Carver sabotaged her little info gathering endeavor? She tilted her head and turned her attention to the man at her side. "I was hoping for a little time off, but I'm doomed not to get it."

"Sure you were." Blue eyes rolled, but there was humor in them.

"Maybe I'll interrogate you instead." She took a drink of her beer. "Or did they teach you how to resist my methods in Special Forces?"

"Pretty sure beautiful women have always been the downfall of weak, feeble men."

She rolled her eyes. "Nice deflection, slick."

He tipped his beer. "I aim to please."

I just bet you do.

He smiled, and she struggled not to stare at the full mouth or vivid blue eyes fringed with the sort of lashes women tortured themselves to emulate. She shifted away from him. Wished she was indifferent.

"You said your dad was a cop too?" Finn asked.

"Family tradition." Holly shook her head. "He's almost sixty and he just learned to dive with me."

"You're never too old to take up diving."

"When did you learn?"

A crease in his cheek told her he knew she'd switched the conversation back to him again, but he didn't clam up. "Thom taught me when I went to live with him. Spent a lot of time drilling safety procedures into my young head and now has to suffer the consequences."

"It must have been hard, losing your family like that, moving in with a stranger."

His gaze locked on hers, and her breathing suddenly felt shallow and tight as warmth rose up to engulf her. His eyes were intense against lightly tanned skin, blond hair ruffled into untidy spikes that made her think of tangled sheets and bedrooms.

She could feel the flush creeping into her cheeks.

His lips twitched then settled into somber. "You really do look like her, you know."

"Yeah." She wiped her palms down the front of her jeans. "I know."

"And you're not even remotely curious?"

"About what?" Holly twisted to look up at him. At five feet ten inches she didn't usually have to look up at anyone. He was closer than anticipated, and although he didn't smell of expensive cologne, he did smell like hot, clean male with a tang of the ocean. She'd always loved the ocean.

"About whether you're Thom Edgefield's missing daughter?"

A flash of something hot surged through her. "I know who I am, and I'm not adopted."

Two men came through the door as the guy she'd met, Mike, and another man headed out. One of them grabbed Mike by the arm and whispered heatedly in his ear. She thought there was going to be a bit of a scuffle, but Mike nodded and left.

Finn put his hand on her elbow and drew her attention back to him. She liked his touch a little too much, so she shook him off.

"You were looking for local color. Now you found it."

Trouble.

The new arrivals changed the atmosphere of the whole place. They wore black roll-neck sweaters and expensive-looking leather jackets. Both carried concealed weapons, and Holly would bet a month's salary neither had a license, but she was after a murderer and the minor stuff could wait—for now. They stood beside a table full of people, who quickly gathered their stuff to leave. One guy didn't move fast enough and earned a little push to speed him on his way.

"Nice." Holly leaned back against the bar.

The barkeep walked quickly over to the table. She twisted around to look at Finn. He sat on his stool, the expression on his face so impassive she knew it was an act.

"Who's that?"

"Someone who doesn't like cops."

"Names?"

"Stop fishing, Holly."

She lowered her voice. "I'm not fishing. I'm a cop, looking for a killer."

"They aren't your guys." He took a swig of his beer.

"What makes you so sure?" She sipped her own drink, but she'd lost her taste for it.

"Well, for one, I don't think they can swim, let alone dive." His eyes flickered, and she spotted the taller of the two men approaching the bar. He stopped behind Finn.

"Mr. Dryzek would like a moment of your time, Mr. Carver. If you can tear yourself away from your pretty girlfriend."

Holly's brows climbed. Dryzek. She'd heard that name in police circles before.

She could tell Finn was going to tell the man to get lost, but then he paused and seemed to reconsider. His glance brushed her face. He nodded as if she'd answered a silent question. "Wait for me, baby. This won't take long." Then he kissed her on the mouth, hungry and hot.

CHAPTER 5

Finn left Holly to choke on her beer while he went over to see Remy Dryzek. The kiss had been a risk. She'd tasted unpredictable and sexy, way too appealing for a guy like him. But hopefully it would keep this asshole thinking she was just a girlfriend enjoying a night out.

Why he felt the sudden need to protect her, he didn't know. It was one of his many flaws.

Dryzek watched him out the corner of his eye. Finn got to the table and stood staring down at the other man. They were about the same age, but Remy was a few inches shorter, more flab than muscle. But the semiautomatic Remy carried gave the man balls he otherwise lacked. Finn ignored Remy's hand that indicated for him to sit. He wasn't a dog. He didn't take orders from Dryzek, and Dryzek knew it.

They'd come to an understanding two years ago, but now it looked like the truce was over. Finn had the terrible suspicion it was all linked to that damned body in the wreck and wished he'd never set eyes on the damned thing. He crossed his arms over his chest and waited.

Dryzek's eyes were narrowed as he picked at the label on his beer. "I seem to have misplaced something that belongs to me."

"A conscience? I'm pretty sure sociopaths don't need one." Finn bared his teeth in a smile that wouldn't fool anyone.

"If I find out you had anything to do with it I'll be coming to pay you a visit."

"Enjoy the fantasy, but I don't know what the hell you're talking about." He was suddenly aware of Holly standing behind him. Dryzek's eyes flickered over her the way a lizard watched a fly. Finn half waited for the explosion where she jumped all over the guy for possession of a firearm—easily visible when the guy's jacket fell open. Instead, she hugged Finn's arm like a barfly. Laying the bait. He refrained from rolling his eyes.

Dryzek had already dismissed her. Gordy Ferdinand, Remy's right-hand man, was smiling at her in a way that made Finn's skin crawl. They'd both underestimated her. A serious mistake.

She stroked cool fingers down his arm. "Going to introduce me to your friends, *baby*?"

"Yeah, introduce us to your girl, Carver. Want to sit with us, sweet cheeks?" Gordy patted the bare wooden seat beside him. She went to sit, but Finn snagged her wrist.

"We're just leaving." Finn slid his hand lower and their fingers intertwined painfully tight.

Dryzek shot him a narrow stare. "Remember what I said; otherwise, your pretty lady might not look quite so pretty."

He probably wasn't supposed to laugh. He turned and left, taking Holly with him. No way in hell was he leaving her in O'Malley's drinking with a creep like Dryzek, even though he didn't doubt she could take care of herself. But being a cop could work for or against her at any moment. Right now, without her gun or her uniform, he figured it worked against her.

Once outside she twisted out of his grip. "What was that about, *baby*?" she demanded.

"I have no idea. If you want to go back in there and chat up those paragons of virtue, feel free, but they don't fight fair, and if they find out you're a cop they won't hesitate to make you bleed."

Her chest heaved. *Hell.* He tried not to notice, but he was just a flesh-and-blood man whose body was rebelling against a self-imposed celibacy that had lasted way too long.

"I need answers, Carver. Why did you blow my cover with the locals but not with Dryzek?" She planted her hands on her hips and leaned forward. He got a glimpse of cleavage and it made him sweat.

How much of what she did was deliberate he didn't know, but he didn't appreciate being played any more than Dryzek did.

He couldn't afford to want this woman. What he needed was to get rid of her before she stirred up more trouble for Thom or his brother, but he didn't want her to get hurt. "The locals won't talk to you no matter how hard you work them."

"Interfering with a police investigation is a chargeable offense."

Anger burned through his veins. She wasn't *listening* to him. "I'm not saying Mike wouldn't have been willing to go outside into the parking lot and bang you senseless." He loomed over her, heat pouring in waves off his body. "But he wasn't about to show you the sights or tell you where the bodies are buried."

Her expression suddenly went stark white as blood drained from her cheeks. "I don't turn tricks to get information."

"I never said you did." He frowned, then figured it out. She thought he was suggesting she was easy because he knew she'd slept with her boss. And though the sharp spur of jealousy that flicked through him was unexpected, that wasn't what he'd meant. Mike was the easy one. The guy couldn't sniff a woman without trying to score. But maybe this was what he needed to drive a wedge between them. He liked her too damned much for comfort.

"Does your team know you're down here alone?" He started walking back to the marine station's docks.

"That has nothing to do with you."

"Yeah, that's what I figured. Where are you staying? Do you need a ride across the inlet, because the water taxi closed up shop ten minutes ago?"

A flash of irritation made that lush mouth compress. But he was done hanging around, waiting for her to make a decision. She was a big girl and could make her own choices. He started along the boardwalk that hugged the inlet. The gentle wash of water drifted on the breeze. She was silently tallying the merits of going back into the bar, unarmed, or following him. Thankfully, she chose to follow him.

"Mr. Dryzek seemed a little bit wary of you, Mr. Carver. Why would that be?"

She was tenacious, that was for damn sure.

"Most people are wary of me. Would you have been happier if we were buddies?"

"I'd have been happier if you hadn't been there at all."

His lips curved despite himself. "Want me to wear a tracking device in the future?"

She snorted out a laugh. "I'll see what I can dig up." The night air was cool, and she drew the edges of her denim jacket tighter together. The stars were bright in the sky, illuminating their path. Frogs croaked in the woods behind them.

It was only a five-minute walk to the dock. He pointed to the rowboat. "Climb in." She didn't hesitate, and he tossed her a life vest, climbed in opposite, and untied the ropes. He pushed off from the side. "If you're really quiet we might see a whale."

"Trying to get me to shut up?"

She'd actually been pretty silent. He wasn't sure this was a good thing. "I figured it was worth a shot."

A peaceful hush settled over this spectacular part of the world, but he could almost hear thoughts rolling like tumblers inside her mind. The current tugged the oars as they sliced the water, and he concentrated on rowing rather than her. The trip took less than a minute, and Finn helped Holly climb out on the other side. He held onto her fingers for a moment too long, savoring the electricity that flicked over his skin whenever they touched.

She swallowed and pulled her hand away. "Thanks for the ride, Mr. Carver."

"Finn," he said.

"What?" Her eyes crinkled in confusion.

"Call me Finn. You did earlier." He didn't tell her he liked how it sounded on her lips. He wasn't that pathetic.

He took a step closer, and her eyes flashed to his. Energy zinged across the distance between them, igniting an awareness and a desire he hadn't felt in months.

He reached out and took hold of the fastener of the life vest she wore. Her lips parted, and he slowly lowered the zipper, wishing he didn't have to stop there. But the barriers between them were thicker than cotton.

He dropped the vest back into the boat.

"Want me to walk you back to your hotel?" The memory of that kiss reminded him he was playing with fire. If she ever figured out he wasn't immune, he was toast.

"This wasn't a date, *Mr. Carver*. I think I can manage." Her tone aimed for frosty but quavered too much to pull it off. They both looked around at the large wooden structure with the big salmon motif out front.

He had no doubt she could manage. "Sleep well, Sergeant Rudd."

She had to be dog-tired from her long day, and yet there was something in her eyes that told him she wouldn't be getting sleep anytime soon. Not his problem. He pushed off from the dock and started rowing back across the inlet. He wanted her gone. He wanted the cops far from here and far from the people he cared about. And if he felt a little pang at the thought of never seeing Holly Rudd again, he ignored it. At least he wouldn't have to lie to her anymore.

Holly handed Jeff a fresh cup of coffee and waited for the next shot of caffeine to kick in. They'd spent the night running background checks on local residents and had turned up quite the colorful collection of misfits, ex-cons, and people searching for a little anonymity. Finn was probably right about them not talking to the cops, but you never knew when one piece of information could leverage another.

Jimmy Furlong walked in the room, freshly showered and shaved. Corporal Messenger walked in a moment later.

"Coroner get back to us yet?"

Holly checked her watch. "I doubt he's even started the post yet." It was only seven o'clock. She and Jeff had been up all night.

"What have you got?" Furlong asked.

"Jeff finished entering witness statements. I've been running names to see what might pop up."

"Anything more on the guys who found the body?" Without an ID on the victim, Carver and Edgefield were still the most viable lines of inquiry.

"A lot of stuff on both of them." The others filtered in. She snagged a muffin out of the box Freddy Chastain carried. "Edgefield started coming out here in 1978 to conduct fieldwork for his PhD. He got a job in Edmonton but still came out every summer to teach courses for the university and do his research. His wife, Bianca, was murdered in 1982, along with their infant son. The body of his young daughter was never found, but they did find her jacket. The assumption was her body was dragged off by a wild animal." Chastain grimaced as he bit into his second muffin. "Ever since, he's been on a crusade to find the killer."

"Was he ever a suspect?"

She shook her head. "Not that I can tell. He was teaching the day she disappeared. He reported them missing when they weren't home for dinner that night."

She took a sip of coffee. It scorched her mouth. "He pretty much moved out here after that, teaching full-time at the marine lab and making the cops' lives hell."

"He'd just lost his entire family. I can understand him going off the deep end," Corporal Malone spoke up.

Holly nodded. "Absolutely." She was still trying to figure out Malone, to discover where his strengths lay. He was one of those enigmatic silent types who always seemed to think a damn sight more than they spoke—like Finn Carver.

She checked her notes. "Carver went to live with Edgefield in 1989 after his older brother killed their father." It had been shocking to read the case files. Photographs had shown a boy severely beaten, with a broken right ulna and radius. Three broken bones in his left hand, where he'd probably tried to ward off the blows, and several fractured ribs. She'd felt an emotional tug on her heartstrings to think about the tall, rugged, capable man she'd met and imagine him as that vulnerable child.

Nothing about him seemed vulnerable now.

"This place is a right hotbed of family drama," said Chastain. "Like *The Young and the Restless* on speed."

"The guy was alcoholic, abusive. He should never have been allowed to raise two boys alone." Reading those files had felt like an invasion of privacy, and she knew Finn would view it the same way. But this was her job.

"What happened to the mother?" asked Furlong.

"Finn—Carver—said she ran off when he was a toddler. I'm trying to trace her now."

"And now these two guys who seem to be surrounded by a constant stream of victims suddenly find another one?" Her boss didn't look convinced.

"There's more." She felt a little odd discussing this. She'd gotten personal with a suspect even though she hadn't gone near any lines, let alone crossed them. Well, except for that kiss, which had caught her completely off guard and nearly knocked her off her stool. But that had been for effect, not pleasure. "Carver joined the army at eighteen and spent six years in JTF2." Canadian Special Forces. "He left unexpectedly a couple of years ago. Didn't give a reason, but it was around the same time a police report stated that Thomas Edgefield was in the hospital and almost died. He was severely beaten and lost a kidney. They never caught the attacker." She didn't mention what she'd witnessed in the bar last night. She didn't want to admit she'd gone there alone without proper backup.

Furlong checked his enormous watch. "I'm going to take a crack at them before I go." He looked excited, like a little kid who'd been promised candy.

Holly climbed to her feet. She wasn't worried about Finn, but if Furlong handled Edgefield wrong, they'd never get another ounce of cooperation out of him. The guy would end up in an asylum.

"You stay here, Rudd. I'll take Corporal Messenger to give her some experience."

"Corporal Messenger is welcome to tag along, sir, but as primary, I insist on being there too."

There was momentary silence.

Jimmy Furlong had a reputation for not being pushed, but a murder investigation was conducted by a group for a reason—to stop tunnel vision and make sure the information was properly disseminated. After a long moment, he nodded, and she had to wonder if it was because of her father or because it was the right choice.

Regardless, she wasn't being left out of the loop.

They strode down to the dock, and Furlong commandeered the local water taxi to ferry them straight across the inlet. "Who the hell builds a town with the sea splitting it down the middle with no bridge or road access?" he complained to no one in particular.

The guy driving the taxi said nothing. Holly had noticed the locals growing more and more taciturn. Maybe everyone who lived here hid a secret. It would make investigations difficult if not impossible, if they remained so closemouthed. Unless they could crack someone into a confession.

On the other side of the inlet Furlong hurried off with Messenger in tow while Holly paid the fare. "Thanks." She smiled.

She looked up and there was Finn Carver leaning against the dive shed doorway, wearing a dry suit stripped to the waist and watching her closely. The sight of that muscled chest stirred things Holly wasn't prepared to deal with. There was something about him that appealed, not just good looks, but the way he handled himself. She wasn't one to bend the rules. Being off limits should have been enough to drown the little yearning noises her body was making. But instead, they were getting louder. Given that her last mistake was already stalking her career, she couldn't afford another one. She jogged up the steep gravel path to catch Furlong. He was rattling the front doors of the marine lab, but they were locked.

"Edgefield lives in a house just down that path." She pointed down a trail that ran beside the marine lab.

Furlong was pissed but trying hard not to show it. He strode off, making Messenger trot to keep up. Holly pinched her lips tight. She was allowed an opinion, but obviously she wasn't allowed to openly argue with the team commander. She should have known better.

One more hour and he'd be gone. Hold that thought. It couldn't be soon enough.

The three of them trekked along the path, down some stone steps to a low, modern-looking building. Furlong pounded on the door, and after a few moments, a weary-looking Edgefield emerged in a pair of blue-striped pajamas. His eyes were instantly drawn to her even though Furlong was the one talking to him.

"Thomas Edgefield?"

Thomas rubbed his eyes beneath his glasses and tilted his head to meet Furlong's purposeful stare. "What can I do for you?"

"We have some more questions for you."

Edgefield laughed self-consciously. "It can't wait until I'm dressed?"

"It'll only take a moment." Furlong brushed him aside and entered his home without being invited. Edgefield looked at her and Corporal Messenger. "You're like buses. Wait a lifetime for one and then three show up at once."

Corporal Messenger gave him a sweet smile. Holly kept her expression neutral. Furlong was on the warpath; she was going to have to watch her step.

"You know Sergeant Rudd." Furlong stood impatiently in the hallway, ignoring the man's outstretched hand. "This is Corporal Messenger, and I'm Staff Sergeant Furlong. I'm in charge of this investigation."

Edgefield shot a look at Holly, which she ignored. He nodded politely, his shoulders gaining that slightly hunched appearance, his hair sticking out at Einsteinian angles. They followed him into the front room, which had huge floor-to-ceiling windows with an incredible view of the Broken Islands all the way across to Ucluelet.

"Please, sit down." The professor sat heavily in an armchair before a fire that burned in the hearth.

She and Corporal Messenger both sat cautiously on the edge of a sofa.

Furlong remained standing. "Why didn't you mention the beating that happened two years ago?"

Edgefield blinked like an owl behind wire-rimmed specs. "I didn't mention the time I broke my ankle tripping over a pair of rubber boots either." His voice sharpened. "Because I didn't think it would be relevant."

"We decide what's relevant, not you." Furlong's attitude was grim and threatening. He was playing bad cop but without any real direction. Holly believed in leaning on a suspect when the evidence backed them up, but it was dubious with a person this unstable.

"Tell me what happened when you were attacked," Furlong ordered.

Edgefield leaned back in his chair. His skin had taken on a scarlet tinge. Embarrassment? Shame? High blood pressure?

A voice startled them all.

"He can't tell you." Finn Carver strode quickly into the room. "He doesn't remember anything." He'd stripped off the dry suit and pulled on jeans and a faded T-shirt that said TRUST NO ONE. "He walked down to the bar one night and someone beat the living shit out of him. He has no recollection of the event itself. The cops failed to collect evidence at the scene or in the hospital. No one was ever caught."

Finn was insinuating, not for the first time, the RCMP was incompetent. Holly bristled instinctively, and yet so far they had failed to do much for Thomas Edgefield.

"Mr. Carver, you weren't invited to this interview." Furlong looked at him long and hard. "I suggest you leave."

Finn walked over to an easy chair and flopped into it. "You weren't invited either, pal, so unless it's a formal interview I'm staying. If it is formal then Thom isn't saying another word until his lawyer arrives."

"Lawyer?" Thom blinked.

"Is that right? Makes it look like he has something to hide." Furlong moved toward Finn, trying to get into his head. If Finn lashed out in any way, Furlong would take him down. Holly couldn't take her eyes off Finn's expression. She willed him to keep his cool, but he wasn't the slightest bit intimidated by the team commander. He leaned back, closed his eyes, and stretched out his feet.

Steam practically hissed out of Furlong's ears.

"We're trying to figure out if Professor Edgefield had any enemies," Holly put in, trying to defuse the tension.

"What difference does that make to your murder investigation?" Those eyes of Finn's opened and raked her skin. "We all have enemies. We all have secrets, or haven't you figured that out yet?" He climbed to his feet, eye-to-eye with Furlong as he delivered his coup d'état. "I bet even you and Sergeant Rudd have secrets." Furlong opened his mouth and then shut it again. Fast.

Finn's lips curled up into a mean smile and, for a moment, she thought he was going to drive his fist through Furlong's face. Holly wanted to curl up on the spot. Embarrassment made her cheeks burn. Finn had used that private information to rein in Furlong, and to her it felt like the ultimate betrayal. "Just because you have secrets doesn't mean you've committed a crime, now does it?"

Furlong shot her a look that promised retribution, and she set her teeth. She hadn't betrayed a confidence, *he* had.

She decided to do her job. "So you have no idea who beat you up?" she said to Edgefield.

He shook his head. "Probably just as well because Finn would have torn them limb from limb."

"Thom," Finn reprimanded him softly.

Edgefield's cheeks turned ruddy. "Sorry. I forget. I make these jokes and forget these people might actually believe me for once." His face lost all expression. "All the times I've sent them positive proof people were lying about where they said they were when Bianca died and no one has ever done a damned thing." He held her gaze and Holly had to look away.

"I'm very sorry for your loss, Professor." This from Cpl. Rachel Messenger who sat quietly beside her. The rookie. The most professional officer here. "I read about the case in school, and it's one of the things that inspired me to join the police force."

Thomas blinked, clearly shocked. "Well," he breathed out heavily. "Maybe you'll catch some bad people and something positive will have come out of it in the end." He rubbed the corner of his eye.

"Jesus." Furlong rolled his eyes and then leaned closer to Finn. "Watch who you're threatening, sunshine."

Holly wanted to lambaste Furlong for how badly he'd handled this interview. But she couldn't think of a single word that wouldn't get her fired.

"You need to leave." Finn's expression was unruffled, but Holly sensed an anger so deep she could almost feel it searing her skin. He held the door wide open. Holly paused for a moment as she passed him. She held his gaze and spotted the submerged glitter in his blue eyes—disappointment? It shouldn't have stung quite as much as it did. She wanted to be pissed. She wanted to say she was sorry. Instead she nodded and turned away. Concentrated on the job she needed to do before she could get the hell out of this creepy little town.

"Jesus, Thom, what the hell were you thinking, letting them in here like that?"

"They didn't exactly give me much choice." Irritation laced Thom's tone.

"You're the director of the marine laboratory. You *always* have a choice, don't you forget that. Just because Holly looks like—"

"Holly?"

"What?" Finn asked, confused.

"Yesterday it was Sergeant Rudd. Now you're on first-name terms? When did that happen?"

Finn stopped talking and regrouped. For all Thomas seemed out of it sometimes, he didn't miss much. Finn had been furious when he'd overheard that asshole Furlong harassing him. He'd dealt with that sort of bully before, but physical violence wasn't gonna work on a jerk with a badge. And he didn't want to explore the unfamiliar feeling of jealousy that had taken root inside him because Holly had slept with the sonofabitch. She was gonna hate him for using that information, even though he'd been subtle.

"Just because *Sergeant Rudd* looks like Bianca, don't let it throw you off and make you say something stupid."

"But I didn't kill that diver. How on earth can I incriminate myself by talking to them if I didn't do it?"

Finn checked his watch. He had five pupils down at the dock ready to do a dive off the pier. *Shit.* He didn't have time to explain the twisted ways of the criminal justice system to a guy who already knew them inside out. "Just promise me next time the cops come calling you won't say a word without Laura present."

"Laura?"

"Laura Prescott," Finn said impatiently. There was only one "Laura" in a fifty-mile radius.

"Laura Prescott the potter?" Thomas's voice was plaintive.

He closed his eyes and counted to five. "She still has her legal license, and something tells me Byron Summers isn't going to have much time for you after you suggested his daddy murdered your wife and child." Finn stared hard at Thom. The man had alienated most of the town's hundred and fifty inhabitants. "We're a little short of options."

"But *Laura Prescott...*?"

Finn tipped his head to one side to examine the man. "What the hell is wrong with Laura?"

"Nothing." Thom bristled, but Finn knew him well enough to know something wasn't right. Thom drew in a big breath into that skinny chest, but the bravado popped as soon as he met Finn's gaze. He swallowed and looked away. "I barely know the woman."

Then he got it. After all these years, Thomas had finally noticed another woman and it scared the crap out of him. Finn knew exactly how he felt.

He headed to the phone and wrote a number on a pad of paper beside it. He also wrote it on another piece of paper and jammed it into the top pocket of Thom's pj's. "You can use this as a way to break the ice."

Thom pulled the number out of his pocket and stared at it. "She'll just think I'm crazy, the same way everyone thinks I'm crazy. How come you know her number?"

Finn laughed. Thom was kind and patient and caring and loyal. He was also scalpel smart and clinically analytical. "You *are* crazy. You know I've always been good at memorizing numbers."

"Yeah, but how come you memorized hers?" Thom was beginning to sound a little pissed.

Finn headed out the door to start work. "You'll have to ask her, now won't you?"

Furlong gave a quick spiel before heading back to the mainland. Basically he told them to keep pressing Thomas Edgefield and Finn Carver about their alibis. He made it personal, and that was always a mistake.

That whole scenario didn't fly with Holly.

Why commit murder, hide the body in one of the most inaccessible places on earth, and then report finding the body a few days later? Why not let the body float off into Barkley Sound or just rot in situ? Neither Edgefield nor Carver seemed stupid. But Edgefield was fragile and an easy target to crack, as Furlong put it. Trouble was, like most good cops, Holly didn't just want to get the case off the books, she wanted to find the killer and get him or her off the streets.

"Walk me to the helipad, Sergeant Rudd."

Here goes. She wasn't fooled by that friendly tone. He carried his overnight bag over one shoulder, walked with long strides that forced her to hurry to keep up. Deliberate. He wanted her off balance. At the bottom of the hotel steps he stopped. The chopper wasn't here yet, but they'd had word it was on its way.

"You've got some nerve." The words were barely a whisper but vehement.

Holly bristled. "Pardon me?"

Furlong moved closer and leaned down. "After everything we discussed, you told Finn Carver about us."

"I didn't tell anyone." She crossed her arms in front of her chest, aware of eyes staring at them through the windows of the hotel.

"I sure as hell didn't mention it." Rage soured his breath.

"He overheard us talking on the boat yesterday morning, put two and two together."

"Shit." He let out a tight breath that seemed to dispel most of his anger, but his frown remained. "Being the deputy commissioner's daughter means a lot of people will be scrutinizing your work. Our past"—he cleared his throat—"*relationship* would cause quite a stir in the wrong hands."

"I didn't get this job because of you or my dad. I got it because I'm a damned good investigator."

"The press doesn't give a damn about how good an officer you are. They care about headlines and cover-ups, and we can't afford any more sex scandals."

"I know that." Dammit, hadn't she had endless discussions with her father about how to improve the force's reputation, especially where woman were concerned? Her voice was so quiet it was almost indiscernible. "Why the hell didn't you keep your pants zipped, or at least keep your wedding ring on? I would never have slept with a married man had I known—"

"Maybe *that's* why I took it off." He held her gaze, and she read something in his eyes that she didn't want to see. "Did you ever consider for a moment that I might have actually had genuine feelings for you?" Oh, god, she didn't want to do this. Not now. Not ever. He'd been a massive mistake, and nothing could change that. This would only make it worse.

He opened his mouth to say more but both their phones rang simultaneously. *Thank god.*

His lips twisted. "It's your father."

Her call was from Steffie Billings. "You've got an ID? Fantastic. Who?"

"Tell me," Furlong ordered, obviously wanting to pass the information on to her dad.

"A guy named Len Milbank." She paused and relayed more information. "He's got a record and acts as a local enforcer for an organized crime gang operating out of Port Alberni."

Remy Dryzek—the guy from the bar last night.

Finally they had a lead.

CHAPTER 6

"What can you tell me about Remy Dryzek?" Holly asked Sgt. Greg Hammond, an officer who worked as part of the British Columbia Combined Forces Special Enforcement Unit, which dealt with the organized crime on the island. He was based in Port Alberni, which was a nightmare drive from Bamfield on agonizingly rutted gravel roads. In his early forties, Hammond had short hair and an unruffled manner. The rest of her team was conducting more house-to-house inquiries, asking if people had seen Milbank in the area. If so—where and when. They were in the process of pulling his financial and phone records. As well as e-mail.

"Second-generation Romanian. Born right here but parents moved to North Vancouver when he was small. He moved back to the island about five years ago when things got a little dicey with the Russian mafia. Served time for assault back in 2005 but managed to fly under the radar ever since."

"What makes you think he's involved in organized crime?"

Cool hazel eyes regarded her. "Oh, he's involved all right." Hammond opened a new computer screen. Pulled up a dozen mug shots, mainly girls who didn't look legal age. "He runs a prostitution ring all over the island and probably on the mainland too. None of the people we've charged will give him up. We inserted an undercover officer into his club once, but they broke out tea and cupcakes and she knew the game was up."

"Did he threaten her?"

Hammond shook his head. "Guy's too smart to mess with the cops directly. They just sat and laughed at her until she eventually walked out."

An idea buzzed in her nerves. "I could go undercover. I was introduced to him in a bar the other day, erroneously, as someone's girlfriend." She might be able to get close, get a confession. Excitement started to whip through her blood.

"No way."

"Why not?" She frowned.

"The deputy commissioner would have my balls. I like them attached."

"How do you know about my father?" Her relationship with the big boss wasn't something she broadcast.

"Your team commander called earlier asking for information on your vic. He happened to mention it." His gaze was bland, but Holly had to wonder what else Furlong had said about her.

Dammit. "What do you have on Milbank?"

Hammond brought up another mug shot. "No rocket scientist, but he knew how to use his fists. Served time for armed robbery and had a bunch of DUIs. Worked the doors at Dryzek's club and generally did grunt work."

At least she now had a face to replace the grisly corpse she'd met yesterday. Square faced, stubbled jaw, eyes only a mother could love. "Can we visit his home?"

Hammond nodded. "But we got a report last night to say the place had been burglarized."

"What time?"

Hammond checked his notes. "Landlord reported it around seven o'clock. He doesn't know when the break-in actually occurred. I've applied for a warrant to collect evidence, but we could do an initial scene examination."

Her heart gave a little flutter. Had the killer been looking for something? If so, what? Remy Dryzek had told Finn he'd misplaced something and threatened him. Had Milbank stolen something from Dryzek? Or was Milbank the thing that Dryzek was looking for? Why was he in Bamfield looking for the guy? What did he know?

Cpl. Steffie Billings breezed through the door. She'd flown back from Vancouver and was catching up with the IFIS people based in this building. "I'm never gonna eat sardines again. Or shrimp."

Floater autopsies required an iron stomach, but Holly had enough professional interest to be sorry she'd missed it. "Bad?"

The other woman held up her hand. "I don't even want to think about it." Her face was a little pale and she wouldn't meet Holly's gaze. Steffie wasn't a rookie. It must have been grim.

"Did the post turn up anything useful?"

"Apart from an ID, not much." Steffie handed her a file to look through.

"Is this my copy?" Holly asked.

"Yes. I've another to give Jeff for the files, and I sent a copy through to the team commander at his request." She raised both brows and dipped her chin.

Shit. Furlong was shadowing the investigation much more closely than most team commanders.

"Knife sliced the left ventricle. Cause of death was massive blood loss. Coroner ordered a bunch of toxicology tests, but it's going to be hard to figure out if he was drugged first, given the condition of the body. It'll take a few weeks to get the results back."

Holly flicked through the file. Seawater was a bitch. No trace evidence. Flesh had been nibbled away. Starfish, shrimp, and crabs had done some damage, although the neoprene had kept the body off the seafloor, which helped. She looked at a photo of the knife in the chest. Something bothered her about the image. "When I was down there yesterday you had to be super careful not to even make the smallest disturbance; otherwise, visibility was wiped out in seconds. A struggle in that hull would have caused blackout conditions and trapped the killer down there too."

Hammond peered over her shoulder. "What happened to Milbank's tanks?"

That was it. The lightning bolt moment. "He must have been killed *before* he put his equipment on—or after he took it off—because with his air tanks on, there's too much gear. The knife would never have penetrated the heart."

"Why would he take his air tanks off inside the wreck?" asked Hammond.

"He wouldn't." She remembered the cold, oppressive feel of that wreck. The disorientating darkness.

"So he could have been killed on land or in the water and then dumped in the wreck?" Steffie asked.

"Or on a boat," Holly said thoughtfully.

"But why dump the body in the wreck?" Hammond rubbed his eyes.

"A wreck no one was supposed to know about..." She shot him a hard look. "Good question. Let's see if we can figure it out. Did the techs finish with Carver and Edgefield's dive equipment?"

"I just spoke to them, and they found nothing. They've already called Carver to tell him to pick it up."

Holly nodded. She could have offered to transport it back to the marine lab, but the less she saw of Finn Carver the better.

Hammond grabbed his jacket.

"We're going to Len Milbank's home," she told Steffie. "You want to tag along?"

"Sure. That way if we find anything I can stick around to help catalogue the evidence."

They headed out in Hammond's SUV. "We really need to track Len Milbank's final movements, find out the last time anyone saw or spoke to him. I'm going to need officers canvassing his neighborhood and hangouts. Can you get me any people to help?"

He nodded, strong hands gripping the wheel. "We're already on it." He cleared his throat. "The team commander requested that earlier." His voice dropped. "Is there something going on that I should know about?"

Holly shook her head. "If you could just keep me in the loop...?"

"Sure," Hammond replied. "But I don't do politics."

Holly smiled. "Good. Neither do I."

Milbank had lived in a tiny apartment above a fishing tackle shop in the middle of town. It was cheap and dirty, with graffiti on the walls in the back alley. Hammond got the keys off the landlord—the guy who ran the shop and who hadn't seen Milbank in over a week. They went up the steps at the side of the building, pulled on latex gloves and paper booties so they didn't contaminate the scene.

Inside, the place was torn apart. Cushions ripped off the couches. Drawers open, contents spilled. But no serious damage and, judging from the enormous flat-screen TV still hanging on the wall with a Blu-ray player beneath, nothing had been stolen.

"Did officers process this scene last night when the report came in?"

Hammond shook his head. "Not yet. We had a little girl lost in Cathedral Grove around sundown last night."

A shiver raced over Holly's skin.

"Don't worry. We found her." Hammond caught her eye and grinned. "The tyke had wandered off when her parents stopped their RV for a coffee break. Thankfully, we had two K9 units available, and the dogs tracked her down in under thirty minutes. Everything else was put on hold."

She nodded. "Glad it had a happy ending."

"Any reason to think he was murdered here and the body transported?" Hammond asked.

"I doubt it." Holly looked around. "I can't see why he'd be wearing neoprene at home, but if you find a pool of blood we'll know I'm wrong."

Hammond nodded.

"Any theories, Sergeant Hammond?"

"Len Milbank made a lot of enemies. Not only was he Remy Dryzek's fist, he freelanced, threatened, and bullied. Generally made people's lives hell." He grimaced. "He was not a nice guy, and not many will be sorry he's dead."

"You ever hear of a guy called Finn Carver?"

Hammond shook his head. "Not that I recall."

She walked through to the kitchen, checked the fridge. "The 'best before' date on the milk is last weekend. Does Dryzek scuba dive?" she asked Hammond.

"Not to my knowledge, certainly not recently. Milbank had a boat, though."

"We need to find it and get a warrant to search it."

She walked back into the living room and hunkered down beside the couch. "Steffie, get some shots of this." There were a couple of books among the jumbled papers. One was on wreck diving. The other on treasures of the deep.

Steffie came over and photographed the books.

"Someone told Len Milbank about the wreck. Someone lured him out there, alone, so they could kill him." Holly was sure of it. "How did he know there was a wreck?"

"I'm pretty sure that's why they pay us the big bucks." Hammond flashed her a quick grin. "Want me to call IFIS in here?"

Holly nodded. "We need to figure out who tossed the place. It's probably connected to his death." She turned to Steffie. "Get them to run fingerprints, check phone records. We need to find his boat, vehicle, and his cell phone, assuming he has them. Did he have a girlfriend?" She directed the question at Hammond.

"Last time I saw him he had one of Remy's girls hanging off his arm. She looked sixteen—maybe. ID said she was twenty-one."

"He sounds like a real prince." Holly pressed her lips into an unhappy line. It wasn't her job to judge the victim, just to find the killer. "I think it's time to pay a visit to Remy Dryzek."

They found him at his house, high on the ridge, overlooking the valley. Two squad cars acted as backup as she and Hammond knocked at the front door.

A housekeeper answered.

"We'd like to talk to Mr. Dryzek. Is he home?"

"I'll see if he's receiving visitors."

"We're not visitors, ma'am," she told the housekeeper firmly. "We are police officers. We can talk to your boss here or we can have him escorted to the station for questioning. Is he here?"

Footsteps echoed down a long, marble-tiled hallway, coming toward them. "What's going on?" Remy Dryzek walked up to the door and put his hand on the woman's shoulder. "It's OK, Elmira, the police officers can come in." It was almost as if he was expecting them. He kissed the woman's cheek, and she bowed slightly and opened the door to let them through.

"Bring some coffee to my study, please."

The good manners made Holly raise her brows. Remy Dryzek beckoned them through the entrance and down the bright white hall. They entered a spacious office where Remy appeared to be hard at work on his computer.

"The housekeeper is my aunt. I told her she doesn't need to work, but she seems to need something to do with her life." He held his hands open in front of him as if he couldn't explain it. Sweet, benevolent nephew.

He wasn't wearing a weapon today, and so far he didn't seem to have recognized Holly from the bar last night. Her cap and uniform certainly made for a different look.

"We believe you have a man named Len Milbank in your employment?" she said.

"I hire Len occasionally." There was a definite air of hyper-vigilance about him. "What's he done? Where is he?" He watched her with laser focus.

"What is it exactly that Mr. Milbank does for you?"

Dryzek settled his weight into the back of his chair, trying to appear relaxed. She wasn't fooled. "He does odd jobs and errands. Sometimes he acts as bouncer at my club, but lately he's been getting into trouble, so I made him take a break."

Made him?

She heard footsteps behind them and turned to meet the brown-eyed gaze of Dryzek's friend from last night.

"Hey," he stopped midstep, "you're Finn Carver's girlfriend."

Dryzek's eyes flashed in sudden recognition.

"No, I'm not." Holly kept her expression neutral and back ramrod straight.

"Carver's working with the cops?" The light in his eyes turned violent. "Bastard."

She didn't want Finn caught up in this, but there wasn't much she could do about it now. She'd have to warn him to watch his back.

Hammond said nothing, but she was aware of him taking everything in. "I'm Sergeant Holly Rudd, RCMP. Sergeant Hammond here and I have some questions about Len Milbank."

"You found Len?" the second guy asked. There was a nervous edge to him too. As if he was bracing to run. This could get interesting fast.

She pulled out her spiral notebook. "What's your name?"

He lowered his chin and stared at his boss. "Gordon Ferdinand. People call me Gordy."

With the twin diamond ear studs, Holly could see why.

"When was the last time you saw Len Milbank, Mr. Dryzek?"

Remy scratched his head. "About a week ago."

"Can you be more exact?"

Dryzek shook his head. "Not really. I don't remember."

Holly leaned forward. "Where did you see him?"

"Down at the club." Dryzek licked his lips. "Why does that matter?"

"Last night in the bar, you told Finn Carver you'd lost something. What was it?"

"You working undercover or something?" He looked her up and down, unconvinced, then crossed his arms over his chest and seemed to be thinking about his answer. "I went looking for Len," he said finally.

"Why?" Holly pushed.

"I'm worried about him. He has a tendency to get into trouble if I don't watch out for him." Dryzek pushed to his feet. "Enough of the questions. Where's Len being held? Did he call a lawyer yet?"

Dryzek was worried that Len might tell them something. It was a damned shame he couldn't tell them anything at all.

"Len Milbank is dead, Mr. Dryzek."

"What the fuck?" His eyes widened and he sank back into his seat. "Shit."

"Carver," Ferdinand said vehemently. Holly frowned.

"When did he die? Where did you find him?" Dryzek demanded.

She hesitated. "We're not sure exactly of the time of death—that's why we need to figure out his final movements."

Dryzek's eyes darted around the desk but finally settled on his clenched fists that rested there. "I want to know everything the police find out." His voice was low and angry. No more pretense.

"You said 'Carver'?" Holly said to Gordy Ferdinand. "Why did you say that?"

But the two men were looking at each other, staring hard into the other's eyes, and Holly knew two things. One, they hadn't known Len was dead until she'd told them. Two, they weren't going to say another word.

"If you know anything, you need to talk to the police. Obstructing a homicide investigation is a criminal offense."

Dryzek's fingers tightened but he didn't speak.

She exchanged a look with Hammond, who shrugged. She took out a business card and slid it across the desk toward the crime boss. "If you have any information…"

He looked up into her eyes, but all traces of warm host were gone. "Len had no next-of-kin. You'll keep me informed and let me know when I can have his body for burial? And his personal effects."

"We'll need to confirm he doesn't have any family and then we'll get back to you."

Gordy Ferdinand climbed to his feet.

"Did you search Len Milbank's house last night?" Holly asked.

"No." The nod of his head belied his words. "But we hung out there a lot." Covering his ass for when they found fingerprints and trace.

"Yeah, I can see why." Holly glanced around the spacious room with its diamond bright windows, view overlooking the water, pristine carpets, and sumptuous furnishings. Why wouldn't they watch movies in good old Len's seedy dive? "Did Milbank have something of yours, Mr. Dryzek?"

Dryzek rose slowly to his feet and she shifted position, her expression remaining hard and blank. Twelve years on the force and she didn't scare easy.

"Len Milbank was a good friend. I'd appreciate some time alone to grieve his death. You have more questions, you give me a call—or ask that boyfriend of yours. He probably knows all about it."

Jeez. She did not like those insinuations on any level. She and Hammond showed themselves out, their footsteps echoing loudly through the luxury mansion. "That got us exactly nowhere."

"Guys like Dryzek know the ropes and don't trip up easy, but the surprise looked genuine when he heard Milbank was dead," said Hammond. He'd been exceedingly quiet in there. Letting her run her own investigation or giving her enough rope to hang herself? She settled into the passenger seat of his car to hitch a ride back to the station. "We've got no suspects and no motive."

"He was pretty anxious to find Milbank. Something tells me love and compassion weren't the reasons behind it. Len Milbank either had something of his or he was a threat in some way. I'll put out some feelers; see what I can come up with. Somebody somewhere knows something." Hammond maneuvered around the quiet streets of Port Alberni and Holly blew out a tired breath.

"And all we've got to do is pry loose those secrets." She said it with her trademark smile, but inside she felt daunted. Secrets were the thing the people of Bamfield seemed to guard most avidly.

The scenery was great—if you liked dirt, trees, and dust.

Holly was on her way back to Bamfield, a bone-jarring trip on supposedly well-maintained logging roads from Port Alberni. She kept her eye on the tiny red mile markers, aware that if she took a wrong turn it could take her a week to find her way out of the vast wilderness. Furlong would *love* that. She hung on tight to the steering wheel as a massive crater almost wrenched it out of her hands. Deep ruts in the gravel meant the seventy-five-kilometer route took two hours to drive.

"Ah, crap." She squeezed over to the far lip of the road and slowed down to a crawl as another enormous trailer-towing logging truck bore down on her. The powerful monster swept past, showering her with dust and stones in its wake. For long seconds she could see nothing, so she sat tight, hating how her heart accelerated from the rush of adrenaline. She gave it another ten seconds for the dust trail to clear and pulled back out onto the dirt road.

Steffie had changed her mind about coming back to Bamfield tonight. The IFIS team had turned up a mass of possible evidence at Milbank's apartment, and she wanted to make sure it was all catalogued correctly before she rejoined the command group.

They'd made good progress today, but were still a long way from catching the killer—or even establishing a solid motive.

She picked up her cell phone to call Jeff Winslow, then swore. No signal. Another cloud of dust appeared in her rearview, warning that another vehicle was hurtling down the road on a death wish. She kept going, slowing down, nudging as far right as she dared, a sharp drop-off just a few feet away on the edge of a thousand square miles of forest.

"Slow down, you moron." She glared into the mirror at the driver of a massive black truck. He wore a ball cap and dark glasses. Her attention was snagged by another cloud of dust up ahead as she approached a single-lane bridge. She judged the distance and figured she had time to cross before the logging truck arrived, so she sped up, jostling as she hit a rut. The truck in her rearview accelerated rapidly and kissed her bumper as she hit the middle of the bridge. The steering wheel jerked out of her fingers, but she grabbed it and fought frantically, accelerating to get off the bridge before the logging lorry that was barreling down the hill squashed her like a fly. Sparks flashed in her peripheral vision as she struck the guardrail. The logging truck blasted its horn as she and the truck cleared the narrow bridge. Holly's heart thundered, sweat dripping off her forehead as the truck nudged her bumper again. She craned her neck to try to make out a plate.

The whack job was going to pay for this. What the hell was he on?

No time to radio for backup. She needed both hands on the wheel. She slammed on the brakes, but the driver of the truck anticipated the move and sped up and smashed into her rear end, twisting her vehicle until it came to a sharp halt in a massive cloud of dust and grit, square across the road. Airbags punched her in the face and thrust her back against the seat. She scrambled to find her seat belt release and her gun, but her fingers weren't working properly and the damn release mechanism was stiff and uncooperative.

Then the sound of a revving engine grabbed her attention. Terror screamed along her nerves as her fingers struggled futilely with the restraints. The truck slammed into her from behind. Rocking the SUV violently, it bulldozed her to the edge of the road. The SUV hung suspended for a breath-stealing moment, then tumbled, gaining momentum as it raced down the bank and into the brittle arms of the uncut forest.

CHAPTER 7

Finn put his foot down, wanting to get home before dusk descended and the wildlife came out on the road and put a crimp in more than the occasional fender. He'd picked up his and Thom's dive equipment from the cop shop. A small rebellious part of him had hoped to see Holly, but she hadn't appeared and he'd had other things to do besides hang around a police station trying to score another kiss. She'd arrest him if she knew some of the thoughts he'd been having.

The backup compressor had blown a seal a few days ago and he'd used the trip to pick up the spare parts. Rob had taken out a small party of experienced divers that afternoon, but tomorrow was jam-packed with novices' first open-water dives. A big day. He rubbed his eyes. He was tired and still had a few hours of work to do when he got back to the marine lab.

Still, busy beat brooding.

Dust trails told him several vehicles had passed this way within the last few minutes. It hadn't rained all week—a minor miracle on the west coast—and that always made the conditions worse. He frowned at the skid marks on the bridge. It never failed to amaze him how boneheaded stupid people could be and that these people were legally allowed to reproduce. He shook his head as the skid marks continued.

Ah, shit. It looked like someone had gone off the road here. Finn pulled over to the side, away from the dangerous bend. A sense of foreboding warned him that he was about to find his second body of the week. Although the last thing he wanted to do was look at more carnage, he couldn't very well walk away without checking for survivors.

He started into the bush and then down the steep incline. Branches were brutally shorn off and a deep furrow scraped through the unstable soil.

He pushed past some thick fir trees and caught a glimpse of something white in the bush down below. The chance of finding survivors was slim. His nose caught a whiff of something else—gasoline, probably leaking from a ruptured gas tank. The slightest spark could start a fire. He started running, slipping and sliding past the massive tree trunks.

Catching a clearer glimpse of the vehicle, Finn's blood turned to ice and his heart pounded like a fresh recruit. The RCMP SUV was upside down, nose wrapped around the trunk of a big old spruce, tires spinning like a kid's toy. The hiss of steam was the only sound in the vast forest. He skidded to a halt beside the driver's door and peered inside, past the deflated airbags. He'd expected blood and broken bones. Expected his worst nightmare. But it was empty. There was no one there.

He spun, searching for a blood trail, and worked his way back up the hillside. Then he spotted something dark lying unmoving in the low brush, and he sprinted up the slope.

Holly, covered in blood.

Absolute terror shot through his veins as he ran to her side.

"Jesus. What did you do to yourself?" He squatted beside her, checked her breath and pulse. Her skin was warm. Pulse fluttering steadily beneath his fingers. Alive. Thank god she was alive. He moved her hair off her forehead to look for injuries. *Dammit.* He was torn about what to do. He couldn't risk moving her. Couldn't risk leaving her behind.

"Holly?" Most of the blood seemed to have come from her nose. Smears covered her chin and shirt, but he knew from experience it probably looked worse than it was. "Can you hear me?" He touched her shoulder gently, and she groaned and started coughing. It was the best sound he'd ever heard. "Steady. Steady now."

He held onto her lightly so she didn't try to get up.

"F-Finn?"

Relief punched his heart. Her gray eyes were cloudy with confusion, the surrounding flesh already starting to swell.

"Yeah, it's me. What the hell happened?"

"Someone ran me off the road."

Anger seared his flesh. She grimaced as she tried to raise her arm.

"Don't move." He ran his hands over her limbs to reassure himself she hadn't broken anything. "Are you saying someone did this on purpose?"

She pushed his hands aside and sat up, squeezing her eyes shut, clearly in pain. When she opened them again, she stared down at the wreck at the bottom of the hill. "Holy crap."

Finn stared too. "You're lucky you're not dead." *Christ,* his hands trembled as he tried to examine her injuries. He was shocked at how much this totally freaked him out. Despite everything he'd told himself, the cop had slipped under his skin like a damn sliver.

"How'd you find me?" She pulled away slightly.

Finn didn't like the suspicion that darkened her gaze but understood the nature of the beast. Why should she trust anyone after what she'd just been through? "I saw skid marks on the bridge; ground was churned up enough I knew someone had veered off the road. Are you all right?"

"No. Help me stand, will you?"

"You shouldn't try to move. I can go for help. Get an ambulance out here." But it would take hours and it was almost dark.

She shook her head, but then grabbed her skull. "I managed to throw myself out of the cab before it rolled and crashed. I didn't hit anything harder than the ground and the airbag." She touched her nose. "But that hurt like hell."

Her cap was gone. Long dark hair strung around her face, which was a mess of stark white skin streaked with dirty crimson. Fuck.

"We need to get you up onto the road and get a crew out here to deal with the wreck."

"That's evidence of the attempted murder of a police officer." Holly pointed at the SUV, her movements shaky. "IFIS need to process it before anyone else touches it."

"As long as it doesn't set the whole place on fire, they can do whatever the hell they want." Finn didn't care. "Let's get you out of here." He eyed the steep incline. Before she could protest, he eased her cautiously into his arms and started the difficult ascent. She wrapped her arms around his neck, and it shouldn't have filled him with anything except relief.

Holly Rudd stirred dangerous feelings inside him, feelings he wasn't used to and did not want. The fact she'd almost died in a car wreck—caused by some frickin' maniac—frayed his usually rock-solid composure. He'd wished her far away from Bamfield and out of his life. But not like that. Never like that.

At the top of the bank he stepped onto the road, breathing heavily, and carried her to his truck. He let go of her legs and leaned her gently against the passenger door. "How do you feel?" Christ, her color looked awful, and she was going to sport one if not two black eyes.

"It's red." Her voice broke and she sagged with whole-body relief.

He squinted at her, wondering how hard she'd hit her head.

"Your truck. It's red." She grinned at him, and although she looked like shit, it was probably the most genuine smile she'd ever given him.

"Yeah." He leaned over and opened the door for her. "It's always been red."

"The truck that ran me off the road was black."

OK. "How do you feel? Any pain? Any sickness?" He stared at her pupils, watched them react to the light. So far so good.

"Don't you get it? I know you weren't the person who ran me off the road."

He squeezed her shoulders carefully and smiled down at her. "*I* already knew that. Do you think I'm the kind of man to run *anyone* off the road?"

Her lips opened. Then she blinked away a sudden shimmer of tears and shook her head. "I'm just used to needing proof, not relying on instincts."

"I'm beginning to think your instincts are pretty damn good, if only you trusted them." He leaned down and, for some crazy reason, kissed her forehead before helping her into the truck. He would never hurt a woman. He would especially never hurt Holly. As confessions went, it was a dangerous one, so he kept it to himself. It wasn't his own secrets he was guarding. And no matter what, he could not afford to get close to this woman.

If circumstances had been different, Holly Rudd might have made quite the impact on his life and his heart. Thinking about the strain lining Thom's face, maybe it was just as well things weren't different. Heartbreak wasn't pretty.

Her hands shook as she tried to do up her seat belt. "I don't know what would have happened if you hadn't found me."

He already knew that admitting weakness didn't come easy to her, so he snorted and made light of it. "You'd have crawled up that hill on your hands and knees and flagged down a passing logging truck and demanded to be taken wherever you needed to go." She had grit and balls. How anyone wouldn't admire those traits, especially in such a beautiful, if battered, package, he didn't know. He leaned over and fixed her belt. Tried to quiet the rage that simmered in his blood.

Hell. She was lucky to be alive, and he didn't want to think about the possibility of internal bleeding or what could have happened if she hadn't thrown herself out of a vehicle careening at speed down a wooded hillside. And what if the person who'd run her off the road had stopped to finish the job?

Fuck. He was so angry it was a wonder his skin wasn't steaming. But Holly didn't need his macho bullshit. She just needed to be taken care of. The cops could deal with finding whatever asshole had done this. He'd make sure no one got the chance to do it again.

He walked around the nose of the cab and got in. "Now I'm gonna give you a choice." Because he knew being in charge mattered to her. "The hospital in Bamfield is only twenty minutes away. It doesn't have all the mod cons of Port Alberni, but it's got the basics. If there's a problem, they can call for a chopper evac, which is probably as fast as driving back to Port Alberni from here." He gave her a flat-eyed smile. "*Or* we can drive back along this road to Port Alberni. What do you want to do?"

"Bamfield." She braced her hand against the dash. Her breath came in sharp, shallow pants. "I want to get off this damned road as soon as possible."

Good. "Who knew you were traveling this road alone? Who wanted to get rid of you?"

Her brow crinkled as he put the truck in gear. "A lot of people want to get rid of me—it's a hazard of the job." Her voice rasped in her throat. He handed her a bottle of water from the groceries behind his seat, and then grabbed his own.

He passed her his jacket to use as a pillow. "Tell me if you're hurting and I'll slow down." He checked the mirror and pulled out onto the gravel, concentrating on avoiding the worst of the ruts so as not to jar Holly's injuries, but wanting to get to the clinic as fast as possible. All the time his mind was whirling. Who the hell would want to kill a cop? A woman? Holly?

"I couldn't see the driver with the sun in my eyes and all that dust flying."

"It must have scared the shit out of you."

"It wasn't my best moment, that's for damn sure."

He put his hand on her thigh. Ignored the electricity and tried to give comfort. "Close your eyes. Get some rest."

She put her hand over his and squeezed; he was disconcerted to feel the sensation echoed in his chest.

"I'm sorry about what happened with Thom this morning. Staff Sergeant Furlong was pissed at me and took it out on the professor," she said.

"Staff Sergeant Furlong is an asshole."

She snorted, then winced and grabbed her ribs. "Unfortunately, until I solve this case, he's also my boss."

"Well, that's a hell of an incentive to solve the case."

"It sure is." She visibly gritted her teeth.

He swallowed a knot of emotion. He wasn't good with other people's pain. In his stint in the military he'd seen too many people suffer. It hadn't taken his fellow soldiers long to figure out that while he was tough on the outside, he was mush in the middle. He might not blink at taking down terrorists or insurgents, but show him a sick kid or injured animal and he was doing everything in his power to help them. Trouble was, nine times out of ten, he couldn't do a damn thing to help without risking the op. It was one of the reasons he didn't miss it. He'd loved being a soldier; hated the associated misery.

"Have you always had the hero gene?"

"What?" he asked, confused.

"You know," she tried to smile, "saving the day, sweeping a girl off her feet?"

He shook his head. "It came to me later in life. God knows I needed saving often enough as a kid." There was silence in the cab except for the constant rumble of the gravel beneath the tires.

"I saw the photos. Of what he did to you…"

He gripped the wheel tighter. Didn't want to talk about it. "It was a long time ago."

"It was during your formative years. You should have turned out to be a complete jerk."

He dropped his voice to a sexy whisper. "Are you giving me a compliment, Sergeant Rudd?"

She groaned even as she held her side. "I have a head injury. No other way to explain it."

He grinned, wishing they'd met under normal circumstances, wishing he wasn't just delivering her to the hospital after someone had tried to ram her into a tree.

Holly closed her eyes. He drove as fast as possible while avoiding bumps in the road and keeping an eye out for deer. They got to the clinic just as the doctor and nurse were leaving.

"Anita. Dr. Fielding. I need your help." He jumped out of the cab and went around and opened Holly's door. Her eyes were open but she looked green. "Pulled the sergeant here out of a car wreck." He took her in his arms and she hung on tight around his neck. Which felt good. Which was a damn shame because she was only here to catch Milbank's killer. "You need to check her out."

Holly fiddled in her pocket as Finn strode through the doors. He laid her gently on a bed in the infirmary and she handed him her cell. "Call Jeff Winslow. Tell him to get a crew out to the site of the wreck. Some bastard tried to kill me and I'm not about to curl up and let him get away with it. And tell him *not* to call my father."

He wanted to ask questions, but the doctor forced her to lie back and started shining a light in her eyes. Then they started undressing her, and Finn knew it was time to leave. But he didn't want to go. He had some crazy-assed notion he was taking care of her now. He gave her fingers a squeeze and wanted to kiss her again. Instead, he went outside and found the number for her colleague the way she'd asked him to, the way she'd trusted him to. Even as he pressed "dial" he knew his life was about to get a hell of a lot more complicated. Somehow Holly had added herself to the list of people he needed to keep safe, and the way things were going it wouldn't be easy.

The village he'd grown up in had always been full of secrets and lies, darkness hidden beneath the quiet, picturesque exterior. Even though he'd known most of these people all his life he didn't trust any of them, except Thom. And Thom was the one person in this place who would never hurt Holly. Because Thom thought this woman was his long lost daughter, which also made the only person he could trust bug-ass crazy.

Two hours later, Finn was exhausted and starving. He'd been interviewed three times, and they still wouldn't let him back in to see Holly. But now all the other cops had left, and he couldn't take sitting around like a piece of meat for a moment longer. Thom had come down and had a local engineer replace the parts for the compressor. Rob Fitzgerald, Finn's assistant, was filling all the bottles they needed for tomorrow's dives.

Finally he'd had enough. He pushed through the door and found Dr. Fielding, who'd already run every possible test imaginable.

"Does she have to stay in overnight?"

"*She* has a name." Holly stared at him with big dark eyes, fragile against the pillow.

The doctor rubbed the lines over his brow. "She seems to have come off remarkably well, considering. No sign of broken bones, internal bleeding, or even concussion." He almost sounded disappointed. "She's going to be stiff and sore and black and blue tomorrow, but"—he met Finn's gaze—"as long as she has supervision, I don't see why she can't be discharged."

Her lips thinned in an unhappy line. "The other officers are going to be working through the night. We don't have time or resources to waste playing nursemaid—"

"I'll watch her," Finn said.

"No." Holly looked appalled.

The doctor looked from one to the other. "It's up to you, Officer. But if you don't have someone on hand to call if necessary, then you're staying here, and I will call your commanding officer to make it official." The doctor slumped. "Which means I'm staying here too. Which means if I'm too tired to treat an emergency patient tomorrow we get to blame you." He beamed, but there was stubbornness to his smile that even Holly recognized.

"I need to get back to work." She tossed back the covers with a wince. "But fine, I'll go with Carver."

Dr. Fielding looked relieved. He headed into his office. "You have my home phone number and my cell. Call if you need me."

She grunted as she moved. "Damn, I don't think I can even get in a boat without a shot of morphine."

"You don't need to. There's a spare room in my cabin. You'll have privacy, but you'll also have me in case you need anything."

She looked uncertain.

"You can call your team. They can stage a rescue anytime you feel scared."

"What am I, eight?" She laughed, recognizing the same tactics she'd tried on him yesterday when she'd been trying to talk him into taking her diving. Christ, was that only yesterday? "I really need to get back to work—"

"Tomorrow," the doctor shouted through the open door, "*if* I approve you." He hurried back and handed her a bottle of meds. "Promise me you'll get some sleep tonight, and you can be back on the job first thing tomorrow." He waited her out with raised brows.

"Fine, but tomorrow starts at midnight." Her eyes took on a spark of fire that had been missing since the wreck. She looked at Finn. "Can you help me with my stuff, please?"

The nurse had found her a hospital gown, which billowed about her like a puffy cloud. She eased her feet carefully to the floor. Finn could barely take his eyes off flashes of naked skin. The doctor walked away, leaving the two of them staring at each other.

"Finn?" She raised a confused brow.

Snapping out of his trance, he strode into the nurse's office and snagged a new set of scrubs off a shelf. "Order some new ones on me," he told Anita as she busied herself shutting down the computer.

He shook out the scrubs—they smelled like warm cotton—and stood beside Holly, bending down so she could slip first one foot, then the other into the pant legs. He held her gaze as he pulled them up over her hips, his fingers brushing the velvet soft skin beneath her gown. Her cheeks got a little pink and her breathing hitched. "Thanks."

The top half was going to be trickier for both of them. "Turn around and face the wall." The curtains were drawn, but there was no way she'd be able to get this over her head without help. If he'd been wearing a button-up shirt he'd have given it to her. Instead, he pulled the string of the hospital gown and held his breath as it drifted slowly to the floor. Perfectly toned shoulders and a delicate spine greeted him. Red grazes covered the tops of her arms and all down one side. It reminded him of how close she'd come to serious injury and how much pain she was probably in.

"Can you lift your arms?" His tone was gruff. Perhaps he should have waited for the nurse to do this, but he could tell Anita was in a hurry to get home. And was he really going to miss out on his one opportunity to see Holly naked?

"I think so." She lifted them slowly.

He could hear the catch in her breathing as she attempted to stir battered flesh. He stood behind her and leaned forward, keeping his eyes firmly on her hands. His chest brushed her back as he whipped the top over her fingers and let the material slide down her arms before drawing it carefully over her head and torso. An electric sizzle snapped through the air between them. He'd never been so aware of another human being in his life.

"Any idea who did this?" He had to rescue his mind from inappropriate thoughts. Like what it would feel like to slip his hands under her shirt and lift those breasts in his palms. *Not* helping.

"The guy I busted for murdering his wife last month? Some local drunk driver with a grudge?" She tried to laugh, but it came out as a gasp. "I'd just paid Remy Dryzek a visit, so officers from Port Alberni are going to question him first. Oh, and you need to know, he recognized me from the bar and thinks you've been working with the cops. You need to watch your back."

"Dryzek doesn't have the balls to come after me. Why'd you visit a lowlife like that anyway?" Was Dryzek involved? Finn could see him stabbing someone, but no way could he see him diving that wreck. It took gumption and nerves of steel. Dryzek had neither.

"Most of the people I deal with are lowlifes." She snorted, then grabbed her ribs. "I need to stop doing that. We just identified the body you found. The name is due to be released any moment." Her feet searched blindly for her boots while her eyes tracked his response. Still doing her job, even here. "Len Milbank. You know him?"

Finn forced himself not to react. "I've heard of him." He dropped to his knees and took her foot in his hands. She'd painted her toenails with little frog decals that seemed at odds with the serious police officer she displayed to the world.

She saw him looking. "I was on vacation."

He said nothing but smiled as he pulled her socks over her toes, then slipped her foot into her boot, then repeated the process with the other foot.

Len Milbank. He should have left the scumbag inside that wreck to rot. "He was a friend of Remy Dryzek's. Nasty piece of work by all accounts." Definitely not a friend of Thom's or his brother's. *Dammit.* Things just kept getting more complicated.

"Any ideas what he might have been doing at the shipwreck?"

He rose to his full height. "Well, I didn't know yesterday and didn't experience any psychic visions overnight, so I still don't know today."

"Funny." She gathered her bloody uniform and equipment belt. Finn held his hand out in an offer to carry them for her. He didn't want her to freak by grabbing her weapons. She let him take them, and he held out his other arm for her to lean on. Strong fingers gripped his elbow. "Well, someone else besides you and Thom knew about that shipwreck because someone told Len Milbank. And that someone probably stuck a knife in his chest. I'm figuring the same someone just ran me off the road and tried to kill me." Her fingernails dug into his muscles as she tried to balance her weight.

He slowed his pace and nodded to Anita, who began stripping down the bed before she left for the night.

"Take care of her, else you'll answer to me in the morning." The nurse smiled with easy familiarity.

"Yes, ma'am."

"Thank you for your help," Holly called to the nurse and doctor, who both shouted responses. She hobbled unsteadily to the door. "Whoever the killer is, I'm going to find that person, and I'm going to put him in jail for a very long time."

Holly woke up to find Thom Edgefield leaning over her, staring intently at her face.

She screamed, sucked in an agonizing breath, and shoved her hand against his chest.

He jumped back in surprise.

"What the hell?" Finn ran into the room, dripping wet with a towel almost draped around a pair of very fine hips. "I told you to keep an eye on her, not scare her half to death."

"I didn't *do* anything." A blush darkened Edgefield's cheeks. He wrung his hands in a clear sign of distress. "I was just looking at her face for identifying marks."

"Jesus, Thom!" Finn slicked back short, sopping wet hair. "Sorry. Thom came by and said he'd listen out in case you needed anything while I was in the shower." His expression was thunderous. "He didn't mean any harm."

"You make me sound like a complete imbecile." Thom threw his hands up in the air.

"Well, sometimes you act like a frickin' moron," Finn almost shouted. Holly was with him all the way.

Thom pressed his lips together as his eyes drifted to the carpet and then away. "I better head home. Good night."

Holly frowned after the man, or she would have, if she could get her face to move. Everything was swollen and sore.

"How are you feeling?" Finn moved to her side. The soap he used drifted on the air, and she was hyperaware there was nothing but a flimsy towel between him and nakedness. She was female enough to be curious. And that was not a good thing.

Her heart drummed uncomfortably against her ribs. When was the last time she'd felt even the smallest hint of attraction? Unfortunately, she knew exactly when it was and that was enough to put her off men for life. But something about this guy—

"Holly?" he snapped. Blue eyes drilled into hers.

"I'm fine." Her voice came out all husky, and he passed her a cup of water from the bedside table. He wasn't just sexy, he was kind and compassionate too. Definitely a heartbreaker, and she liked hers intact. She grabbed the cup with relief and glanced around the room, avoiding looking at him as he just stood there, nearly naked except for the water droplets that glistened against his tanned skin.

"You look like shit," he told her.

She almost choked on the water. That should banish any fantasies of naked mud wrestling from her head. He took the glass from her hand and placed it back on the table.

"But a hell of a lot better than you should, considering."

Someone *had* tried to kill her. When she considered the shape the SUV was in, that person hadn't been too far from succeeding. "Did I remember to thank you for getting me to the hospital?"

"You promised me sexual favors for life." His grin was wicked.

"Ha, ha. Funny man." But her heart thumped crazily in her chest. She didn't want to like Finn. She certainly didn't want to want him. "I like what you've done with this place." Avoiding the thoughts that swirled inside her like an unhealthy cocktail, she checked out her surroundings. The walls were wood. Two desks set into the walls. One single bed, which she was lying in, another set of bunks pushed against the opposite wall. He seemed to care little about material things. There were no pictures on the walls. Nothing but plain utilitarian space. She wondered what his bedroom looked like and put a rapid halt on those thoughts. Blood filled her cheeks, but she doubted he'd notice considering the mess that was her face. Both eyes were swollen. Her nose throbbed like a beacon. "Exactly how bad do I look?"

"Like you've gone ten rounds with a heavyweight champ." He grimaced, and the towel slipped an inch. Mesmerized by the dark blond hair that arrowed down from his navel she couldn't look away.

"I guess I'm going to have to cancel the photo shoot with French *Vogue*."

He laughed. Relaxed and ridiculously at ease. Almost naked with her in bed.

Great. Just great.

She felt the heat building in her cheeks and tried to shift up the bed, ignoring her protesting ribs. This guy was still involved with this case. She could not be having carnal thoughts about his incredibly ripped, smooth-skinned, and definitely hot body.

"The cabins are set up for grad students and visiting profs. I'm here all year round, but I let people stay in here if the lab is short on space." He kicked up those wide shoulders, and muscles flexed beneath taut skin. Her mouth went dry, and it had nothing to do with pain meds or whiplash. "I guess I could get somewhere better, but I spend most of my life working so I don't see the point.

It's cheap, convenient, and beats the hell out of what I had in the military."

"You were in the army for sixteen years." She latched on to this tidbit.

He raised a brow and waited.

He did that, she'd noticed. Kept his silence and waited for the actual question rather than fill the expectant quiet. Not many people had the nerve for silence.

"You weren't that far from a full military pension. Why'd you quit?"

His lips twitched, barely. "I'm not quite ready for retirement."

"*Was* it because Thom got beat up?"

He shrugged and distracted her with the sort of smile that got women in serious trouble. Even smart women. "Not everything in life is about money."

Finn Carver had a knack for avoiding answering her questions. As a cop and a woman, it put her on edge.

Annoyed, she tried to throw off the covers to get out of bed and away from the effect he had on her, but they were tucked in so tightly she could barely move. There was so much to do. The last thing she needed was to be in bed, ogling man candy when there was a murder to solve.

Jimmy Furlong was going to love this.

"I have to go," she said.

"Nuh-uh."

"Where's my gun? If I shoot you, you'll have to let me up."

From the determined look in his eyes, he was ready for a fight, which suited her perfectly. But every movement she made shot streaks of pain into her ribs and up her side. Her neck felt like she'd been unsuccessfully lynched. He sat down on the edge of the bed, trapping her.

With a snarl of frustration she lay back against the pillows, breathing hard. She tried not to notice his flat abs or smell his clean, soapy scent. The man was totally gorgeous and *she* was a primary investigator in a homicide. She didn't have time for distractions.

"I could arrest you," she growled.

"I thought you owed me a favor?"

For the dive, she remembered. "*This* is your favor?" She gestured to the bed.

"Getting you into bed was definitely on the list." His eyes heated, then he looked away. Broke the connection. "I set up an oh eight hundred meeting here for your team."

Her eyes widened a fraction. Even that hurt like a bitch.

He reached for the bottle of tablets and shook out two, handed them to her. "I have to be at the dive shed by quarter after eight, so you'll have the place to yourselves." Steam billowed through the open doorway behind him. The shower was still running. "You can search the place if you like, eliminate me from your inquiries."

But she knew from the intelligence in his eyes that all his secrets were hidden inside that finely packaged mind of his. And suddenly she wanted inside—inside that mind, and closer still. She swallowed the pain pills with another gulp of water.

Her phone rang. He picked it up, looked at the display, and handed it over. "Your father."

She recoiled and her head started screaming. "I don't want to talk to him."

"He already knows about the accident." Those blue eyes of his were cool now. Dark and cool, like the deep ocean. "He called earlier, and I apprised him of the situation."

"You had no right." Her fist clenched around the cell. She had to answer it. But she didn't want to be yanked off the case.

"I told him you were a bit beat up, but the doctor said you'd be ready to return to work first thing in the morning."

Her mind whirled. She'd assumed Finn would have done his best to get her off the case, and she didn't know why the fact he hadn't made her feel all warm and fuzzy inside. She pressed the answer button, never dropping his gaze. "Hi, Dad. No, I'm fine. Sore, but fine."

She covered the mouthpiece as Finn turned to leave the room, that damp towel clinging to his butt in an erotic display. "Hey," she called. He glanced over his shoulder. "Thanks."

He nodded and she heard him going back into the bathroom. She turned her attention to her father.

"How are you really feeling?" Her father's voice was deep and rich as hot chocolate and always filled her with warmth.

"I ache all over, but nothing's seriously damaged except my pride."

"Well, we all have to deal with that at some point or other." There was a pause. Her dad was good at saying a lot with his silences too. "We've got people working the scene, trying to catch this person. Do you think it's related to the homicide you're working?"

Holly squinted out the windows into the solid darkness. "It seems the obvious thing, but you're the one who taught me to look at the facts and not jump to conclusions."

He blew out a gusty sigh. "I'm not happy about this, Hobbit. Not only has one of my officers been attacked, but the fact you're my daughter makes it hard to sit back and follow procedure. It was bad enough you getting stabbed last month…" Her father had always been the most honest person she knew. "I want to fly over there and rip off someone's head. Instead, I have to sit behind a desk and let others do the job for me."

"Dad, I know how to handle myself—"

"I know that. But," there was a thick swallow, "after losing your mother, you're all I've got left, and I'm damned if some joker is going to take you away from me."

"Never gonna happen."

"Staff Sergeant Furlong suggested you step back from the case until you're feeling better."

I just bet he did. Holly swallowed the instinctive retort. "There's nothing wrong with me that a few hours' sleep won't fix."

"Humph." Thankfully he changed the subject. "Who's the guy playing nursemaid?" As if he hadn't already run a zillion background checks.

"Finn Carver is a former Special Forces soldier who found me minutes after the crash happened and drove me to the hospital. Only way they'd release me was if I had someone on call if I needed help. The command group has work to do. He volunteered."

"He's the one who found Len Milbank's body."

"Correct. And he took me down to the shipwreck to look at the crime scene too."

"Alone?"

"That's right, Dad. Alone. And I'm still alive and breathing."

"Any chance he's the person who ran you off the road?"

"None."

"You're sure?"

"Actually, Dad, I am totally one hundred percent sure, and you can tell the deputy commissioner the same thing."

"Smart-ass." But he laughed.

"I learned it from you."

That silence again. Holly decided to wait it out in case she blurted something stupid.

"I spoke to his former commanding officer."

Of course he had.

"Guy said he was an excellent soldier, one of his best. You know I have a great deal of respect for our armed forces, right?"

There was a "but" in there. "Of course."

The silence took on a cautious quality. "Just make sure you're both on the same side before you trust him too much—understand?"

A quiver of embarrassment rolled over her skin. "I would never do anything unethical, sir."

"Hell, Holly, I'm not talking about sleeping with the guy— although, jeez, that's not what a father wants to think about. He's a former Special Forces soldier. He can do things most cops can't even contemplate. Remember that. Until you know more about him, keep your guard up."

She didn't tell her father she trusted Finn—it sounded foolish and naive on such short acquaintance. If she was wrong she didn't want to look like an idiot, and she'd been wrong before. These were dangerous waters, and she had no intention of drowning in them.

Her father let out a low rumble of frustration. "If I could get over there and nurse you myself I would. I'm in the middle of a meeting with a bunch of feds from across the border—I just slipped out for a moment. I could try to find someone from the agency that looked after your mother..." The words brought the usual pang of loss, a thousand different memories stretching between them.

"No." She ran her fingers over the cold metal of her gun. "Finn Carver has the eyes of the entire RCMP watching him tonight and he knows it. I'll be fine."

"If I hadn't had at least fifteen different reports that he was a trustworthy guy, I wouldn't contemplate leaving you there, you know that, right?"

"I'm not a kid." She smiled. "I love you, Daddy."

Another big sigh blew into the phone. "I love you too, Hobbit."

They said good-bye, and she clicked off thoughtfully. There was another good reason to stay here tonight. Gaining Finn's trust was a good way to dig deeper into this town's secrets. She wasn't about to fall for the golden boy good looks or protective charm. She was disciplined enough to admire the beauty without succumbing to temptation—wasn't she?

Only one thing mattered to her, and that was the quest for justice, even when the victim was a two-bit thug who'd probably got exactly what he deserved. But there was a reason justice was blind and cops didn't try cases. It was all to do with men like Len Milbank and Finn Carver.

CHAPTER 8

Jeff Winslow knocked on the bedroom door just as she was pulling on her equipment belt. "Come in."

All her belongings—complete with a new uniform—had turned up sometime during the night. As she'd slept like the dead, she assumed one of the guys had brought them over, and she didn't want to ask who'd seen her snoring. She had to move with extreme caution so as not to jar her sore ribs. Thankfully, the pain meds made her feel less like she'd been sawn in half.

She could do this.

"Thanks for meeting me here. I just needed a solid sleep to get back on my feet."

"You shouldn't even be on the job." Jeff's eyes crinkled in sympathy as he took in her bruises. "Are you sure you're up to this?"

"It looks worse than it is." *If only.* "Let's go into the living room and set up."

Finn—fully clothed, *thank god*—had left a pot of coffee, which dripped and sizzled, releasing a mouth-watering aroma. She'd seen him briefly before he headed out the door and had managed to pin down her hormones so she could view him with a little more detachment this morning. Sure, he was gorgeous and brave, but she dealt with that sort of alpha male every day. Normally it didn't affect her.

The chivalry was an unexpected turn-on.

Mentally she kicked herself.

The car accident must have shaken her up, made her a little extra vulnerable, but everything was back under control today. He'd left out the makings for toast, so she made herself some while Jeff set up his laptop and screen projector. Corporals Messenger, Chastain, and Malone rolled in, their booted feet shaking the floor as they climbed the stairs and pushed in the door. Tiredness edged everyone's features.

She felt them all weighing her abilities by her battered features and determinedly held her hand up. "I know I look like crap, but I'm perfectly fine. Just a few colorful bruises and a hell of an incentive to bring this guy in. Where's Steffie?"

"Still in Port Alberni." Freddy Chastain helped himself to coffee and so did the others. She used the opportunity to sneak into one of the chairs. She didn't want to bump against anyone and let them know how fragile she was really feeling.

"A separate team is investigating the crash incident," Jeff commented.

Holly nodded and sipped her coffee. She'd already sent them a statement, but one of the officers would be tracking her down later today.

"Steffie stayed to cross-reference any evidence they came up with. They've already figured out a black Ram truck was stolen yesterday afternoon. They're checking surveillance cameras and are looking for it, but if someone dumped it in the woods—well, there's a lot of area to cover."

She swore under her breath. "Let's get on with finding Len Milbank's killer. What do we have that we didn't know yesterday?"

"We've interviewed most of the local residents, although we've still got a few key people to get around. Most people knew who Len Milbank was, and not one of them looked sorry he was dead."

"Yeah." She nodded. "I got that impression yesterday too."

"And no one remembers seeing him around here the last few weeks."

Holly thought about Thomas Edgefield's assertion that people had lied about their whereabouts the day of his wife's murder. He'd been chasing the truth for nearly thirty years and still hadn't found it. People here did not want to talk to the cops.

"What else do we have?"

Jeff opened another file. "The eyeball is definitely Len Milbank's. They found no DNA or prints on the knife except from the victim. We now have photos we can circulate." He handed them each a picture of a ten-inch dive knife with a six-inch blade. He also handed them a picture of Len Milbank before he'd become fish food.

"Anything on the suit?" she asked.

"Nothing yet."

"Vehicle?"

"Nada."

"Boat?"

"Nyet. West Coast Marine Service is starting a search of all the coves and inlets, but it's going to take some time." Jeff raised a brow. In this light, she saw his light brown hair was starting to thread with gray. Why was a smart guy like Jeff still a corporal but she was a sergeant?

"So what *do* we know?" She grabbed a piece of chalk, grateful there was a blackboard on the wall. "Victim: Len Milbank. Stabbed in the heart and found inside a supposedly undiscovered shipwreck at a depth of thirty meters.

"He couldn't have been stabbed during the dive itself because the tank harness would have gotten in the way of the blade." She went through each point. "The killer must have stabbed him just before or after a dive because there's no way you can wrestle a corpse into neoprene. And unless he had some weird rubber fetish, there's no reason for him to be wearing a dry suit unless he was diving. Whoever killed him was his dive buddy."

"So the killer is a diver, probably has a boat, or access to one, or used Milbank's," said Chastain.

"Which rules out exactly no one in this region," Malone added with a scowl.

"Whoever it is must be physically strong and a good enough diver to drag that body into the heart of the shipwreck and get out again alive. Corporals Messenger and Malone—I want you compiling a list of all the scuba divers between here and Port Alberni."

Malone groaned.

"I thought no one knew about the shipwreck," Messenger said quietly.

"Someone sure as hell knew about it. Did you find out anything yesterday?"

The officer slumped, defeated. "Nobody knows anything for sure. Coast Guard got pretty excited because they *think* she might be a windjammer." She read from her notes, "'An iron-hulled sailing ship made in the late nineteenth century.' But they said there's a wreck for every mile of coast around here. They're going to try to measure and identify it as soon as they get clearance to dive."

"Should be soon," said Holly.

"Maybe there's someone with an old family connection who knew about the wreck and kept it secret?" Jeff suggested.

"It's a hell of a coincidence that a few days after the scientist finds his shiny new sea slug some guy's body gets dumped there."

Cops were never big on coincidence. Holly pinched her lips together. "There are two possible reasons why the killer would hide the body down there. One," she ticked the number off on her fingers, "they didn't know the wreck had been found and didn't want Milbank washing up unexpectedly. Two, they knew the wreck had been discovered and wanted Carver and Edgefield to be in the spotlight for finding the body."

"They got their wish." Chastain tapped his pen on the arm of the sofa. His phone rang, but he ignored it. He saw her looking. Pulled a face. "Fiancée, probably wanting to know what color ribbons I want on the flower girls' dresses."

Malone laughed.

"So we're essentially back to square one?" Corporal Messenger said quietly.

"Not exactly. We've got Milbank's associates in Port Alberni acting suspiciously, and someone tossed his place. I'm thinking Milbank might have been involved in drug or alcohol smuggling for Dryzek, which is why he got so antsy when he didn't show up."

These small coastal communities were rife for exploitation by criminal organizations, Holly knew. They also served as distribution centers for smugglers. Maybe Milbank's death was just a drug deal gone wrong. "Jeff, can you talk to the guys from West Coast Marine Services and see if they've heard any whispers along the coast?"

Jeff nodded.

"I think we're making someone nervous. Otherwise, they wouldn't have tried to run me off the road yesterday." She touched her nose, which was sore as hell.

"Unless that was personal?" Malone ventured.

"No one hates me that much," Holly said. But she couldn't silence the whisper of disquiet that ran through her mind. Something didn't feel right. She needed more information, and the quiet, secretive nature of the village made it unlikely she was going to get it.

Jeff was reading files on his laptop. "Len Milbank was in VIRCC in the early nineties. Served two years for armed robbery with violence."

"Two years?" Holly shook her head. Some days she wondered why they bothered to turn up.

"And it turns out there was another local resident in prison with him at the same time."

Her veins constricted as she held her breath in anticipation.

"Brent Carver. Finn Carver's older brother."

She remembered Dryzek and Ferdinand saying *Carver* yesterday. She'd assumed they meant Finn, but maybe she was mistaken. "Brent was serving time for killing their father, correct?"

Chastain nodded. "Hit him once over the head with a beer bottle. Must have had a hell of a swing. He was charged as an adult and convicted of second-degree murder. Served twenty years."

Most days, criminals didn't get sentenced to enough time, but given the extenuating circumstances, it seemed a little harsh. Holly didn't like the pang of agitation that went through her thinking about the sort of childhood those kids must have endured. She couldn't let it cloud her judgment.

"Brent Carver got out three years ago." Chastain checked his notes. "He's not even forty yet."

"I think I'll go and talk to him today," said Holly.

"You?" Malone asked dubiously.

She gave him what was sure to be her ugliest smile. Damn, she could barely see through the slits of her eyelids. "That's right, Malone. Me. You think I can't do my job?"

"I'm not the one with the techno-colored face, Sarge."

She grinned for what seemed the first time in days. "You should see the rest of me. OK, let's get out of here. Malone, because you're so worried, you're with me. Messenger can work on the list of divers on her own. Let's find this bastard and get out of here."

Mike glanced up and down the road. Except for the bald eagle staring at him from the high branches of a fifty-foot pine tree, there was no one around. At this time of day, everyone would be in lectures or classes or at work. He headed purposely up the steps to Finn's cabin, tapped the door, and walked inside.

"Hello. Anyone here?" he called. When no one answered, he cautiously opened both bedroom doors and peeked inside. No one here. With a glance at the front door, he went into Finn's bedroom with its neatly made bed.

He dropped to his knees and checked under the bed. Nothing, not even dust motes. He opened the bedside table. Books. Lots of them. On top of the nightstand was a lamp, a clock radio, and a copy of *Invertebrate Identification in the Pacific Northwest*. Mike rolled his eyes. The guy never gave it a rest.

Nothing on the two desks except for a laptop and paperwork. Not what he was looking for. Sweat started to trickle down his spine. Remy Dryzek had asked a favor, and he had no illusions what would happen if he didn't produce results.

For a long time, Milbank had been pressuring him to come on board with some smuggling activities, but Mike hadn't been interested. Remy had helped him out with some trouble he'd got into with a bookie in Port Alberni, but it wasn't enough of a debt to throw his life away. After a few weeks, Mike had paid back the money he owed. He'd assumed Milbank would stop hassling him, but if anything, things had gotten worse. Len had threatened to kill him if he didn't start doing him a few favors.

Now the guy's unexpected death had left Dryzek in a rage and Mike up shit creek, trying to paddle the depths with his little finger. Someone had killed Milbank and stolen Remy's coke or money—the guy didn't even know which because he didn't know if Len had made the exchange or not. Dryzek was now a fire-breathing maelstrom of retribution.

What made Mike break out in a sweat was Gina had told him she thought Finn had found a shipwreck in that cove, and while trying to avoid imminent death, in an attempt to get on the guy's good side, *he'd* told Milbank. They'd planned to check it out together—and yes, Mike had been half hoping Milbank might suck in a lungful of water and maybe get lost on the way up. But Milbank had never shown, and the dive equipment Mike had borrowed from the dive shed had walked. The cops were asking a lot of questions that made him very nervous.

He opened the wardrobe doors, wincing at the noise, and pulled out a small case from the bottom beside a neat row of boots. The case was locked. He went back to the bedside cabinet and rifled through the drawer. Found a small key, and fitted it into the lock. *Bingo.* His heart drummed so fast there was a quiver in his chest as he unclipped the latches. But inside wasn't a haul of coke. Instead there lay a matte-black semiautomatic pistol and a shitload of ammunition. Mike slammed the suitcase shut and thrust it back into the cupboard. Finn was a trained soldier. He knew how to protect himself if need be. Mike checked the top shelf, but there was nothing there.

An itch started at the nape of his neck. He stepped back and made sure everything looked the same as when he'd come in. He was just about to leave the bedroom when he heard the front door open. He eased behind the door. What the hell was he gonna say if Finn caught him in here? Come clean? Then Dryzek would kill him for sure. He was stuck between a rock and an erupting volcano.

Shit.

He pressed himself tight to the wall behind the door and peered through the thin slice between it and the frame. It took him a moment to recognize the uniformed figure of Holly Rudd striding into the other room. *What the hell?*

Then he remembered what his mother had told him about Holly going home with Finn from the hospital. She grabbed something off her bed, turned, and went right back out the front door. Her face was a mess. *Christ.*

Mike counted to a hundred and then moved cautiously into the kitchen. He searched the cupboards rapidly, but there was no way Finn would keep contraband in the kitchen cupboard if he had the cop camping out.

The idea of Finn stealing didn't fit with what Mike knew about the guy, but Remy had been adamant. His throat went dry because if Finn found out, he was going to look a lot like Holly Rudd. Worse, Finn wasn't the only Carver residence Dryzek had ordered him to search. Chances of getting inside Brent Carver's new place without the bastard catching him were slim to none, and he didn't want to wind up like their dear old daddy. Mike needed a miracle, but heaven seemed a little short recently. Pausing, he went back to the suitcase in the bedroom and took the gun out of the case. It felt heavy in his palm. He slipped it into his waistband and covered it with his T-shirt, pocketed some ammo, and closed everything up the way it had been.

Finn was going to kill him if he found out. But at least the pistol gave him some hope of coming out of this mess alive.

He checked the windows and headed down the stairs with an easy grin stretching his mouth, just in case anyone was watching. Sweat soaked through his T-shirt under his arms. He'd done something foolish and gotten involved with some scary people. Now he was paying for it.

There was a knock on his door, and Thom looked up from his computer monitor. His secretary came in with a cup of coffee. Despite the massive difference in their salary, he was merely the figurehead and it was she who ran the inner mechanisms of the marine lab.

"What would I do without you, Gladys?" He smiled as she settled his favorite mug on the coaster on his desk. Even on those days when he slipped into obsessive mania, she made sure everyone else did what they were supposed to do.

"Laura Prescott called."

His heart gave an involuntary flinch.

"She said she was going to be late for today's lunch meeting."

His throat constricted to the size of a straw. "We have a lunch meeting?" he squeaked.

Gladys smiled and went back to the door. "One o'clock. Your place. From the expression on your face, I'm guessing Finn set it up."

He tugged at his shirt collar that suddenly felt way too tight. "I don't want a meeting with Laura Prescott."

"You need to think about your future. You're so focused on the past. What if the police decide you did kill that diver you found? You need to be prepared." Gladys stared at him from his office door. "Anyway, Laura's a sweetheart."

"She scares the crap out of me," he admitted.

Her kind brown eyes softened. "Bianca died a long time ago. No one's saying you have to forget her, but…"

Thirty years. Thirty years of grief and misery and bone-gnawing frustration. He stared up at Gladys and realized he'd spent most of his adult life chasing a fool's errand. "I can't." He thought of the freckles on Holly's forehead matching those on the photograph of his beautiful lost daughter, Leah. "Not yet."

She didn't look surprised by his answer. "We get one chance at this thing called life, Thom, and none of us knows how long we've got until it's over. You think about that."

Thom stared down at the trailing wisps of steam coming off his coffee. He didn't want to think about it. Which meant he was stuck in that nightmare day from three decades ago. Reliving the panic of not being able to find his wife or children, the fear that she'd left him, the terror of knowing something was wrong, the despair at finding their bodies, and the endless search for his daughter.

He caught his gaunt reflection in the monitor as his screen went black and jolted as an old man looked back at him. Saliva pooled in his mouth and he almost choked on it.

Would Bianca have wasted her life searching for his killer had the tables been turned? He knew she wouldn't. But in some ways it made it even more imperative he find the villain. She hadn't loved him the way he'd loved her and she'd stayed with him anyway. She'd come to Bamfield because of him; therefore, she'd died because of him. And the thought of giving up on his children, of finally letting them go…

He flicked his monitor back on and stared at the only family portrait he had. Taken in the grass outside this very building, the day before they'd been stolen from him forever. How could any father give up on his family? He'd rather die.

"What the hell does this guy do for a living?" Holly and Malone looked at one another and then back at the enormous luxury cabin that overlooked the ocean. Malone's face showed disgust. Holly's expression should have shown surprised suspicion, except all her features were now padded by painful swelling and colorful bruises. She was going to have to rely on more than her friendly smile today.

She knocked on the door again, but no one answered. They shrugged at one another and tramped around the back.

"Now *that's* a view." Malone whistled.

There were some tree-topped rocky islands nearby, and far northeast were the mountains in the island's interior. But stretched out west to the horizon were the deep indigo waters of the Pacific.

"They grew up here." Holly looked around. There was nothing to suggest the grinding poverty or violent death of the past. Instead, the massive, million-dollar home with huge windows facing the sea sat in isolated splendor. She knocked on the door again, harder, and this time there was a noise from within.

The door opened abruptly, and there stood a tall, rangy man, blond hair sticking up on end, eyes bloodshot and blurry. Barefoot, in jeans and a ragged T-shirt, his face was drawn with deep crevices that carried a damn sight more experience than his years warranted.

"Mr. Carver? Brent Carver? Can we come in?"

His eyes took in her battered appearance, sparking with interest, but he said nothing, just shook his head. He turned and walked wearily away. She and Malone exchanged a look and followed him inside. The house was dazzling bright, skylights making the most of the morning sun. They ended up in a huge, open-plan kitchen that would have looked right at home in a magazine.

Brent Carver pointed to the coffeepot. "Help yourself." Then he slumped into a navy couch, holding his head in one hand as he slugged back coffee.

He looked like a man who'd gone on a bender ten years ago and hadn't stopped since.

Even though the coffee tempted her, Holly refrained from accepting a cup. "We've got some questions about a man named Len Milbank."

"I heard they found his body out at Crow Point."

The RCMP hadn't released that the body had been found inside the shipwreck. In fact, they hadn't even released details of the new shipwreck to the public yet, but this was a small town. They'd all know soon enough.

"We're trying to figure out what Mr. Milbank was doing out there."

Brent Carver opened his eyes and looked straight at her. She blinked because his eyes were the exact same color as Finn's but his were bleak. Empty.

"Why would you ask me?"

"You were in Wilkinson prison at the same time as Mr. Milbank."

"Me and three hundred–plus other inmates."

"But you knew him?" Holly pushed.

"We weren't friends." He put his cup on the solid oak table beside the sofa.

"That's not what I asked."

A line creased his cheek as one side of his mouth twisted up. "I knew him."

"When was the last time you saw Mr. Milbank?"

"I don't rightly recall."

"Have you seen him since you left prison?" Holly watched that face closely.

A shrug. "In passing."

"Do you scuba dive?"

His face scrunched up, and he stretched out all his limbs in an all-body yawn. "Sometimes. Not often, though."

"Can we see your equipment?"

"Get a warrant."

"You got something to hide?" asked Malone.

He cracked out a sharp laugh. "Something to lose. Something I've grown attached to, this time around. My freedom."

"You haven't talked to Mr. Milbank during the last two weeks?"

His eyes watched her the way a tiger watched a bunny. It had been a long time since she'd felt like the bunny. "No."

"What do you do for a living, Mr. Carver?"

"How's that relevant?"

Holly tried to smile, but it tugged at all her bruises. *Ouch.* "Just trying to get a picture of your life, Mr. Carver. And figure out how you can afford all this." She waved at the gleaming wood and sparkling new appliances and enormous original oil painting of the view outside that hung over the fireplace.

"You're trying to take the easy route in your investigation and pin it on the ex-con." His lips curled. There was no love for the police in those eyes.

"You did kill your father." Malone paced around the kitchen island. "You must have known you'd be top of our list of suspects."

"Oh, I knew. That's the only reason I let you in the door. Lack of imagination has always been a problem for police officers." Brent Carver unwound from the couch and climbed to his feet. "I'm going to have to ask you to leave now. I've got work to do." His smile was fixed and cold and crept up Holly's spine in a silky wave of unease.

Malone shook his head with a smile and turned to leave.

A frown touched Brent's brow. "What happened to your face?"

Holly touched her nose. "Car wreck. Someone ran me off the road."

He laughed, chilling her blood. "So your next question is where was I yesterday afternoon?"

"How did you know when the wreck occurred?"

He raised a hand as if to touch her face. She froze. He dropped it. "Let's just say I have a lot of experience with bruises."

She suddenly found herself on the back porch, standing beside Malone, staring up at the closed door of the luxury log cabin.

Malone rolled his shoulders. "I'd say we've found ourselves a potential suspect, Sergeant. Shall I see if I can get a warrant?"

She shook her head. "Right now we've got nothing on him, not even circumstantial. Let him sweat. We'll keep digging."

Finn stood outside the store, petting a local family's English bull-dog while waiting for Laura to put aside some groceries for her return trip home. The supply boat had come into port today and fresh stuff didn't last long. She lived alone on the west side of the inlet, just down the road from where he'd grown up. Last summer he'd bumped into her in this store, and she'd asked if he knew anyone who could rebuild her dock for her. He'd volunteered because it kept him occupied in the little time he had off, plus it kept him fit.

He glanced along the boardwalk. Holly and another RCMP officer were heading toward the front door of the hotel.

Holly glanced toward him, her skin maybe a fraction less swollen than when he'd checked on her that morning, blue-black all around both eyes. Sore as hell. She said something to her buddy and changed direction to walk toward him.

She gave him an uncertain attempt at a smile, and he suddenly realized she was knocked off balance because she could no longer use her beauty to bamboozle people. Good job she hadn't figured out he was attracted to her no matter what she looked like.

"How are you feeling?" His gaze rested on her swollen lips and damn if he didn't want to swoop down for another taste.

"I've had better days," she admitted.

They both hung over the wooden rail and stared at the ocean. A seal bobbed up and down in the wind-ruffled water.

"Do you make a habit of rescuing damsels in distress?" she asked after a moment.

Finn laughed and shook his head. "You're definitely my first."

An amused gleam lit her eyes. "Somehow I doubt that."

"Seriously, most people I'd leave floundering in a ditch. Obviously, I have a thing for women in uniform."

Her eyes flashed as if she couldn't quite believe he was flirting with a woman who looked like she did. He couldn't believe it either. Damn, the memory of that wreck had haunted his dreams last night, along with a few erotic musings of just how many bruises he could kiss better. Among other things.

"You must have saved people in the army."

One shoulder kicked up. She knew he couldn't talk about it any more than she could talk about her investigation.

Gray eyes watched him. "I met your brother earlier."

His entire being froze. Her words were like a kick in the gut. The people he cared about couldn't afford the attraction he felt for her. Hell, he couldn't afford it.

"Family reunions are always a blast." Why couldn't someone have dumped Milbank's body in the open ocean? It would be in goddamn Alaska by now.

Laura came out of the store wearing black slacks and some sort of arty purple sweater with a matching scarf draped around her neck. In her early fifties, she exuded a relaxed beauty that was incredibly easy to be around. He hoped Laura and Thom might hook up, although he wasn't exactly renowned for his matchmaking skills.

"Laura, meet Holly. Holly, meet Laura."

"You must be the police officer involved in the car wreck yesterday." Laura held out her hand to shake Holly's.

"What gave it away?" Holly joked. "The wild hairstyle? Crazy makeup?"

Christ. He started shaking. Some bastard had tried to kill her yesterday, and today she was laughing about it. He'd done it himself in military situations where bullets had missed their target by inches and they'd had lucky escapes, but to see Holly doing it today was more than he could physically stand.

"I need to get back to work ASAP." He checked his watch. "Come on." He took Laura by the arm and strode to the top of the gangplank.

"Any chance we could borrow a boat to shuttle across the inlet?" Holly called after him.

Inside he was torn by conflicting emotions. The mindless male inside him wanted to look after her, protect her, even though she was the one packing heat. The suspicious friend and brother wanted to get as far away from her as possible. He set his teeth for a moment. "I'll send Rob across."

Holly followed them down onto the dock. Despite everything, he didn't want the connection to end.

"Thanks again for looking out for me yesterday," she said.

"No problem." It was terse and it was a lie. Thanks to yesterday's accident his emotions had been involved. Circumstances were bringing them closer all the time, but his loyalty to Thom and his brother had to top any feelings of attraction.

He helped Laura into her seat, handed her a life vest, and didn't look back as he rowed them across the inlet. When he got out on the other side and glanced across, the cops were gone. Laura was watching him, and not a lot got past her.

"What?" he asked sharply.

"I've never seen you be rude to a woman before."

"I wasn't rude."

"She unnerves you." Her eyes sparkled. "You like her."

He grunted.

She kept quiet but grinned and ruined it.

"She's only here for the investigation." He reminded himself as much as her. He walked her up to Thom's house and, when no one answered the door, realized that he'd been outmaneuvered.

A nervous tic started beneath his right eye. He called the office, but no one answered.

"Sonofabitch." He kicked a stone and it shot along the path.

"Maybe an emergency came up?" Laura suggested. But he could tell by the shadow in her eyes she'd figured it out too. Thom had blown off their meeting. Finn was going to kick his boss's ass when he tracked him down.

CHAPTER 9

As the RCMP SUV was now a crumpled lump of steel, Holly decided to walk to the local library from the marine lab. They'd had another vehicle assigned to use as a runabout, and Steffie was driving it out later that afternoon. For now, Holly was just glad it had stopped raining.

Jeff was typing up notes. Corporals Malone and Chastain were conducting more door-to-door inquiries using the photographs as visual aids. Messenger was trying to compile a list of divers. She had other plans.

The sound of a branch snapping just beyond her line of sight in the woods had her swinging around, heart hammering. *Just the wind or Bambi playing in the woods.* Tall trees loomed overhead, and the wind whispered through the needles and made them rattle. Primal fear slipped into the marrow of her bones and lengthened her stride.

Sweat pearled on her brow. Her hand rested on her Smith & Wesson and she started jogging. It hurt, but she needed the exercise. *Yeah, that's the only reason you're running.*

She turned a corner and there was the school, which also housed the library. Relieved, she slowed to a brisk walk. Some of the kids looked her way and she waved.

See, kids, not scared at all, although I'm pretty damned scary judging from the expressions of horror on their faces. No wonder Finn's attitude had done an abrupt one-eighty today. Not that she wanted to explore the electricity that had sparked between them last night, but the unexpected coldness when they'd parted company earlier had hurt—and *that* had been a shock to the system.

Men had lost the power to hurt her when the guy she was falling for had left her bed to pick up his cell phone and find out his wife had gone into premature labor.

Jackass.

The urge to gag, even now, rose up in her throat. She ignored it. Today was all about pretense and getting the job done. She wasn't sore, wasn't humiliated to her core, and she looked like a million dollars.

She skirted the building and went in the front door. No one was in the first room, so she continued into the atrium of the school, where there were chairs and rugs and shelves of kids' books. She glanced about, tapped on the glass door of an office. "Hi there, I'm looking for the librarian."

The woman sitting there was in her late thirties, early forties. Wavy brown hair and pretty eyes. "That's me. You must be the Mountie who got run off the road."

News traveled fast in this place. "How'd you figure that out?" Holly moved her lips into what should be a smile but didn't know whether or not she pulled it off. She laughed and was glad she still sounded like herself.

"The panda makeup." The woman's voice was sweet and clear. "It was all over town that Finn Carver rescued you and carried you into the hospital like some white knight." She fanned herself dramatically, but the smile and gentle humor seemed genuine. "I always thought he had heroic tendencies."

Most women might appreciate the fantasy of a strong man "saving" them. Trouble was, Holly came from a long line of cops and preferred to save herself.

"I'm Gina Swartz. How can I help you?"

Holly asked her about the maps and documents Finn had been researching last week. Gina showed her where the maps were kept but didn't remember anything except which day he'd been in.

After thirty minutes and a dozen sneezes that made her ribs shriek, Holly realized there was nothing here. Dead end. She put the maps away and smiled at Gina, who was talking quietly on the phone, left the building, and headed into town.

She entered the tiny community hospital/clinic and saw the nurse from yesterday.

The woman shot her a look over her reading glasses and winced. "You survived a night of Finn's ministrations?" Her smile was warm and sympathetic.

The cut on Holly's lips tugged painfully. "He's not the worst nurse I've ever had."

"Plus he's easy on the eyes." The woman smiled again. "Now, I need a little information from you."

Holly leaned over the desk giving her home address and medical number.

"Your full name is Holly Rudd, right?"

"Holly Francesca Rudd."

"That's a beautiful name."

"Thanks. Francesca was my mother's name."

"Was? You lost her?"

"Nearly two years ago." She pushed through the break in her voice.

"I'm very sorry." The nurse unexpectedly touched her hand. "I had a dream once where I thought my son was dead. It was so real I thought I'd die from the pain. When I woke up I ran to his crib and there he was smiling up at me like a little angel. Losing someone you love is hard."

Holly nodded and shifted away from the well-meaning nurse. Talking about something so private, so personal was not on Holly's agenda. Cops were suspicious by nature. It wasn't that her family didn't talk about their feelings, they just didn't talk about their feelings with people they didn't trust. And they didn't trust strangers.

Maybe this was part of Holly's problem right now. She couldn't talk about how she felt about losing her mother with her dad because they were both still too raw. But keeping her emotions bottled up wasn't helping her any either. An image of Finn Carver's smiling face flashed through her mind. And *that* was exactly the same sort of stupid-ass impulse that had led to the monumental fiasco with Furlong.

"Next of kin?" the nurse asked, filling out the form.

"Terry Rudd. Lives in Vancouver."

"Husband? Father?"

"My dad."

"Have you always lived in Vancouver?"

Holly frowned and tried to look at the paper.

The nurse blushed. "Oh, it isn't for the form, I'm just curious. Probably because you look so much like—"

"Bianca Edgefield." The doctor came out of his room and smiled. "I don't know why I didn't see the resemblance yesterday—although considering the facial bruising, maybe it's not such a surprise. Glad to see you're still with us." He glanced at the waiting room. "I think, given the circumstances, you better jump the queue."

There were a few sour glances from people, but Holly wasn't going to complain or be noble. She had work to do, so she followed the doctor to the exam room.

"You knew Bianca Edgefield?" She sat on his examination bench, and he started going through all the usual stuff: heart, lungs, blood pressure.

"She was a patient of mine, although, only when she and Thom were in Bamfield. Those kids were so sweet..." His voice trailed off in sadness.

They were both silent as the blood pressure cuff released its tight grip on her arm.

"Did you know Len Milbank?" she asked.

"Who?"

"Len Milbank is the murder victim we found—"

"Ah, the man in the shipwreck." His eyes widened with excitement. "It's all over town, but no, I hadn't had the dubious pleasure of Mr. Milbank's company." He smiled and slapped a cold stethoscope on her back. *Jesus.*

She'd known the information would leak soon. She hadn't expected it to leak quite this fast. She asked a few more questions but basically got nothing except small talk. Ten minutes later, she was dressed and out of his office. As she walked down the hall, a man walked in carrying a bunch of bloodred roses.

She nodded a greeting.

His step hitched momentarily as he took in her battered appearance. Then he nodded and swept past her to knock on the nurse's open door.

Compelled by curiosity, she turned to watch. The nurse came out from behind her desk with a huge smile on her lips. "Oh, honey. You shouldn't be wasting money on me."

He leaned down and kissed her on the lips. "Buying flowers for my true love is never a waste." He winked. "Plus, I got a great deal."

There was a little quiver in the region of Holly's heart. The nurse grinned up at her husband, then, realizing people were looking at them, she put her hands to her flaming cheeks.

Holly turned away.

Her dad had bought her mom flowers every week for as long as she could remember. The scent of roses brought an upwelling of longing so strong she wanted to cry. She hurried outside, sucked in a couple of deep breaths. Noticed Mike Toben sitting in his truck, looking impatient. She waved at him, and he gave her a slow grin.

Needing something to do as opposed to mourning her mother, she went to talk to him. Finn wasn't around to censor her today.

"Well, aren't you a sight for sore eyes."

"You should see the other guy." She propped her hand on the open window and leaned into the cab.

"I can well believe it." He winced in sympathy.

"So how well do you know Remy Dryzek?"

He gave her a lopsided grin that was all bedroom eyes and easy charm. "I know him well enough to say *hi* to when I meet him in a bar."

"What about Len Milbank—you know him well enough to speak to in a bar?"

His hands tightened on the steering wheel and he stared ahead through the windscreen. "Len was an asshole."

"So you did know him?"

"I knew him," he admitted. "I avoided him as much as humanly possible."

"Why?"

He turned those chocolate eyes back on her. "Because the guy was trouble, and most sane people avoid trouble whenever possible."

Mike's lips pressed tight together. He was film-star handsome, and Holly waited for a little kick of attraction. There was none.

"When was the last time you saw him?"

He ran a hand through his short dark hair, thought about it for a long moment. "Probably week before last. I took Mom into Port Alberni to get groceries. I drove past him on the street."

"Any idea who his friends were out here?"

"Len didn't have friends, period."

Mike was telling her more than the entire town put together.

She leaned closer. "Do you have any idea how he found out about that shipwreck, Mike?"

His nostrils flared. "No idea."

A bang of metal made her jump as the man with the roses slapped the hood and strode around the front of the truck to jump in. "Sorry to hold you up, son. Looks like you managed to entertain yourself while I was gone, though." His tone held a little censure. "One of these days your girlfriend is gonna get pissed off with all the goddamn flirting you do."

Girlfriend, huh?

Mike started the truck. He sent Holly a hellfire grin that would have melted the bones of a lesser woman. "Flirtin's part of my charm, Pop."

His father *harrumphed* as Mike sent her a wink before pulling away and driving off down the road.

She watched them disappear over the crest of a hill, then pulled out her phone because she had to update Furlong. She dialed her father instead, relieved when it went to voice mail. "I got the all-clear from the doc, Dad. No reason to give yourself an ulcer worrying over me, OK? I'll call you tomorrow. Love you."

Eyeing her phone with distaste, she decided to go question the bar owner again. Everyone knew she was a cop now. Maybe if she sat on the barstool long enough he'd start talking just to get rid of her.

Finn had ten first-year students to take on a dive off the pier. Usually these were some of the best dives. Low effort. Huge reward. You literally stepped off the dock into the channel, which dropped rapidly away. All along the sides of the inlet were starfish the size of dinner plates, mussels longer than his hands, and often an inquisitive seal checking out what they were doing. It was a fantastic training ground.

He'd split them into pairs, and each pair had an advanced diver with them. He nodded to Rob to take the first group down. Two minutes later, he nodded for the next team to go and checked his watch. He watched his surface safety spotter note on her clipboard at what time the second group descended. Good.

He moved away to his group, got them organized and filing along the wooden boards. They helped each other with their fins and last-minute equipment check, then stood ready for the signal.

Out of the corner of his eye he saw a cop—the pretty young woman who'd been kind to Thom yesterday—heading his way.

"I'm Cpl. Rachel Messenger, Mr. Carver. I need to assemble a list of people in the area who scuba dive. I thought you'd be a good source of information." Tall and willowy, the woman exuded keen politeness. How long would those qualities last in the big bad world?

Yesterday he was a suspect; today he was helping compile lists of other suspects? Part of him wanted to say no, but that wouldn't speed them on their way out of here. He regarded her with a rueful smile as he stood there in full scuba gear.

"I'm a little busy right now. I'll be done in about an hour. You'll find me in my cabin after that. I've got a list of people who've dived with the marine lab, and I guess I can tell you the people in the area I know who dive regularly." He adjusted his mask. The safety officer caught his eye and gave his group the signal to go.

"Thanks," the cop called after him brightly.

The regret in his heart as he stepped into the deep, cold water was that it was Corporal Messenger, not Holly, asking for his help. He turned to his wide-eyed students and flashed them the OK signal, which they both mirrored. Their excitement and nervousness was palpable.

He forced himself to concentrate on a job he took seriously. People could die if he got it wrong. They descended the sheer drop-off, him pointing out goose barnacles, which gently fanned the water with skeletal fingers, and an octopus that sat in a hollow and seemed to watch them just as avidly as they watched it. And still a bone-deep awareness of Holly filtered through the edges of his mind. Women did not affect him like this. He didn't do relationships past the basics and never got involved with women who thought he might. In his experience, life was filled with blood, death, and disappointment; happily ever after was part of the fairy tale that died as soon as reality set in. His reality had set in from day one.

He gave the signal, and they went deeper, cold water pressing around him and forcing him to concentrate on these students, this dive. To live in the moment because life had also taught him that was all anyone really had. Just this one moment in time.

He deliberately flooded his mask to show the students how to clear it ten meters down, in the murky reality of the Pacific. Then he made them do it.

One of the girls grinned at him when she successfully got rid of the water and he smiled back. But even then it was Holly's smile he was thinking about, the perfect line of her bare shoulder, the gentle curve of her waist. He pictured her battered face, and that only made things worse. With a frustrated shake of his head, he finally figured out he couldn't simply ignore Holly while she was here. He had to help catch Len Milbank's killer and help her on her way out of town. Protect her, protect the people he cared about. Then they could both get on with their lives.

Holly walked into Finn's cabin and kicked off her shoes at the door. "Goddamn misogynistic, hairy, smelly—"

"Whoa, Sergeant Rudd, you startled me." Corporal Messenger stepped out of Finn's bedroom, and Holly felt like she'd been slapped in the face by a two-by-four. The heat that suffused those cheeks and the bright sparkle in Messenger's eyes told their own story.

"I'm just collecting my stuff so I can go back to the hotel." Holly sounded defensive even to her own ears.

She stalked toward the bedroom she'd slept in last night. As she passed the open door, she glanced inside and there was Finn, leaning his chair back on two feet, hands behind his head, hair ruffled, SCUBA DIVERS GO DOWN LONGER T-shirt clinging to honed muscle. No wonder Messenger's eyes were twinkling. Holly hooked her door shut with her ankle and winced when the wind caught it and slammed it home. She cursed when there was a quiet knock on the door less than two seconds later.

"That could be a problem." Messenger's pretty ruby lips pursed. "The hotel sprung a leak, and the whole second floor was water damaged, so they've only got two rooms habitable. Steffie and I are sharing one. Jeff, Ray, and Freddy are sharing the other. I thought you'd just stay here."

"I can't do that," Holly snapped. Christ, the thought of staying this close to Finn was already making her sweat. "People might talk."

"I don't know why, under the circumstances." Messenger dropped her gaze to the carpet. "But *I'll* take the couch at the hotel. I really didn't think it would be an issue."

Holly blew out a tight, hot breath. "No. I'm sorry. Stay where you are. I'll take the couch." She wasn't going to be getting much sleep anyway.

"How did the interviews go?" Messenger asked, eyes intent. Holly had the feeling she was going to be a great cop one day, if she could just get over her "nice."

Holly opened her mouth to say something rude about the local, tight-lipped, stubborn, unhelpful population but closed it again when Finn walked up to Messenger and handed her several printed pages. Holly watched the two of them together—so perfect, so beautiful it hurt the eyes. Messenger was almost Finn's height but looked all waif-thin and elegant standing next to him.

Holly didn't remember ever being jealous in her life and didn't want to start now, no matter how golden Finn's smile. She caught her reflection in a mirror and grimaced. The grotesque bruises and unsightly swelling were beginning to recede. Looks didn't matter, although resembling a monster hadn't helped her chances in the bar. The barkeep had been a complete ass-wipe. She stripped off her vest and tossed her cap on top of the blanket. Wiped her sweaty forehead.

"That everything you need, Corporal?" Finn asked the other woman.

"Yes. Thanks, and please, call me Rachel."

Holly pulled faces to herself as she listened. Then the other woman left and she could hear Finn in the silence. It wasn't Messenger she was pissed at. It was the whole goddamn world and total lack of answers in this murder investigation. She heard the creak of a floorboard.

"Come on. I want to show you something," Finn said, watching her from the doorway.

"What?" She was almost too tired to move.

"Come on."

"About the case?"

"What else?"

With an exaggerated sigh she pushed herself up and off the bed. Her bruises were so tender she wanted to weep, but she wasn't about to give the bastard who'd pushed her off the road the satisfaction of slowing down.

Finn's red truck was parked next to the cabin, for which Holly was eternally grateful. She hauled herself up and settled into the comfortable seat, setting her teeth against the constant ache of day-old injuries.

Finn started driving, through Bamfield and out of town.

"Where are we going?" Her voice was hoarse—with fatigue or frustration she didn't know.

He looked at her, sun slanting over those rugged features, turning his hair and skin to gold dust. "Do you trust me, Holly?"

She blew out an exasperated breath. "If this is the moment where you turn into an ax murderer, I *will* shoot you." She closed her eyes and leaned back against the head rest. Ten seconds later, she was fast asleep.

Finn pulled into the parking lot at Pachena Beach and drew in the fecund scent of the rainforest, trying to drown out the sweet scent of Holly, whose gentle breathing made him want to sit there until the sun set and just watch over her. Her face was starting to regain its normal shape, although her skin looked like a tattoo artist on oxy had gone on a binge of self-expression. Black was easing into purple edged with mottled green. The split on her lip was healing fast. And she hadn't let it stop her.

He'd lied to her, and she was going to be pissed. And it bothered him only because watching Holly get riled up turned him on. Not what he'd had in mind when he'd dragged her out here.

He silently eased open the door, but her instincts were honed, and her eyes snapped open.

"Where are we?"

"North end of the West Coast Trail."

She followed him out of the cab and stretched out her back with an audible crack. "What are we doing here?"

"I need to show you something." He led her along the path, past the A-frame visitor center.

They crossed the clearing and walked down another sandy path that opened up onto a half-mile stretch of the purest white sand this side of the northern hemisphere. The sea smelled as fresh and clean as ozone. The sun inched west in inexorable fashion. He used his hand as a shade and watched three ospreys taking turns diving into the surf. He kicked off his shoes, and after a taut pause, she did the same with her boots and socks. They abandoned them, and she wiggled her frog-tipped toes in the sand.

"What did you want to show me?"

Finn scratched his jaw. "Nothing. You just looked like you could do with a break."

Her lips parted, and Finn told himself to stop watching her mouth, but somehow he couldn't drag his gaze away. She closed her eyes and seemed to be counting to ten to stem her temper. He snagged her wrist. "Walk with me."

Her hands formed fists, and he felt the strain in her sinew as she pulled against him. From the glint in her eye, she was thinking of flipping him onto his ass. He was thinking about letting her.

"Please," he added.

"I have a murderer to catch and some bastard tried to kill me. I have a boss who wants to make sure I screw up my first case as primary. I *don't* have time for a walk."

But she took a reluctant first step and he tugged her again. "Sometimes you need a break so you can see things more clearly."

Holly glared through shadowed eyes. "I'd see more clearly if people in this goddamn town would talk to me."

Finn pressed his lips together.

"See?"

"What?" he protested, but one side of his mouth curved as she fell into step beside him. "What is it that you want to know?"

"Everything. Anything."

"Like what?"

"Your brother. How does he make a living?"

Finn slipped his fingers down to interlace with hers. He'd made a decision to help. He might as well take advantage of the fringe benefits. "I have no idea."

"See? See!" She tried to pull away, but he didn't let her.

"We haven't been close in years." He didn't mention the conversation they'd had the day before yesterday. "Once he was arrested, he refused to see me." God, what a time that had been. Freed from his tormentor but cast adrift by the only person in the world he'd loved. For a thirteen-year-old boy it had been a critical period, the confusion and rage crippling. He could so easily have slid into the downward spiral of a life of crime. "Thom took me in." He'd saved him. "He figured out I was dyslexic and taught me to read."

She blinked. OK. Finn knew he was telling her more than he'd planned to, but none of it was relevant to the crime, just to why he owed these two people so much. He'd be dead without Brent, and he wasn't sure anyone would have noticed, let alone cared. Without Thom, he'd have been locked into a life of confusion and frustration. Which of them he owed most, he couldn't say.

"Thom told me that the first thing Brent did when he got out of prison was burn down the shack where we'd grown up. He lived in a trailer for a few years while he built the house."

"*I* couldn't afford that house."

Finn shook his head. "Me neither." The sea's detritus lined the beach. Palm-sized, bone-white bivalves, some ragged and broken, others pristine and whole.

"I wrote to him. Probably a thousand times over the years." And back then, writing hadn't been easy.

Holly said nothing, but her fingers tightened in his. Her skin was like satin, her flesh warm and soft despite her prickly exterior.

"He sent back every single letter unopened." Every time he'd mailed one, he'd steeled himself for the return envelope. Every time he'd gotten one, it had pierced his heart like a speargun. "Eventually I stopped trying."

"Why won't he talk to you?"

Finn huffed out a breath that should have been a laugh. "I destroyed his life—"

"It wasn't your fault."

"Of course it was my fault!" He dropped her hand and immediately wanted it back. Too damn bad. He walked faster, but she kept pace despite the fact she'd taken a beating yesterday. He knew how the hell that felt. "Usually when the old man was on a bender, we ran and hid until he sobered up. This time I'd fallen asleep and he caught me. Then I said something stupid to set him off."

He picked up a piece of driftwood carved by waves, drew back his arm, and hauled it far out to sea. "I'd missed the signs, been careless, and Brent paid for my mistake."

Holly hooked his elbow, and he had to use every ounce of self-restraint not to pull away from her challenging grip. Or not to grab hold of her and ravage those poor swollen lips just to change the subject. Yeah, that's the only reason he wanted to kiss her.

"That's the child talking, not the rational-minded adult."

It was hard to separate the two when it came to his relationship with his brother.

"That man should never have been allowed to keep you boys when your mother left." She suddenly looked fiercer than ever. "He was the monster, and you and your brother did what you had to do to survive."

"You're right." Finn sucked in air and tried to keep his eyes on the ospreys, not the memories. "But Brent didn't have to save me. He should have just saved himself. Then he wouldn't have spent all those years rotting in jail."

She laid a hand on his chest and his heart stumbled. He brought his hands up to clasp her shoulders. Her lips moved, and it took a moment to figure out what she was saying because the blood was rushing south so furiously he couldn't hear a damn thing except his body telling him how desperately he wanted to be inside her.

"I never had a little brother." Straight white teeth caught her bottom lip. "I always wanted one, even sometimes pretended I had one, but Mom couldn't have any more babies after she had me." Her eyes went dark as charcoal. "If I'd had a brother I'd have protected him the same way Brent protected you." She shook her head. "It doesn't make it right, but I get it." She looked directly into his eyes. "I do get it."

She took a step away, her chest heaving as if she'd been running—or was in pain. "It doesn't change the fact that I am looking for a killer, and I will not let sentiment get in the way of doing my job. No matter *who* is guilty."

As he tried to get his pulse back under control—the same pulse that was usually unmoved—he figured something out. "You can find out how Brent makes his living from the tax offices, right?"

"Assuming he's telling them the truth, yeah." She looked at him, and he knew she'd already spoken to them. She'd been testing him. He wanted to feel angry, but all he felt was this odd mix of hot and numb. Hot for her. Numb to the memories.

"He's self-employed." A small smile touched her mouth. "Want me to tell you what he does?"

The urge to know was so strong he almost choked on it. "No. I want him to tell me himself." And that would never happen.

Her eyes softened. "Did Brent know Len Milbank?"

He took a step toward her and hooked his finger around a lock of her hair. "Not to my knowledge." He'd burn in hell for that one.

"Did he know about the wreck?"

Integrity was something he'd always treasured, but he might be losing his own. He leaned toward her, gazes locked, as his lips lowered toward hers. He whispered in her ear. "Not to my knowledge."

She swallowed hard, and he got satisfaction from seeing a shiver flicker across her skin, goose bumps forming in its wake. Then she grabbed two handfuls of his T-shirt and tried to shake him. "Would your brother have run me off the road?"

He wanted to lie again. Couldn't. "I don't know." He closed his eyes, his whole body shaking from the effort of not pulling her close and sinking himself into her warmth. He dropped his head. "I wish I did."

There was a fierce cry overhead as two golden eagles swooped in and chased away the ospreys. He gathered his strength and moved away to face the ocean. A burst of spray in the shallows told him a whale was feeding on the baitfish that swam close to the shore. Holly came up behind him and they stood in silence. They were in nature's paradise, but the oppressive weight of secrets haunted everything he loved.

How the hell could he keep Brent and Thom safe? What if one of them was a killer? What about Holly? What if Brent *had* forced her off the road? "Tell me what you need to know. I'll try to find out," he said quietly.

"You'll help me?"

He nodded. "Yep."

"Why?" Suspicious to the end.

He turned and held that smoky gaze. "Because the sooner you leave, the sooner I can get you out of my head."

Her eyes flared, and for a moment he saw the same hunger that ate at him, burning away at her resolve. Then she looked away, clenching her fists. "You and I can never happen…"

"I don't want it to happen either, but I'm damned if I can stop thinking about getting you naked." He pressed his lips tight together to prevent himself from revealing more. He turned his back on her and stared at the seemingly endless ocean.

He felt her behind him. Her hand tentative on his arm. Forehead heavy against his back. "Sleeping with you would destroy my career." There was a long pause until finally she whispered, "But I can't stop thinking about it either."

CHAPTER 10

Finn drew clean air into his lungs, but it did nothing to stop the desire that flooded him. Heat swam through his flesh, and he gritted his teeth against the image of them entwined around one another. *Hell.*

He turned, hands resting on her waist as she looked at him with stormy, conflicted eyes. He leaned closer, expecting her to break the connection even as his lips found hers and gently coaxed a response. Her tongue flicked across his, and he was instantly, painfully aroused, like a horny teenager with his first taste of female. Her hands clasped his neck, tunneled up and into his hair, drawing him deeper. She groaned in the back of her throat, as if wanting more, wanting him.

Dark and sultry, she tasted like hot summer nights and sweet, sexy temptation. His head was about to explode as urgency drove through his blood and made his heart hammer against his ribcage. His breath came in ragged gasps. Heat poured off his skin. He strained against his zipper, jeans suddenly two sizes too small as one of her hands slid down his chest and her palm spread wide against his heart. He wanted her to keep going lower. To touch the aching length of him that burned for her. When was the last time he'd felt this way?

He dragged her closer, taking care of her bruises as he squeezed the sweet curve of her ass, sculpted the indentation of her waist, then moved higher, until his thumbs found the hard peaks of her nipples that thrust eagerly against her uniform shirt. He'd never found uniforms particularly sexy until he'd met Holly. She shuddered as he circled both tips smoothly and firmly, making her whimper and her knees sag. She fell against him, and he gathered her to him, letting her feel exactly how much he wanted her. He thought it would jolt her back to reality, but she rubbed herself against him with a low groan, obviously as aroused as he was—a massive turn-on for a man already on the edge. It felt like a million years since he'd made love to a woman, and he had to hold on tight to his control.

He nipped at her mouth. Palmed her breast while his other hand cupped the curve of her ass and pressed her more firmly against him. It felt *so* good, and yet he knew it was nothing compared to how he'd feel sheathed in her hot, wet heat. He was shaking. Muscles trembling with the need to hold back.

He wanted to lay her down in the sand before either of them remembered who and what they were. This attraction was scorching hot, achingly sweet, and heartbreakingly wrong. They both knew it. Breathing hard, he pulled his mouth away. They were on a public beach, for god's sake.

The chime of a cell phone shattered the moment. She swallowed hard, squeezed his arm for a long moment before she answered.

"Rudd here." She sounded breathless. It filled him with a fierce sense of male satisfaction because he'd done that. "Where? Damn. Yes, I'll check it out." Her eyes swung to his as she talked to her cell. "I don't know how I'm going to get there, though. I don't have a vehicle."

"I'll take you."

She covered up the microphone. "You don't know where I need to go."

After what had happened yesterday, the thought of her driving alone on these remote roads made him feel ill. "Doesn't matter. I'll take you."

There was a strident rap on his door. Thom stood in the kitchen and hoped whoever it was would go away. He didn't get much time to himself, and frankly, lately, he was sick of everyone interfering and telling him how to live his life. Then the thought that it might be Holly had him scurrying to the door like a frantic rabbit. He yanked it open only to be confronted by the person lowest on his list of lovely-to-see-yous.

"You missed our lunch appointment." Laura Prescott raised one arched brow and used her briefcase to bludgeon her way inside. "I'll put it on your bill."

Bill?

She wore black slacks that clung and revealed a shapely figure. Her hand-knit purple sweater had a pretty little ruffle and she wore a flowing scarf loosely wrapped around her neck.

"I never arranged an appointment, so you may as well leave." He followed her into the living room where she sat on the sofa where Holly had sat, just yesterday morning. OK, he had to stop obsessing about the young woman, but last night he'd been examining her moles and noticed she definitely had some in common with his baby girl.

But Holly said she had a family, so he had to be wrong. What if it were just a coincidence that she looked like Bianca? A phenotypic aberration?

"Finn arranged the appointment."

"He shouldn't have interfered," said Thom.

"Why not? He does everything else for you," she snapped. "And he's paid me up front so you may as well just sit down and discuss this with me—"

"There's nothing to discuss!"

"Then for god's sake get me a glass of wine because I'm fed up with being treated like a leper whenever we're in the same room."

Heat spread up his back and neck. "I don't treat you like a leper, I barely know you."

"Exactly." She raised her face to the ceiling and swore. "In a town of only a couple of hundred people, it's the same damn thing."

Thom's mouth went dry, and when it was obvious she wasn't going to move, he stalked into the kitchen and popped the cork on a nice bottle of white he had in the fridge. He carried two glasses back and found Laura staring at a photograph of Bianca and the kids that hung on the living room wall.

She turned, a direct blue gaze following him across the room. "Did you kill the guy you found in the wreck?"

"I didn't think lawyers asked their clients if they were guilty." He watched the way the light fell over her face. She had soft-looking skin.

She laughed. "I was never a *defense* attorney. " She shuddered. "I worked prosecution. I don't believe in working for people I already know are guilty."

Did she really think he might be dangerous? He found he rather liked the idea. "So if I say I killed him, you'll leave me alone?"

"Did you?" She didn't let up.

"No." His throat was dry. "I didn't kill him. I don't *kill* people. It's not my thing."

Laura took the wine he held out, her fingers brushing his in the process.

"You're cold." Thom immediately went and lit the fire.

"I have vampire blood," she said.

He laughed, but then she moved closer to him, and he felt slightly hunted. Women did not pursue him. He had no real idea how he'd ever ended up with someone as beautiful as Bianca—it was another great mystery in his life.

"So what *is* your thing, Professor? Besides mourning yourself into an early grave? Wasting decades looking for a murderer who will never be found? Is that *all* you want out of life?" Dark blue eyes pinned him, demanding answers. "Or do you still have a heart beating inside that scrawny chest?"

"I've been doing it for so long I haven't really thought about it," he answered honestly. Until these last few days. Suddenly he was tired. Tired of the constant struggle to solve a mystery that no one else seemed to care about. He inhaled and looked down at his lean frame. "And I'm not scrawny. I'm wiry."

A smile curved Laura's lips and she sat on the sofa. Opened her briefcase. "Let's go through some basic facts in case the police decide to try to hang this on you."

"I can't believe a prosecutor would ever think the police might go after the wrong guy."

Another tinkling laugh filled the room. "I'm a lawyer, I'm not stupid. But I can only do my job if I know the facts."

"You want the whole truth?"

"Nothing but."

Thom blew out a sigh and sat, keeping her briefcase between them.

She raised her glass for a toast. "To a new business relationship."

He clinked her glass and took a long swallow of his chilled wine and found he rather liked that idea.

"Who knows where it might lead."

He almost spat it all back out again.

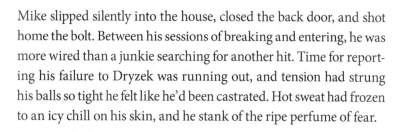

Mike slipped silently into the house, closed the back door, and shot home the bolt. Between his sessions of breaking and entering, he was more wired than a junkie searching for another hit. Time for reporting his failure to Dryzek was running out, and tension had strung his balls so tight he felt like he'd been castrated. Hot sweat had frozen to an icy chill on his skin, and he stank of the ripe perfume of fear.

The sound of the shower going full blast rammed his senses with a mixture of gratitude and self-disgust. He needed to forget his troubles for an hour. He needed release. Unbuttoning his shirt, peeling it over his head, then undoing his pants as he strode down the hall. He slipped a condom out of his back pocket, kicked off his boots, and slipped soundlessly into the tiny bathroom of Gina Swartz's two-bedroom bungalow. The room was thick with steam, hot and cloying in his lungs. The scent of sweet strawberries filled the air. She was singing loudly, and from her silhouette he could see she was distracted, washing her hair. He tossed the condom on the side of the sink. Silently he eased past the curtain, moving soundlessly until he stood right behind her. She suddenly froze, and her elbow bumped into his hand as he grabbed her around the waist. She drew in breath to scream, but he slapped his other hand over her mouth and pulled her flush against his painfully aroused body. She bit him, shampoo streaming over their skin in a slick trail. He held her tight, whispered low in her ear, threatening. "I won't hurt you as long as you do *exactly* as I say."

Her eyes were enormous as she stared at him over her shoulder. He released her mouth, carefully gauging her reactions. His fingers slipped up into her wet hair, then he kissed her neck. "I need you, Gina. I really need you, baby."

He hadn't meant to get so involved with Brent Carver's ex, but now he was finding it harder and harder to leave her alone. He hadn't touched another woman in months and, despite his flirting words, hadn't wanted to. She turned in his arms, slippery and wet. He dove into the passion and heat of her mouth and wished he could go public with their relationship. But if Brent didn't kill him, Finn might. And with Dryzek threatening his ass, he couldn't risk Gina getting caught up in the tangled mess of his life.

He pushed her against the tiles and manacled her wrists above her head, looked down into those pretty eyes. "I've only got an hour." He swallowed the emotion that caught him off guard. She deserved better than this, and he had the terrible feeling he was starting to fall in love with her. Not only was she the most sexually adventurous woman he'd ever met, she was soft and gentle and kind.

She was also hot. Really fucking hot.

She ran her leg up his thigh, and he almost dropped to his knees. Never had he imagined that beneath those plain cotton blouses and knee-length skirts was a creature so full of simmering sensuality he could barely look at her without getting a hard-on. And naked in the shower with water drenching her skin, running over those full breasts? He was a goner, pure and simple.

She stood on tiptoes and nipped his ear. "So what are you waiting for?"

Holly sat between Finn and Malone as they peered through the darkness. She tried not to think about Finn's thigh pressed snug against hers in the close confines of his truck.

"Where exactly was it spotted?" Finn leaned over her shoulder to stare at the topographical map she'd spread across her knee. All three wore headlamps, and it was like being stuck in a damn laser show. The thing that had happened on the beach made this situation even more difficult because she still had a job to do. And she still wanted him.

"We have two hikers reporting an abandoned boat anchored just south of the Klanawa River Ecological Reserve, just north of where it meets up with Blue Creek." She stuck her index finger on the spot. "The numbers on the side match the boat Len Milbank owned."

"So you figure the killer dumped the body in the wreck, boated up here, ditched the boat, and either got a ride or walked home?" said Finn.

Malone gave him a cranky, bloodshot look that screamed too many hours spent upright with his eyes open. "That how you'd have done it?"

Finn glared back, landing Holly smack bang in the firing line of two pissed-off alpha males.

"If I'd killed Milbank, I'd have dumped the body out in the open somewhere nice and remote"—the fastest place for decomposition—"and then I'd have taken his boat out into the sound, scuttled her, and swum home in time for beers and burgers. You wouldn't be sitting here wetting your pants about crime scenes and trace evidence." Finn's lip curled in disgust.

Malone pushed open his door. There was a path through the woods, just visible as a denser patch of forest. "You stay here with the truck, Rambo."

Finn got out on his side. "In your dreams, Barney."

"Finn." Everyone was tired and stressed and this wasn't helping.

He looked furious. "There are thousands of acres of bush out here. If you guys get disorientated and lost, it could take the authorities weeks to find you. And that's even if they know your starting point." He grabbed his jacket from behind the seat. Stabbed his arms through the sleeves. "Plus, the island has the densest population of cougars in the world, not to mention black bears and gray wolves—"

"I was just going to ask if you had another flashlight. Malone's winding you up," Holly said patiently.

"Successfully," her colleague muttered with a smirk.

She glanced at her fellow officer, who raised an innocent brow.

"You know this area?" she asked Finn.

"Some. We used to fish up here when we were kids." Finn pulled another flashlight out of the back of the truck and retrieved a rifle case too. She and Malone watched with interest as he unpacked the gun and slung it over his shoulder.

"Got a license for that?" Malone asked.

"You got a license for your mouth?"

She planted a hand against Finn's chest before the testosterone ignited. "Corporal Malone is just doing his job, although," she raised her voice and aimed her next comment at the usually taciturn cop, "he could be a damn bit more polite to a man who's just spent the last hour driving us out here, especially if he wants a ride back again."

"Now there's a thought." Finn smiled.

Malone grinned, unrepentant.

"You *do* have a license for that, right?" she asked Finn.

His teeth flashed. "Remind me to pull it out and show you if we meet a *Puma concolor.*" But he opened his wallet and showed her the license anyway.

"I might just steal the rifle and shoot you both. I like *cats.*" She rolled her eyes. "Finn, lead the way. Malone, bring up the rear and stay close. I don't want to lose either of you tonight."

They set off through the dense black forest. Tree branches creaked overhead in the low wind that was slowly building from the west. Holly could see nothing beyond the rifle draped across Finn's red jacket and a foot of jungle when she shone her lamp that way. It felt like the set of a horror movie. Even though she carried a gun and a Taser, she was glad to have Finn, and Malone, close.

"This place gives me the creeps," said Malone.

"Me too." Holly spoke loudly, hoping to scare away anything with canines sharper than her own.

"At least it isn't raining," Malone commented. She saw Finn shake his head as, a moment later, the first drops hit.

"Fuck a duck," Malone squeaked. The rain was gentle at first, just the odd large drop splattering on the wind. But that was just the scouting party. Thirty seconds later, the heavens opened and a sheet of water lashed out of the sky. It got heavier and heavier, in waves, like a monsoon. At first her coat and hat kept off the worst, but after five minutes, water began to seep in along the seams, and rivulets dripped from her nose and chin. Her pants stuck to her skin, and she was starting to shiver. She sneezed. Finn looked back at her, lips tightened with concern.

They kept going, pushing through the overgrown bushes until Holly heard a rush of water above the hammering of the rain. Finn stopped, and she almost ran into him. He steadied her and spoke to Malone. "There's no real path here, but it looks like there's an animal track along the edge of the river. The boat should only be a few hundred yards that way, assuming it hasn't come loose from the anchor."

Malone nodded miserably.

"Let's get this done," Holly said.

The need for banter had dissolved into wretchedness as they trudged through the growing mud puddles that formed out of nowhere. Her feet were wet and cold. Jesus. Nothing about this case had come easy so far.

"There she is." Finn shone his powerful flashlight across the fast-flowing water and picked out the tiny cruiser. "What now? There doesn't look like there's anyone on board, but they'd be below deck in this weather anyway." Water raced down his face, dripped down his jacket and onto his soaked jeans.

Damn. The boat was in the *middle* of the river. They'd have to swim to get on board, and they couldn't risk getting on board that way because they might contaminate evidence. Holly had hoped she could look it over. But at this distance, in this weather, it was impossible.

She took some photographs, praying her camera didn't crap out because of the downpour. Then she exchanged a look with Malone. "We've established Milbank's boat is actually here. We'll head back and call in the IFIS team to retrieve it."

"Or you could swim out there and tow it to Port Alberni with your teeth." Malone aimed another jab at Finn.

Finn swiped some more water off his face and finally relaxed enough to smile. "So that's it?" There was an unholy glint in his eye. "You don't wanna leave a cop guarding the thing overnight?"

"In this weather?" Malone scoffed.

"It's only a bit of rain."

And Niagara was only a trickle. Holly bit her lip and pretended to think about it.

Malone pointed a finger. "That river is rising fast."

"Then maybe you *should* stay, just in case the boat starts to drift away, you could follow it..."

He finally figured out she was joking. "Ha ha."

"If we had another officer out here I'd consider it, but not alone, not in this storm." Once again the rain intensified, and they all hunched deeper into their already soaked clothes.

She took some crime tape out of her pocket and tied it to a branch. "This should give us a visual reference point."

Finn pulled something out of his pocket and pressed a button.

"What's that?" Malone jerked his chin at the thing.

"Satellite GPS. I just e-mailed you a signal from this location."

Malone peered closely at the device and whistled. "I want one."

Finn handed it over so he could check it out.

"How sweet." Holly shook her head, droplets of water spinning off her nose. "Boys, bonding over gadgets."

"Hey, there's nothing wrong with gadgets. Thanks." Malone handed it back to Finn and turned to lead the way out.

Finn caught her arm before she could follow him, leaned close to her ear. "For your information, Officer, I'm a man, not a boy. And you can bond with my gadget anytime." He wiggled his brow, pleased with his joke. That sexy grin was oblivious to the rain and wind and bleak atmosphere of the ancient forest.

Holly backed up a step and would have fallen over a tree root if he hadn't steadied her. "What is it? What's the matter?" His urgent eyes scanned her face.

"Nothing." She sneezed and shivered and stumbled away. She was in deep trouble. Very deep trouble. Because she didn't know the last time her heart had felt such giddy delight. Didn't remember the last time desire had pounded through her bloodstream like a narcotic. And the combination of those two factors scared her more than all the cougars and all the bears in the goddamn universe.

Mike needed a beer more than he needed breath. Gina had taken the edge off, but he was now back to being terrified. The gun he'd stolen from Finn rubbed his spine, and after a moment of indecision, he pulled it out of his jeans and stuffed it back in his glove box. If Dryzek saw he was armed he'd kill him for sure. He couldn't appear to be a threat.

At least it had finally stopped raining. His hands shook.

Another car slid in beside him, no lights. A malevolent black shadow in the deserted parking lot in the middle of nowhere. Mike forced himself out of his truck as Dryzek rolled the passenger window down an inch.

"Did you find it?"

Mike put his hands in his pockets. "I searched Finn's place, but it isn't there. It wasn't in his truck either."

"What about Brent?"

Fear made his mouth dry. "The guy never leaves the house. I can't get into the place without him seeing me—"

"I don't care how you do it. Kill him for all I care. I just want my stuff." Dryzek's voice was a furious hiss.

He could feel his heart punching his ribs. "I can't hurt anyone, Remy. You know that. Brent Carver will beat the shit out of me the moment I step on his land."

He heard the driver's door slide open, and Gordy Ferdinand climbed out and walked around the car. The man was a massive, threatening hulk of meanness. Mike backed up a step, but Ferdinand drove his sledgehammer fist into Mike's stomach. His knees crumpled and he wanted to hurl.

"Jesus," he gasped, sitting in an inch of mud on the ground. How the hell had he got into this mess? "What the fuck was that for?"

Ferdinand picked him up by the collar and rammed him again. *Holy mother.* His vision blurred. Pain twisted his insides into a rigid knot.

Dryzek slipped the window down all the way as Mike, on his knees, braced one hand on the ground, the other arm trying to shield his body. In the darkness he couldn't see a damn thing, but the proximity to Ferdinand's boots scared the shit out of him. One good kick could snap his neck, and he'd suddenly figured out—five minutes too late—that he should have just taken off until the cops found Len's killer.

"Set up a diversion. Hell, get the guy arrested if you have to. Just find a way to search Carver's place. I want to know if that fucker is trying to take over my turf, and if he is, I'm going to take him down, along with that piece-of-shit brother of his."

"And if I don't find anything?" His voice was shaky and weak. *Dammit.* When had he become lowest on the food chain?

Ferdinand grabbed him by his shirt collar and hauled him to his feet. "Then we'll figure out where you're gonna look next."

His whole body shook. "What if the police find it first?" There was no way he was hanging around Bamfield to get screwed over by Remy Dryzek.

The sharp edge of Remy's profile became visible as he stuck his head out the window. "Now that would be a shame…because Gordy's been dying to pay your old man a proper visit."

Mike's tongue stuck to the roof of his mouth as all the moisture in his mouth disappeared.

"I don't normally let him pound old men or women, but this is important to me." Mike finally saw the guy for what he was—evil. "Like your parents are important to you."

His heart stopped beating.

"You understand?"

He nodded, and a fist like a brick smashed into his jaw.

"Answer him, you little shit!"

White light flashed through his eyes and his vision faded in and out. He staggered to his knees, tensed as Ferdinand grabbed his hair and pulled his head back for another strike.

"Wait," Dryzek ordered. "Do we have a deal, Mikey?" he asked quietly.

"Yeah, we have a deal." The words grated out from between locked teeth.

Ferdinand shoved him to the ground. A moment later the hot blast of engine fumes whipped over his face as he lay panting in the mud.

He was so fucked.

CHAPTER 11

Pictures of violent death were spread out on the table as they all gathered around, drinking coffee. The fact she was still hungry meant she was getting a little too used to the job.

The command group had convened for another meeting. She and Malone had dried off, changed, and towel dried their hair—his more successfully than hers. She sneezed.

"Bless you," said Messenger.

"Thanks." Holly sniffed, then sneezed again so violently it tore through her bruises with a nice sharp kick.

"*Gesundheit.*" Malone grinned then sneezed himself. "Fuck."

"Phone records show no outgoing calls from Len after Monday, April second," Jeff Winslow carried on.

"Can we get access to his incoming calls and voice mail?" Holly asked.

"Already did." Jeff distributed copies. "We've got a lot of activity from a burner phone out of Port Alberni on that Monday; same burner was used in Bamfield but hasn't been used since. Several messages from Remy Dryzek asking where the hell Milbank was, one in particular telling him if he didn't get his ass back by Friday he was personally going to rip his balls off."

"When was that one left?"

"Thursday the fifth."

Holly looked around at the other officers, trying to shake off the pervasive cold that had fused with her bones. "According to the pathologist, Milbank was probably already dead by then. I want a list of names of everyone who called Milbank or who he called during the last six months and we'll cross-reference them with locals who said they didn't know the vic."

"Can we get a fix on where he made his last call?" asked Holly.

"Yep, but it doesn't give us anything except Port Alberni."

"Which we already had." She pressed her lips together. "Any trace evidence at all on the vic, Steffie?"

"Not a damned thing."

"Think someone knew how much seawater messes up evidence?" This from Chastain, whose eyes were bloodshot and shadowed. Steffie had told her he'd just been dumped by his fiancée via text message. She'd told him to go home and fix it, but he'd been determined to stay. Being a cop and having a personal life wasn't easy. Everyone on the team needed a power nap.

A wave of hurt hit Holly head-on. She pulled out her pain meds and swallowed another two with a mouthful of coffee. Damn. "I don't know, but whoever murdered Milbank had to have screwed up somewhere. Can they locate Milbank's cell phone now?"

"Phone company has been trying to ping it, but they found nothing. My guess is it's in ten feet of water," said Jeff.

"Or out of cell tower range," suggested Steffie.

Too many options in an area this remote. "What do we have from Milbank's apartment?"

Steffie shuffled her notes. "We've got traces of narcotics. Fingerprints from Dryzek and associates and several females who have records for prostitution. Found a few diving manuals and books borrowed from the local library."

Chastain laughed. "Len Milbank had a library card?"

It didn't fit with his character. "When did he join the library?" asked Holly.

"Friday, March thirtieth," said Steffie.

Excitement burned a hole in Holly's chest. "So Finn Carver and Thomas Edgefield find the wreck on Wednesday, March twenty-eighth, and by Friday Len Milbank knew about it?" She snorted. "No matter what they said, someone else knew they found that wreck."

"You still believe them when they say they didn't tell anyone?" asked Steffie.

"I do, but..." Her thoughts turned to the librarian. "See if a woman called Gina Swartz shows up on any of those phone lists. Did Milbank have an e-mail address?"

Malone nodded. "I'm checking out those messages right now."

"Anything suspicious that hinted at shipwrecks during that time period?"

Malone checked his notes. "Nothing."

Holly's brain was firing, and she knew she'd missed something. She snapped her fingers. "Finn Carver said they wrote down their coordinates on the dive sheets. Did you check that?" She looked around, but everyone shook their heads. She checked her watch. Crap. "I've got to go pick up my stuff anyway. I'll go check." She eyed the couch balefully, and everyone avoided her eye. "Let's see how closely the coordinates they left match up with the site of the shipwreck and if someone could have used it to pinpoint the exact location—especially if someone overheard them talking about what they'd found."

Her phone rang. Almost midnight. Staff Sergeant Furlong. Tension squeezed all the air out of her lungs. "Yes, sir?"

"What's the progress, Sergeant Rudd?"

She cleared her throat. "We've narrowed down the timeline for time of death and believe he was killed on Monday, April second."

"Do Carver and Edgefield have alibis for Monday?"

She stretched out her stiff neck. "I'm not sure yet, sir. We've only just narrowed it down—"

"Find out," he snapped. "I want them to account for every damn minute."

"Yes, sir." Holly could feel her cheeks burn. Malone eyed her steadily and Chastain went to grab himself another coffee. They'd be peeing pure caffeine at this rate and had more chance of coma than sleep.

"Have you checked the dive shops regarding the knife?"

"The knife was old, sir." Christ.

"Well, maybe the killer had to buy a new one to replace it. Get on it, Sergeant." He disconnected, and the ensuing silence made her agonizingly aware of how one lapse in judgment could screw with her whole career.

Shit. The man was going to waste their time focusing on suspects that her gut was telling her were innocent. But she had to follow orders, which meant if they got a lead from those lines of inquiry, Furlong got the praise. If they got nothing, she'd get the grief. Damned if she did and damned if she didn't.

"Rachel." It was the first time she'd used Messenger's first name. "The team commander wants us to circulate a photograph of the knife to all the local dive shops. See if anyone recognizes it. And ask if any of the BMSC staff or Bamfield residents bought a new knife recently."

The woman looked annoyed but didn't complain.

"Did you talk to the guys investigating yesterday's crash?" Malone asked.

"I gave them a statement, but they don't have much new. They're canvassing the drivers of logging trucks. I also asked them to check to see if the drivers had seen anyone walking along Klanawa Road over the last two weeks too because whoever dumped that boat had to get home somehow."

"Unless they had an accomplice," Chastain put in.

"It's worth a shot."

"Pity you didn't get a better look at the guy who ran you off the road."

One side of Holly's lips drew up in a rueful smile. "If I'd known what was going to happen I'd have shot the crap out of his truck, but I was too busy trying to keep my vehicle on the road."

"And look how well that worked out for you," said Malone with a serious expression. "Next time, shoot the damn truck and screw the paperwork." No one liked it when a cop got hurt. It brought back the awareness of all the dangers of the job.

She rubbed her forehead. "You guys get some sleep. I'm going to go down to the dive shed and check those coordinates."

"I'll come with you," Malone said.

"I don't need a babysitter." Her voice got hard. She didn't need protection or special treatment. They had a motorboat to cross the channel now, so it wasn't like she'd be rowing. "I'll be thirty minutes, max."

"Don't forget your gun," said Chastain.

She snorted, hand on her pistol. As if she would after yesterday. They all stood and headed off to steal a much-needed couple of hours of rest.

Steffie came to stand beside her and eyed the couch. "You can't sleep on that wretched thing; it's four feet long." They both eyed it distastefully. "Stay where you were last night. No one's gonna say anything. Carver isn't even a suspect except in Furlong's tiny brain."

"I need to check his alibi for Monday to know that for sure." Plus, no way could she risk being alone with him overnight again. Every time she saw him she wanted to touch him, and every time she touched him she wanted to kiss him and…not a good idea. "I'm not allowing anything to cloud this investigation." She dropped her voice. "I can't take any chances, Steff. Furlong would bury me if there's any sort of impropriety."

Steffie shook her head. "Finn Carver isn't our guy and you know it."

Holly mumbled under her breath.

Steffie gripped her forearm with strong fingers and shook her slightly. "You always feel like you have to work harder than us because of who your father is. Better test scores, better fitness, better marksmanship, better clearance rates, higher ethics, longer working hours—everything. Did it ever occur to you that *those* were the reasons you got promoted so fast?" She smiled sadly. "That you might actually deserve the position you're in?"

Holly watched her go and wanted to believe her. Trouble was there was no way she could ever prove she'd got as far as she had on her own merit, and she'd made enough mistakes to last a lifetime. "Well, you can't fix stupid." But she didn't have to do anything to make it worse. She headed out the door and into the enveloping darkness.

Finn lay in bed staring at the ceiling. He could hear the guys downstairs having a beer outside, but that wasn't what was keeping him awake. Images kept circling his mind. Holly in street clothes the day she arrived. Bloody and injured after the wreck. Those tiny frogs on her toes. Sleeping across the hall last night. Kissing him on the beach.

Why had she freaked out on him back there in the woods? Had he overstepped some invisible line by joking with her like that? Her face had turned ghostly white under her bruises and she'd barely spoken to him the whole drive back. After the connection they'd shared, her sudden pulling away had confused the hell out of him. But he was dealing with a woman, so it wasn't exactly new or unexpected territory. He had to stop thinking about her. He punched the pillow under his head to try to reshape it. Launched it across the room when that didn't work and laid his arm across his forehead. What the hell was he thinking anyway? That a woman like Holly would fall for his charm? What the hell did he have to offer besides a quick slaking of some red-hot lust?

Goddamn it. He didn't need to be thinking about any slaking. She was so rule oriented and dedicated. His imagination whirled. What would it feel like to shatter the professional façade and reveal the woman beneath? To touch her naked body as he laid her on a blanket. To take her against a wall, rough and sweaty, hard and slow. Those lips. Those eyes. Those long, slim limbs that looked like they'd been made to wrap around his body. He groaned and sat up, knowing sleep was as elusive as a five-legged goat.

The creak of a footfall had him rolling out of bed to his bedroom door within a split second. He pressed his ear to the wood. Boards groaned gently. Someone was in his cabin. Remy Dryzek? Ferdinand?

He glanced at his wardrobe and thought about getting his handgun, then dismissed the idea. No time. Plus, he didn't need the gun when he had darkness. Silently he eased open the door. A silhouette was outlined against the window, black on black. He immediately recognized Holly's shape, or maybe he knew her scent on a cellular level.

"I was just going to borrow your keys to the dive shed." Her voice was gruff, almost nervous sounding.

Something was wrong. "Everything OK?"

Her chin rose and he heard her swallow thickly.

Shit. This was about him. He walked toward her. "I don't know what I did to freak you out—"

"You haven't done anything—"

"Then why the hell are you backing away from me?" Loud, vehement, frustrated. Definitely frustrated. He tried to dispel the lust that scratched at his veins.

She froze, but he'd gotten close enough to see the expression in her eyes. Not fear. Something else. He released a breath that had been trapped tight in his chest. He took another step so she was within arm's reach, and her gaze ran over his body. Right, he'd forgotten he was wearing only boxers. Thankfully, it was dark and he had some measure of self-control.

"What happened out there in the woods?" He kept his voice low. "What did I do, besides be an idiot?"

She turned away and rested her hands on the edge of the stainless steel sink. He took another step closer and, drawn like a magnet, lifted the thick tresses of her hair over one shoulder.

"Nothing." But her voice vibrated.

"I was just joking with you about the gadget thing." Her hair smelled of rain. He tried not to inhale her.

"I know." She shuddered.

Unable to resist, he reached out a finger and ran it down the line of her neck. Her skin was both hot and satin smooth. He took her shoulders gently in his hands and turned her around to face him. "I thought we'd reached some sort of working relationship?"

She nodded quickly. Too quickly, too quietly, too damn easily. Her eyes had lost their swollen puffiness. The skin was discolored, but at least she looked like Holly again. Something widened her eyes and her breath hitched. Definitely not fear.

Attraction.

Lust.

Want.

He didn't think. He just kissed her; hand cradling the back of her head, fingers sinking deep into her hair. He angled his mouth and opened her lips, diving deep into wet, volcanic heat that made him groan. She kissed him back, tasting like coffee, dark and heady. Addictive. Still hanging on tight to the sink as if scared to let go.

Every hair on his body stood erect. His skin tingled, blood raced through his veins.

Working relationship? Right.

Need rocketed through his body, making his legs shake. When had a woman ever affected him like this? It wasn't normal, wasn't rational, wasn't sane. He pressed forward, and her hands shot up and braced against his chest, fingers curling against his pecs, small noises coming from the back of her mouth that demanded deeper, harder, more. And if he could just keep doing this all night, his life would be fine. He brought her fully against him and she squeaked, just enough to let him know that he'd hurt her.

He jerked his head up and let go of her waist, still pinning her against the kitchen counter. "Sorry. Christ."

She struggled away from him and he watched her go. She wiped the back of her hand over her mouth. "Finn…" Regret burned across her features. "That can't happen again."

Couldn't happen again? The same way he didn't need to draw in oxygen? He made himself laugh softly, didn't want to scare her by dropping to his knees and begging. Rejection wasn't new to him, but he didn't remember the last time a woman had said no. *No* was fine. *No* was a personal choice. But this *no* hurt on a different level.

"It was just a kiss, Holly." He was gratified to see her eyebrows rise.

"If that was just a kiss I can't imagine what full-blown sex would be like." She slapped a hand across her mouth and then laughed, dissipating the tension that had built to almost snapping point. "I didn't say that."

"Hey, no big deal. People kiss. People even have sex." He looked out the window into the night. "But I'm not the kind to kiss and tell." He immediately knew he'd said something wrong. The silence got strained. He pretended what had just happened was perfectly ordinary, instead of just perfect. "Give me two minutes and I'll get dressed and take you down to the shed."

"I don't want a chaperone." Her voice was subdued. Eyes hooded and watchful.

"My keys, my shed." He held his hand out for his keys she'd picked up from the bench.

Holly hesitated. The kiss had been amazing. The fact he wanted to keep it secret as much as she did should have reassured her, but actually bothered her at a fundamental level—as if once again she wasn't worthy of a real relationship, just some dirty messing around on the side. Which was crazy, because if he told anyone she'd have to shoot him and bury the body deep.

She realized she was still staring at him, drooling, even though he terrified her. His muscles well defined even in the shadows. Pecs and abs hard as a bronze statue, long legs solid with muscle, boxer shorts that didn't disguise the impressive maleness that had pressed so wonderfully against her just moments ago. She dragged her eyes away and figured she should be grateful he was wearing anything at all, considering it was after midnight and he'd been in bed.

She dropped his keys into the palm of his hand and walked to the door. That kiss had stirred up the hormones in her blood and she wanted him. Really wanted him, like drop him to the floor, straddle, slide him home, and ride him until they both screamed.

Not happening.

She pulled at her collar, heat pouring off her skin in waves. She didn't do this. Didn't fall for guys she barely knew. Didn't fantasize about having sex with them on the floor. Most of her friends said she was repressed, but right now she was about as repressed as a schizophrenic on a psychotic break.

If anyone found out they'd been fooling around, her career would be irreparably damaged.

She was nothing without her badge. Nothing without the long line of family tradition holding her up by the bootstraps. She needed that. Needed that sense of belonging. Needed the acceptance. No matter how mouthwateringly gorgeous he was, she didn't want to fall for Finn Carver, and right now she was desperately close.

And she didn't want to think about what it would do to her heart or pride when he finished, rolled over, and walked away.

He went back into his room and came out dragging a shirt over his head that said AIR SUX, NITROX ROX.

She rolled her eyes and gave him a grin, forcing herself to relax. To hide her disquiet.

They'd kissed. It hadn't gone further, and she didn't intend to let it. She needed to make like it was no big deal so they could move on. "Let's go."

He grinned back, and Holly wished to hell her vision was still blurry because the guy was the most stunning male specimen she'd ever encountered, and considering her line of work, she encountered a lot.

The two guys from downstairs were gone when she and Finn went down the steps. They crunched along the gravel road to the dive shed, her breath steaming the chilly air. He didn't seem to notice the cold. They passed a couple of students. There was obviously a party going on somewhere.

"What did you do last Monday?" she asked.

He shot her a look. "We were jammed. Two different schools arrived for field courses and one of the staff went down with appendicitis. The whole week was a train wreck. Why?"

Holly held her tongue even though she wanted to answer him. "That's when you think Milbank was killed, isn't it?"

The guy was so sharp. So smart. Maybe that's why she'd fallen for him, not the hero good looks. She pressed her lips tighter together, glad for the relative darkness. "I can't discuss the case with you." She sounded miserable and wanted to kick herself. He wasn't her boyfriend. She didn't need to apologize to him for doing her job.

"I get it, Holly. There's a lot of stuff I can't talk about either."

Special Forces. Of course he got it. It made her feel even more wretched.

"Talk to Thom's secretary, Gladys. She had to rework the schedule at the last minute. Get our timetables and then get someone else to verify we were doing what we were supposed to be doing. Hell, I don't think I was alone even taking a…bathroom break." He coughed.

Did that include at night? Jealousy ate at her like some sixteen-year-old with a high school crush. Thankfully he was oblivious.

"You can cross us off the list once and for all."

"I know how to do my job." Holly bit her lip, annoyed she sounded so defensive. Why was she giving him grief? Because he'd made the same mistake she had? He might have kissed her first, but she hadn't exactly been throwing out the stop signals.

Lights reflected in the water of the inlet but the night was silent. Neither spoke again. She'd killed the earlier intimacy and she was glad. They were back on a professional footing.

They reached the dive shed and Finn moved ahead of her. Opened the door and turned on the light. The fluorescents flickered for a couple of seconds before they reluctantly sparked up. Finn went to the desk and pulled off a clipboard and handed it to her. Avoiding his watchful gaze, she peeled back the pages until she got to March 28, the day he and Edgefield claimed to have first found the wreck. Above it were notes about the sea otter sighting.

"Do you have a photocopier?" She twisted around and found him next to her, way too close for comfort. Holly's mouth went dry and her heart tripped over her racing pulse. His eyes flared and he took a step back. Then he schooled his features to reveal nothing.

"In the marine station's library. Come on, I've got a key to that too. Let's get this finished." That sounded as final as any death knell.

Outside, the air temperature seemed to have cooled ten degrees and had nothing to do with the weather. They started back up the steep slope, the silence thick between them. Then she stumbled, and every hurt from the car crash shot along a million neurons simultaneously. Her sharp gasp of breath had Finn reaching for her. She'd almost forgotten about her injuries—those kiss endorphins were *that* good.

"You OK?" The heat from his hands burned through her shirt.

She nodded, breathing rapidly. "Just caught myself awkwardly."

"Considering you almost died yesterday and have been working nonstop since dawn, you might want to go a little easier on yourself." His hold tightened, and she found herself staring at his lips again with all sorts of off-duty thoughts shooting through her mind. But until this case was done she wouldn't be off-duty.

His Adam's apple slid up and down his throat, and he let out a low groan. "If you don't stop looking at me like that…"

She forced down her reaction and pushed out of his arms. No one ever said being a cop was easy, but she didn't think this was what they'd been talking about. "Come on," she said.

There were distant sounds of music and carefree laughter.

"One of the field courses finished up today," Finn explained. "Party time."

They went all the way around the front of the main building, and he unlocked a side door that led straight into the library stacks adjacent to the study area. He entered a code and the photocopier sprang to life. "Here," he took the clipboard from her hand, "I'll make two copies and the office can keep one too." His lips pressed hard together and she was sure he was about to add "just in case."

The attitude toward the cops around here was a little insulting, but maybe, considering what Professor Edgefield had been through, she understood. It made it even more imperative they catch Len Milbank's killer.

The machine spat out two copies, and Finn handed her one, which felt warm in her hand, and then headed toward the office. He unlocked another two doors and left a copy on Edgefield's secretary's desk. They were heading back to the door when he stopped dead and she slammed into his steel back. *Whoomph.* He whirled and caught her before she fell over.

"Ouch." She touched her smarting nose.

"Sorry." But his attention was elsewhere. He sniffed. "Do you smell smoke?" Suddenly he was on his cell, calling 911. "We need the truck up at BMSC."

Holly sniffed the air. The very faint tinge of smoke caught her nostrils. "We should wait outside."

"*You* wait outside for the fire brigade. They're volunteers, and sometimes it takes them awhile to get here. Tell them to head down to the basement."

"No."

He tried to push her out the door, but she broke his hold, caught his arm, and twisted it up behind his back. He froze, solid and immovable, but something about the way he held himself suggested he could break her hold if he wanted to. And suddenly, she instinctively knew all her police training would prove worthless if Finn ever decided to challenge her.

It should have scared the crap out of her. Didn't.

"Fine, come with me, but it could be dangerous. And we need to move fast."

She let go of his arm, and he turned and smashed the glass in the fire alarm. He wedged the front door open. "Follow me. Do *not* go off on your own. I just want to check no one's in the building. No playing hero," he warned her.

They headed downstairs at a run, Holly struggling to keep up, puffing like the Hogwarts Express.

In the lower levels, they encountered thicker smoke, and he ripped off his T-shirt and wrapped it around her face before she could protest. "I wasn't the one in a car accident yesterday," he told her. It was warm on her face, and his scent enveloped her. It was like being injected with pure male pheromones.

They carried on, opening every door along the way. All the labs and rooms were empty. At the end of the corridor was the exit door that led outside. The smell of smoke was strongest here. Finn touched the doorknob and jerked away. "Shit, it's roasting. The fire is on the outside. Come on!" He dashed back to the stairs, and Holly ran after him, bracing herself for the torturous climb.

He threw her a sympathetic glance as he pulled out his cell. "I'd carry you if I thought it would help."

She gritted her teeth and nodded, too distracted to speak when every breath felt like one of her ribs was stabbing into her lungs. They climbed quickly, and she heard him talking first to the firemen, then to Thomas Edgefield, telling them there was a fire on the south side of the building that was threatening the structure.

"Thank fuck it rained tonight." He stuffed his cell in his jeans pocket and grabbed an extinguisher off the wall, and they ran outside just as a fire engine arrived, all sirens blaring.

They started rolling out hoses as she tried to follow Finn. But he leapt over a railing and scrambled through thick bushes down the slope. There was no way she could get through that tangle, not even at full strength. Instead, she ran down the gravel path, half slipping and sliding. Flames were erupting fifteen feet high out of a metal trash can that had been pressed up against the side of the building.

Why hadn't they seen it on the way up the hill? Had it only just ignited?

Sparks flickered in the air. One landed in the thick scrub, and Holly saw embers starting to smolder in the darkness.

"Get some water over there," she yelled to the first fireman to catch up with her.

She jerked back in surprise as Finn's assistant, Rob Fitzgerald, grinned at her. "Yes, ma'am." She stood out of the way. Finn had emptied the contents of the extinguisher into the trash can, and the flames seem to have subsided. He glanced over his shoulder and stepped back as the firemen took over.

Sweat dripped off his brow and darkened his hair. They both stank of smoke.

"Arson?" she asked. She handed him back his T-shirt, pretending not to ogle his muscles.

He blew out a breath, wiped his face on his shirt before dragging it over his chest. "More like stupidity. Probably someone smoking down here and throwing a cigarette butt in the trash when it wasn't fully out."

Holly's heartbeat was gradually slowing down. She still clutched her notes. If they hadn't gone to the dive shed in the middle of the night, that fire could have caused some serious damage. As it was, the flames were all out and the fire department was ripping their way through the bushes to make sure there were no stray embers.

He blew out a huge breath. "You should just sleep in my cabin." She jerked up to look at him.

"Alone." His eyes glowed with all the things they were trying to ignore. "I'm going to be here for most of the night, chewing my way through students." The determined look in his eyes made her grin.

Finn looked pissed as hell and she couldn't blame him. If they hadn't caught the fire, it could have spread and destroyed not only the marine lab, but also potentially thousands of acres of forest and god knows how many lives. Exhaustion hit her head on and her vision started to whirl. The thought of walking down to the dock and boating across the inlet was more than she could bear. Plus, all her stuff was in his cabin, not that she had much. It made sense. She put her hand on his back. It was supposed to be a slap of appreciation for a job well done, but her fingers lingered and turned it into something else entirely. "Er, right. I'll, hmm, see you tomorrow."

He watched her, face expressionless even as his eyes burned. "Good night, Holly. Lock the door, and sleep well."

Mike sat absolutely still beneath the branches of an old pine, staring at the back door of Brent Carver's home. Hopefully the small fire he'd set in the trash can would be enough excitement to get the ex-con out of his house while at the same time not doing any real damage. The earlier downpour should stop the flames spreading, but, bottom line, Mike was desperate. His phone vibrated, but he held still. The fire department was going to have to cope without him tonight.

The door opened and Brent stepped into the darkness. The guy kept an eye on everything that happened in town. He even slept with some sort of radio receiver or scanner set up next to his bed. When he slept at all.

Gina said he didn't, not anymore, but Mike didn't want to think about the fact that he was in a relationship with the woman everyone considered Brent Carver's girlfriend. The guy had dumped her, and Mike had been there to pick up the pieces. Carver's loss. His gain.

Gina had been all for his role-playing games, which had been a bit of a surprise. In fact, she'd told him some of her secret fantasies, which had culminated with her being tied to the bed earlier. Considering the rest of his day, he wished he could do it all over again. Maybe she could tie him up next time and keep him there for a week as her personal sex slave.

Footsteps echoed through the darkness as Brent went down to the dock and started his small motorboat. Mike waited until he was out of sight and around the bluff before he sprinted to the back door. He turned the handle and the door opened, unlocked. Thank god. He didn't know anything about locks, and he didn't want Carver knowing anyone had been here, which he would if Mike had to smash a window.

His jaw ached from Ferdinand's fist as he walked into the huge open-plan space. Not bad for an ex-con. No way he could afford all this without some illegal activity. Maybe Remy was right?

That bastard. Threatening his parents? Motherfucker was gonna get his. Mike touched the gun in his waistband. He wanted to go over to Remy's and blow them both away, but not only did Dryzek have top-notch security, Mike wasn't really killer material. Unless they went near his folks or Gina, because then all bets were off.

Mike wore black leather gloves and carried a flashlight. He started opening cupboards and searching every crevice large enough to stash a hold-all. Nothing in the kitchen or living room. He decided to search upstairs next, just in case Brent came home sooner than expected. He checked his watch. He'd been here five minutes already.

The wood on the stairs shone like honey. Jeez, the entire place gleamed. It seemed wrong. Wrong that a convicted murderer got to live like a king while god-fearing, hardworking people like him and his parents made do with a small, rickety house and ancient appliances.

Upstairs were five closed doors and a weird smell. Mike headed for the stink and opened a door onto a massive room that had huge windows facing the sea. There was a couch, and there were hundreds of stacked canvases in various stages of development propped against both walls. Mike's lower jaw dropped.

Holy hell, the guy was an artist? Brent Carver was a fucking painter?

He went across and touched a canvas showing a blue-black lake at the base of a mountain. It was abstract but beautiful. He drew in a breath through tight lungs. He was an artist—and a damn good one. He squinted at the signature in the corner of a finished canvas. B.C. Wilkinson. Holy mother.

Brent Carver was some artist called B.C. Wilkinson?

Shit. This was how he made money. He wasn't going to start dealing coke.

He backed away, and another sound registered. The motor of a boat. Mike looked out the window and saw Carver's boat pull up to the dock. His distraction hadn't worked. He turned off his flashlight and ran downstairs, sprinting like an Olympic athlete to the door nearest the road. He skidded to a halt and then silently eased open the deadbolts. Mike opened the door just as Brent came in the door at the rear of the house. He slipped out and silently closed it behind him. And then he ran. Faster than he'd ever run in his life as his lungs pounded and his heart exploded.

CHAPTER 12

Gina used to have a dog, but it had died about six months ago. Sentiment had overruled common sense and she'd never replaced it. Now he opened the back door and slid soundlessly into the kitchen. Years eroded memory. Time eradicated fear. Bad things happened to other people, in other places. Not safe little towns like Bamfield.

So trusting, so naive, so flawed.

He stood silently on the worn linoleum floor, clock ticking in the darkness. The refrigerator rattled to life, and he looked at it for a long, grateful moment. It would help mask his footsteps.

Rage burned in his chest, expanding his lungs to bursting. Human beings were inherently flawed. Most of them were foolish, fickle creatures who didn't stop to think about the consequences of their actions.

His fists clenched.

He'd been like that once. He'd learned his lesson early and never forgotten. Paid the price. Never screwed up again. Then Milbank had come crawling around his place like a cockroach, and he'd been forced into action again, trying to contain the mess.

She was the last of it.

He walked down the dark passageway. Brent Carver's little whore was bound to go running back to him at some point and then everything would get screwed up. He'd made a tactical error stuffing Milbank's body in the shipwreck. He'd thought he was being clever, but so few people knew about the damned thing that Gina Swartz was a potential loose end. If she opened her stupid mouth, he was sunk. He wasn't about to let that happen. The walls pressed as heavily against his skin as the walls of that shipwreck had, but at least here he could only drown in guilt.

It wasn't his fault. She'd done this to herself. They always blamed others for their own mistakes, but this was on her. Loose lips sank ships, and he wasn't willing to take any more chances. Not with the things that mattered.

The scent of laundry detergent drifted from a room to his right. The bedroom door was slightly ajar. He paused as he tried to pick out the woman in the shadows. Then a shaft of moonlight cut over her face as she lay on her back in bed, lips parted.

She was naked.

The lack of clothes made his job easier, but he didn't appreciate the bolt of arousal that shot through him from just looking at her. The sight of her dragged him back to another place, another time, when he'd only cared about fucking any skirt with a pulse. He'd been disgusting. An animal. But the memories made him hesitate, wondering if those velvet nipples would taste as good as they looked.

He bit his lip.

How would those breasts look, all plump and swollen? With those womanly nipples condensed into tight little buds of desire as she panted for him while he pumped inside her?

His hands shook just thinking about it.

Her skin looked as soft as rose petals. Pale as milk, except for the dark thatch of hair between her legs.

The room smelled of sweat and sex. Christ, he was so hard his dick strained against his zipper, but he wasn't that man anymore. He stood there, tempted until he hurt, looking at a woman he had no right to be looking at, wanting to have her, knowing he could get away with it. No one would ever know. No one would suspect. Wasting time, increasing the risk that he'd get caught.

He moved carefully across the creaky old hardwood planks until he stood so close he could reach out and touch her. She'd have liked it too. This type always did, no matter who was doing the touching. His breathing grew tighter in his lungs as he thought about all the things he'd like to do to her. Of all the ways he could take her that a *lady* didn't like.

Covers were tangled around her legs, trapping her. God, he wanted her. To take her, to punish her for making him do this.

But sex wasn't everything.

In fact, sex was nothing against the all-consuming power of love.

Sweat beaded on his upper lip as he fought temptation and ruin. Her chest rose and fell in the rhythm of deep sleep, oblivious to the mess she'd made.

Women like her were not decent or good. They were designed to drag good men to their knees and make them beg. He drew out the knife and held it two-handed above her chest. She was nothing but a threat who could destroy everything he'd worked so hard for. There was no regret and no sorrow. He drove the blade down through her ribcage into her heart. Her eyes and mouth opened on a silent, gut-gurgling scream. Her body bowed rigid against the mattress in pain and death. It wasn't instant, but it was damned close.

CHAPTER 13

"Yo, boss."

Holly jerked awake. She'd fallen asleep lying half on the couch, half on the floor. Given the pathetic state of her already battered body, she now felt as stiff as a pine tree in an Alaskan winter. She unfolded one inch at a time and wondered if she could take a shot of morphine and still do her job. Probably not, but hell, it was tempting.

Freddy Chastain stood grinning at her with his Italian good looks in direct opposition to how she felt.

"You OK, Freddy?"

He shrugged one shoulder. He obviously didn't want to talk about his personal life, and as long as it didn't affect his performance she was fine with that. None of her business.

"Your face is almost completely green now," he said.

"Thanks for the update. No wonder you made detective." Then he handed her coffee and all was forgiven. "Any news from IFIS on the boat?"

"They're scratching their heads trying to figure out the best way to get it to Port Alberni. Said they'd call you when they'd decided a course of action. What were you looking at?" He sat beside her and glanced over the information she'd pulled on Remy Dryzek last night.

"I went back to basics." The coffee soothed her sore throat and gave her heart a little shove. She dragged her hair out of her eyes and caught a whiff of sweat. Ew. She needed a shower. From the hiss of water through the hotel's pipes she'd missed her early morning opportunity. Last night she'd desperately wanted to sleep in Finn Carver's cabin, which had made the need to return here imperative. She hadn't even fetched her stuff because she'd known the moment she'd stepped over his threshold she'd have sunk into a deep, exhausted slumber in the bed in the spare room, and if he'd come back, if he'd kissed her, anything could have happened.

Nothing was going to happen.

"To catch a killer you have to understand the victim, so I dug a little harder into Milbank's dealings with our resident Al Capone and came up with a few ideas."

"Such as…"

"We found traces of narcotics in Milbank's apartment." Holly leaned closer. "The first night we arrived, I checked out the local bar while you guys went bye-bye."

Chastain watched her with eyes that were almost completely black. She'd never realized what a great-looking guy he was until now. Thankfully, he didn't stir up anything except professional coworker feelings.

"Dryzek turned up in the bar with his sidekick Gordy Ferdinand. He told Finn Carver he'd misplaced something and he wanted it back."

"But they didn't hint what *it* was?"

Holly shook her head. "That would be too easy."

"And the apartment was turned over earlier the same evening?"

"Yep, by a couple of hours."

"Circumstantial, but…"

"I know." She raked her fingers through her hair.

"If Dryzek trashed the apartment, what do you think he was looking for? Drugs?"

"That's what I'm betting on. Either Bamfield was a drop-off point for smugglers or a distribution point for moving drugs on up the coast. And Milbank was the middleman."

"Shall I reach out to narcotics? I've got a couple of buddies there."

"Do that. And dig into Milbank's past and see if you can find *anything* that links Milbank to someone in Bamfield. We need to figure out what Dryzek was looking for and where the hell it is now because that might be the key to Milbank's murder."

Chastain narrowed his eyes. "Do you think Finn Carver has something to do with this?"

"No." Holly squeezed her eyes together to try to banish the fuzziness, and then realized it was her brain not her vision that needed waking up. "He seemed genuinely confused by what Dryzek was talking about in the bar, but there was no love lost there."

Holly stole a piece of toast from Chastain's plate before he whipped it out of her reach. "From what I can gather, Finn Carver left the army when Thom Edgefield was beaten to a pulp. Because of Edgefield's crime-stopper mentality—which we could use more of—he'd made it difficult for organized crime to get a foothold in Bamfield. Sergeant Hammond says RCMP get weekly reports on any suspicious activity in the town."

"So you think Dryzek was responsible for beating up Edgefield and Carver came back to level out the playing field?"

"And they ended up in a stalemate." Holly nodded. "But with Milbank turning up dead in the neighborhood and Dryzek losing his stash of whatever, I get the feeling the truce might be over."

"It still doesn't make any sense for Finn to find the body and report it."

"Criminals aren't always smart." Holly was playing devil's advocate, curious as to Chastain's take on Edgefield and Finn.

"But those guys are both scalpel sharp. I mean the professor is screwy, but the man's a member of Mensa, and Finn, man." He grinned. "I like that guy. Decorated soldier. Respected diver leader. He seems straight up."

"I think so too." It was just good to hear it from someone who wasn't dazzled by all that testosterone. "So what I'm thinking is that Milbank finally found someone to work with in town—hence all the calls to the burner cell we can't find here in Bamfield."

"Wouldn't Dryzek know who Milbank was working with?"

"Maybe. Maybe not." Holly had been turning things over in her mind on and off all night. That and reliving those kisses. "Perhaps Milbank was trying to make himself more valuable to his boss by keeping a few things secret. Or going freelance."

"Or maybe it's a new contact Milbank was trying to exploit but hadn't nailed down yet," Chastain added.

Holly remembered something else about the night in the pub now too. "Dryzek knew Mike Toben. He had a quiet word with him when he walked into the bar."

Chastain nodded. "I'll go talk to him first thing this morning."

"See if we can examine Mike's financials." Chances of warrants at this stage were slim. Holly's phone screeched. She winced as she realized it was Furlong on the line at six in the morning. Fantastic.

"Good morning, sir." She spoke calmly even as she stood stiffly and eased the cricks out of her back.

She half zoned out as Furlong started telling her all the things she had to do that day. Instead, she thought about the couch. Taking an ax to it wasn't enough. Tonight she was going to sleep in a bed, even if it was in the bedbug-infested rooms at the local dive motel. Her skin shivered in revulsion, but anything was better than feeling like she'd been stuffed in a trunk and left to die.

Finn's lungs bellowed and his feet pounded the ground. Thoughts of Holly wanted to push all other images out of his head. He couldn't stop reliving those damn kisses. Could not get her off his mind no matter how much he pushed himself physically. She hadn't slept in the cabin, but her stuff was still there. It told him she was still thinking about those kisses too, thinking about her job and how much it meant to her—as if he'd ever jeopardize that. He wasn't some selfish prick. But he hadn't had anything to do with Len Milbank's murder, so it was a nonissue.

But what if Thom had? Or Brent?

Then it definitely became a problem, and he was glad Holly hadn't stayed in his cabin last night because he didn't think he had the strength to resist her, and he didn't want to cost Holly her job.

The sun had risen as he'd pounded up and down Pachena Beach, the ospreys breakfasting on rockfish. An hour spent running and he still burned. He forced her out of his mind and started back along the road.

The marine lab had dodged a bullet last night. If he hadn't been right there when the fire started, if he hadn't smelled smoke, the whole place could have gone up.

Had this been another attack on Thom? Or just one of life's random accidents? He'd spoken to each student. Interrogated the ones who'd had cigarette smoke on their breath. Not one of them had admitted to being on that side of the building or using that garbage can as an ashtray. But considering he'd looked like the grim reaper, smeared with soot and bursting with sweat and attitude, maybe it wasn't surprising.

A car passed him and hooted, but he ignored it.

He hit the town marker and pushed himself harder down the hill and up the rise. Past the hospital. There were plenty of bears in the area, so he constantly scanned the thick woods on either side. Most of the creatures around here left humans alone. Cougars were another matter, but they hadn't had a sighting in over a year.

He passed the school/library and hit the road to the lab. Last night's rain looked like it was going to settle back in for the day. The sky had turned gray and overcast. He'd always hated gray, and yet now it reminded him of the storminess of Holly's gaze. And if that wasn't the most pitiable observation he'd ever made he didn't know what was. It was one thing to imagine what she looked like naked, another to start composing sonnets about the color of her eyes. He pushed his pace, swore when his shoelace came undone. Drawing to a stop, he bent down and tied the lace, then spotted a trail of footprints heading into the forest. That's when he realized exactly where he was. Frowning, he followed the trail through the morning dew. His heart thumped that slow, constant beat, harder and harder as the silence pressed against his eardrums so tightly it started to punch his temples.

He pushed past bushes and saplings that were growing up along the thin trail and stopped in a small clearing. The exact spot where Bianca and little Tommy Edgefield had been found murdered thirty years ago. Sorrow sat heavy inside his chest.

What had happened to the little girl?

He remembered her vaguely, had been jealous of her even, with her sweet mommy and respectable dad. But the mystery of Leah Edgefield was probably the saddest thing of all. They'd found her jacket and a drag trail. Probably a cougar. But no one really knew. She'd just disappeared.

A flash of yellow caught his eye. A tightly bunched bouquet of daffodils lay at the base of a towering pine.

Grief squeezed his heart like a vise. Thom had been through hell all these years and still left tributes to his lost family. Some days it broke his heart.

What would that sort of love feel like?

Finn didn't know.

His family made dysfunctional look beautiful. He had friends from the army. Good friends. Soldiers he'd die for. Just the same way he had Thom and, in a twisted way, Brent. But what would it feel like to really fall in love? To commit to a woman and have her love him back?

He swallowed. Pushed away all the images that wanted to crowd his mind. That wasn't for the likes of him. A boy who'd grown up in poverty and desperation and had been lucky to make it through alive. It would never be for the likes of him.

He shoved back through the bushes and started pushing hard, finishing his long run in a full-out sprint with every heartbeat reinforcing the terrible feeling of loneliness and need that seemed to fill his core. Concentrate on the big picture. Concentrate on keeping Thom and Brent out of jail and then he could think about his own needs and wants. Later, when all this was over, when Holly was long gone. When everything got back to normal, then he'd think about what he wanted from his life. The sharp edge of a Pacific breeze made his eyes water. He blinked it away, turned around, and started another lap.

"You can verify that?" Holly asked.

"I just *did*." Thom's secretary, Gladys Hildebrand, gave her a hostile look over square-framed glasses. "I can get you twenty witnesses for both of them, plus the boats were in full use that day. No way could they have gone off diving when we had so much to do here. This isn't a holiday camp, you know." Clenched teeth, slight growl. Pissed as a rattlesnake.

Holly hesitated, her pencil hovering over her notepad. "Do you have a problem with me trying to catch a killer, Gladys?"

"I have a problem with you going after two innocent people while the real murderer is probably in Mexico by now," the woman snapped.

"This will help eliminate them from our inquiries," she said patiently.

Gladys huffed. "Until the next time."

Holly reminded herself not everyone liked the cops. "Is the professor in?"

"He's down in the lab." There was an edge—not just of anger, but also of hurt—in the woman's voice that was starting to make her uncomfortable. Like *she* was the bad guy rather than the person who'd stuck a six-inch blade through Len Milbank's ribs.

Holly tried a little small talk. "Did you have any serious damage from the fire last night?" Her question was met by stony silence. Christ.

"Right then." Holly blew out a tight breath. She loved her job. Really, she did. She loved champagne too, which also gave her a headache.

She headed off to find the professor. Police work often involved asking the same questions of different people over and over and seeing if the stories matched. She headed outside into the cool, oppressive west coast morning. Dew was so thick it hung on the tips of the short green grass like teardrops. She skidded on the loose gravel and swore. Her bruises were healing, but her neck was stiff with whiplash, and sharp movements still hurt.

She dialed her father on the walk down the hill.

"How's my favorite girl?" He picked up on the first ring.

"Almost as good as my favorite deputy commissioner."

He laughed. "How's it going out there?"

She put her hand on her head—she'd left her cap behind at the hotel, which reminded her she still needed to get her stuff from Finn's cabin—and wished she could lie. "It's gonna be a tough one to crack, Dad. IFIS are trying to figure out a way to haul Milbank's boat to Port Alberni without losing any potential evidence. The Coast Guard will probably have to tow it around."

"Tell them to cut down trees if they have to."

"Yeah, well, unfortunately the boat is in a protected old growth forest, so I think the government might have something to say if we did that. Anyway, they called me first thing to say they'd do an initial examination in situ. DNA, fingerprints, etc." She could hear her father talking to someone in the background. He must already be at work. She stared out across at the Coast Guard station. Thick clouds banked on the horizon. Another storm heading this way.

"What makes it tricky is the victim's organized crime buddies probably couldn't have pulled off stashing his body in the shipwreck. We're pretty sure Milbank had someone in the town working with him smuggling either drugs or counterfeit money." That was a new angle Sergeant Hammond had come up with after talking to his contacts. "Apparently, there've been a few phony ten-dollar bills surfacing in Victoria. Good forgeries, not easy to spot."

"I'll talk to ICET," her father said, referring to the RCMP's experts on counterfeit currency. "See if there are any known links to Vancouver Island."

"Until we figure out who Milbank was working with we're stuck looking at anyone able to put on a dry suit." Which was almost everyone in this part of the world, Holly thought grimly.

Her father cleared his throat. "Couple of loggers found a black Ram truck burned out near Saltiss Lake."

The information had her flashing back to the accident, to the moment her car had gone over the edge and started smashing through the forest. Her heart contracted forcibly. "Anything there?"

"We had IFIS all over it, but whoever torched it did a good job."

They had nothing on the person who'd tried to kill her. If only she'd stopped sooner. Got out of the vehicle and confronted the attacker. He'd have mown her down like a fly hitting a windscreen, but she might have been able to give him a few bullet holes in the process. "IFIS sure are busy right now."

"I'm sending some extra people to help out. Keep following the leads. Something will come up."

"I don't want to let you down."

"Honey, you will never disappoint me. Never."

But that wasn't necessarily true. "I love you, Dad."

"I love you too, Hobbit. Now go solve this case." He hung up.

No pressure.

She looked up at the squat utilitarian building and tried the door, surprised to find it unlocked. She retraced the steps Edgefield had guided her along before. Through the labs and up the stairs. The slightly odd chemical smell and white noise of the freezers made her feel on edge. Suddenly the hair on her nape snapped to attention.

"Boo!"

She pulled her gun and whirled around.

Professor Edgefield stood there with a huge beaker held in both hands and a shocked expression on his face. "I—er—sorry." He looked terrified, of her, of the weapon, of the consequences of his ill-thought-out actions.

Holly's heart was still jammed in her mouth, and she couldn't speak for fear of yelling at the idiot. After a few moments of staring at each other, she stuffed her gun where it belonged and gritted out, "Don't ever do that to someone who carries a loaded pistol. Ever. Again."

His Adam's apple bobbed. "Right. I won't." He walked past her and into the lab that held his precious sea slugs. Holly followed, but her heart still raced.

The tank was shrouded in a black cloth.

She'd planned on putting him at ease, buttering him up. Mice and men and all that. "Have you confirmed you found a new species yet?" she asked, trying to regain her equilibrium.

He glanced over his shoulder, looking torn between wanting to talk and worried he was going to say the wrong thing. "I have a colleague in Edmonton who's going to run some DNA samples for me. I don't want to kill any of these specimens if that's all there are in the world. So he's going to try to get a profile off the slime first." His eyes brightened. "Do you have any idea when we can dive the wreck again? I want to do a population survey." He frowned, clearly lost in his underwater world. "I should start grid diving that cove and seeing if they are anywhere else in the area. It would make sense for them—"

"Professor."

He blinked.

"I'm not sure when the wreck will be released. I'll talk to the Coast Guard and my boss about it, but—" He opened his mouth to speak but she rolled right over him. "What I really need is a detailed account of your whereabouts on Monday the second and Tuesday the third of this month."

He closed his mouth and frowned. "Did you ask Gladys? She knows my schedule—"

"I asked Gladys."

"Oh." He looked uncertain. "What did she say?"

Holly couldn't believe this guy ran an internationally renowned marine lab. "I need you to verify what she told me, sir." Her voice softened. "I need your help proving you didn't have the chance to kill Len Milbank."

"Ah." His eyes narrowed as he thought about it. "OK, let me figure it out. Last week was…" He concentrated so hard his pupils contracted. "I remember now. Last week was a nightmare. We had two university field trips and a short school program booked. Then, about an hour before they were all due to arrive, one of our chief instructors took seriously ill. She needed a chopper to get her to the hospital in Victoria. She's still sick actually. Had an emergency appendectomy so *she* has a solid alibi for that whole week. Nasty thing, a ruptured appendix."

Patience. "So you were in the lab all day, teaching?"

He shook his head. "I was in the lab, then the lecture theatre. I even took a turn out on the boat, taking some of the kids dredging. And I had to keep up with all the other BMSC stuff too." He smiled. "I think I was in bed after midnight every single day that week, and I was so frustrated." He shook his head.

"Because...?" she urged.

"Because I was desperate to get back to these babies." He indicated the tank with his hand. "It's possible they're a previously undocumented morph of *Polycera tricolor*, but not likely. Another option is they hitched a ride on that ship and formed a new isolated colony when it sank, but they aren't familiar to me, and if there's one thing I know, it's nudibranchs—" He broke off, pinching his lips together before turning away from her to look out the window. "I know it's not life and death, but it's all I've had since my wife died."

It was the sadness that drenched his whole being that got to her. Holly felt the questions on her tongue dry up. What did you say to a man who'd lost everything? Delivering death notices was probably the hardest part of the job. She hated it. They all did. And looking at the aftereffects of violent loss that feeling was only ever going to get worse.

"You gave me hope when I first saw you, Sergeant Rudd." His eyes were clear and bright. "That was unfair of me. You have your own family, and I would never steal you away from them the way someone ripped mine away from me. But if you get the chance to look at my wife and children's case," he swallowed audibly, "would you do it?"

The quiet desperation, the newfound dignity dug into Holly's heart and wrenched at her soul. "Send me the file. I'll look at it when this is over."

Her phone rang and she checked the caller display. Finn. Her pulse skipped, but she was glad to have an excuse to leave Edgefield to his sea slugs before she promised him something else. Like a goddamn DNA sample.

Finn stood on Gina Swartz's front step and fought the urge to vomit. Holly answered her phone on the second ring.

"One Deerleap Road. Turn left at the crossroads. Get up here now." He hung up.

There was a pain in his chest, a burning that throbbed with every beat of his heart. Anger and grief rode his veins, but he was dry-eyed. Clearheaded. Like the bastard who'd stabbed an innocent woman through the heart with a blade.

Knife to the chest, just like Milbank. But Milbank was a depraved sonofabitch who'd deserved every inch of steel. Gina had been kind. *Nice.* What kind of monster would do that to a fucking librarian? He looked out at the forest that surrounded her house. No, not a monster, just a man. Ordinary and evil. Invisible.

He walked over and sat on the swing she'd set up to face the sunset. You couldn't see the ocean from here, but it was tranquil and quiet. Real quiet. No one would have heard her scream, although he'd be surprised if she'd gotten the chance.

Tears wanted to fall, but anger pushed them aside. It wasn't the first time he'd seen violent death. Hell, he'd killed people more efficiently than someone had disposed of Gina. But they'd been military targets, and he'd been under orders and had never taken their lives for granted. Never forgot those he'd killed.

A bald eagle screeched as it flew overhead with a dead rabbit hanging from its talons. The town had its fair share of predators, but this was different. Someone in this dark little place was an ice-cold killer, and the thought unsettled him all the way to his gut.

They'd had the occasional unexplained death over the years. Was it possible they'd had a serial killer in their midst the entire time? That they were so green, this person chatted, joked, drank with them every day? Hiding the compulsion to destroy beneath a thin layer of sociability?

Had he or she killed Thom's family thirty years ago?

He heard a rumble of tires coming along the road. Gina would have been tuned into that rumble. She'd have heard her killer. Had she known him? Was it her new boyfriend? Or her old one?

Shiiiiiit. He hated himself for the thought, for that smidgen of doubt.

Holly pulled up in a new RCMP 4x4. He stuck his hands in his pockets and watched as she jumped out of the cab. She'd picked up Malone, thank god. He wouldn't want her going in there alone, not that he'd be able to stop her. The guy shot him a look, and Finn motioned him toward the house with a stiff nod.

He wished it wasn't Holly investigating this stuff, seeing this carnage. But Christ, she wasn't the sort of woman to sit home baking muffins. If she were, they'd never have met.

The wind chilled the sweat on his skin. He was starting to get cold. He didn't move. Didn't care. Brent...*How can I tell Brent Gina's dead?*

He'd loved her. He'd always loved her. No way would he have killed her, not even over another guy.

But Brent had a notorious temper. And he was rash. *Shit.* He squeezed his eyes shut. What the hell should he do? Tell Holly that Gina and Brent used to be involved? If he didn't, someone else would, but this was Brent he was talking about. His brother, the man who'd killed their father. The man who'd saved his life.

Gina was dead.

He buried his face in his hands. There were no easy answers to this mess.

Holly came out of the house a minute later, although it felt like hours since he'd last seen her. A lifetime. The expression on her face was stark, the wind tugging her hair out of its neat braid. It was surreal to see her standing like that, beautiful and whole, knowing that Gina was just a few yards away laid out like a sacrificial virgin.

Holly stood on the back step for a very long time and stared at him. He stared right back.

"What are you doing here, Finn?" Her voice reached across the clearing and she followed it. Walking slowly.

"I stopped by to talk to Gina." Was he a suspect for this too? Fuck. Probably.

He didn't even care anymore. Maybe he should confess to keep Brent out of jail? But then the real killer would still be loose, and who knew who would be the next target. Thom? Laura? Holly? He closed his eyes. He knew almost everyone within fifty miles. He should just *know* who'd done this.

When he opened his eyes she was standing right in front of him, lines around her eyes making her look tired. Bruises making her look fragile.

The beat of silence was tense.

"I thought you'd be at work." She checked her watch. *If* Brent had done this, and no way did he believe his brother was this sick, but *if* he had, he deserved to go back to prison. He deserved a lot more.

He let his head fall back so he was staring at the canopy over the swing. Poor Gina with her little love swing. "The students have lectures till midday. I was up all night, so I figured I'd skip off this morning. I wish I'd stayed in bed."

"Did you find out anything about the fire?" He could feel her mentally working her way around him, trying to get him to relax and spill his guts.

He shook his head. "You think it's connected?"

"I don't know. There's a lot of weird stuff happening around here lately. It can't always be this exciting."

It wasn't. "You think someone used the fire as a distraction?" He frowned.

Holly looked away. Not answering. "Did you know the victim?"

Victim.

"We grew up together. We were friends." He sucked in a deep breath because this was the moment. "She was Brent's high school sweetheart. They were an item for years." He saw her eyes narrow and loathed himself now more than ever. "I'd hoped to figure out a way to maybe get them back together again. She'd mentioned she was seeing someone else."

"Who?"

"Never said. But if he did that to her I'm going to rip him apart."

She touched his arm, not even withdrawing her fingers when Malone came out of the bungalow, cell phone glued to his ear. "It's important for us to figure this out without going vigilante or panicking the whole town."

"Why shouldn't they panic? There's some bastard running cops off the road and stabbing people through the heart. What's not to panic about?"

"You're right. I just don't want to see you arrested for hitting the wrong guy—"

"I wouldn't *hit* him, Holly. I'd put a pair of bullets between his eyes."

Her eyes turned hard. "I need you on my side. Finn—I don't want to have to arrest you." Her voice broke.

Breath sagged out of his chest. He was being selfish. A fool. But the need to act crawled through his belly and wanted to explode. He reined it in. Pushed down the raging inferno that demanded retribution.

"So I'm not a suspect here?"

Her eyes told him the truth. Of course he was a suspect. "We need to question you further. But I did verify your alibi for Len Milbank's murder."

"Great." Finn crossed his arms over his chest and stretched his legs out in front of him. He couldn't believe this mess. Get cleared of one murder and in the frame for the next.

"But she's in full rigor, which means she was probably killed between six and twelve hours ago, give or take."

Finn felt his stomach twist.

"You were with me during a lot of that time last night, driving out to Klanawa River and then dealing with the fire for the rest of it."

"We both know there's a gap in the middle where I could have snuck out and stabbed her. It wouldn't take more than twenty minutes to drive up and down from the lab." Had someone raped her? Christ, the thought of Gina suffering made him gag.

"When we came back from finding Milbank's boat there were two students from the cabin below yours sitting on your bottom step. They were still there when I came back to get the keys for the dive shed." A tinge of red bloomed in her cheeks, probably remembering that wasn't all she'd gotten. She eyed the surrounding bush warily. "Did you leave the cabin?"

Finn shook his head.

"Then give me their names and I'll confirm that ASAP. Pretty sure those two are going to provide you with a solid alibi. We'll know more when the coroner gets here and establishes an accurate TOD, but for what it's worth, I don't consider you a suspect." The wind blew strands of her hair across her face. "But I've got to phone Furlong, and he will."

He clenched his teeth. "I'd forgotten about that asshole."

"I haven't."

Finn jolted.

"I don't mean—" She pressed her lips together and stopped saying whatever it was she'd been about to say. He watched her swallow nervously. "Until I solve this case, I'm stuck with him."

"You could ask your father to remove him from the case."

"Yeah, I could." Her gray eyes watched the sky again. "But I don't want any special favors because my dad's the deputy commissioner of E Division."

"Just make sure Furlong's on your side, Holly. He'll screw you over as soon as look at you."

Holly smiled. "Yeah. Good advice."

He needed a drink of water but welcomed the soreness of his throat. A little discomfort reminded him he was still alive while Gina was definitely and irrevocably dead. "I went for a run to Pachena Beach this morning because I had someone I couldn't get off my mind, so I did another loop, trying to forget her, and ended up here." Life was too damn short for playing games and he didn't want to hide from what he was feeling anymore.

Eyes darkened, but she didn't look away.

He curled his fingers into fists. "But I don't want to forget her anymore." He pushed away the image of Gina's dead body. "I'm done running from whatever it is between us, Holly."

"It's just lust," she said quietly.

That did nothing for his pulse. "No, it's not. Anyway, people kill for less."

"If you know anything at all about Gina's relationships, you need to let me know."

She was avoiding the personal conversation he was trying to have. Although, damn, he owed it to Gina to put a sock in it and let Holly do her job and find her killer. He wasn't at the fucking prom.

She stood as another vehicle rumbled along the track.

"Who the hell?" Finn rolled to his feet. "Oh, jeez."

But he was too late, and Brent had pushed past Malone with an animal roar and was running toward Gina's open door. Finn sprinted harder and took Brent down in a tackle that smashed them both onto the deck so hard the house shook. Brent, fighting hard, shoved his palm into Finn's nose, elbow into his ear, and knee into his crotch, but Finn dodged the worst of it, holding onto his brother with every ounce of strength he possessed. He whipped Brent onto his front, facedown against the wood. He could not let his brother see what someone had done to Gina. It would destroy him.

Brent roared like a bull and almost succeeded in dislodging Finn from his back. "Gina," he gasped. "Is she all right? Tell me, Finn. Fucking tell me!"

He drew his brother's arms high up to try to just hold him still, calm him down long enough to talk to him, to break the news. Malone snapped cuffs around both Brent's wrists.

"Hey!" Finn grabbed Malone by the arm.

Malone shook him off. "Don't make me arrest you too."

"You can't arrest him!"

"He assaulted a police officer." He dragged Brent to his feet. Muscles bunched in Malone's jaw. Holly shook her head slightly, and Malone backed down a millimeter.

"Where is she? What's happened to Gina?" Brent's gaze never left Finn's face. "I got a phone call. Something about a homicide on this road." His voice got super quiet. "Where's Gina, Finn?"

He forced out the words. "She's dead, Brent. Someone killed her."

His brother dropped to his knees and screamed as if someone was ripping out his heart. The sound stabbed through Finn like a bayonet. Howls filled the air. Great big sobs of grief as if nothing else would ever matter.

"We're going to need to ask you some questions, Mr. Carver." Holly leaned closer to Brent. "We're going to take you down to Port Alberni and record an interview. You're not being arrested for assault, and Corporal Malone is going to let you out of those restraints just so long as you behave." Malone gaped at her. Holly ignored him.

"You know how this works. If you resist us or run into this house and contaminate our crime scene, it will look bad for you. Very bad. So if you've got nothing to hide and want to help us find who killed Gina, you need to stay calm and tell us everything you know. Do you understand?"

The whites of Brent's eyes were bright red. He raised his chin.

"Do you understand, Mr. Carver?"

Brent's eyes died right in front of him. Finn shivered. They'd looked cold before, but now they looked like the inside a freezer in the morgue. Brent nodded. No emotion, no more tears. No more roars of pain. He walked quietly to the SUV and Malone helped him climb in the back, his wrists still cuffed.

Finn's heart cracked. "You want me to go too?"

Holly pursed her lips and shook her head. "I'm going to take down a statement from you while I wait for backup and the coroner. I want you to give me the names of the guys from the downstairs cabin. Then you can go back to work at the marine lab. I'll question you later."

"I'm going to get Brent a lawyer."

Her eyes flashed.

"He's my brother, Holly, an ex-con, and he didn't do this."

Her eyes narrowed. "Do what you have to do. Just don't tell anyone about what you saw in there." She pointed her finger. "Right now we're the only ones who know what happened to her—"

"Except her killer."

"Exactly."

Finn looked from his brother's desolate expression to Holly's slender back as she walked away. They were suddenly as far apart as the Pacific Ocean, and barreling toward them at five hundred miles per hour was a category five hurricane.

CHAPTER 14

The wound in Gina's chest gleamed darkly, blood crusted and dried against pale skin. Blood had run down her chest and soaked into the bedding. The coroner bent over her, peering closely at the wound, pressing turgid flesh with a satisfied grunt, working his alchemic magic. "I can only give you a wide ranging time of death at the scene, you know that."

George Margolis was a methodical and careful man who measured words as carefully as the corpse's temp.

"She's still in full rigor mortis."

"Hmm."

Holly held on to her patience. When she got a pathologist who'd commit to more than a cup of coffee at a crime scene she was going to do a jig on the spot.

"George, give me something to work with here. I've got two dead bodies, both with knife wounds to the heart, and a town full of suspects. If you can give me a TOD, I can start eliminating people from the suspect list." She dug her hands deep in her pockets, reining in her frustration.

He threw his head up dramatically and gave her a pitying look. "And when I change the TOD after the autopsy you'll be pissed and back to square one, correct?" Supercilious brows rose over ruddy cheeks.

"Yes," she gritted. God, she hated doctors in all their forms.

"Hey, what happened to your face?" He'd obviously only just noticed her bruises. He was much better at dealing with the dead.

"Kissed an airbag."

"You don't get out enough." He turned back to the body and Holly resisted pacing. She had Chastain and Messenger outside Brent Carver's house waiting on a search warrant.

Maybe she was going soft, but she didn't like the guy for this one. The grief had been too raw, too potent. A search warrant would actually help clear his name as long as they didn't find any bloody clothing or knives hidden away. She doubted Finn would see it that way.

Jeff and Malone had taken Brent into Port Alberni for questioning. Steffie was working her ass off, cataloging all the evidence from this crime scene on top of all the others. Holly had put a request in for more officers, because with a double homicide and multiple crime scenes, they were stretched as thin as plastic wrap.

She answered her cell on the first ring. "Yes, sir?" Furlong. Again. Christ, he was certainly keeping this investigation under microscopic scrutiny.

George rolled his eyes. He was one of the few people in the world who thought Staff Sgt. James "Jimmy" Furlong was a complete prick. She gave him a half smile as Furlong started in on her.

"Coroner got a TOD yet?"

"Not yet, sir."

"Useless piece of—"

"You're on speeeaker," George sang loudly in the background, then grinned evilly.

"What the fu—"

"You're not on speaker, Staff Sergeant Furlong." She rolled her eyes and walked out of the bedroom, away from what remained of poor Gina Swartz. "George is messing with your head." And frankly, she liked it.

Furlong paused. She could actually imagine him tilting his head in consideration and realizing he'd lost some of his vaunted cool.

"I just spoke to Malone, and he said Finn Carver found the body. I want that man in custody—"

"That would be a waste of our time and resources, sir. Finn Carver's whereabouts can be vouched for almost all of last evening—"

"Well, people lie."

"*I* don't lie."

"You're his alibi? After everything I said to you before I left about causing a scandal?"

Holly tried to find the calm center of the raging storm that swirled inside her at his insinuations. She'd come close to crossing the line with someone involved in the investigation, but she'd resisted. Thank god. "He *drove* Malone and me out to find Milbank's boat because we didn't have a vehicle at that time." A small dig, but a dig nonetheless. "Then, after midnight, he was getting the dive logs for me when we spotted a fire outside the marine lab. He helped put it out and spent most of the night questioning students to see who'd been stupid enough to almost burn the place down." Her voice had risen and rang out over the trees. She was outside, standing next to the flowery-patterned garden swing that sat in a small patch of sunshine. Gina Swartz had sat there, had read there, relaxed there. Hell, maybe she'd even made love there. Her eyes narrowed. She needed to make sure the DNA on the sheets and mattress was analyzed ASAP. She needed to know who her most recent lover was.

If Brent Carver's DNA was on those sheets, he was lying about his relationship with the vic. Maybe this had been a crime of passion? Most women were killed by partners or ex-partners.

She zoned back to hear Furlong talking about coming out there as soon as his schedule cleared. Dammit. "I can manage, sir."

"Funny, because I thought you'd requested more people?"

"But I know how busy you are." Her stomach churned. Ripples of unease rolled through her.

"I'm coming out there, Holly. It isn't just your reputation on the line, and this thing is starting to get out of control."

"I can manage."

"Well, you're doing a piss-poor job so far."

Maybe he was right. Maybe she hadn't done a great job on this case. There were so few clues and no one was talking. But what the hell could Furlong do that was different and still legal?

"I look forward to seeing you, sir."

After she hung up, she stared fixedly at the bare patch of ground under the swing. No way was she letting Furlong elbow her aside. She dialed another number. Usually she didn't pull strings, but she was going to solve this case any way possible.

"Hey, Cassy. I need a favor." Cassy was a friend who worked for IFIS back on the mainland.

"Hey, chica, how you doing out there in the wilderness?" Cassy DeAngelo was five feet and one inch of sheer, unadulterated sexiness. Guys fell for her the moment they set eyes on her and vied for her attention like groupies at a rock gig. She treated them all with indulgent indifference.

"Truthfully? I'm struggling."

"Uh oh. How can I help?"

Holly smiled. "I'm going to courier you some bed linen." Which would hopefully give them the name of Gina's current lover—assuming he, or she, was in the system. They could cross-reference her phone records. See if they could obtain voluntary DNA samples for all her acquaintances, which would help whittle down the suspect pool to a manageable number. "If you could get back to me ASAP on DNA and run it through every database you can think of, I would be *forever* in your debt." If she waited for normal channels, they wouldn't see results for at least a month, and she couldn't bear another month of the commanding officer from hell.

"Is this favor worth a weekend away with me to NYC?"

"Anything."

"Anything? Wow, I should have asked for a fortnight in Hawaii, seen if we could hustle us up some cabana boys." Holly could hear her friend's grin. She was irreverent and unrepentant and the master of decoding genetic secrets of biological material in all its many forms. "Tell 'em to mark the package *urgent* and with my name, not just the lab. I'll get on it as soon as it arrives."

"Thanks, Cass. I owe you."

"And I will collect."

Thom hovered behind Finn as he pushed inside Laura's back door. He'd tried to get Finn to calm down, but for once the unflappable ex-soldier was too riled for reason.

"I need your help," Finn said to Laura.

She stood there in old jeans, a faded pink sweatshirt, and both hands covered in clay. The outfit was all potter, but the angle of her chin and glint in her eye was pure prosecuting attorney. He caught her gaze. She nodded at him, that silent communication all they needed to convey the importance of this moment. Finn asking for help. She turned, wiping her hands on a crusted rag.

"Gina Swartz was found dead, and they've taken Brent for questioning."

Her hand went to her chest and Thom watched her nostrils flare before she swallowed. "They used to date, right?"

"Yeah. But he broke it off a couple of months ago. She told me she'd just started seeing someone else."

"Who?"

"I don't know." Finn ran both hands over his face. The guy had been up all last night and probably hadn't got much sleep the two nights before that. Thom clasped his hands together wanting to do something to help. Finn had long ago stopped being the vulnerable teenager Thom had rescued. But right now he was remembering everything he'd gone through to become the man he was today.

"Does he have an alibi?" Laura asked Finn.

Finn's lip curled. "Brent? How would he? He's almost a recluse."

"Hmmm…" She headed for the tap and started running hot water and then soap over the red clay that was trapped in the margins of her fingernails. She got the scrubbing brush to work, clearly figuring out what she was going to say.

Finn's expression hardened. "I know he's not the nicest guy in the world."

"Not *nice* barely covers it." Laura looked over her shoulder archly.

So she'd met Brent Carver.

"Look, I know he doesn't conform to all the social niceties." Finn's voice was tight, his actions jerky.

Laura's eyes flicked to Thom. She seemed to be looking to him for guidance. He opened his mouth, but nothing came out.

"He loved Gina. He wouldn't hurt her," Finn said.

"Hmmm…" She dried her hands on a soft peach towel beside the sink.

"OK." Finn rammed his fingers through his hair. "Just give me the name of another lawyer in Port Alberni who has a chance of keeping an ex-con—who's on parole—out of jail. And lock the doors and windows from now on because Brent didn't do this. Someone else did." He turned and shouldered his way past Thom.

Thom exhaled a breath and stared at Laura, strangely at ease with her, considering she jumbled him up inside. "It would mean a lot to him," he said. "You might not have noticed, but he rarely asks for anything for himself."

"I noticed. But this isn't for him; it's for his cranky brother."

"Well, that's why it's important to him. You know what happened when they were kids, right?"

Blue eyes pierced his. "I don't listen to gossip."

Why that pleased him he didn't know. He suddenly felt like he was about to step off an emotional cliff. "If you agree to help him, I'll tell you what happened. Not gossip. Just the facts."

Her eyes widened and she looked thoughtful. She tugged off her sweatshirt—the clingy top beneath revealed lots of curves—and she flung it over the back of a kitchen chair. She picked up a pretty woolen cape thing that she pulled over her shirt. "Do you think Brent Carver killed Gina Swartz?"

Thom pressed his lips together. "I don't know," he admitted. "He scares the crap out of me. But the way he stood up for Finn all those years ago? It's got to count for something, don't you think?"

She narrowed her eyes and they gleamed like polished sea glass. "I'll take his case, but I want that story over dinner. In a fancy restaurant. A *very* fancy restaurant."

"It's a date." A weird feeling entered Thom and he stood a little straighter. "Now how do we get started?"

Laura slipped her feet into suede boots that were sitting by the front door. She balanced herself by holding his arm. "Brent's house first. First thing the cops will do is get a warrant to search it. I want to be there when they do. Plus, I always wanted to look around that guy's place." She grinned. "And you need to call the RCMP in Port Alberni because I want Brent to give his permission for the cops to go in without a warrant."

How did she know he knew the number by heart? Inwardly he cringed.

"Tell them not to question my client about anything else until I get there."

He fumbled with his phone. His heart raced as she strode down the lane toward Brent's house, and he couldn't help noticing the sway of her hips and curve of her backside. Sweat broke out on his brow as he realized his life had shifted on its axis.

But for better or worse, he had no clue.

Finn was jogging back to the dock when he realized two cops were sitting on Brent's back porch. He did a quick one-eighty and strode down the driveway.

"What are you doing here?" Finn asked.

The Italian-looking cop lifted his cap and ran his hand through his black hair. "Waiting on a warrant to search the property."

Rachel Messenger gave him a look he was sure was supposed to be reassuring. "This is the best way to clear your brother's name."

He swallowed a snort. The crunch of gravel made him swivel around. Laura walked up the steps to stand next to him. "Any news on the warrant?" she asked.

"They're still waiting." Finn turned away from the cops impatiently.

"It's yours too, isn't it?" she asked.

"What?" Finn blinked.

Laura gripped his arm. "If we're going to save your brother you need to get your head in the game."

He bit back a wince as her fingers dug deeper. "Yeah, on paper the property belongs to me and Brent, but—"

Laura held up her hand. "The *but* doesn't matter." She pushed past him and spoke directly to Chastain. "My client is going to let you take a look around without a warrant." Finn started to interrupt, but she shot him a stony look. "My client has nothing to hide from the authorities, but I want to ensure you only look in plain sight—no evidence collection at this point. Finn here is the co-owner of the property and has allowed us entry. Correct?"

Her eyes said that if he wanted her on the case this was how it was going to be.

He nodded stiffly and complied, putting on latex gloves the cops provided before turning the door handle. Unlocked. He blinked against the glaring white light, so at odds with the dim, grimy shadows of his childhood. The whole place was sparkling clean. Not a speck of dust anywhere.

"Wow, this is not what I was expecting." Laura looked around with admiration. There wasn't a dish in the sink. Not a cup on the draining board. She walked up to a massive oil painting that dominated the wall over the fireplace. Finn couldn't take his eyes off the piece. He walked slowly toward it.

"B.C. Wilkinson." Laura whistled. "Way out of my price league. You sure your brother isn't a crook?"

Finn couldn't stop staring at the picture. He'd grown up with pictures like this pinned to the wall of their falling down shack. Neither he nor Brent had been good with letters, but they'd both spent a lot of time drawing and painting. "That's not B.C. Wilkinson," whoever the hell that was, "that's Brent."

Laura's eyes went round. "You're telling me your brother is B.C. Wilkinson?" She slapped herself on the forehead. "B.C.— Brent Carver."

"And Wilkinson is the prison where he served his time."

"No wonder the artist is such an enigma."

Chastain came to stand at their shoulder. "We want to go upstairs."

Finn and Laura exchanged a look, and he nodded. He trailed the cops up the stairs. First room they entered was clearly an artist's studio. Finn stared around at the canvases. Huge landscapes that bled emotion. "I'd forgotten he liked to paint." A hard knot formed in Finn's throat. He'd forgotten. And maybe life hadn't been quite as hellish in prison as he'd feared. Brent had found a release in his art, found a career and a vocation. "So these are worth money?"

Laura gave him a sad smile. "I bid on one in an auction last year. Had to drop out when they got to eighty thousand."

Emotions swelled inside him. Wonder and grief, both fierce and sharp. "Bianca Edgefield gave him his first set of paints when we were kids." There was a catch in his throat. "Brent drew a picture of a bunny for her little girl, and she must have recognized his talent." Surely a boy who drew bunnies for little girls wouldn't slaughter his ex-girlfriend in cold blood. All the muscles in his chest grew tight, and it was a struggle to breathe.

Laura gently stroked his arm.

These paintings went way beyond the pictures they'd drawn as kids. They were deep and fathomless and full of dark, morbid beauty. Pride filled him. Pride and shame he'd doubted his brother even for a second.

He'd never doubt him again.

There was a cry from down the hall. He and Laura rushed along the hardwood corridor and skidded to a halt in what looked like the master bedroom. The room was monastically simple. A bed with a huge white and black and purple seascape above it. Some sort of radio beside it. Built in wardrobes, no other furniture in the room. The bed was neatly made. The deep charcoal bedspread pulled snug and tight over each corner. And smack bang in the middle of the bed lay a knife with a gleaming edge, encrusted with something dark and ugly.

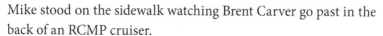

Mike stood on the sidewalk watching Brent Carver go past in the back of an RCMP cruiser.

Hot damn! He grinned. He pulled out his other cell phone. The burner one he'd got to communicate with Dryzek. He didn't want to talk to the bastard, but would rather be the bearer of good news while it was still news than call with nothing at all.

Someone picked up, but no one said anything.

"Guess who I just saw go by in the back of a police SUV?"

The silence continued.

"Brent Carver." Mike let him think he'd gotten Carver arrested. It might keep the bastard off his back for a couple of days. A rustle of air told him someone was there. "Did you search his place?"

"Yeah." A shot of panic swept through his veins at the thought the cops had found Dryzek's stash inside Brent's house. His palms started to sweat. "There was nothing there, but now he's out of the picture, I'll go back and search it again."

"Thoroughly, Mikey. No mistakes. You know what'll happen if you make a mistake."

His mother chose that moment to come out of the supermarket with a cart overflowing with groceries. Her blond hair danced around her face as the wind blustered out of the west. There was a storm coming, and the first splashes of rain hit the dust on the sidewalk with a solid splat. Her soft, shining eyes reminded him exactly what was at stake, as did his aching jaw. "It isn't going to be an issue."

"Good." The phone went dead, and Mike wished he could dropkick it into the water.

During the drive home his mom chattered about everything from redecorating the living room to getting another dog. He mentally figured out how soon he could slip away and cross the inlet to search Brent's house. But when they got home, his dad was sitting on the front steps of their house with his head in his hands, looking pallid and ill.

"Grant?" His mom jumped out of the truck so fast she tripped, but didn't fall.

He ran to his father's side. "What is it, Pop? You OK?"

His father got shakily to his feet. "There's been some bad news, son." He planted his hand on his shoulder and squeezed.

Shit, the cops had found out he'd told Milbank about that shipwreck. Or someone had found the damn drugs or cash Dryzek had lost and pointed the finger at him, and now the cops had come calling. He braced himself, donning his most innocent expression. "What?"

"Gina Swartz." His dad sucked in a gasp of breath.

He frowned. "Gina?" Damn. "What about Gina?"

His dad gripped him by both shoulders now. "She's dead, son. That bastard Brent Carver killed her."

He shook his head, confused. Then his knees buckled, and just like that he was on the ground. He'd seen Gina last night. She'd been fine. Better than fine. She couldn't be dead.

His hands shook with palsy. "Oh, god. I have to go talk to the cops, tell them what I know." *Who'd hurt someone like Gina?*

"Don't you dare!" His mother slapped his cheek.

His jaw dropped as he stared at her.

"No one knows about the two of you. No one!" Her eyes filled with tears. "If you go telling the police you were lovers, you become a suspect. Don't get involved with this, Mike. I don't want to risk losing you." Her lips wobbled. Mike registered her lipstick was smudged. They might live in the boonies, but his mother's makeup was always immaculate. It disconcerted him to see her so visibly shaken.

"When did it happen?"

"Sometime last night. After midnight, I think." His dad's moustache splayed wide over his lips as he grimaced. "You got an alibi, son?"

Before or after he set that fire and searched Brent's house? He shook his head. "I couldn't sleep. I went for a drive." He felt hollow. Numb. Gina couldn't be dead. He'd never lost anyone close to him before, and he wasn't even able to mourn her publicly or show her the respect she deserved.

He looked up at his dad. "Why would I need an alibi? I thought you said Brent killed her." His heart kicked. "Did the bastard kill her because he was jealous?" Grief ripped through him, gouging his insides until he felt like he was going to puke.

"They haven't charged him yet. Those Carvers are no good. They'll figure out some sort of way to wriggle out of this and pin the blame on someone else if they can. Anyone see you last night?" his dad asked with a sideways glance at his wife.

He shook his head. His mother's fingernails dug into his neck like talons and dragged him back to reality. "You were home with us, understand?" Her grip loosened and stroked. She dropped to her knees beside him, wrapping him in her arms. "I'm never going to let anything happen to you, you know that, don't you?" She held him tight, just as she had when he'd been a little kid.

Mike sniffed and wiped his eyes. From now on he had to remember what was important to him. "I was home all night. I never went out." Slowly he climbed to his feet, hugged his mother back, trying to comfort her. He wasn't going to jail; he wasn't leaving them vulnerable.

There was no way he'd be able to get close to Carver's property now, and Dryzek was going to come after him regardless. Another thought struck him. *Dryzek.* Had he killed Gina? Was he laughing at Mike behind his back while quietly setting him or Brent up for murder? The guy was cunning enough.

No more doing favors for Remy Dryzek—not even to save his own skin. His dad had been right about him. His dad was always right. He thought of the gun he hid in his glove box. If Remy or Ferdinand came near him or his family, he was going to blow matching holes in the rat bastards.

CHAPTER 15

Thom paced the waiting room of the police station in Port Alberni. The sound of a door opening had him whirling to face Laura, who looked tired and frayed. She headed outside without a word, stood and inhaled a massive lungful of fresh, clean air. The sky was overcast, clouds burdened with the threat of rain.

"Are you OK?" he asked quietly.

She looked at him over her shoulder. Mouth pinched, eyes etched by horrific detail. "I gave this up for a reason."

Her words cut through him. She'd walked away from death and violence, and he'd forced her back into that world. He inched closer. For the first time in decades, he wanted to put his arms around a woman and offer comfort, and his body didn't know how to do it.

"But there's no way Brent Carver would be dumb enough to leave that knife on his bed in a double dog dare." Her eyes hardened as she shook her head. "He didn't even flinch when they told him about the knife." Lines gathered between her brows. "I don't know if he even heard them." She started walking to his SUV with a brisk, purposeful stride.

Thom followed, fascinated by the contradictory nature of the woman. Softness and steel.

"What I don't understand is why he dumps a woman he clearly loved?" She was blinking rapidly. "Why would he push away the woman he cared about?"

"To protect her," Thom said with surety.

"Women don't need protecting if it means their hearts are going to get obliterated." Her words were sharp and bitter.

"Someone hurt you." Anger stirred inside him. Some men had no clue what a privilege it was to love a woman. Absolutely no clue.

He pulled her against him. She felt supple and warm in his arms, and for the first time in this lifetime he felt strong enough to give comfort. After a moment, she pulled away and swiped at the moisture that threatened to spill from her eyes. He reached out and touched a tendril of hair that had escaped her haphazard bun.

She stilled. Stared at him. Said nothing.

There was a lot going on inside that brain of hers, and Thom suddenly wanted to figure her out. And instead of the expected guilt, all he felt was a colossal weight lifting off his shoulders.

"Where are we going now?" he asked.

A smile curved her lips, and she was back to being bossy Laura again. "We are going to go to the store and buy a few essential items, then we're going to grab a fast dinner—not our date dinner, just something to eat—and I'll head back for further questioning while you find us a hotel. I'm not sure how long this is going to take."

Thom nodded nervously. She didn't tell him how many rooms to get and he daren't ask. He was going to have to get his head together and figure this out. "Man up," was what Finn called it. He stood a little straighter.

She paused beside the car door. He opened it for her to get in, but she just stood there. "I don't know why I care more about him now that I know he's a famous painter than when he was just a grumpy, ex-con neighbor. It certainly isn't his sunny personality." Lines creased her brow. "Maybe I'm shallow? It's not because he's rich. I think," she said slowly, "it's because I relate so viscerally to his art that I find it hard to believe someone who can move me that profoundly, on such a fundamental level, would be a killer, let alone a dumbass killer."

"He didn't do it," Thom said.

Her eyes picked at his soul. "He could have killed your wife and children. He was old enough back then."

Thom shook his head, suddenly certain. "The only time that boy killed was to protect his little brother. And he got the world's worst attorney and ended up doing more time than anyone deserved. He's got a good heart." But it was buried deep and it was doubtful it would help his cause.

Laura nodded. "I'm counting on it." Then she grinned. "And believe me, I'm *not* the world's worst attorney." And he found his gaze glued to her lips. "I rock, in *every* way. If you're lucky you might just find that out for yourself."

Holly rumbled down the lane toward Mike Toben's house. They were re-interviewing everyone regarding Gina Swartz's murder, and she wanted to personally talk to this guy. They didn't have enough probable cause to get a warrant for his financial or phone records, but she was convinced from the night she'd seen him in the bar that he had some connection to Remy Dryzek. It was a pitifully thin lead, one of those cop hunches that were often a waste of time, but impossible to ignore.

The wind swirled the upper branches of the trees and made them sway wildly. The Tobens lived down a track just outside Bamfield proper. She drove out of the forest and saw a narrow inlet, house up on the hill to one side, dock at the water's edge, several boats tied up, along with an old float plane that caused a curious prickle inside her chest. Mike's truck was pulled to one side, next to a small silver sedan. A small motorbike sat in the lee of the porch.

A dog barked. A chocolate lab that made himself hoarse even as he wagged his tail so hard in welcome he almost fell over.

Mike's mother—the nurse from the local hospital—came out of the house, wiping her hands on a dishtowel. "Hush, Topper. Hi there, Holly. You don't mind if I call you Holly, do you?"

Holly shook her head. "Nurses, doctors, paramedics can pretty much call me anything they want." A smile curved her mouth. Creating unity with people was what she did best—unity and trust as she mined for information.

"You can call me Anita." She blinked and looked away. "Well, you certainly look a lot better than you did the other day, thank heavens." A fine shudder ran over the woman's frame. "You catch that maniac yet?"

Which one? They had a lot to choose from.

Anita's eyes darkened. "I guess you've had more important things to think about with Brent Carver killing poor Gina. Such a sweet girl." Her gaze was avid on her face, searching for clues to feed the gossip mill.

"No one's been charged yet." Maybe people around here believed that if you said something often enough and loudly enough it became fact. Better than thinking the monster was still out there among them. "I'd make sure your doors and windows are locked at night. Just in case."

The woman went white.

"We're still checking everyone's whereabouts last night. Ruling people out of our investigation."

"We were all here last night," Anita said quickly. Too quickly.

"From what time?" Holly pulled out her notepad.

Anita bit her lip. "I finished work about five thirty. I only work late if we have an emergency." She nodded pointedly to Holly's face.

You owe me, loud and clear.

"Mike and Grant came back from the hardware store about the same time." Anita laughed, a little high pitched. "We all stayed in and watched *American Idol*. Had an early night."

"I love that show." Not that she ever had time to watch it. "So where can I find the men of the family?"

"Grant's at the store and Mike's down at the dock." Anita bit her lip.

Holly turned and, sure enough, a somber-looking Mike Toben had just come up on the deck of a small charter fishing boat.

Holly said good-bye to Anita and went down to talk to Mike. The dog followed, still wagging his tail but getting distracted by a good smell in the grass.

"Hey," Mike called, without his usual sparkle. He had a bruise on his jaw, as if he'd been socked.

"How you doing?" Holly smiled. "Been in a fight?"

He touched his chin, shrugged, and turned back to wiping down the surfaces of the boat. "I don't know why I'm bothering," he eyed the ominous clouds, "but we've got a booking from some anglers this weekend, and I wanted to get it clean."

There was no flirting grin today. No levity at all.

"Did you know Gina Swartz, Mike?"

He stilled and then went back to cleaning the boat. "This is a small town. I know everyone."

"Even Brent Carver?"

He clenched his jaw, muscles bunching. "Brent Carver is a murdering asshole, and if I ever see him again I'm gonna rip off his head." Dark fury rolled off him.

Was that protective male posturing or something more, something deeper? "Did you ever have a sexual relationship with Gina?"

"We were friends, nothing more." But his eyes shifted, and suddenly Holly didn't believe him.

"You ever been in her house?"

His lips pressed firmly together and his eyes glittered as if trying to decide what to tell her. "She asked me to upgrade her plumbing a few weeks ago. Every damn tap in the house dripped."

"I'm going to need your fingerprints so we can eliminate them from the scene. I've got a kit in the SUV. I'd like to take DNA too, eliminate you from all our inquiries."

"I don't want my goddamn DNA in the system like some common criminal."

She grimaced. Unfortunately, Mike wasn't alone in his suspicious nature. They hadn't had a single volunteer for their database yet. She'd need warrants, which meant more headaches and more delays. "At least you've got a decent alibi, huh?" She smiled, trying to put him at ease.

"What?" He stood straight and glared at her. She kept her reaction light, but was balanced on the balls of her feet for any sudden moves. Had Mike been Gina's new lover? "You and your mom, watching TV together. It's rather cute, although I figured you for more of a hockey fan." Given every T-shirt he wore bore the Canucks' logo.

"I watch whatever she wants to watch." His face was hard. Eyes flat. Giving nothing away. No more charming rogue. The guy was pissed.

"Come up with me now so I can get your fingerprints and eliminate them from our investigation, OK?"

Anita leaned on the door frame and watched them.

"Fine." He swallowed, then asked abruptly, "D-did she suffer?"

"Gina?"

He nodded rapidly. There was a fine sheen of sweat on his brow. Plenty of nerves. Why? Lover? Killer? Distraught friend?

"I'm sorry," she told him gently, "I can't disclose any part of the investigation."

He flinched.

"But, no," she said quietly. "I don't think so. I think it was probably very quick."

"Good." He blew out a long breath. Sniffed loudly. "That's good."

Holly took his prints under the watchful gaze of his mother. Then she got in her SUV and drove away, watching them in the rearview. Mike—tall, dark, and handsome, beside his petite, blond mother. Something was definitely up with that family, but Holly didn't know if it had anything to do with her case or not.

Her cell rang, and she saw it was Furlong. She answered, wishing like hell she had enough seniority to ignore the guy and knowing she didn't. "Yes, sir." Every syllable hurt.

"Coroner's given us a pretty firm TOD for once, mainly because the victim spoke to her sister in Vancouver just before midnight. Gina Swartz was murdered between midnight and one o'clock." Her heart gave a little leap of thanks because that put Finn in the clear. "You still interviewing locals?"

"Yes, sir. Just spoke to Anita Toben and her son, Mike. Something seemed off about them. It's possible Mike Toben could have been Gina Swartz's mystery lover. I'd like to apply for a warrant to obtain a sample of his DNA."

"Yeah?" Furlong sounded distracted. Tired. "That sounds like a good plan."

"You OK?"

"Nothing an arrest wouldn't cure."

She wanted to kick herself for asking. "IFIS get anything else from Brent Carver's place?"

"They got a few fingerprints. Get your ass back here and let's see what we've got."

"On my way, sir."

"And, Holly?"

Her heart gave a painful spasm, expecting more criticism.

"I was out of line before. I let things get the better of me." His voice dropped. "I've been having a few problems at home, and I allowed that to spill over into my work. We need to work together on this, start over. Concentrate on the case."

Her breath stuttered. An apology? Not exactly, but *wow...* "Let's catch this killer so we can all go home," she said.

He laughed with such pained irony she got a glimpse of why she'd briefly fallen for him.

"If only that would solve my problems. See you soon, Sergeant Rudd."

Back in the hotel, Holly was working through the list of people from the village who had solid alibis for last night. The vast majority of folks at the marine lab were accounted for, although not everyone. Thomas Edgefield didn't have an alibi; neither did Rob Fitzgerald, Gladys, or half a dozen others. Still, it felt good to knock a few people off the list of potential murderers—assuming the killer was a local. She was looking to see if they could get any information from cell towers that might pin down locations of the others. Unfortunately, the fire brigade hadn't been called until twelve thirty, which gave all of those volunteers thirty minutes in which to commit the murder, so none of those guys were necessarily in the clear. The arson investigator couldn't say for certain if the fire was started deliberately or not, but it had all the feel of a diversion.

"We finally got records from the phone company who confirmed there was a call to Brent Carver at nine thirteen in the morning. It came from the public call box in town," Messenger shouted out to her and Furlong, who grunted. They were working in the lounge.

"See if we can get a warrant for all the calls made from that call box. Outgoing and incoming," said Holly. In the age of cell phones, public pay phones were often overlooked. "Call IFIS and get a technician back here to see if we can get any DNA or fingerprints that might give us an ID on who made that call." She checked her watch; she was exhausted but couldn't afford to slow down or take a break.

"Get Chastain and Malone to guard it until the tech gets there. It won't do much good in court, but it might give us a name," Furlong muttered, running his fingers through salt-and-pepper hair. There were loaded bags under his eyes. Everyone on the team was starting to look hollow-eyed with fatigue. "We need a break in this case."

Holly looked up. "You don't fancy Brent Carver for this one?"

His mouth twisted. "Before we found the knife I'd thought he was a good bet, but what sort of asshole leaves a bloody murder weapon on his frickin' bed? Doesn't fly, and it stinks of a setup."

"Unless it's a bluff."

He laughed. "You need balls of steel to make that bluff, and no one likes prison that much, especially not this guy. I'm thinking we need to identify Gina Swartz's lover as a person of interest, but the lab is swamped. I tried strong-arming them earlier." He had the grace to look sheepish. "Didn't work. What can I say? I'm an ass sometimes." The look in his eyes was almost haunted.

Still, she wasn't about to feel sorry for him. Or tell him the local lab didn't have those particular samples. Instead, she went out the front of the hotel and called Cassy to see how it was going.

"I'm getting there, but no matter how brilliant I am, I still have to give it a few hours in the PCR machine. I found skin cells and semen." She sounded excited. The nerd. "I also tested different blood drops. Amazing how much people leave behind on a sheet when they have sex."

Especially when one of them ends up dead.

"How long do you think before you can start trying to type it?"

"I'm going to go grab a couple of hours' sleep while it amplifies and then come in early to get this started before I start my real shift—"

"Thank you *so* much."

"I'm sending flight details and a list of hotels to you as soon as I finish this, BTW. Three full days, got it?"

"I've got it. Your birthday is coming up next month, right?"

"Ugh. Don't remind me." Cassy didn't want to be thirty. But she brightened. "NYC will be a great place to take my mind off it."

Holly hung up, glad to have pulled this particular string. She jumped an inch off the ground when she realized Rachel Messenger was standing in the darkness just a few feet away.

"Sorry," Messenger said quickly. She looked over her shoulder. "I just found out something about the knife," she whispered.

"What?" Holly frowned and stepped toward her. Her heart started a slow pound. Whatever it was didn't sound good. Messenger motioned her to come closer. She was acting weird, and Holly hated people who acted weird.

"What is it?"

"The hotline got a tip about who the knife belonged to and passed the message on to me."

Holly crossed her arms. "Who?"

"Thomas Edgefield." Messenger's eyes ping-ponged off the entrance.

"Shit." Holly's jaw locked.

"I've also got a record of him purchasing a new knife in Tofino the day before Milbank was killed."

Finn had lied to her. Holly firmed her lips together. Anger was flowing along her veins, and she didn't want it to escape yet.

"But the most interesting thing is this. I listened to the call, and I recognized the voice of the guy leaving the tip."

"Who was it?" Holly snapped.

"Rob Fitzgerald. Finn Carver's assistant."

She mulled it over. Either Rob was being a concerned citizen while trying to not lose his job or he was trying to pin the murder on Edgefield, which meant maybe he was involved. "I want you to dig into Rob Fitzgerald's background. Everything from phone records to financials." She looked across the inlet, the anger gaining ground now. Searing her skin. Simmering inside her heart. "I'll be back in an hour."

"Where are you going?" Messenger asked.

"I'm going to re-interview Edgefield and Carver about that knife. Let's figure out exactly who is lying about what before we tell the boss."

Rachel nodded rapidly. "I won't say anything. Just report in, OK?"

Holly snorted. Messenger was worried about her. She tapped her Smith & Wesson. "I've got you on speed dial. But don't worry, I can take care of myself."

Finn sat on his deck sinking a cold one. He'd had bad days in his life, plenty of them, but they never got any easier. First finding Gina dead, fighting with Holly, and seeing Brent carted away like some piece-of-shit criminal. He clenched his fist and held back the fury that burned through his veins.

Idiot. Getting close to Holly after he'd told himself not to. And what had happened? Within hours of figuring out he cared about her, his brother was sitting in an eight-by-eight cell. He tipped back the beer and downed the lot. Christ. Emotions burned his eyes, but he didn't cry. He wasn't that stupid little kid anymore. He would fix this.

Boots stomped up the stairs. About goddamn time. He flipped the cap off another bottle and leaned back in his chair, letting his gaze rove insolently over her body. Because he didn't have anything to lose anymore, and pissing her off was a bonus.

She leaned down until they were eye level, hers as hot as lava. Her teeth didn't move as she ground out, "You lied to me about the knife."

He went dizzy for a moment. He'd forgotten he did have something else to lose. Thom.

He stood, forcing her to take a step back. He opened his door and dragged her into his living room. This was not a conversation he wanted anyone to overhear.

"Let me go."

He dropped her arm like a stone. "How did you find out about the knife?" And what exactly did she know?

Anger rolled off her in waves. Well, hell, they were even. "That's classified information. Tell me about the knife."

Shit shit shit.

"Fine. The knife was Thom's old dive knife. He said it went missing a couple of weeks ago." He dragged his hands through his hair. "Anyone could have taken it out of his locker. We don't lock them up, and even if we did, it—"

"I understand that." He watched the line of her throat ripple as she worked to clamp down on what she really wanted to say. "What I don't understand is that when I asked you about that knife, you lied."

"Thom wasn't involved in Milbank's murder, but if you'd known his knife was the murder weapon you'd have hauled him in for questioning the same way you hauled in Brent."

"With good cause—"

"My brother would never lay a hand on Gina!" He always kept control of his temper. Always. But right now he was ready to punch the wall. "You already eliminated us from Milbank's murder because of the timeline. I. Did. You. A. Favor."

"Impeding a police investigation is an offense."

Thunder rumbled in the distance. He held his wrists together in the moonlit room. "Then why don't you arrest me?"

"You're impossible." She whirled away, stalked back. "What else have you been lying to me about?"

He pressed his lips tightly together. He didn't believe Brent had killed anyone, but he wasn't giving the cops fodder to make a circumstantial case against him.

"If you know anything, Finn, you *have* to tell me."

"I don't know anything." He went to the sink and filled a glass with water, downed it, and filled it again. Heard the fat drip of rain as the sky finally unleashed the storm it had been promising all day. "Except Thom and Brent are not killers."

"Where is he, the professor?" She followed him and leaned against the counter.

He was hyperaware of them being alone together. Cocooned as the lightning flashed across the sky. His anger left him feeling raw and exposed. Emotions pulsing too close to the surface.

"He's staying with Laura Prescott, Brent's *attorney*, in Port Alberni until they get him released." Thunder boomed, making the windows shudder in response. "No way would Brent risk going back to prison. He said he hadn't seen Milbank in months."

"And I thought you hadn't spoken to Brent?" she said archly.

She was sharp. He'd give her that. Slowly the rage was filtering out of his body, leaving him tired and angry. "I went to speak to him after I found that body in the wreck. I asked if he'd heard anything."

"Had he?"

"Only that someone was asking after Milbank."

She hissed. "So you knew the identity of the body before we did?" The skin around her mouth went white.

Finn rested his hand on her shoulder. "It wasn't like that."

She shook him off. "Then what was it like?"

He took a breath. Looked for his Zen mode and found it pretty damn elusive in Holly's company. "I suspected it might be Milbank because Remy was looking for him and the size of the body was about right. That's all I knew. That it *might* be Milbank."

She turned away from him. "Did you tell Gina Swartz about the shipwreck?"

Shock jolted through him. "No. No! She was in the library, but I didn't talk to her about it. If you want to keep something a secret in this town, you don't tell a damn soul."

"Could she have seen what you were doing?"

"No." He shook his head and then froze. "Shit." He swallowed. "I left to get a book out of the main library—the side room near the front door. When I got back, she was in her seat after getting back from lunch." He closed his eyes, trying to visualize the moment. "I had a list of local shipwrecks on the PC and a large map of Crow Point spread out."

He dropped the glass and it shattered in the sink. "Did I get Gina killed?"

Holly grabbed his hand and pulled him away from the glittering shards. "Careful, I'll help you clear that up."

He jerked his hand away. Lightning lit up the sky and thunder boomed. "Is it my fault she's dead?"

CHAPTER 16

Finn towered over her, dark and threatening, but somehow she knew he'd never hurt her. How the hell did she know that? Was she psychic or just plain old-fashioned stupid?

"You didn't kill her, Finn. Whoever planted that knife in her chest killed her."

"But it's my fault she died." The fury inside him was a palpable thing, like a tiger trapped beneath the surface of his skin.

"You can help me catch her killer. You know these people."

"No one I know would butcher Gina like a piece of meat." She wanted to comfort him but did not dare touch. He was so beautiful she ached just looking at him, all blond, scruffy, and gorgeous. The planes of his face were sharp in the dim light. Shoulders broad enough to carry more than their fair share of trouble. And he did. She knew he did.

There was a solid core of honor and compassion that ran through him that propelled attractive into irresistible. She wanted to reach out and test the strength in those arms, feel the hardness of his chest pressed against the softness of hers. Her body was on fire, and it made it hard to breathe, let alone think.

"What do you want from me? A meaningless apology for something I'd do again?" he asked.

What she really wanted was to feel the rough scrape of stubble over her naked skin. Not exactly appropriate. She stalked away.

"So I lied about the knife—big deal."

It *was* a big deal. She threw up her hands. "Don't tell me we suck at our jobs when everyone thinks it's OK to lie to us." All she wanted to do was catch a killer and get the hell out of this nightmare. Romping with this guy was not on the menu, no matter how hungry he made her. She rested her hands on her hips, remembering she was a professional, a solid cop with a hell of a track record for catching bad guys. "I wanted to tell you your brother hasn't been charged and is just being held for questioning at this time. He's OK—"

"OK? O-*fucking*-kay!" He took a step back. "You've got him in jail." Silver sparked in his eyes. Thunder cracked and a bolt of lightning split the night. "He's already spent one lifetime in that hellhole, it'll kill him to do more."

Holly stared up at him, trying to penetrate the fury. "I don't think he did it," she said quietly.

"And what about that asshole boss of yours?"

"He doesn't think he did it either."

"Seriously?" He stared at her wide-eyed, as if he didn't believe her. "Then why the hell did you haul him off?"

"He's a convicted felon, Finn, with a previous sexual relationship with the victim. I wouldn't be doing my job if I didn't bring him in for questioning." She clenched her fists and relaxed her jaw. "He's got a great lawyer, and that knife on the bed shows your brother is either a complete megalomaniacal psychopath or he's being framed. Cops aren't stupid, you know."

His lip curled and he snarled as he turned away.

Because he was hurting, she realized. Because he was in pain, and for some reason that made her hurt too.

He rested his head against his forearm as he leaned against the kitchen wall. "When I saw your boss earlier." His voice was low and gravelly. "I wanted to take him apart."

"Join the club."

He whipped around to face her. "Why did you sleep with him?"

Her mouth went dry. *Christ.* She should tell him to go to hell, but they were involved in something here. Something that didn't involve police procedure and defied convention. Something elemental and essential. Like blood. And oxygen.

There were plenty of reasons she'd slept with Furlong. Loneliness and foolishness being prime among them. "My mom had just died."

Muscles bunched in his jaw, and his breath escaped as steam that heated the air around them. The wind started to howl. Trees braced against the onslaught of the storm outside and an equal storm battered her senses, weakening her defenses. She swallowed uneasily. "I needed someone to hold me."

"Bad choice."

"Yeah, bad choice." Her heart stuttered. "I don't usually make mistakes." She stepped forward and placed her hands on his chest.

His hands gripped her waist, and it wasn't a gentle caress. The heat of his touch burned through the thin layer of her uniform shirt. "Am I another mistake, Holly?" His voice was a whisper against her lips. His eyes were like fire against her soul.

She shook her head and stood on tiptoes, needing just one kiss. Her fingers sank into his hair, and suddenly she was pressed up snug against his lean, hard body as she caught his lips with her own. She ran her tongue lightly over the seam and then, just as she was about to pull away, he slanted his mouth over hers and plunged.

Oh, hell. Desire ignited along her veins, and she sank both hands into his hair, dragging him closer, absorbing every detail of their kiss—the essence, the sensuality, the unexpected tenderness.

Her knees shook. He tasted like magic. Like someone had cast a spell of enchantment over her, making her want him with every particle of her being. She felt drunk, or drugged on nothing more than a simple kiss that was as complex as the universe.

It's just a kiss, Holly.

The hard planes of his body felt solid and strong against the softness of hers. His hands slipped into the waistband of her pants and cupped her bottom, pulling her up against the firm ridge of his zipper. Fireworks exploded through her at the contact.

Busy fingers undid tiny buttons on her shirt with more dexterity than she could manage even when she wasn't burning from the inside out. He pulled it off her shoulders, impatiently found the clasp of her bra, and the cool air wafting over her flesh told her she was naked from the top down. His fingertips fluttered over the faded bruises, and for a moment she thought he was going to stop. "Does it hurt?"

She shook her head, unable to speak.

He stripped off his T-shirt, and Holly slid enthralled fingers up the solid slabs of muscle, scraping a fingernail up over bumpy abs, then over first one nipple and then the other. She watched the slide of his throat as he swallowed. Eyes, colorless in the night, but no less intense, watched her with a combustible heat—fire waiting for oxygen.

His mouth dropped to her breast, soft hair brushing her skin an instant before pleasure shot through her. He sucked deeply, swirling her nipple with his tongue as his fingers plucked and played with its mate.

The sensation was so incredible, so erotic and magnetic. Her head spun, and the gentle rocking motion he made with his thigh had her so desperate to have him inside her she was rubbing against him with the need to get closer. Her fingers found his zipper, and she eased it carefully down, admiring the length and width of him as he sprang into her palm. *Oh, god.* She hummed as she ran her fingers up and down and around him until she could feel heat start to build just beneath the surface of his skin.

He undid her belt, top button of her uniform pants, and slid the zipper down. She bent her legs against the wall so she could undo her boots, first one foot, then the other. The weight of the equipment belt took the trousers the rest of the way to the floor. She kicked out of them and her shoes and stood there in nothing more than her panties and a splash of moonlight. The storm lashed against the windows with indignant fury, leaving them isolated in the darkness. Finn moved closer, spreading her thighs with the sheer bulk of his.

There was a tiny voice at the back of her mind whispering that she shouldn't be here, shouldn't be doing this. Then she watched him shuck his jeans, grab a condom out of his wallet, and the little voice was roped, gagged, and sidelined into oblivion. He stripped off her nothing panties, lifted her onto the kitchen counter, and she gasped as the cold surface connected with her bare skin. He smiled and kissed her again. Long, slow, mesmerizing kisses. His fingers touched her everywhere, driving her up, driving her wild until she was panting and writhing, wanting him closer, wanting him buried deep inside her.

She picked up the condom from beside her hip and rolled it over his thick length. A fine shudder ran through his body, and she was relieved to know her touch affected him too. He positioned himself against her, the swollen head of him big and bold. She tried to move toward him, but he wouldn't let her. He leaned down and ran his tongue between her breasts before closing once more over her nipple. Her toes curled, and she sank back against the wall, trembling and so turned on she was going to melt. She could feel him, right there, his body straining with the need to be inside her. It had been a long time for her, but she didn't remember ever losing control before, didn't remember being so frantic.

"Tell me I'm not a mistake."

Her throat went dry when she realized what he was asking and why he was asking it right now. Because she could still change her mind, because she hadn't totally crossed the line. Yet.

But she didn't care about the line. She sank her fist into his hair and dragged him closer, wrapped her legs around his hips and brought just the thick tip of him inside her. Muscles started to clench, needy, grasping, wanting him to fill her, wanting to take him deep.

"Tell me," he demanded, not moving an inch even as the tendons in his neck grew taut.

"You're not a mistake."

He took hold of her hips and thrust deep and hard, and every color of the rainbow shattered inside her mind. She moaned, and he captured the sound with an openmouthed kiss that drew her into him again. He pulled her to the edge of the counter, straining to get deeper. Sweat coated both their bodies. Skin about to ignite. He moved in and out of her wet heat, but he couldn't get all the way inside her, and it was killing them both.

"Do you trust me?" He rested his head on her forehead.

She almost laughed except she couldn't find the breath. She was naked on the guy's kitchen counter. Her gun and Taser on the floor, and he was asking if she trusted him?

He pulled out and she gritted her teeth with frustration. Then he flipped her, and she yelped as cold Formica connected with her stomach and breasts. Then heat spread slowly over her body as inch by inch he toed her legs wider apart. *Oh…*

"Tell me if you hurt, *at all*," he ordered roughly.

She swallowed. *Whoa.* She felt exposed and vulnerable and so turned on it was like being in some erotic movie. His breath was in her ear as his chest curled over her back. "You're the most beautiful woman I've met, did you know that?"

She felt the prickle of the hair on his thighs against hers, felt the engorged head of his penis as he probed her hot, wet core.

"I'm not beautiful," she denied. She sucked in a gasp, and suddenly he was filling her, deeper than before, and she didn't care about being beautiful or any other damned coherent thought. So deep, he filled every corner of her body and mind with the sort of mind-altering pleasure that robbed her of speech and brainpower. He was gentle, sliding in and out with long, smooth strokes that built a tangle of need inside her until she was writhing and panting and clutching at his thighs with her fingernails. "More."

He laughed, breath hot as dragon's breath over her neck as he ran his tongue down her spine. And then, finally, he started pumping harder, driving deeper and cupping her breasts as he drove and drove and drove, and she was flying again, spinning out of control and shattering into a million pieces of glitter that sparkled like stardust before it too exploded. And she felt his climax pulse through her, and her muscles quivered and rode and milked his orgasm as if it was her own. She collapsed into a mass of boneless jelly and waited for her heart to restart.

It restarted with a bang.

CHAPTER 17

Oh, hell.

What had she just done?

His body was still draped over hers, heavy, solid, their skin sticky with sweat and sin. His breath was in her ear, heart pounding against her back, still deep inside her, pulsing, their hearts beating in rhythm. Part of her craved that closeness, that connection that fused them like metal alloy. She'd never experienced anything like it before and didn't want it to end. But no matter what she thought of Finn Carver, his brother was still a suspect in jail. She closed her eyes and pushed back against his bulk. "Let me up."

He was watching her with raptor-like intensity. He could read her expressions as easily as she read his. "Dammit, Holly."

She shifted restlessly. He withdrew and dealt with the condom. A freakin' *condom* because they'd had freakin' kitchen countertop sex, and she'd never had kitchen countertop sex before with anyone, let alone someone involved in a murder investigation.

"I can't believe I did that."

"*We.* We did that."

"I know, but if anyone finds out I did it with you, *I* will lose my job. You'll probably get a goddamned high-five."

His face went hard. Eyes cold and brilliant like Arctic sunshine. She tried to take his hand, but he pulled away.

Cold air brushed across her bare skin, and she grabbed her bra and panties, struggled into them in the close confines of the kitchen as he watched her with a gaze that turned molten again and made her feel weak inside. What was wrong with her? She didn't do this sort of thing. She didn't have time.

He reached out and untwisted her bra strap, and she froze, wishing she could melt into him as he ran a finger over the bare skin of her shoulder. She wished circumstances were different. That she could drag Finn to bed and go for seconds. That she could kiss him in public and hold his hand and, hell, just lick him all over.

But she couldn't.

She'd screwed up.

What had she done? What kind of cop behaved like this?

If she had any integrity at all, she'd step down from her position as primary investigator. She started to hyperventilate, the air never quite reaching her lungs. Each breath getting tighter as panic spiraled. She held on firmly to the sink in case she fainted.

His fingers squeezed her shoulders. "Don't."

She swore and then struggled into her uniform, doing up her belt, heavy with equipment and responsibility. A headache throbbed through her temples as she tucked in her shirt, pulled her hair back into its ubiquitous braid.

"Are you OK?" Finn asked, sounding level and resigned.

Her heart squeezed and she thrust away from the sink. "I'm good, but I need to go—"

"Wrongs to right, bad guys to catch." His eyes glittered in the darkness as he stood back to wave her through. Not level and resigned at all. Pissed as a two-headed rattler.

She walked past him and he let her go. Out into the darkness where cold air bit and remorse flooded her.

"Come back anytime, sweetheart," he called after her. "Always happy to take one for the team." He slammed the door, and the sound echoed through the night like leftover thunder.

She ran down the stairs, not mad with Finn, but heartbroken. Because she hadn't just hurt him, she'd lied to him about it first. And she knew from personal experience that was the deepest kind of betrayal.

Her cell rang just as she hit the bottom step. "Rudd," she answered.

"I missed it." Messenger sounded agitated and on edge.

"Missed what?"

"Rob Fitzgerald used the call box to phone the hotline with the tip about the knife."

Holly's heart pounded and she stopped moving.

A truck drove past, going from the dive shed toward town, and the hairs on Holly's nape snapped taut as she recognized Fitzgerald behind the wheel. He waved, and she nodded and held his gaze as he drove past.

"The call was made only an hour before someone used that same call box to lure Brent Carver to Gina Swartz's house."

Probably to try to frame him for murder.

"I want everything on Fitzgerald. *Everything.*" She stared after his taillights.

All the turmoil and uncertainty about what she'd just done with Finn evaporated as her heartbeat steadied. She radioed Malone to come pick her up in the RCMP vehicle. They were getting closer, she could feel it. And she was about to spend the night with memories of Finn keeping her warm as she staked out their prime suspect.

The next morning, Holly watched through the hardware store window as an IFIS guy with circles the size of Kansas around his eyes sampled the town call box for DNA and fingerprints.

"Do you remember anyone using that phone yesterday morning, Mr. Toben?" she asked. She'd spent a sleepless night watching Fitzgerald's house from a high point in the motel parking lot. But his truck hadn't moved until 7:30 a.m. when he'd headed off to work.

Grant Toben scratched his iron-gray hair. "I don't spend my time gazing out the window, young lady."

Young lady?

"I appreciate that, sir." She smiled, but it was getting harder and harder to use her charm when she had a weapon and a badge. "However, you have a great view from here." The store sat just across the parking lot from the public phone that had been used to make both calls yesterday morning. Had the murderer expected cops to already be on scene or had they scored a lucky break? Had the killer wanted to hurt Brent Carver, place him at the scene, or just get him out of the house long enough to plant the murder weapon? Maybe it was all of the above because he made a hell of a slam-dunk murder suspect.

"Where's Mike? Maybe he saw something."

"I do remember seeing that young man from the marine lab down here." He scrunched up his features, lips disappearing beneath his thick moustache.

"Which one?" Holly pressed.

"Don't know his name. Tall, lanky fellow. Brown hair hanging down over his shoulders like a girl."

Holly hid her excitement behind neutral features and held up a photograph of Rob Fitzgerald.

"Yup." Grant Toben nodded nonchalantly. "That's the guy. And I remember thinking it was strange because I know he has a cell phone because whenever he's in here he can barely take his eyes off the damn thing long enough to carry on a normal conversation. Scourge of modern society, those damn things."

"I'm going to need you to make a statement, Mr. Toben." She nodded to Rachel Messenger to finish conducting the interview, and although the news was exactly what they'd hoped for, it was hard to feel excited. Deep inside, she felt like a fake. Someone impersonating an officer. The sort of cop she and her father had always derided over dinner because even though the evidence pointed the other way, she had been intimate with someone involved in the investigation, and no matter how incredible it had been, it was still wrong. She glanced outside and caught Furlong's glance. She thanked Toben and headed outside. "He identified Rob Fitzgerald as using the call box yesterday morning."

"Nice one. Let's pick him up. Any idea where he is this morning?"

"I assume he's still at the dive shed." Freddy Chastain was supposed to be keeping an eye on him without tipping him off. Not easy in this part of the world.

Furlong looked at her oddly. "You OK?"

The thought of seeing Finn again was unsettling. She'd treated him the same way Furlong had treated her, and she knew how bad that felt.

"Just tired." Right now she was so busy keeping up her own deception she couldn't really condemn anyone else's, not even Furlong's.

"Let's go pull this guy in for questioning."

She should be buzzing. They had a viable suspect, one who wouldn't tie her up in an unwinnable conflict of interest. But she felt hollow. Ashamed of how she'd treated a man she cared for. *Really* cared for. Messenger came out of the hardware store, and they all climbed into the SUV and headed back to the marine lab.

She'd messed up everything. She'd finally fallen for a guy, and not only had she screwed up her job, she'd walked out on him after mind-blowing sex. And now she was going to have to pretend nothing had changed. That he hadn't rocked her world and hadn't moved her so deeply she was still shaken to the core. She was going to have to pretend he was just one in a long line of people she'd interviewed who meant nothing to her. Because otherwise, everything she'd ever worked for was in jeopardy.

She couldn't risk it. Not even for Finn Carver—who might just be the goddamn love of her life.

Finn surfaced, the seawater on his lips failing to obliterate the taste of Holly imprinted there. She'd walked away. Hell, he'd always know she wouldn't stay, but somehow last night had caught him like an uppercut to the heart. Unexpected. Raw. Pain.

Which was the other reason he should have steered clear of her in the first place.

He'd worked his balls off, first prepping for the day's dives. Cleaning and double-checking equipment. Getting two boats ready for an easy wreck dive on the lee side of one of the Broken Islands. Then he'd maxed out on dive time, spent as long as he could under the clear, blue water. Pushing his body, pushing the limit. And still he felt like a damn fool for giving a shit about what a woman had done to him.

They'd had off-the-charts sex. She'd got off. He'd got off. Everything should be golden.

Which was *not* what he was feeling right now.

He spat out his regulator and pushed his mask onto his head. "Darren—watch your ascent rate next time. Otherwise, you guys did great." He swiped water off his face and kicked toward the boat where the rest of the students were already on board. Rob was in charge of the second boat and flashed him the hand signal to say everything had gone as planned. Finn hauled himself out of the water.

The eyes of his fellow divers glowed; mouths hovered on the brink of jubilant grins. Nothing could beat a good dive except, maybe, spur-of-the-moment kitchen sex.

"Everyone have fun today?" Inside, his body hummed with unreleased tension. Brent was in a goddamn cell, and Finn had been shagging the cop who'd put him there. He was an ass. He knew better than anyone not to let people get too close. So why the hell had he made such an elemental mistake with Holly? Why couldn't he resist the pull that existed between them?

Once everyone was sitting down and the equipment secured, he opened the throttle on the way back to his suddenly stagnant, frustrating life.

Rob followed him closely, and they both slowed down when they got inside the inlet. They drew up to the dock and tied up. He made sure the students grabbed their gear to wash it down before hefting his own equipment over his shoulder and striding up the wooden boards.

The RCMP cruiser rolled down the hill, heading toward them at a slow crawl. He could see Furlong driving—bastard—and Holly sitting beside him, avoiding his gaze.

What the hell did they want now, or were they just en route across the inlet, going back to the hotel? He turned away, didn't care.

Sure.

The students milled around waiting for Rob to unlock the dive shed. It was a pain in the ass to have to be so much more careful than before. He heard car doors slam, boots crunch as the police started doing whatever the fuck they needed to do.

He felt Holly at his side but was too stubborn to acknowledge her.

"Rob Fitzgerald?" she called.

Finn gave a little shake of his head. She wasn't even here for him. Must be Rob's time for a roasting. He watched the young man he'd worked with for the last eighteen months turn toward Holly. Rob's face drained of blood and he lunged toward her sidearm.

Sonofabitch! Finn caught Rob's hand, swung him around by it, and had him facedown in the grit, foot on the back of his neck, with Rob's arm bent at what he knew to be an excruciating angle, in under a second.

Holly and the other officers were staring at him a little wide-eyed, as were his students.

"What the hell is going on?" he demanded. Rob liked a good time, but had always been reliable and easy to work with. *Didn't mean he wasn't a killer,* his brain taunted.

Holly nodded to Messenger, who put handcuffs on Rob's one wrist.

"We just need to talk to Mr. Fitzgerald," Holly said calmly, still not looking him in the eye.

Finn handed over Rob's other wrist for the steel band. "Why?" he demanded, getting in Holly's face. *Why did you walk out last night? Why will you not talk to me?*

She narrowed her eyes at him. But at least she finally connected.

"We've got some questions to ask him." She looked beyond him into the dive shed. "I'd appreciate it if you'd find us some dry clothes for Mr. Fitzgerald so we can make his interview more comfortable."

Suggesting they were going to question him for some time. Finn turned his gaze to Rob. The guy looked like he was about to open his mouth and start begging.

"If you had *anything* to do with Gina's death you better hope they keep you locked up nice and safe." Anyone who lunged for a gun had something to hide. Not even Finn had been that desperate—no, he'd just lied and manipulated his way into the investigation. Finn shook his head at himself as he walked into the dive shed, grabbed Rob's bag, and stuffed in jeans and T-shirt that he knew belonged to his assistant. When he walked outside, Furlong, Messenger, and Rob were already heading back to the SUV.

He handed the bag to Holly. "And how are you this morning, Sergeant Rudd?"

She took it, head down, muttering, "If anyone finds out about last night, I'll get suspended."

"Who exactly am I gonna tell?"

"People will just *know*." She shot him a sideways glance. "I can't talk about it right now."

He gave her a look that let her know he thought she was insane. "So that's it?" He leaned closer. "That's all you've got to say to me?"

"Right now it's all I *can* say. I'm sorry." She marched away with Rob Fitzgerald's stuff under one arm. The car door slammed and they drove away.

His heart felt as if it had spent the night in the deep freeze and then been hit full whack with a sledgehammer. And in the blink of an eye he was once more the little kid who nobody wanted. Well, fuck that.

Rob Fitzgerald sat at the interview table with an insolent jut to his jaw. The charm had fallen away to reveal a surly, whiny individual with a sealed—until now—juvenile record for drug possession and theft.

"You knew about the shipwreck. didn't you, Rob?"

His eyes hardened. "I don't know what you're talking about."

"I'm talking about the fact that you talked Len Milbank into going down there to look for treasure, and as soon as you got him there, you stuck a knife in his chest and then dumped the body."

He pressed his lips together. "I didn't do that."

"So tell us what you did do," Holly urged.

"I never killed Len." He started chewing his lip, a sure sign of nerves.

"But you knew him." Half an hour ago they'd gotten phone records, going way back, that showed a series of phone calls between the two men. The calls stopped when Rob started working at the marine lab, but Holly would bet a month's pay they'd used a burner cell to communicate after that. "You were the inside guy for his smuggling operation."

Rob started tapping his feet on the floor, making his knees bob rapidly. "I don't know what you're talking about."

"Oh, come on." Holly paced, unable to settle in the chair beside a glowering Furlong. She'd do better without him here, could finesse Rob Fitzgerald with a few friendly smiles. But right now she didn't feel like smiling. She felt dead inside. Blackened and charred as if a forest fire had swept through her heart. She'd told Finn from the beginning they had no future, nothing but some weird chemistry. But she'd hurt him. She'd seen it in his eyes and felt it reflected in her own feelings. She'd messed up. He must hate her now.

"We know you made a call about that knife," she said.

Rob's blue eyes met hers, and she read calculation in them, guile. "I made the call about the knife. I recognized it, but I didn't want to just up and say anything in front of anybody. It was my boss's knife." He leaned forward over the desk, all boyish sincerity. "I *need* this job."

"You made another call not long after that one."

He frowned.

"That call was to Brent Carver. Someone told him there'd been a murder on Deerleap Road—"

"What?" His eyes went wide. "I didn't make any calls to Brent Carver. That guy is not someone I'd be messing with." He shook his head, then his eyes whipped forward. "You don't think I killed Gina—"

"Did you?"

"No! I liked Gina."

"But you didn't like Len."

He slumped back in his chair. "No one liked that motherfucker."

"So why'd you work for him?"

He rubbed long-fingered hands over the back of his neck. "I never had a choice," he admitted. "I managed to kick drugs after I got busted a few times. I went away, but as soon as I came home the scumbag got me hooked again."

Did he force them down your throat or into your veins? It was always someone else's fault that users couldn't resist temptation.

"He told me that if I moved down to Bamfield and just acted as the occasional go-between with a guy he knew from down the coast, he'd make sure my life was rosy." He scanned the interview room and rolled his eyes. "Milbank always was a fucking liar."

"So you killed him?"

Rob pulled his long hair out of his eyes, incredulous, or a damn good actor. "I worked for him because he scared the shit out of me. I didn't kill him, for the same reason."

"What about Gina?" Furlong spoke up. He slipped a photograph across the table.

Rob's eyes bugged and he put his hand over his mouth. "Whoa. I never hurt Gina. I don't need to attack ladies to get some, you know." He shot Holly a god's-gift-to-women smile and she wanted to slap him. But he'd assumed from Gina's naked body that she'd been sexually assaulted, and as far as the coroner could tell, she hadn't been. Or he was a hell of a liar. She pressed her lips together and studied him carefully.

"We have a witness that says you used the call box yesterday morning. There were only two calls made from that phone around that time. One was about the knife. The other was about Gina."

His skin bleached and he shook his head. "I never touched her, or Milbank. Where's my lawyer!" he started yelling and bumping the table with his legs.

"Tell me what happened with Milbank," she asked when Furlong had gone out the room to "look" for the guy's lawyer.

"Milbank was convinced he was being watched by the cops, though if that was true he probably wouldn't have wound up dead." He stopped moving. "Look, I'm not admitting anything. But it is possible Milbank gave a certain someone drugs destined for up north, which they might have swapped for money way out to sea. And a couple of days later, it's possible that same someone met up with Milbank to give him his cash and then went quietly home with a small payment for services rendered, only to hear the ugly bastard had got himself killed and the cash was nowhere to be found." The guy wiped his nose on his hand.

So he had been Milbank's connection. "That someone is going to have to come up with a few names and times."

"I'm not fessing to anything until I talk to my lawyer." He shrugged a bony shoulder.

"Lawyer's coming. Did you ever have sex with Gina?"

"She wasn't my type. Too old. Although she was hot under those old granny blouses—who knew?" He whistled as if remembering Gina's naked body from the photograph they'd shown him. Even if he didn't kill her he was a sick puppy.

She hid her disgust. "Would you willingly provide us with a DNA sample to eliminate you from our inquiries?" They could get a warrant. They already had his prints. "It'll go a long way to proving your innocence if we don't find your DNA at Gina's house. Or you could just come clean and tell us what really happened." Her impatience leaked out, or maybe it was pure exhaustion. She didn't remember the last time she'd slept.

He leaned back in his chair, considering her with a hard, calculating gaze. "You think you're something special, don't you?" He sneered. "Better than me? I don't think so."

"Pardon me?"

"I know what you did last night." His eyes gleamed with a sly edge. "I saw you getting drilled by Finn last night. Cut me some slack." He eyed the door. "And I won't tell your boss."

Numbness crept up around Holly's heart. He was bluffing. He had to be bluffing.

His eyes started to dance as he read her reaction. "You don't believe me? I went to see him last night, during the storm."

Her nerves buzzed.

"Got quite an eyeful, Officer. Nice ass, by the way."

She gritted her teeth. "You're full of shit, Fitzgerald, and you are going down."

His gaze slithered over her skin. "Unlike you guys, huh. Oh well, maybe next time?"

Her chest squeezed so tight she thought she was having a heart attack. The interview was being recorded, and he'd just fried her career with a few careless words. What was worse, he'd watched her and Finn making love. She felt violated. Dirty. Revulsion flooded every cell in her body.

Her legs wobbled as she got to her feet. She didn't deserve this job. She'd never deserved this job. She picked up the case file and left the room. On the other side of the door, Furlong stood staring at her, openmouthed.

"I'm done. Someone else can take over as primary." Her hands were shaking. "I'm not jeopardizing putting that asshole in prison."

Furlong snapped his mouth shut, his eyes dark and troubled.

"Don't worry," she said bitterly, "*I'll* call my father."

"Finish your vacation." He took the files out of her arms. "Lie low and don't talk to anyone about this. I'll handle things."

"Handle things?"

"I'll figure something out. Don't tell *anyone*." He stepped toward her and lowered his voice. "How could you be so *fucking* irresponsible?"

"Believe it or not, I don't make a habit out of it." She glared. "I don't want you to *handle* anything. I'm going back to Bamfield to grab my gear and then I'm going to Victoria. I'll call my dad. That little shit is not going to blackmail cops or wriggle out of everything he deserves."

"Holly..." He touched her arm and grimaced. "I wish I could ignore this. But if he's guilty, if he goes to trial, he could twist the evidence to make it look like a conspiracy theory to clear the name of the primary investigator's lover's brother."

She closed her eyes. It was *so* goddamn sleazy. Drained from lack of sleep and plain, old-fashioned humiliation, she wanted to curl up on the floor and die. "I'm taking myself off the case. I never interviewed him until after his arrest. The case is rock solid. You'll have to decide if I face disciplinary action or not, but…" Her throat felt like crushed glass as she swallowed. "Just give me a few hours to talk to my dad, OK?"

"I'll handle it," he repeated.

She marched away with her head high. How could she have thought she'd get away with such a massive error in judgment? She burst into the reception area, and there was Thomas Edgefield, waiting patiently on one of the chairs. Brent Carver was still being questioned. *Christ.* She ran her hands down her face. It was a nightmare.

"Holly! Sergeant Rudd." He held up a flash drive. "I heard you were here and thought I'd take the opportunity to give you all the details from my wife's murder investigation."

She snatched it off him and sailed out the door. Her fingers curled over the small flat object. She may as well look at Edgefield's case. Christ knew she had nothing better to do.

CHAPTER 18

She hired a car to drive back to Bamfield. She could have asked Steffie or Messenger to ship her stuff to Victoria, but she'd be damned if she'd ask for any favors. And she wanted to face them. Apologize—rather than slink away like a rat. Trouble was, there was no one at the hotel, and she figured they must still be re-canvassing the locals in the wake of the second murder.

Was Rob Fitzgerald their killer? She hoped so. The sick voyeur could rot in prison, and people here could get on with their lives without living in fear.

She used Steffie and Messenger's room to get changed out of her uniform and into plain clothes and made it back across the inlet to the bar where she'd left the rental car. She leaned against the hood. The thought of another two hours on that god-awful road just to get to Port Alberni brought her to a standstill. She couldn't do it. Could not climb behind that wheel. She glanced up at the painted wooden structure of the motel at the back of the bar and walked inside the small reception area. A young girl, about sixteen, manned the desk.

"I need a room for the night."

"You look like you've had a rough journey. That road's a killer, huh?" The girl popped gum.

Holly blinked. The girl didn't recognize her. Thank god for small favors. "It is." She handed over her credit card and waited for the sky to fall in.

"Room seven." The girl smiled, a small gap showing between her front teeth.

Holly blinked as she was handed a key. "Thank you." She hefted her bag and headed back outside. Trod the sagging boards with their peeled white paint and unlocked the door of number seven. She braced herself and then walked into a room that, while it wasn't anything special, was clean, warm, and thankfully quiet. She tossed the bag onto the chair, plugged her phone into the charger. She was thirsty, so she put the mini coffeepot on and brewed herself a mug.

The sun slanted in the window, so she closed the curtains and dragged her laptop onto her thighs as she lay propped up in bed.

She inserted the flash drive Edgefield had given her and pulled up the initial police reports. They'd put in a lot of man-hours interviewing people but, like her, they hadn't gotten much info out of the locals. She recognized most of the names, and though there'd been some newcomers to the area, a lot of the townsfolk were the same.

Holly found it strange living somewhere so remote. The thought of facing that damn road every time she wanted to see civilization? No way. She liked the wilderness, but for visits, not for normal everyday living. Which reinforced the fact that she and Finn could never be anything except a casual hookup. So why was the desire to go find him and apologize digging into her mind with needle-sharp claws? Did she want a repeat of last night? Her body said hell yes while her mind said solidly no.

Did she want to hurt him, mess with him more than she'd already done? Not that he'd tried to chase after her last night or call her after their run-in today. Why would he? She'd treated him to a classic slam, bam, thank you…man.

And even though most guys wouldn't care, she knew he did. They'd shared a closeness that she had ruined because she'd laid hands on him and he'd kissed her. Then they simply hadn't been able to stop, and now she didn't know who she was anymore.

Am I another mistake, Holly?

She squeezed her eyes shut because she could still feel the pleasure of his touch and still wanted him so badly, on so many levels, that her pulse revved. Why would he want her now? He wouldn't. No one would. And that was fine. But it didn't stop a raw ache from opening up inside her and filling her with a yawning gulf of emptiness.

He was done. History. And a damn sight better off without her screwing up his life.

She clicked on the crime scene photos from the Edgefield double murder. The images were black and white for the most part. Some color. The first images were of the forest, only a rifle shot away. The first close-up of the victim made her stomach clench.

It could have been her, lying there with her head smashed in. The next shot zoomed out to show the baby who'd also received a blow to the front of his tiny face. Holly wiped a hand over her eyes as her throat closed up. She pulled her coffee mug off the nightstand and took a drink to steady herself.

This was how Thomas had found his wife and son?

So the report said.

But why had the killer placed the baby so carefully in his mother's arms, snug against her breast? Protected in death as he wasn't in life? Bianca Edgefield hadn't been sexually assaulted that the coroner could tell. Someone had simply smashed a hammer into her skull and left her to die. An up close and personal murder.

She flicked through more of the images, but they all showed the same thing. And no sign of the two-year-old girl. No blood.

Just her little red jacket and what looked like drag marks. Holly squinted at a picture of the kid.

Shit, they could have been twins except for the massive smile on the girl's face. Most of Holly's early photographs showed her on the verge of crying. She hadn't liked to sit still for long. She touched the plump cheek of the kid.

"What happened to you, Leah? Where did you go?"

She brought up the autopsy report. Bianca had been a young, healthy mother of two, still nursing, who'd died from blunt force trauma to the head. Autopsy on the baby proved inconclusive. Although, really, the crushed skull revealed more than any investigator could ever need.

She couldn't find any DNA evidence. Then she realized DNA profiling hadn't even been invented back then. Maybe Edgefield was right about reopening the case, although who knew what condition the evidence was in after all this time. She picked up the phone and called Cassy.

"Hey." Cassy sounded miserable.

"What's up?"

"The results of those DNA tests are back."

Excitement stirred. "You've run them already? Seriously?"

"What can I tell ya, I'm good. I found two sets of DNA on that sheet. The vic's and an UNSUB."

"In the system?" Holly asked before she could stop herself.

"Not *ex*actly," Cassy said slowly.

"Ugh. You shouldn't be talking to me about this. I'm off the case."

"What?"

"Cassy." Holly cradled her head in her hands. "I screwed up."

"How?"

Holly swallowed. She wasn't going to lie about her mistakes. Not anymore. "I had sex with someone involved in the investigation."

"No buckin' way."

"Oh, yes. I really did. And I had two, maybe three, orgasms to prove it. And the worst thing? I want to do it again. And I can't. Ever. Go near. Him." *Christ.* She hugged her knees as sweat beaded her brow.

"But," Cassy spluttered, "you're usually so staid…and boring!"

Holly blew out a soft laugh. "Thank you, so much. I appreciate it. Staid, boring, highly unethical, and borderline criminal. A winning combination for a cop."

"Holy crap, Holly. You can't be serious."

"I am serious." Inside she went cold again. Humiliation welled up. She had to tell her dad the same thing, and the thought was killing her.

"Oh, god…" Cassy sounded like she was going to faint.

"You OK?"

"I just…I just…" Holly could hear her friend taking deep, settling breaths. "I don't know how to tell you this."

"If it's about that DNA, you need to call Furlong and fill him in."

"You need to hear it first."

"I'm off the case, Cass." She paced the floor. She shouldn't have started talking about sex because now she felt raw and edgy. She needed to get back on track. "I do have a question about old DNA though—"

"Holly—"

"What?" she said impatiently. Thinking about Finn, missing Finn, unsettled her. She needed to work.

"The DNA for the UNSUB on that bed sheet you sent me. I looked at the mitochondrial DNA in the skin cell samples—mitochondrial DNA is passed on *only* through the mother. I found a full maternal match with someone in the system."

Anticipation burned along Holly's nerves. She hoped it was Rob Fitzgerald, the smarmy little prick. "You have to tell Furlong, not me," she insisted.

"Listen. I ran it through CODIS and against every DNA profile I have in the system just like you told me to, breaking probably more privacy laws than you need to worry about."

Holly winced.

"Remember your last case when we had to take your DNA to eliminate it from the knife that bastard used to cut you?"

So they could separate her DNA from that of the wife he'd killed. "Yes." They were getting way off course here… "What does that have to do with—"

"The match was with *you*, Holly. A full maternal match. So I compared nuclear DNA too, which wasn't a full match. But enough to tell me you have a half brother out there, and I hope to God you didn't just have life-altering sex with him because the victim sure as hell did."

Holly dropped the phone and stared at it, frozen. When she picked it back up, Cassy was still there. Patient. Silent. A true friend. Holly's voice quivered, "I don't understand. Mom said she couldn't have any more children. I told you that." She was getting hysterical. She could feel it bubbling under the surface of her skin.

"I know, hon. That's why I checked something else—"

"What? Who?" Holly snapped.

She heard a thick swallow. "Your father's blood type is AB positive."

"So?"

"You are type O negative, Holly."

She didn't understand.

"It's simply not possible for the deputy commissioner to be your biological parent."

Holly covered her mouth and sank down onto the bed, curled over. "There must be a mistake."

"No mistake."

Holly's head started pounding. "You're telling me my mom had an affair? My dad isn't my dad? And she had another kid?" None of this made sense.

"That's possible, I suppose." Holly could hear the doubt in the other woman's tone. "It's also possible you were adopted."

"But I have baby photographs!" Sweat streaked Holly's face. It trickled down her temple, down her neck, corrosive as acid.

Cassy said nothing for a moment. "If you can get me some of your mom's DNA, an old hairbrush or some clothes, I can do another comparison. But the easiest thing would be to just ask your dad."

The thump of her heart was so loud she thought the other woman must hear it. She had no memory of her early childhood. It was like that part of her life was wiped clean. Or blocked? But how many people *did* remember their infancy? She pulled up the photograph of Leah Edgefield and stared at the little girl. Gray eyes. Like her. Like Thomas Edgefield. The man she'd looked down on since the moment she'd met him. The man she pitied.

Could he be her father? Could *she* be Leah Edgefield?

"Holly? Are you all right?"

God, she'd forgotten about Cass. "I'm OK. I need to call my dad…" Her tongue turned to dust. What should she say to him? *I slept with someone involved in the investigation and, by the way, am I adopted?*

"Still want me to call it in to Furlong?"

God. This was too personal. More personal than some pervert watching her have sex—and that had been bad enough. The room swayed in and out of focus. But the thought of being adopted threatened her very identity, every belief she'd ever held about her worthiness as a person, as a cop. Without that heritage, she had nothing. Was nothing. Nausea rose up her throat, but she forced it back. "I just need a bit of time to process this."

"I understand, sweetie. It's a lot to handle, but…"

"What?"

"The guy you slept with. Could he possibly be the guy who slept with the dead woman?" And Holly's brother?

"No." She remembered what they'd done together and her insides spun. *Christ, if Finn was lying or mistaken...* "His name is Finn Carver, aged thirty-six—he was in the military, so his DNA *might* still be in the system if they haven't already destroyed it. His brother, Brent Carver, thirty-nine, was just questioned in relation to Gina Swartz's murder. I know he gave a voluntary sample to IFIS in Port Alberni. It's not him, but would you...Could you... Just to make sure." *Favors.* She had no right to ask for favors.

"Double-check his profile and compare it to yours? Sure. It won't take long. I'll call you back ASAP. You're sure these two are full-blood brothers?"

She remembered how alike they were in looks—both blond and blue-eyed. Knew they'd grown up together. Couldn't imagine that his mother had dumped them and run off to become the beautiful and caring woman who'd raised her with such love and grace. Her stomach somersaulted. "I'm as sure as I am about anything right now." Then she dropped the phone and ran to the bathroom and vomited.

Finn kept the marine lab's dive program running despite the skeletal staff. He'd roped in a post-doc from the lab and Scotty Wolf, the hotel owner, both experienced divers, to partner some of his students. Paid them in cash and beer. He'd had a crap day, but he'd gotten everything done. He didn't quit and he didn't fail. Except when it came to a five-foot-ten-inch brunette with eyes of steel.

Now his brother was home. Released without charge.

They climbed into the boat, Brent, then Thom and Laura. Finn was so grateful to have Brent home he was willing to do anything to try to re-forge the bond they'd once shared. He cast off and buzzed them across the inlet, the sharp wind a welcome blast of ice that helped keep him awake after another near-as-damn-it sleepless night.

Brent wore the same clothes he'd worn yesterday morning. The lines around his eyes were grooves of fatigue edged with grief. Finn tied up the boat, watched Thom help Laura safely out.

"Time to go," Finn ordered Brent, who hadn't yet moved or spoken.

Instead of objecting the way he'd expected, Brent stepped out onto the dock and stood there. Shoulders stooped.

Lost.

"I'm going to see Laura home." Thom touched her arm, and Finn's eyes widened. It looked like he wasn't the only one who'd gotten lucky last night, but Thom might actually have gotten *lucky*.

Unlike him.

Don't think about Holly.

He stepped closer to his brother. "You need to thank Laura for getting you out of that hellhole."

Brent stared dully at the weatherworn planks of the dock.

"It's OK." Laura pulled her shawl tighter around her shoulders and smiled at him with tired eyes. It had been a long twenty-four hours. She adjusted her briefcase then Thom took her bag from her. "Astonishingly, I was actually glad to help." She turned on her heel and strode away. Thom followed with a lightness in his step Finn hadn't seen in years. Someone was coming out of this mess more intact than when they'd started, and for that he was glad. He'd even be content with his own fucked-up love life if he could ease the heartbreak that pummeled Brent like Pacific rollers.

Brent started up the gangplank with a weary tread. A couple of the guys were leaning on the railings watching them but saying nothing. Finn gave them a stare that told them to mind their own business. Thom and Laura veered left into the shop, but Brent ignored everyone, arrowed straight for home, slipping into the dense woods with the ease of a man long adjusted to the shadows.

"You should give her something for helping you. Most people would have let you rot," Finn called out as he kept pace. He wasn't letting him go this time.

Brent snapped off the top of a sapling as he snaked along the trail—the only indication he'd heard Finn bitching at him. He stumbled over a fallen pine—looking exhausted and worn. They'd come this way so many times as kids, Finn felt like he'd been catapulted back to simpler times. Grimmer times, when surviving a beating had been the only thing that mattered.

Given the current state of their lives, maybe he was mistaken to think they'd moved on. They got to the cove where they'd grown up and both stood looking at the small patch of wilderness that they could rightfully call their own. Brent's log cabin sat up on the hill like a testament of resilience and strength against all the bad things that could happen in life.

A shiver passed over his shoulders when he saw how Brent was looking at the place. With loathing and revulsion.

"You gonna burn it down the way you burned down the shack?"

Flat eyes regarded him.

"Dad would enjoy that." Finn got in Brent's face. Shoved him, wanting a response. Got nothing. "Dad would have laughed his drunken ass off if he saw you burn this place to ashes and all your paintings with it."

"What the hell do you know about my paintings?" The first flash of fire out of the embers of grief.

"I saw them when the cops searched the place."

Brent's eyes swung to the studio on the first floor.

"I recognized them from when we were kids. You were always good." Emotion started to strangle his throat. "I can't believe how great you've become."

"I'm not great." Brent's lip curled. "People are just stupid enough to pay top dollar for a bit of paint splashed on a canvas."

"You don't believe that."

"Don't tell me what I believe!" His voice rang off the ocean, angry and loud. At least he was feeling now, although that might not be such a good thing.

"Dad used to tell you they were a waste of paint. Even as a kid you knew better. You were smarter. Kinder. Better than he was."

Brent swallowed. Finn watched him flex his fists and hoped he wasn't about to get a meaty jaw sandwich. Although he'd take it. Hell, if it got his mind off Holly long enough to get some sleep, he'd welcome it.

The wind blasted them with a lick of fury.

"Whoever killed her put the knife on my bed." Air crackled around them. The agony in his eyes intensified. "I met people like that in prison. They liked playing mind games. They liked hurting people—women—more than killing them." Brent closed his eyes. "Did she suffer?" His voice broke.

"She died quick." A hell of a lot quicker than their father had. Finn curved his hand over his brother's shoulder and squeezed. "One stab wound to the heart. She died instantly." Finn didn't want to think of her naked or dead. She'd been his friend, and his last memory of her was savage. Brent didn't need any of that in his head. He had nightmares enough.

His brother's eyes flashed open, so like his own but with a darkness deep inside. "I never wanted to hurt her. I told her over and over to move on, to find someone else." He released a quiet snarl. "She waited for me, but I wasn't the same boy she'd loved. I tried to make it work, but the demons…" He shrugged out of Finn's reach. "They never let go." He faced the ocean. Their ocean. "She deserved better than a two-bit convict who couldn't stand the sight of his own face in the mirror." His features twisted. "But if I hadn't pushed her away she might still be alive."

"If I hadn't fallen asleep when we were kids, if I hadn't told him to go fuck himself, things might have been different, and she'd probably still be alive, and you wouldn't have spent years in prison."

Brent blew out a breath through his nose. And shook his head. "I was always gonna kill the sonofabitch. If I'd been smarter, I'd have just made sure no one found the body."

Finn didn't correct him. Saying that was easier than admitting the truth. Brent had loved their dad. In a perverse way, Finn had loved him too. That was the power of being a parent. Didn't matter what shit they did to you, you still loved them.

It was a sick evolutionary joke.

A figure stood on the road behind the house. Thomas. Waiting for Finn.

Finn put his hand across his brother's back, half expecting that punch in the jaw. "You going to be all right?"

Brent gave a choked laugh. "I doubt it."

"You gonna do anything stupid?"

"Probably." But Brent smiled, and Finn forced back the emotions that threatened.

"Don't forget to thank Laura."

Brent said nothing.

"The biggest painting you have should do it."

Brent ground out a reluctant laugh. "If I find out who killed Gina, she can have them all."

Finn wanted to tell him not to be stupid, not to throw away his life. But what would he do in Brent's place? He knew exactly what he'd do.

He left Brent standing there and went to meet Thom on the gravel road. "You not staying with Laura?" Finn asked pointedly.

Thom's back stiffened, but there was a glint in his eyes. "I was just escorting a lady home."

"Sure you were." At least Thom was giving the thought of a relationship with Laura a shot. Finn should be ecstatic. Thom and Brent were both clear of the investigation despite someone—presumably Rob—trying to implicate them. And that had been his objective ever since he'd found Len Milbank's rotting corpse.

But inside, he felt as if someone had stolen his heart and replaced it with a clockwork toy that didn't really work properly.

"I can't believe Rob Fitzgerald had anything to do with this." He'd worked with the guy pretty much every day for a year and a half and he hadn't had a clue.

"You OK?" Thom asked him suddenly, a worried look in his intelligent gray eyes.

"Yeah," he lied. "Let's go get a drink."

They walked silently as the dusk settled. Shoes crunching gravel. They got to the hotel just in time to see the cops trailing up the front steps. Finn braced himself to face Holly, but as he scanned the group, he realized she wasn't there. Where was she? Chasing a lead alone? The thought made him crazy.

Malone jumped down the steps and approached him, eyes flashing rage. He got right in his face. Finn stood his ground.

"What the hell were you *thinking*?" Malone yelled.

Finn held up his hands in front of him, eyeing the other man warily. He liked cops—one in particular—but he knew it didn't take much to provoke an arrest when they were pissed. Malone was red-mist pissed.

"I don't know what you're talking about."

Malone smacked his arm. Finn's eyes narrowed. "Touch me again and it'll be the last time." He held Malone's gaze. Frowned. "Where's Holly?"

The punch to the gut caught him unexpectedly. Next thing he knew he was on his front in the dirt, Malone trying to get the cuffs on him. He flipped the guy on his back and had him pinned in under a second. "Where the fuck is Holly?"

The other officers rushed over. None of them looked happy. He climbed off Malone, figuring he'd just earned himself a night in the lockup.

Holly's boss, the fucker, stood there with something like empathy in his gaze.

What the hell?

Malone got to his feet, looking like he wanted to punch him again, but Finn kept his eye on the man. He'd made a vow when he was thirteen that he wasn't letting any asshole lay a hand on him. Not without a fight.

"Rob Fitzgerald's been making some unsubstantiated accusations about witnessing Sergeant Rudd having a liaison with *someone* involved in the investigation." Furlong's gaze told him to put a lid on anything he wanted to say. "Sergeant Rudd took herself off the team so she didn't jeopardize the case."

Rob, the weasel, had been spying on them. The thought turned Finn's stomach. He wanted to know what else Fitzgerald been involved in, but more importantly, he wanted to know about Holly. "What does that mean?" This case meant everything to her. Being primary meant everything. "Where is she?"

"She headed back to Victoria. Her stuff is gone." This from Rachel Messenger, who bit her lip, looking upset.

Thom went white. "She promised to look at Bianca's murder."

"Well, she'll have time to do that now, won't she." Furlong's derision flicked like a whip.

Finn turned away. She'd warned him they couldn't do what they'd done last night. Told him, and he'd done it anyway.

"Will she lose her job over this?" His voice was gruff. He felt hollow. She loved her job. She would never forgive him for this. He was nothing compared to her career. He was obviously nothing, period. It stung that she'd left without a word.

"Fitzgerald wants to make a deal with us, giving up Dryzek and Ferdinand's drug running operation in exchange for immunity—"

"From murder?" Finn bit out. He could barely draw breath. Thom looked aghast. Rob had seemed like a decent guy. Neither of them had had a clue.

"He's not copping to murder, yet. Just drug running." Furlong shook his head. "I've made sure he understands the deal involves keeping his mouth shut about every other aspect of this investigation or the whole agreement is blown."

"So that's it? She's just gone?" Finn didn't know what he was supposed to do now, but he was wrong about the clockwork heart. This thing being ripped from his chest hurt too much not to be real.

The cops turned away. Malone looked like he wanted to punch him again.

"The first one was free, but the next one you have to pay for," Finn warned him.

Thom put his hand on Finn's shoulder. "This isn't what you need right now."

No, what he needed was Holly on his doorstep, or in his bed, and a week without interruption. "Let's go."

On the other side of the inlet, he told Thom he needed to check on something quickly. He sprinted to his cabin, blood pumping with hope as he burst into his bedroom. But the room was empty, the bed made. No note. No phones messages. No Holly.

He snagged a bottle of scotch off the shelf in the kitchen, trying not to remember what they'd done in this very space. But because of his weakness, she was gone for good, and unable to face the memories, he headed to Thom's, determined to get completely and totally wasted.

CHAPTER 19

Mike sat at the bar and stared into his beer. It was quiet. No one was laughing. Just grim and sober when all everyone really wanted to do was get drunk and forget. A week ago his biggest problem had been the frustration of not being able to get away from this boring little town and maybe finding the stamina to keep up with Gina in bed so he didn't come across as a dud. Now Gina was dead. Dryzek was on the warpath looking for things that had fuck all to do with him, and cops were crawling over every inch of town. They should have made him feel safe. Didn't.

He swigged back another mouthful of beer.

He needed to get out of town, but until Dryzek was dead or in prison, he daren't leave his parents unprotected. He pushed the bottle away and shoved to his feet. He wasn't doing them any favors sitting here. He headed for his truck across the road by the hardware store, but something caught his attention outside the motel. He found himself peeking around the side of the building just in time to see a jean-clad Holly Rudd walk into a room and close the door behind her.

He frowned. Why was she staying there? Were the cops doing some sort of undercover operation?

His phone rang. The burner. *Dryzek*. Uncertainty had him digging in his toes. He hovered on the verge of knocking on Holly's door and confessing everything. That he'd been Gina's lover. That Gina had told him about the supposed shipwreck and he'd foolishly told Milbank. That he'd stolen scuba gear from the lab so they could go take a look, but Milbank had never shown up. That he'd broken into Finn's and Brent's places, stolen Finn's gun. But he hadn't killed anyone. Hadn't run the cop off the road.

Who'd believe him? It sounded insane. Like someone was setting him up. And no way did he want to lose possession of his gun until Dryzek was locked up.

Another option was to tell Dryzek there was a cop set up in the motel. And from what he could see, she was alone. The barkeep was in Remy's pocket, so getting into the room would be a cinch. Maybe the gift of a cop would be enough to keep Dryzek off his back. Maybe a tip-off to the police about what was going down at exactly the right moment would result in Dryzek and Ferdinand going down for a long stretch of time. Or maybe Holly would do something he seemed incapable of and shoot the bastards dead. Either way, it didn't seem as if he had a lot to lose by making her a sacrifice. Except maybe his soul.

Cassy called back five hours after they'd last spoken. She sounded out of breath. "Sorry it took me so long. I had a serial rapist come in who couldn't wait. I've been waiting to get this guy for a long time and think we finally have his DNA."

Holly couldn't speak. She felt as if she'd been stuck in limbo since they'd last spoken, a thousand possible scenarios running through her head. She hadn't called her father. She needed to talk to Cassy before she figured out how to deal with any of this.

"Finn and Brent Carver are full brothers and don't share anything with you or the UNSUB except carnal relations, apparently. Well, only in the case of the former, unless you have something to tell me involving two hunky brothers and every woman's fantasy threesome."

"What?" Relief expanded inside her at the news. She lay on the bed and held back the tears that wanted to pour out and drown her.

"I'm disgusting, I know, but I want details. Is Finn as hot as his photo suggests? His brother is smokin'. And, honey, I'm getting desperate. I haven't had a date in weeks, possibly months, and he looks gorgeous—"

"I think I'm in love. With Finn. Not his brother." She sucked in a shocked breath as Cassy shut up. "I really messed this up. I've probably lost my job, and he's never going talk to me again." And really, that was the least of her problems even though it was the one that made her feel like a lead weight was pressed down on her chest. "And apparently I have a half brother in town." She sat up. God, the implications. She pulled up the crime scene photos from the Edgefield case. "I think I might be a girl called Leah Edgefield."

How weird was that?

"What?" Cassy asked.

"Thirty years ago there was a double murder in this town. A woman, who looked so much like me her husband fainted when we met, and her infant son were bludgeoned to death." *Or was he?* Holly thought suddenly. They had no DNA reference for the baby, just the assumption he was Bianca's son because he was the correct age and had been found in her arms. But his features had been crushed by a hammer—*why?* Had it been a random act of violence or calculated illusion? She heard Cassy typing in details. "Her daughter, a little girl called Leah Edgefield, disappeared on the same day. Everyone assumed she was taken by a cougar or wolf."

"Heck, you do look like her."

Something was cracking open inside her chest. A wild and terrible theory. "I need to test their DNA. The woman and the baby." Bianca Edgefield could be her mother. She looked at the image and tried to imagine that scenario. Tried to imagine Thomas as her father. Couldn't.

"It's possible the murder has nothing to do with you and your half brother," Cassy stated.

But it was a hell of a coincidence.

She licked her dry lips. "I'm going to call Dad. Tell him what you found. Ask him to order exhumations of the bodies of Bianca and Tommy Edgefield." Assuming they hadn't been cremated.

She flicked through the files Edgefield had given her. "Jesus. He got his and the daughter's DNA profiles worked up in the early nineties—from her umbilical cord. He listed it with the BC Coroners Service." Her throat convulsed. She could imagine him, channeling his energy, trying to find his daughter, never giving up.

How would he feel if the daughter didn't want to be found?

"I'm sending you the case file." She looked at her watch. It was ten o'clock. "Go home. It's waited thirty years. It'll wait another day."

"You're kidding, right?"

"You must be tired." And Holly wasn't ready to face the answers to these questions.

There was an odd silence. "You don't have to do this, Holly. I can send Furlong the DNA from the bed sheets, and we can do a voluntary sample collection and whittle down the candidates. He doesn't need to know about the match. No one needs to know," Cassy insisted.

"*I* need to know. Thomas Edgefield needs to know. I need the truth." And if Bianca was her mother, she wanted to be the sort of daughter who cared enough to hunt down her killer. The sort of cop who sought justice, whatever the cost—the way her father had taught her. "Maybe Bianca Edgefield had another baby before she met Thomas, or maybe the whole thing was to cover up the death of that little baby boy." She touched the photo of his poor, battered cheek.

"I'll work on it, but it might not be as simple as it sounds. Techniques have changed. It might take time to match the profiles or I might need to retest."

"Whatever you can get, Cass. I'll talk to Dad and get to work on that angle."

They said good-bye.

Her phone rang and she froze. The stupid girlish fool inside her hoped it was Finn, but it was her father, and she couldn't put this off any longer.

"Dad."

"What's going on, Holly? I spoke to someone who said you'd taken yourself off the case because some guy made lewd accusations against you."

"They weren't lewd, Dad. He was right. I crossed the line. Got involved with someone who was a witness." This had been her worst nightmare earlier. But she felt numb. And had bigger issues to deal with. "I messed up, Dad, but I need to talk to you about something else."

She heard him splutter but ignored it. "We found DNA on the murdered woman's sheet. Cassy did me a favor and ran it and came up with some odd results."

"Why are we even talking about this if you're off the case?" She could hear the fury in his voice. She'd let him down. Good cops did not sleep with witnesses. Well, she'd done it and now they had to deal.

"Cassy ran it against all the databases and," she took a deep breath, "it turns out I have a maternal half brother out here in Bamfield. And you're not actually my biological father."

She heard a whoosh of air as if he'd collapsed onto a sofa. She hadn't realized she'd been hoping for some sort of outraged bluster or flat-out miracle, that this was all a terrible misunderstanding and Cassy—brilliant Cassy—had actually made a mistake.

"Oh, god, Holly." The silence stretched out with growing horror. "I never meant for you to find out like this."

She felt as if she'd been shot. "I was adopted?"

"Oh, god. Oh, god, I'm so sorry."

"Was I adopted?" Her voice was sharp, angry, but she didn't know how to do this any other way.

"Yes. We adopted you from an orphanage in Calgary when you were little. Your mother…" She heard him crying and felt her own tears stream down her cheeks. "I wanted to tell you, but she wouldn't let me. She just kept saying you were ours now. *Ours*." Great wracking sobs wrenched her heart. "I wanted to tell you, but when she died, she made me promise I wouldn't. She said we needed each other more than ever. She worried we'd drift apart."

"Oh, Daddy, I would never drift away from you. You're more likely to disown me because I have totally screwed up my life."

"You always felt like my own. From the moment I held you in my arms, you were *mine*," he said grimly.

"But you lied to me my whole life. The baby photos…"

"Your mother knew you'd need proof. She used photos from some obscure relative in France. She worried you were going to remember where you came from and start asking questions—the idea tore her up."

"I don't have any memories apart from us together as a family." Emotions churned, swamping her, making her wish none of this had ever happened. But then she wouldn't have met Finn, and although she wished they'd met under other circumstances, she wouldn't miss knowing him for anything.

But her memories felt like a huge swindle, a massive con. How could she trust her dad again? Then she remembered exactly who she was dealing with. He was the most honest person she'd ever met. He'd never deceive her unless he thought it was for her own good. She just needed him to realize she was a grown-up now, not an abandoned child.

He cleared his throat. "This guy you got *involved* with, is it Finn Carver?"

"Yes."

"Do you love him?"

She bit her lip. No more lies. "Yeah, I love him." She braced herself for a lecture.

"Then don't waste it. The job, that's one thing. But love—" She was crying so much she couldn't see, but her dad was speaking fiercely, "True love is rare. Don't let him go. Not even for the job, not if he's as special as people say he is."

She nodded into the phone. "I won't, but now I need you to do something for me, and it's going to be hard. Really hard. I need you to order the exhumations of Bianca Edgefield and a baby who was found with her, believed murdered."

"Why would I do this?" He was back in cop mode.

"I think she might be my birth mother. There's someone else running around this town sharing my maternal DNA, and given how much I look like this woman who was murdered thirty years ago, I have to assume it's a possibility, right? So she either had *another* kid who's now living in Bamfield..." Looking at the time-line of when Bianca met and married Thomas Edgefield and when she died at age twenty-four, it wasn't likely.

"Or..." the idea that had started to nag at the corners of her consciousness seemed so far-fetched, so outlandish she could barely put it into words, but she needed to say it out loud to hear her father's reaction, "...someone killed her to steal her baby and replaced him with another dead infant."

The silence was heavy. Not a good sign.

"Maybe their baby died of natural causes or maybe they killed it, but whatever happened, I was excess baggage. Or maybe they sold me, hell, maybe they sold us both. I don't *know*." She took a huge gulp of air to steady her nerves. "But my gut is telling me Bianca's baby boy is still alive."

"Oh, jeez."

"I might be wrong."

"But you've got good instincts. You get them from me." He laughed, but it was forced and hollow. "You want her murder investigation reopened?"

She thought of Thomas Edgefield, a man who'd waited a lifetime for answers. A man who might be her biological father. "Yeah, I do. And I need to see if I can figure out who that dead baby might be." And find out if her newly discovered half brother was also a cold-blooded killer.

Finn lay in bed and swore he was dreaming. The scotch-overlaid fatigue certainly managed to make this particular fantasy vividly alive. She was warm and smelled like Holly.

"Whoa, you're skunked." She even sounded like Holly.

He wrapped his hand around her wrist and pulled her toward him, just in case she decided to disappear. Dreams were like that.

He laid her down on the sheets and traced her brows with his fingertips. "I thought you'd gone." His voice was gruff.

She just stared up at him with huge, troubled eyes.

He ran tentative fingers over her lips. "I thought you'd left me."

Her eyes shimmered. "I'm sorry." She cupped his cheek. "I'm pretty sure you won't remember this in the morning, but I think I love you and that's a first."

He kissed her then, even though she was a dream. Because the real Holly wouldn't be putting her heart in *his* hands after the way he'd messed up her life.

He ran his fingers down her body and wished to god he hadn't drunk so much, although if he hadn't, she might not be here. And maybe he was losing his sanity, but right now he didn't care. She tasted like whiskey-soaked longing and desire. He slipped his hands under her tank top. Silky skin. Warm flesh. He cupped bare breasts. Definitely his fantasy. With nothing to lose except his mind, he slipped his hand into the waistband of her pants, lower, over her mound and dipped into her hot, wet core. She groaned away from his mouth, her fingers digging into his arms. Considering this was his dream, she had way too many clothes on. He stripped her top over her head and reared back just to look at her. She was so beautiful. Pale skin, slender lines, full breasts, slim waist. The sort of bellybutton that begged for a taste.

He kissed his way over her body. Sipped her skin as if she was nectar. He dealt with her pants and threw them to the floor, along with silky panties that got tangled on his fingers. She lay there stretched out on his bed. He took her foot in his palm. Bent her leg and raised it higher as he kissed his way to her knee. If this was a dream, it was more vibrant than any he'd ever experienced before. She opened for him, and he put his mouth on flesh that defied any dream.

Holly.

He pulled her closer. Inhaled her scent. She was here. In his bed. And he thought she might have said she loved him.

Her hands skimmed his shoulders with sweeping strokes. His tongue rolled over her, back inside that hot piece of heaven. He kept his arm across her waist to stop her bucking him off as she came. He thrust deeper, wanting to steep in her essence, in the taste of this woman. *His* woman.

There was no one else in this world for him. It had taken a lifetime to find her, now he wasn't letting go.

When the quivers stopped, he knelt between her thighs and she reached for a condom from his wallet on the bedside table and rolled it over him.

Hell of a dream. He grinned. Smoothed his hands over her hips and pulled her close. She wriggled, trying to adjust their positions and get even closer.

"I'm still scared I might actually be dreaming." If he woke up alone right now he was going to be so fucking sad.

She curled her fingers around his length and squeezed hard enough to make his eyes cross as she guided him home. And suddenly he was all the way inside this woman, the way he'd been last night, but this time they were face-to-face and he couldn't stop looking at her. Those eyes, that sweet nose, lush mouth, perfect body—bruises and all. She shifted her thighs, took him deeper.

"I never want to lose you." Any minute he was going to freak her out with a marriage proposal. *Shut up, stupid.*

Harder, faster, a solid rhythm of sex that was building and gaining momentum inside his blood, echoed in her ragged breathing and skipping pulse. She locked her ankles tight behind his back. He caught that small, sensitive nub of her femininity between two fingers as he moved inside her, over and over, applying just the right pressure to make her buck and writhe. She screamed, sweaty and panting, and still he didn't let her rest. He rolled them so she was on top, boneless, lax, and sated.

He started laughing, his hands playing with high nipples that pleaded for attention. She twisted her hips and he broke out in a sweat. She took his wrists and held them over his head, dipping one breast enticingly near his mouth. He reared up to savor as she teased him. Then she sank back down along his length, taking him slow and deep, leisurely letting him feast on her breasts and then driving him up again until he thought he might die from fiery, desperate lust. And then she sat back and raised her hands in the air and rode him. Slowly at first. Then faster and faster, driving his brain to white-out conditions. His fingers dug into her hips as she pushed him closer and closer to that elusive edge.

Then she touched herself. Her hands drifting sensuously over her breasts, cupping their weight, pinching those pretty pink nipples with pale, graceful fingers. His mouth went dry. Her long dark hair fell across her shoulders like tendrils of silk. One slender arm drifted lower as she hummed and slipped her hand through her dark curls, until she gripped him firmly while he was still inside her. He exploded, white light burning through his lids as he threw back his head and yelled. He felt her shudder in response, and she rode out another climax while he watched her with dazed wonder and awe.

She collapsed in a warm heap on top of him.

He pulled her close and stroked her hair off her shoulder.

"I love you. I didn't think I'd ever get to tell you that. Don't leave." Christ, he was drunk and pathetic. He banded his arms around her, and they went to sleep with her on top of him, still joined.

When he woke up the sun blinded him, and she was gone.

CHAPTER 20

"I know it's an imposition, but I really need to see the files of all the children born in nineteen eighty-two." Holly stood on Dr. Fielding's front step and stared into his sleep-blurred eyes and figured steely cop stare would work better than smiles at five in the morning.

"It can't wait?" He looked at his watch with a grimace and Holly sympathized. But she wanted this over with, and the itch at the back of her neck, combined with her newfound knowledge, meant she couldn't sleep. She had a case to solve. A promise to keep.

"No. It can't wait. A warrant is being faxed to your office as we speak." Hopefully.

His mouth dragged down at the corners, eyes resigned. "Give me five minutes to get dressed."

She nodded and stepped back. She hadn't been suspended— as far as she knew. So she'd put her uniform back on to make this official. Maybe getting run off the road had been personal. Maybe it was all about Bianca Edgefield's murder, not Milbank's. Someone had suspected she was Leah Edgefield—and didn't want anyone asking too many questions about that long ago crime.

Her father had gotten a judge to grant the exhumation, and someone was supposed to track down Thomas to ask for his permission. She didn't think it would be a problem given his zealous desire to find the killer. But regardless, the bodies would be reexamined. She hoped he approved.

Cassy hadn't gotten back to her yet on matching Leah Edgefield's DNA to her own. Holly wouldn't be surprised if she'd fallen asleep over her sequencer. She tried not to think about Finn and the sweet, drunken declaration of love he'd made. She found it hard to imagine he really meant it. And concentrating on solving a crime helped ground her, offered her a measure of redemption on a day when she badly needed it.

Dr. Fielding followed her to the tiny community hospital in his SUV and parked beside her, almost blocking her in. Maybe he was pissed she'd dragged him out of bed. She got out, careful to not scratch the paintwork on her rental car.

Fielding's face looked drawn as he unlocked the doors and tapped in the alarm code. "Here, you can use the computer in the nurses' office, but not everything was put into electronic format yet." He pointed to a row of filing cabinets along one wall. "Most of the records from thirty years ago are still in there."

Holly pressed her lips together. This could take awhile, but *this* was the job.

"Thanks." She started on the computer, decided to see what the databases showed her. Records went back to 1985. She made a note of all the names of the kids and dates of birth. Tommy Edgefield had been six weeks old when he supposedly died.

The phone rang, strident and loud in the silence of the clinic. She heard Dr. Fielding answer just as she slid open the first drawer of the first filing cabinet. She checked the date on the file—1950. Oh, hell. Still, she had a good idea of the time window she wanted to examine in detail—assuming her hunch was correct. Whoever the baby found in Bianca Edgefield's arms was had to have been born within a couple of months of Tommy, but she decided to check every baby born within a year of the murders, which had occurred in July 1982. She worked her way through the files and pulled out all the files on newborn babies during that period. Eliminated the girls.

Unbelievably, a stack of fifteen boys remained. "Must have been a bumper year."

Anita stuck her head in the door and Holly jumped. "Dr. Fielding called me in. Said you were here and he had an emergency out at Eagle Ridge. Jeb Granger had a hypoglycemic attack last night. Diabetic. Dr. Fielding didn't want to leave you here alone because you might run off with the narcotics." She grinned, and her eyes ran over the files Holly held. "Martin made a pot of coffee. Want some?"

Martin must be Dr. Fielding. "Sure."

She went away, and Holly heard the stirring sound of a spoon inside a ceramic mug. Footsteps came back toward the office. Anita's office. She looked around. Damn, there wasn't room to swing a cat in here. She glanced at her watch. Not even six. She needed to be done before the place opened for business. "I threw in a lump of sugar because Martin thinks coffee and tar taste equally good." She placed the mug on a coaster beside the small pile of files.

Holly picked up the mug and slurped some down. Considering she'd barely eaten over the last week sugar was a good thing.

"Can I help you find something or is it top secret?"

She eyed Anita carefully. "I'm looking at the birth of babies in the early eighties."

"Oh my god, why?" Her hand gripped her throat. "It isn't some issue with medication is it, because my Mikey was born in eighty-two?"

"I didn't see his file." Holly frowned.

"I had him in Victoria, not a homebirth. Those are the home-birth records."

Holly swore. She shook her head, reassured the anxious mother. "Just some irregularities is all, but I need the records of all the male babies born around that time. How many were there?"

"There used to be a lot more families in the area. Number of kids we have in town has dwindled considerably..." she trailed off. "Anyway, I can pull all the inoculation files from the computer, that'll cover most of the kids." She nodded to the PC. "There are a few families—New Agers—who don't believe in immunization. Rely on the rest of us to put our children at risk so they can skip around being all righteous. Not that I'm bitter or anything," Anita grimaced into her coffee. Holly finished hers, suddenly parched after a night of stress and red-hot sex.

"There's more in the pot if you want some," Anita told her. "Go help yourself." She pointed to the files Holly had pulled. "Want me to copy those for you? And then pull up the inoculation records?"

"Thanks, that would be great." She should have asked for help in the first place but had wanted to do it alone. Bad police procedure; *this* was why they had a command group. So no one got tunnel vision or went off half-assed. Holly shook her head, more tired than she realized. She definitely needed more coffee. "Do you want another cup?" she asked. Anita shook her head. Holly stood, her head whirling slightly. When was the last time she'd slept more than an hour? Coffee pot was near the front door she remembered. She turned and stumbled down the hallway.

Her legs felt wooden and suddenly collapsed beneath her. Her fingers were nerveless. Toes numb. Her bones dissolved. She tried to open her mouth as she crashed on her face. Ouch.

She watched someone step over her and unlock the front door of the clinic. A car was backed right up to the door with the trunk wide open. *Help.* Her eyelids felt as if someone was physically pulling them downward, but she fought the soporific demands of her body.

Anita Toben came back and took both her hands and dragged her to the door. She looked around and then, with a strength belying her size, hefted Holly across her shoulder and tumbled her into the truck.

Holly's need to achieve had once again overridden good police procedure. She'd been a damned fool the whole time she'd been in this town and still hadn't learned her lesson. The trunk closed and trapped her in complete and utter darkness, and then the drugs took her deeper.

While Mike finished cleaning the boat they needed for the anglers tomorrow, he realized they didn't have a fire extinguisher in the galley. Too tired to go into town and pick up one from the store, he jumped in their little speedboat to grab one from one of the compartments and got the shock of his life.

An unfamiliar bag was stuffed into one of the hidey holes.

What the hell?

He eased back the zipper, even more confused when he realized it was full of cash.

A creak behind him made him spin around. His dad stood there watching him with a grim expression on his face. "I had to get rid of Milbank before he dragged you down with him, son."

"What?" Mike asked. It was as though his father had suddenly started speaking in Mandarin.

"I heard what he said to you. That he was going to kill you? No one threatens my family. No one." Grant Toben spat into the water, both hands stuffed in his sweatshirt pockets. "He came here that day on his boat looking for you, but you were watching the store."

"He was supposed to come out on the Sunday but never showed…"

Grant's moustache bristled. "He said you were supposed to take him diving to Crow Point and kept looking at his watch as if he didn't have much time. Turns out he was right." His father's smile turned cold. "The scuba gear was right here, so I offered to take him out."

The implications of what his father was telling him finally hit. "You *killed* him?"

"He attacked me." His father straightened, indignant. "I defended myself. I lashed out, caught him in the chest."

Mike eyed his father as if he'd never seen him before. "But you took Edgefield's knife; you deliberately set him up." Why would he do that?

Grant's eyes shifted. "Guy's a nut-job. I was trying to do the town a favor."

Which meant he'd planned it. A terrible sense of impending disaster ate into Mike's chest. "Why didn't Len show up that Sunday?"

His father's cheeks reddened, nostrils flared. He didn't like being called on his actions. Mike didn't care.

"I called him," Grant admitted. "Told him you were sick and to come on Monday instead."

His father had made sure he'd gotten Len alone, and then he'd killed him. "Oh, sweet Jesus, Pop. Do you know what you've done?"

His father shrugged. "I protected my family. Way I was brought up to."

"I was handling it!" Mike yelled.

"Not from where I was standing, you weren't."

Mike walked over and grabbed his dad by his shirt and shook him. "You fucking killed a man. Now every cop on the island is trying to hunt you down. How could you do it?"

The spit and vinegar evaporated, and his father suddenly looked old. Mike realized he was gripping his dad so hard he was probably hurting him. Slowly he unlocked his fingers. "Oh, god, what are we going to do?"

"He was no good. You know he was no good." Grant scratched his thinning hair and cleared his throat. "Figured the money might come in handy if that bastard Dryzek started leaning on you again. Maybe give you an escape route."

"He threatened you and Mom." His dad had murdered a man in cold blood. To protect him. Mike shook his head. The leaden sky pressed down upon him. "I'm not going anywhere until he's put away, and the cash might not even be real."

"Well, shit."

The man he'd known his whole life as a fine, upstanding citizen had taken a life and barely seemed bothered by it. The sound of an engine had them both scrambling to close the cubbyhole. They looked up, relieved, as his mother pulled up in her sedan. She got out, wringing her hands. "She figured it out." There was fear in her eyes, agitation to her movements.

Mike jumped out of the boat, strode over to her, and gripped her shoulders. "What is it, Mom, what happened?"

"She figured it out." But she wasn't looking at Mike, she was looking at his father, and his father had gone white. "She's in the trunk."

His father nodded calmly, as if he knew what she was talking about.

Mike stood openmouthed. "What the fuck is going on? Who's in the trunk?"

"Don't use that sort of language around your mother," his dad snapped. And then, surreally, popped the trunk to reveal Holly Rudd, cop, lying twisted and unconscious inside.

Mike's whole being rang with shock. He'd decided against telling Dryzek about Holly last night. Couldn't bring himself to get a woman hurt, and here she was today, in his mother's trunk. He pinched himself hard, but nothing changed. He looked at his mother. "What have you done?" His mom and dad were looking at one another and not at him. Whatever silent communication was going on between them didn't include him.

"Take your mother inside. There's been a misunderstanding, and I'm going to take care of it. Get everything straightened out."

His mom shook so hard she started to sag at the knees. Mike caught her around the waist and helped her walk around the car and up the porch steps. When he turned around, his dad was already driving away. He looked at his mother who had tears smeared across her cheeks. He froze and swallowed an awful, rising dread. "What did he mean by take care of it?"

She tried to grab his hands when he released her. He ran for his truck. He hadn't counted on her coming with him but didn't have time to fight about it when she climbed in the passenger side.

Finn was in the dive shed with the sort of hangover that usually involved a bed, a jug of water, and a bottle of Tylenol, when Malone walked in.

"If you've come to have another go, give me a minute so I can finish this log sheet. Then you can have at it."

"I can punch you?" Malone asked with a glint.

One side of Finn's mouth curled up. "You can try."

Malone grunted. "I've got instructions."

Finn frowned. "For me?"

"For Holly." Malone gave him a sly grin. "Me and the deputy commissioner play squash together occasionally."

Ding. "He sent you to keep an eye on her."

Malone snorted derisively. "I suck at bodyguard duty. Anyway, she's supposed to be at the motel, but she's not. And she's not picking up her cell, so I figured maybe you knew where she was?" He raised his brows knowingly.

"I saw her last night." At least he thought he had—he wasn't one hundred percent certain it hadn't been a dream. "She left before I woke up."

Malone frowned. "I don't like her being out there alone. Not with everything that's going on." His cell buzzed and he listened for a minute. Finn shoved the dive records aside.

"OK, I'll be right there," Malone said. "They picked up Remy Dryzek and Gordy Ferdinand last night, got enough out of Rob Fitzgerald to hold them. Also got some surveillance photos of the black truck that ran Holly off the road. There was a tarp in the back that didn't belong to the owner. They reckon the attacker had a dirt bike ready for when he ditched the truck. Only distinguishing feature was the guy had a moustache, but that's not exactly uncommon around here."

"A lot of planning went into running her off the road."

"We're checking out all the people who have bikes in the area."

"Not everyone registers them."

Malone nodded, then held his gaze. "I was tough on your brother. I'm sorry."

Finn shrugged. "I guess I'd have done the same in your shoes."

"No diving today?"

Finn shook his head. "Finished up yesterday. The students have a lab this morning and then they're done."

Malone cleared his throat. "I shouldn't be telling you this, but, well, at least I'm not doing you." He grinned evilly. Finn gave him the eye. "Anyway, you might want to go see your buddy, the professor. Deputy commissioner is going to exhume the bodies of his wife and child. They're reopening the case."

"Thanks to Holly?"

"Yeah." Malone's expression darkened. "So you don't know where she might be?"

"No clue. Thom's in lectures all morning." He stood. "I'll drive around, see if I can track her down."

Malone handed over his phone number. "Call me if you find her. I'm starting to get a bad feeling about this. I'm gonna round up the troops."

Finn nodded and locked up the shed. Then he ran to his truck and stepped on the gas.

The sound of an engine revving made Holly float to the surface. Her head felt full of rocks, and wherever she was lying was cramped and stank of cheap plastic carpeting and exhaust fumes. The car stopped. A door opened. She tried to move her legs, but they were dead weight. A wave of dread washed over her as the catch clicked open and she instinctively closed her eyes. Even with her mind disconnected from her body it was hard to pretend she was unconscious and unaware while at someone else's mercy.

Light flooded the interior of the trunk, bright sunshine warm on her cheek. That felt wrong. The weather shouldn't feel so nice when you were about to die.

Rough hands reached beneath her and yanked her out. Digging into her bruised flesh. She didn't flinch. She was going to get an Oscar for this performance. Pity she'd be dead.

Her fingers started to tingle.

Maybe if she delayed long enough, she could get the drop on whoever had her slung over their shoulder. Chances were they had her weapons, but they'd overestimated the power of the drugs because she was definitely coming around, and she wasn't the sort to roll over and die.

There was the sound of more car doors slamming and feet rushing through last year's dead leaves. The cavalry?

"Go home."

Not the cavalry.

"You can't do this, Pop." Mike Toben's voice rang around the forest.

"There's no other way, son." Mike's father, Grant Toben. Sonofafreakingbitch.

"We can run. Take that money of Dryzek's, buy new identities and build a new life." He caught up with them, and there were more noises in the background. More feet. Damn. It was a goddamn murder club.

"You said the money was counterfeit."

"I don't know for sure. Maybe Remy put that rumor around so no one would steal it. He's going to a lot of trouble to get it back."

Grant Toben shook his head. "I can't risk it. I'm not dragging your mother around in a life on the run."

He dropped her on the ground and the effort not to cry out was too much.

"She's awake. Knock her out, Pop. Quick, before she recognizes you."

Grant Toben gasped a tired laugh. "It's a little late for that, son. Your mother drugged her and stuffed her in a trunk. I think she's gonna remember us."

She tried to open her eyes, but her lids wouldn't cooperate. She rolled onto her hands and knees and waited for the world to settle, struggling to gain control of her body. "It was you who ran me off the road." Her voice came out raw.

"No, I didn't," Mike insisted hotly. A wave of pity for him rose up inside her. He was about to lose everything he cared about.

"Not you, Mike." She sat up on her knees, knowing it was too soon to stand. Her legs wouldn't hold her yet, but the muscles were starting to come alive. She was in dense forest, no visual reference points. "I was talking to your dad."

Mike gaped at his father. "Pop?"

Grant's moustache twitched. "She was asking too many questions."

They'd taken her weapons and radio, but missed her cell. She slipped her hand into her back pocket and fingered the keypad. Dialed what she hoped was 911 and prayed there was a cell tower within range.

"She's a cop. It's her job!"

"You don't understand," Grant snapped.

"I understand," Holly told him. "Mike, these people aren't your real parents—"

"You lying bitch." Grant pistol-whipped her across the side of the face and pain exploded. She went down like a cement slab.

"Jesus! Pop. Stop that." Mike crouched beside her. Concern evident over his stark features. Features that, now she'd figured it out, were so like her own.

"We've got the same nose and mouth," she whispered.

He touched her forehead as if searching for a fever. "You're as crazy as he is."

She dared Grant to hit her again as she voiced her theory. "You're Bianca Edgefield's son, Tommy Edgefield."

Mike shook his head and rose back to his feet. "He died. Remember?" He turned to his mom. "What the hell did you give her?"

His mother refused to meet her gaze. The muscles in Grant's jaw kept bunching as he tried to hide his reaction to her words. They didn't deny it.

"We tested DNA from Gina's bedding and found a match with someone in the system. A cop. Me." Holly grasped his pant leg. "You were Gina's lover, right?"

He pinched the bridge of his nose and squeezed his eyes shut. Then he nodded.

So Mike *was* Gina's lover, and given the physical similarities between her and Mike, they were almost definitely related. Nice to know her instincts were on target despite not being her father's biological daughter—maybe it wasn't all about DNA.

"You're my half brother. We had the same mother. Different fathers."

"What's she talking about, Pop?" Mike broke her grip and backed away a couple of steps.

"She's lying." Grant spat on the ground. *DNA*, her cop brain registered. "Bianca Edgefield played Thomas Edgefield for a fool every chance she got. Could have been any number of people who killed her."

"You had an affair with her..." said Holly. The missing piece snapped into place.

They'd had an affair. She'd gotten pregnant and told him the baby was his. When his wife's baby died, he'd decided to take

Bianca's. *Did Thomas know?* "Must have freaked you out when your wife and your mistress both got knocked up at the same time. Or was it a thrill? Quite the stud back then, weren't you?"

Grant aimed her Smith & Wesson at her, and earth spat just inches from her face. She rolled. *Crap.*

Anita Toben was standing just a few feet away along the narrow, twisting trail. "That's a lie. She's lying. Mike. Don't you fall for it." Her expression remained carefully blank.

"How else do you explain Mike being my *brother*, Anita? You killed our mother and stole him."

"Someone else must have been sleeping with Gina Swartz besides my Mikey." Anita's expression grew mulish, arms tight across her chest as she half turned away from them. "You don't know what you're talking about."

"Grant killed Bianca after your baby died," she insisted. Hadn't Anita told her about the dream she'd had when Mike was dead? And then she'd woken up and he was fine? Because Grant had stolen her a new baby.

But she must have known. A mother *knew*, surely?

There were massive trees all around and dense undergrowth. Christ. No one would ever find her out here. Dead or alive. Stall, stall, stall.

The lines around Mike's eyes crinkled as he tried to work through everything she was telling him.

"Grant ran me off the road because he was scared I was going to ask too many questions about Bianca's death, stir up the past. He's nothing but a coward. Doesn't mind murdering innocent women, but doesn't want to pay the price, do you?" She clutched her sides as she started to laugh. Hysteria probably wasn't conducive to escape, but she couldn't stop.

"I took no pleasure in killing Bianca. I did what I had to do to protect what's mine." His eyes grew icy and hard. "I should have killed you when you were too young to know better. Do I get thanks for sparing your life? No. I just get grief for protecting what's rightfully mine. Well, this time I'm in no mood for mercy."

Grant raised the gun again, but Mike stepped in front of her.

"She said *women*, Pop. Who else did you kill?"

Finn headed to the grocery store and asked the shopkeeper if she'd seen Holly this morning.

"No." She charged a kid for a quart of milk.

"There's a rental car sitting outside the clinic, any idea who it belongs to?" The place was locked up. It was possible that car was Holly's rental.

The woman shrugged. "Despite what everyone might think, I don't constantly stare out the window keeping tabs on people." She had a perfect view of the crossroads from here, though. "However," she gave him a beady stare, "I did happen to see Anita heading home from that direction not long ago."

Facts started to click into place. The Tobens had a dirt bike. Grant had a moustache. Finn remembered something else—Gina had said her new lover was a boy toy with no scruples. When it came to women, Mike Toben had no conscience.

But he had to be mistaken. They were nice people, weren't they?

"Thanks." He stopped at the hardware store and tried the handle despite the lack of lights and CLOSED sign on the door. No one answered, so he got in his truck and headed to the Toben family home. Anita's car wasn't there. Nor was Mike's truck. Where could they be? Then he remembered the old track that led through the back of the Toben property. It was used more by ATVs than cars, but that's the route he'd take if he was trying to avoid being seen. Hell, he had nothing else to go on.

He headed off, feeling like the biggest fool until he saw the cut off and tire tracks in the mud. Vehicles had definitely come this way recently. He called Holly's cell and experienced a sharp kick of adrenaline when it went straight to voice mail. So he left a message. She might be in someone's house having breakfast. She'd probably laugh at him and they'd have to figure out exactly how he was going to deal with the inherent dangers of her job. Assuming "I love you" was the same as "I want to get to know you and spend a little time with you"—fifty years should just about do it.

When he found her he was going to drag her to bed for a week. Do nothing but have sex and go diving and have more sex. Maybe eat and drink beer. And, OK, that was a pretty lame guy fantasy, but *where the hell was she*?

He wound down his window, scanning for cars pulled off into the bush. He eased on the brakes as a big black bear ambled in front of his truck. It turned and gave him an unimpressed sniff. Finn eyed the creature warily. Then a gunshot made them both startle, and every drop of blood exited his veins. The bear took off, and Finn caught sight of two cars up ahead on the track. Anita's little sedan and Mike's truck. He turned off his engine and slid quietly out the door.

He moved silently through the damp, impenetrable forest, reined in the desire for speed over stealth. What if Holly had been hurt? Every second mattered. But bursting on the scene without a clue wouldn't save anyone, and instinctively he knew Holly was in danger.

He dialed Malone, belatedly remembering to fill him in on his location.

"Holly dialed nine-one-one about five minutes ago. We're trying to narrow down her location," Malone told him, sounding out of breath.

"I think I've got her." He gave him directions and rang off, stuffed his phone in his pocket, creeping through the bush, peering around massive pine and spruce trees, climbing over downed cedars without a sound. Finally he spotted them. Holly on her knees and Grant Toben holding a gun, while Mike Toben wandered around, looking confused. Anita was there too.

Holly tried to stand up. He didn't see any blood, thank god. Then Mike pulled a pistol from the back of his pants, and Finn's blood froze.

Time was running out.

"She's lying. I didn't kill anyone." Grant Toben sounded pissed because she hadn't died like a good girl.

Holly laughed and struggled to her feet, staggering and woozy. If she could get close enough to Mike to grab that gun, she'd take the chance. Otherwise, she was going to plunge into the bushes and run through the trees where she could at least try to lose them. Legs and stomach were a bit wobbly still, so it was a slim chance. But better than waiting to catch a bullet between the eyes.

She thought about Finn, hoped he didn't end up as desolate as his brother, and felt tears prick. She forced the thoughts away. Thinking about Finn wouldn't save her right now. Being pessimistic wouldn't help either. Focus.

"You already told me you killed Len Milbank, Pop."

Good to know.

She watched Mike swallow convulsively. He stood between her and his father. She didn't think Grant would shoot him, the boy they'd sacrificed so much for, but would Mike really defy his father? She doubted it.

"Stand aside, son. Let's put an end to this."

"You killed Gina too, didn't you?"

"Gina was a tart who was going to get tired of you, run back to that asshole Carver, and open her flapping lips right along with her legs."

"I loved her!" shouted Mike.

Grant looked startled for a moment and shifted his feet. "Now, son, you're just upset—"

Mike flexed his hands into fists a split second before he lunged for his dad. They went down in a pile of arms and legs and spraying leaves. Mike's gun went flying. She dived toward it and ended up flat on her face in the dirt.

Anita Toben leaned down and picked up the matte-black pistol and pointed it at her. "Don't move." Hands rock steady.

Holly finally accepted she *was* going to die. This woman had kept quiet while her husband committed atrocious acts. The cold, calculating gleam told her that killing someone who looked exactly like the woman who'd seduced her husband would be as simple as immunizing a baby.

"How did it feel when you found out he'd been unfaithful, Anita? That he'd had sex with other women? I bet she wasn't the first, was she? How did it feel to know you weren't good enough in the sack to keep him satisfied?"

"Shut. Up." Anita's hands shook violently. "It wasn't like that. He wasn't like that. She came sniffing after him like a bitch in heat. Wouldn't leave him alone!" Saliva sprayed from her lips, and she wiped her mouth with the back of her hand, but the gun didn't waver.

"Did you kill your own baby? Smother him in his sleep because he wouldn't stop screaming?" Holly pushed.

Her mouth dropped open in horror. "No! It was SIDS. I left him for less than an hour, and when I went back he was...cold." Wide, horrified eyes stared at her as if she'd finally realized what she'd admitted. What both she and Grant had done.

Grant staggered to his feet, still holding the pistol. His lip was bloody. Holly cursed when she realized Mike was lying unconscious. Christ, she hoped he wasn't dead.

"Is he all right?" Anita asked in a high, concerned voice.

"He hit his head on a branch."

Anita took a step toward her son.

A figure came out of nowhere and tackled Grant to the ground. *Finn.* Anita pointed the pistol toward the fighting men and pulled the trigger.

Holly's heart screeched. She used every ounce of strength she possessed to climb to her feet and snatch the gun out of Anita's hand, knocking the stupid woman over. The men were still fighting. Holly swayed but used her momentum to wedge her knee between the woman's shoulders, pull out her cuffs, and snap them tight around Anita's skinny wrists. The woman lay crying in the dirt next to her stolen son.

Finn punched Grant in the mouth, and the man went flying. Grant lay on the ground, breathing heavily, his eyes wild and desperate. "Stupid asshole, interfering in something that has nothing to do with you!"

"That just so happens to be the woman I love you're trying to dispose of, you bastard." Her heart soared even as Finn picked up her pistol from where it lay in the leaves. "So it has *everything* to do with me. But you're right. I must be pretty damn stupid compared to you. I mean you got away with murder for decades. Fooled everyone. Probably laughed your ass off at Thom. You must have had heart failure when Holly turned up."

Grant spat out an expletive. "You've got some nerve. The Carvers are nothing. A bunch of drunken, inbred wastrels."

"Yeah well, at least my brother had the balls to admit his crimes and serve his time, not to mention we don't have any baby snatchers in the family."

"Your brother is an illiterate moron and you're no better."

"Doesn't make him any less worthy than you, Toben." Sweat dripped off Finn's temple. He was white with rage.

Holly hobbled toward him, touched his shoulder. "He's trying to rile you. He wants you to shoot him so he doesn't have to face what he's done. Give me the gun. It's my job to arrest him."

"But it's my job to protect the woman I love, or don't you get that yet?" Finn said.

Holly let out a little laugh. "I'm not sure we can argue the relationship dynamics right at this exact moment, but we will discuss this." She pulled out her phone. Showed it to Grant, who went pale. "I called nine-one-one earlier. They got everything. The whole confession. They know you killed Bianca Edgefield, Len Milbank, and Gina Swartz. You kidnapped two minors. Assaulted and kidnapped an RCMP officer. Grant Toben, I'm arresting you—"

"No!" Grant screamed, but Finn got hold of his arms and flipped him on his front.

Holly dug out a pair of flexi cuffs she kept in her pocket and cinched them tight around Grant's wrists. She turned to face Finn, surprised when he stumbled away and sat in the muck and the leaves. And then she saw the blood soaking through the side of his T-shirt. "No."

She forced him to lie back, pulling at the waistband of his jeans to get a clear look at the wound.

"We don't have time for this now, baby." His big hand cupped her cheek. He looked impossibly handsome in the heavy gloom of the forest. "But pencil me in for later."

"Funny man." She shook her head. "Why didn't you tell me you'd been shot?" She tore off her shirt, and his eyes widened, and he was obviously about to add another inappropriate comment. "*Don't* start with me." She pressed hard against the oozing wound at his side, and his eyes rolled back in pain. She looked around. She needed both hands to apply pressure to stop the bleeding, and her phone was in her pocket. Sirens were close. "We need an air ambulance. Man down! I repeat, man down!" She yelled into the ether and hoped someone somewhere was listening. She could hear bushes thrashing. Grant stood up and tried to take off. He wasn't going to get far.

"Your fellow officers are about to get an eyeful." Finn's mouth curved into one of his handsome smiles, but his skin was pasty, and his eyes were starting to glaze.

"They'll survive." She could be stark naked for all she cared.

"Holly." His eyelids started to drift.

"Don't you dare die on me, Finn Carver."

"I'll do my best. This isn't the first time I've been shot, you know." He gritted his teeth, grabbed her hand. "This one was worth it. To save you, anything would be worth it."

Cops finally burst on the scene. They confiscated weapons, restrained the prisoners, checked poor Mike, but she didn't care about anything except Finn. Someone wrapped a shirt around her shoulders and medics arrived, firefighters. Pretty much every person in Bamfield converged on this isolated expanse of forest that was supposed to be her burial place.

She watched them work. Finally, what seemed like hours later, the throb of rotors beat the air as a Coast Guard chopper flew over and landed somewhere nearby. They got Finn onto a stretcher and she held his hand.

"I'm coming too."

"Only to the chopper. Not enough room on board and no time to argue," one of the medics told her.

Finn reached out and squeezed her hand as they ran for the ambulance. "I'm not gonna die, Holly. I've got a lot of years that I want to spend wrestling with you in the sheets." He grinned as she shook her head, then they piled inside the makeshift ambulance and started reversing along the rough track.

"Holy fuck that hurts!" he yelled when they hit a rut.

The medic laughed. "Well, at least your lungs are fine."

Finn ignored the guy. Stared into her eyes. "I'm not going to go anywhere important without you for many years. Got it? We're a pair—you and me—from now on you don't get rid of me that easily." She figured out she was crying only when tears dropped onto their joined hands.

"But you've got to finish what you started here, Holly. You've got to talk to Thom."

She closed her eyes. He was right. She had to finish this. Write the reports, close the links, finish this thing.

"You'll wait for me?"

He squeezed her fingers so hard they hurt, but she didn't complain. She kissed him, then stood back as they loaded Mike Toben—who was probably really Tommy Edgefield—and Finn, the goddamned love of her life, onto a cherry red chopper.

Someone dragged her back away from the helicopter, and when she turned around she realized it was Professor Edgefield, his eyes full of concern, especially when he looked down and realized she was covered in blood.

The helicopter took off and blasted them with downdraft. Suddenly Holly didn't want to be here. "Oh, god. I've got to go after him." She whirled around and yelled at Furlong, who was striding toward them. "We need another chopper here ASAP."

Instead of arguing, he nodded and spoke into his radio. Suddenly aware she was cold, she wrapped the shirt she was wearing tight around her body. She started to shiver hard.

"I'm so sorry, Professor Edgefield." Christ, that sounded odd now, but she could hardly call him "dad." "I found out who murdered Bianca. It was Grant Toben. I'm sorry to tell you the boy Bianca gave birth to might not have been your son—Tommy was probably Grant's child, and he stole him when Anita's own baby died."

His mouth had dropped open in shock. "Tommy's alive?"

She nodded quickly and felt a fresh onslaught of tears hit as an ecstatic smile lit up his face.

"And Leah?" he asked hopefully.

Holly opened her mouth several times, but nothing came out for a full ten seconds. "I might be Leah. We need DNA confirmation." She held out her hand to him. "I'm sorry I messed it all up." She bit her lip as he just stared at her.

He pulled her in for a full body hug. She expected to feel weird, or uncomfortable, but the tight squeeze of his embrace actually felt right. She heard more rotors in the distance. "I need to go after Finn." She gripped his hands, stared into comforting pewter eyes. "I promise we'll have time to get to know each other, but right now I need…"

He nodded. "I love Finn like a son. I'll follow as soon as I can." He grimaced. "First I need to tell Brent what's happened. That'll be fun."

Holly nodded, and a numb feeling of cold stole over her. The chopper arrived, and she ran toward it, bending low. To her surprise Furlong got in beside her. Once they were settled in with headsets, he told her, "This way I can interview you without any delay." He gave her an almost regretful smile. "You ended up solving the whole damn thing on your own."

"I did everything wrong—"

"But you found the murderer, Holly. And that's what the job is all about. Getting the bad guys off the street."

She could barely speak, but she started talking him through the events of today, even as her mind focused on the man in the other helicopter. If he died, she didn't think anything would ever matter again.

CHAPTER 21

Mike opened his eyes to find Thomas Edgefield standing beside his bed. His head throbbed and pain sliced through his eyeballs.

"What happened?" But then the memories flooded him in a wave of horror and he wished he could slip back into a coma.

"Your parents…" Edgefield tripped over the word. "Grant and Anita were taken into custody." His features pinched tight as he took the chair beside the bed. "This must be a hell of a shock for you—"

"I'm not your son," Mike bit out angrily.

Thom rocked back slightly in his chair. "I watched you grow in your mother's tummy and helped deliver you into this world. You think I care whose sperm created you?"

"Bianca betrayed you. Don't you even care?"

The pallor in Thom's skin deepened. "I care, but it was a long time ago."

"They raised me." Mike's chest tightened, and he felt like someone had driven a sword through his heart but it just kept beating.

"I loved you, Mike, as a baby. I still do even though you probably don't want to hear it."

Mike flinched. He didn't deserve love. He thought about Gina and what his father had done to keep his cruel secrets. He'd killed two women in cold blood. Two women who'd done nothing but fall for Toben men. His chest quivered as he thought about Gina's pretty eyes and soft smile. If he hadn't gotten involved with her, she wouldn't be dead. The knowledge seared his brain like a branding iron.

A wealth of sadness was visible in Thom's eyes. "I thought Grant was my friend. I can't imagine what you're going through right now."

Except he could.

Mike knew that if anyone understood misery and suffering it was this man. And it was his father's fault. His father was a killer, and his mother—the woman who'd raised him—had known about it. All those years he'd admired their happy marriage, it had hidden a rotten core of brutality and murder.

Where did that leave him?

"You have a sister…"

Holy mother, he'd forgotten about Holly. He tried to sit up. "Is she all right?"

"She's fine and said she'll come talk to you later." Thom grimaced. "Finn got the worst of it. He was shot, but he's going to pull through."

Shit. Like a dark shadow, Brent Carver passed his doorway. The usual fear had disappeared. Nothing Brent did to him could make him feel worse than he already did.

"Finn's a good guy. I'm glad he's going to be OK." He frowned. "I stole his gun."

Thom cleared his throat. "I think the cops do have a few questions."

Mike looked toward the door and noticed two Mounties, jaws clenched, waiting patiently by the door.

"You better let them in." Mike braced himself.

Thom stood and handed him a glass of water. "Just give it another minute, until your lawyer gets back from the restroom."

"Lawyer?"

"Laura Prescott has agreed to represent you." He gave him a look. "You're not alone, Mike."

Mike didn't know how to respond. He felt alone. In fact, he'd never felt more alone in his whole goddamn life, but that was what he deserved. It was what he wanted.

Thom reached out and squeezed his hand. "Give it time, son. Give it time."

There was enough pain packed inside his head for Finn to wish he wasn't drifting into consciousness. Then he opened his eyes and saw Holly sitting beside his bed, staring at him intently, holding his hand so hard his fingers hurt. And the pain was fine. Better than fine. Because it meant he wasn't dead and she did, in fact, love him.

"Hey," he said.

She blinked rapidly. "Hey, yourself."

"Are you OK?"

She shook her head. "Yes." She pressed the call button for the nurse.

He laughed, but fuck, that *hurt*. "How am I?"

"Thankfully, the bullet missed all vital organs."

"Well, it wasn't *that* low."

"Hey," she raised her voice. "I'm being serious here. You could have died. What the hell did you think you were doing, throwing yourself at a man with a gun?"

He stared at her until she stopped being angry. "There is never a time when that's not what I'd do. If you can't deal with that part of me, you better get out now." Although there was no way he was letting her go.

She held her face in her hands, looking beyond exhausted. His getting shot hadn't helped. "How are we going to make this work?

Your job is in Bamfield. I don't even know if I'm still going to have a job when this whole thing is over. Maybe I should just quit."

"Don't you dare quit. I'm *so* proud of you. You are such a good cop." And like that she was back with him in the present. Dealing with him rather than her fears and worries. Who didn't have fears or worries? He stroked her fingers with his thumb. "I can work anywhere. And something tells me Thom doesn't need me to protect him anymore."

"Dryzek and company have been arrested," she confirmed. "He told officers that Milbank was responsible for beating up Thom that time before you got out of the army. Both he and Ferdinand deny smuggling, but the cops from narcotics are all over them. They are going down." She offered him a small smile. "Mike Toben has a nasty concussion, but he's going to be fine— well, as fine as he can be, considering what he just learned about his parents. I still need to talk to him." She bit her lip, clearly reluctant after everything that had happened.

He spotted Thom in the corridor with Laura. But what made him stare was Brent, in deep conversation with a tall, broad-shouldered man in a police uniform. Talk about worlds colliding.

He turned back to the complex and special woman at his side. "I don't care much about money, which might make me a bad bet for the long term. Trust and loyalty are all that have really ever mattered to me, and now love. I love you. I trust you and I will be loyal to you until the day I die. We can figure out all the other stuff as we go along, except for me jumping in front of bullets for you. That's a given."

She tried to smile, but she was an absolute mess, hair straggly, faded yellow-tinged bruises around her eyes. Wearing a blood-splattered shirt—his blood, thank god.

"I should just ask you to marry me right now. The guilt from getting me shot should carry you down the aisle before you get cold feet and change your mind."

She opened her mouth, indignant. "I did not get you shot. And if that is your idea of a healthy relationship—based on guilt—you've got a lot to learn."

He swallowed the huge lump that formed in his throat. "I know. I've never done this before."

Her eyes swam in tears again, but thankfully they were saved by the heavy tread of the big guy in the fancy uniform heading their way. Holly turned and looked up and threw herself into the man's arms.

"You must be Finn Carver." The man held out his hand to shake.

"You must be my future father-in-law."

The man laughed, and Holly rested her hand on the man's uniformed arm. "You need to teach him the art of romance, Daddy."

"Oh, I don't know, from what I hear you guys have got that covered."

Holly colored up fire engine red, and even he felt heat in his cheeks.

"I wanted to thank you, son." Brown eyes shone with sincerity. "For saving the life not just of one of my officers, but for saving the life of my child."

Finn was pretty sure he was crying now too and figured he could probably get away with it because of the gunshot wound. "You're welcome, sir."

And then his brother came forward. Followed by Thom and Laura. Brent said nothing, but leaned down, ruffled his hair, then went to stand by the window.

"Dad." Holly touched her father's arm. "I want you to meet my other father. Thomas Edgefield."

The two men shook hands, both visibly upset.

"I'm sorry for what happened to you and your family, Professor," the deputy commissioner said.

"Thank you. And thank you for raising her so beautifully." Edgefield's eyes shone like silver. "She turned out absolutely perfect."

"Hardly." Holly rolled her eyes.

"Perfect for me," Finn said.

Brent grunted. Holly shook her head and Laura smiled. Everything was going to work out, Finn realized suddenly. After years of being alone, he now had a family. A big, funny-looking family and Holly was the center of it.

The beginning.

ACKNOWLEDGMENTS

I set this story in the gorgeous community of Bamfield, BC, but feel the need to reassure anyone who might visit the area that the locals are, in fact, very friendly, the scenery is stunning, and the wildlife bountiful. Also note I tweaked some of the local topography to fit the story so I apologize if you fail to find my mythical shipwreck, or if you inadvertently ground your boat trying to navigate a too-shallow river.

A special thank you goes to Cpl. Darren Lagan, senior media relations officer, BC RCMP, who answered my many questions about murder investigations with painstaking detail, enviable patience, and a much-needed sense of humor. Any mistakes are mine though I hope I'm forgiven a little artistic license.

Writing can be a lonely profession but I'm lucky to have numerous, wonderful, online writer friends who keep me relatively sane. Especial thanks go to Loreth Anne White, Skype buddy extraordinaire, who always forces me to ask the hard questions. Also my incredible critique partner, Kathy Altman, who sees the roughest first draft and doesn't tell me to quit while I'm ahead.

Massive amounts of love to my family who support me every single day and thankfulness to my readers who make me strive to write a better book each and every time.

Huge gratitude to Jill Marsal at the Marsal Lyon Literary Agency, LLC, for believing in me and this story, and to my editors, Kelli Martin (Montlake Romance), Charlotte Herscher, and Renee Johnson for their diligent eyes and boundless enthusiasm. Thanks also to the rest of the team at Montlake Romance who have been wonderfully helpful.

ABOUT THE AUTHOR

JAMES HARE. © 2012

A former marine biologist who completed her PhD at the Gatty Marine Laboratory in St. Andrews, Scotland, Toni Anderson has traveled the world with her work. She was born and raised in rural Shropshire, England, and, after living in five different countries, she finally settled down in the Canadian prairies with her husband and two children. Combining her love of travel with her love of romantic suspense, Anderson writes stories based in some of the places she has been fortunate to visit. When not writing, she's busy walking her dog, gardening, and ferrying the kids to school, piano, and soccer games. She is also the author of *Storm Warning* and *Edge of Survival*.